# The Case of the Curious Corpse

# The Case of the Curious Corpse

the endless

Chronicles of Brother Hermitage

by

# Howard of Warwick

From the Scriptorium of
The Funny Book Company

The Funny Book Company

Published by The Funny Book Company

Dalton House, 60 Windsor Ave, London SW19 2RR

www.funnybookcompany.com

Copyright © 2020 Howard Matthews

All rights reserved. No part of this publication may be reproduced, copied, or distributed by any means whatsoever without the express permission of the copyright owner. The author's moral rights have been asserted.

Cover design by Double Dagger.

ISBN 978-1-913383-13-8

Also by Howard of Warwick.

**The First Chronicles of Brother Hermitage**
The Heretics of De'Ath
The Garderobe of Death
The Tapestry of Death

**Continuing Chronicles of Brother Hermitage**
Hermitage, Wat and Some Murder or Other
Hermitage, Wat and Some Druids
Hermitage, Wat and Some Nuns

**Yet More Chronicles of Brother Hermitage**
The Case of the Clerical Cadaver
The Case of the Curious Corpse
The Case of the Cantankerous Carcass

**Interminable Chronicles of Brother Hermitage**
A Murder for Mistress Cwen
A Murder for Master Wat
A Murder for Brother Hermitage

**The Umpteenth Chronicles of Brother Hermitage**
The Bayeux Embroidery
The Chester Chasuble
The Hermes Parchment

**The Superfluous Chronicles of Brother Hermitage**
The 1066 from Normandy
The 1066 to Hastings
The 1066 via Derby

**The Unnecessary Chronicles of Brother Hermitage**
The King's Investigator

**Brother Hermitage Diversions**
Brother Hermitage in Shorts (Free!)
Brother Hermitage's Christmas Gift

**Howard of Warwick's Middle Ages crisis: History-ish.**
The Domesday Book (No, Not That One.)
The Domesday Book (Still Not That One.)
The Magna Carta (Or Is It?)

Explore the whole sorry business and join the mailing list at
**Howardofwarwick.com**


Another funny book from The Funny Book Company
Greedy by Ainsworth Pennington

*With thanks to Umair (No relation) and Janine*

| Caput I | Surprise! | 1 |
| Caput II | Day Trip to the Body | 16 |
| Caput III | The Curious Corpse | 29 |
| Caput IV | Tales from The East (Not Norwich) | 43 |
| Caput V | Le Pedvin Did What? | 60 |
| Caput VI | If In Doubt, Read a Book | 74 |
| Caput VII | The Mahuqiq Are Coming | 88 |
| Caput VIII | Hereward the Wake (Not) | 104 |
| Caput IX | Friends in the Woods | 116 |
| Caput X | Deceive the Deceivers | 131 |
| Caput XI | Where's the Rest of Them? | 149 |
| Caput XII | The Investigator Investigates | 164 |
| Caput XIII | What a Rude Book | 176 |
| Caput XIV | Haven't You Finished Yet? | 192 |
| Caput XV | The Green Man | 208 |
| Caput XVI | Discoveries All Round | 222 |
| Caput XVII | Suspect Number One Please | 232 |
| Caput XVIII | Not Him Then | 246 |
| Caput XIX | Tied Up at the Moment | 261 |
| Caput XX | Accusation | 274 |
| Caput XXI | Doom | 287 |
| | **The Case of the Cantankerous Carcass** | 307 |
| Caput I | Visitation | 307 |

## Caput I

## Surprise!

The attack by the force of Normans was unexpected. But then, Brother Hermitage reasoned, could an attack that was expected still be called an attack? Everyone talked about surprise attacks and he had naturally assumed that all attacks were surprises. He had been attacked himself, who hadn't in these difficult times? And he was still only a young man of, what was it now, twenty-three? Something like that. Every one of those attacks had come as a complete surprise.

He couldn't imagine that people sent word of an attack, or made arrangements for a time that suited everyone. Surely the attacker would not want their opponent to be prepared. He couldn't imagine anyone arriving for an attack and then having to rearrange the whole thing because it wasn't convenient.

But presumably, if something had to be called a surprise attack there must be attacks that were not surprises, otherwise what was the point of the nomenclature?

'Pay attention,' Cwen snapped as she smacked him lightly on the back of the head.

He came back to the real world in which the real attack was making a lot of noise outside Wat the Weaver's workshop.

'What do they want?' he bleated, observing the organisation of horsemen taking place to the front of the building.

'What do the Normans always want?' Cwen sneered.

'They've only just arrived in the country and here they are throwing their weight around.'

Hermitage's appraisal of Cwen comprised the usual contradictory evidence. An excellent weaver in her own right but no more than a young girl really, elfin thin, small and, when it appeared, with a smile that could light the darkest chamber; and a temper like the same dark chamber set on fire with a pack of mad dogs inside. And a scowl that could clean rusty metal. Her willingness to take on the entire band of Norman attackers on her own was absolutely clear. And she wouldn't be worried about whether it was a surprise or not.

'How many?' Wat's voice called as he scrambled the stairs to this upper chamber.

'At least a dozen,' Cwen called back from her place at the window overlooking the front of the workshop; the window from which Hermitage's immediate response to the sight of a dozen well-armed Norman soldiers had been to consider the linguistic proprieties.

Wat joined them at the window. His wild smudge of black hair perhaps presenting an unintended target if the Normans had brought archers. He straightened his very well made jerkin, brushed the dust from his exquisite leggings and flicked a smudge from the toe of his well-fitting left boot.

He was the oldest of them by a small margin, and the richest by a whole collection of very large margins laid end to end. He didn't get to have his own workshop by being a humble weaver of cloth. No, he got to be a very rich weaver by making tapestries with images the like of which Hermitage had only seen in a book of something called anatomy. And in the anatomy book at least the bodies had the decency to be dead. There was no decency in Wat's

# The Case of the Curious Corpse

tapestries at all. And people paid ridiculous sums for them. Very bad people and very bad tapestries, as Hermitage frequently pointed out as he persuaded Wat to stick to more wholesome works.

In the face of the oncoming Norman onslaught, Wat would make sure he looked his best, Hermitage would check that everyone addressed one another properly and Cwen would do any actual fighting.

'What do they want?' Wat asked with some exasperation.

'That's what I wondered,' Hermitage put in. 'Perhaps they've come to buy some tapestry?'

Wat looked over the band trampling around outside and took account of their rough appearance, their grizzled and careworn faces and their use of language that would make a pig blush.

'They don't look the tapestry buying type,' he concluded.

'Tapestry stealing, probably,' Cwen huffed.

Wat faced Hermitage with an explicit look. 'Could they want you?' he asked.

'I hardly think so.' Hermitage was shocked at hearing the idea out loud, having come to roughly the same conclusion about their uninvited guests.

'You are the King's Investigator,' Wat made the title sound very grand.

'Don't remind me,' Hermitage replied. And he meant it. Being made King's Investigator had been awful. First King Harold, and then, when he was dead and Hermitage thought it was all over, King William went and renewed the appointment. Doing the investigations was terrible and constantly living in fear of being summoned to yet another scene of violence and sin kept him awake at night. 'The king is hardly going to send a whole band of horsemen just to fetch me. He's just sent a messenger in the past. Or even a simple threat on its own. I'm hardly likely to put up a fight, am I?'

Wat shrugged that this did seem out of keeping with King William's usual ways.

'Pillage, violence, robbery,' Cwen determined, with a grunt. 'The usual. Just a gaggle of Normans out for what they can get. Although why it takes quite so many of them to do anything, I have no idea. Probably because they wouldn't be safe if they went out on their own.' She made it quite clear that she would be one of the main causes of harm to a lone Norman.

'Perhaps they're just passing and are going to make us provide hospitality,' Hermitage speculated, hopefully.

'We could always get Mrs Grod to poison them,' Cwen said, suggesting that Wat's cook could do what she did best.

'I don't think they'd line up like that and draw their swords to get an invitation to a meal.' Wat nodded out of the window where the Normans appeared to be making themselves ready for a significant fight.

'What were you doing downstairs?' Cwen asked. 'Barring the door?'

'No,' Wat replied, 'opening it. Don't want that lot knocking the thing down when there's no need.'

Cwen snorted her contempt.

'Be reasonable,' Wat went on. 'There's no way we can keep them out. You, me, Hermitage, Mrs Grod and old Hartle with the apprentices at his back? That meal would be us on a plate. If they find the door's shut it'll only make them angry, and they'll probably just burn the rest of the place down so they don't have to use it.'

'Why don't you just go down and invite them in?' Cwen's

opinion of Wat's strategy was clear. It was lower than a very low thing.

'Because I suspect the first person to speak to them could end up with the bits of their body a lot less joined up than is usual. You know the Norman approach, chop first and ask questions later. In fact, why bother with the questions at all?'

Hermitage studied the visitors again. They had arrived in a flurry of dust and noise having thundered up the road from nearby Derby. Goodness knew what state they'd left that place in, but they were clearly prepared for a major confrontation.

Even now, the one who appeared to be in charge was ordering the others about, moving them into the right position and checking their equipment. He was clearly unhappy with something as he was shouting orders and deprecations in language which, apart from being quite revolting, occasionally slipped into some local dialect akin to Norman French; the sort of kin the rest of the family doesn't talk about any more.

Hermitage knew an order and deprecation when he heard one though. That raised fascinating questions about the role of tone and expression in language.

Cwen hit him again.

'Will you keep your mind on the problem at hand,' she ordered and deprecated all at once. 'What was it this time? The Norman approach to the care of horses?'

'Not at all,' Hermitage protested, having very little interest in horses. Nasty, bad-tempered animals, just like the people riding them, in his experience. Which gave him another thought. And quite a good one this time. 'Who do they think they're going to fight?' he asked.

'Does it matter?' Cwen indicated that the three of them

would not make for a very long battle.

'Well, of course it does. Look at them.'

They all looked.

The leader now seemed relatively satisfied with his troop's turn out. All the horses were lined up side by side, the men on top had swords in hand and reins were at the ready. The leader turned his attention to the building in front of them and seemed to be waiting for something.

'They've obviously prepared for a major confrontation. It's as if they've come to this place specifically for quite a significant battle.'

This did give Wat and Cwen pause for thought. Despite Cwen's protestations, it was quite common for a single Norman to cause an awful lot of trouble on his own. Everyone knew that if you provoked a Norman sufficiently, another thirty would turn up within a day or so to make sure that you, your family, your village and probably several of the neighbours never provoked anyone again.

A dozen Normans constituted quite a force. Twelve professional soldiers on horseback could take most small towns unaided. It was only when the object to be defeated was a lord or a king that serious forces were required.

A Norman child on a dog could probably conquer Wat's workshop. And not a very healthy dog at that.

Wat slapped his hands to his thighs in anger and frustration. 'Don't say they've arranged to have a fight in my front yard.'

Hermitage didn't like to answer, as he couldn't immediately think of anything else these men would be good for.

'Why me?' Wat howled his protest. 'If they want to take over the country and defeat all the local forces, why don't

# The Case of the Curious Corpse

they do it in a field, like a proper army?'

Now Hermitage was lost. He looked to Cwen and Wat for some explanation.

Cwen sighed at the impracticality of monks, and of this one in particular. 'If some local lord has refused to submit to the new king, there's going to be a fight.'

Hermitage could follow that. It still seemed to be a very poor way to organise a country, but it was tradition.

'So,' Cwen went on. 'Said lord and king agree where and when they're going to sort it all out.'

Ah, thought Hermitage. So attacks could be organised and not surprises at all. How fascinating. 'But, why here?'

'Exactly.' Wat protested.

'No point in ruining the lord's manor,' Cwen explained. 'The king will want that.'

'But,' Hermitage held his finger up as some scintilla of information about battles wandered into his mind. 'Doesn't the lord stock up with provisions, raise his drawbridge and fight from behind his walls?'

'If he has any,' Cwen gave a short laugh. 'Castles are for the very rich. You don't send a dozen disorganised Normans to fight someone with a castle. No. This is most likely some petty landowner who is either mad or an idiot.'

'An idiot?' Hermitage raised an eyebrow.

'King William?' Cwen asked Hermitage to recall who they were talking about. 'The one who has just conquered the country and defeated Harold sends word that he'd like you to swear fealty, and you say no thank you? You'd better have a thousand Vikings at your back.'

This was a whole new world to Hermitage, and he hadn't really got the hang of the first one yet.

'Perhaps the local lord has changed his mind?' Hermitage

suggested, looking out of the window again and seeing no sign of any opposition turning up for the Normans, who had clearly gone to a lot of trouble.

'Very sensible,' Wat said as they cast their eyes over the Norman force, which was starting to look a bit impatient.

Hermitage considered that as armed Norman warriors were bad, impatient armed Norman warriors were probably worse.

'Pah,' Cwen dismissed such defeatism.

'I thought you said they were either mad or stupid to fight in the first place,' Wat pointed out.

'At least they should see it through,' Cwen said. 'You can't put your defiance down when it gets difficult.'

'Die with honour, eh?' Wat said as if it was an invitation.

'Perhaps we should go and ask,' Hermitage interrupted what might become one of Wat and Cwen's loud and awkward arguments, or "discussions" as they called them.

'After you,' Cwen beckoned towards the stairs. 'I'm sure they won't stab a monk. Not straight away.'

They gathered and looked out of the window some more.

It was inevitable that they should be spotted really. You can't sit at your window staring at the soldiers in the garden without one of them noticing. It was too late to duck out of sight, so Hermitage just raised a timid and half-hearted hand. 'Hello,' he mouthed.

'Hello?' Cwen turned to Hermitage, aghast. 'Hello, indeed.'

'Maybe they'll realise they've come to the wrong place,' Hermitage suggested. 'If they're expecting this defiant lord and all they get is a monk, they may go away.'

'Normans don't do going away,' Wat said.

They chanced another look out of the window. Now that

he had their attention, the leader raised his sword and pointed it at their vantage point.

'Well done, Hermitage,' Wat sighed.

They all raised their hands to acknowledge that they had only just noticed a force of armed men had appeared at the front door.

'You,' the Norman leader barked up at the window. 'Bring out your forces.'

Hermitage turned back to the others. 'Bring out our what?'

'Forces, Hermitage, forces,' Cwen said, sounding rather annoyed. 'When a force wants a battle they usually have another force to do it with?'

'We haven't got any forces.'

'We know that,' Wat said. 'Not sure they're quite so up to date.'

'Why do they think we've got forces?'

'Normans think everyone's got forces.' Cwen was grim. 'I suppose we're going to have to go out there.'

'Really?' Hermitage could see quite well from where he was.

'If we don't send out our forces they'll think we're insulting them,' Wat explained. 'And there are better people to insult than a dozen armed Norman horsemen. Come on. There's only one tactic that will work in a situation like this.'

'And that is?'

'Abject surrender.'

Hermitage was in a bit of a daze as he realised that he was walking down the stairs and towards the door, outside of which a band of mounted warriors was waiting for him. He'd never been a force before.

'Aha,' Wat said, in a loud, friendly greeting, holding his arms wide as if he could embrace his new best friends who had turned up on their horses.

'Who are you?' the leader barked.

'Wat the Weaver,' Wat announced, bowing low. 'Pleased to make your acquaintance.'

'You won't be,' the Norman grumbled with a nasty smile.

Cwen and Hermitage strode bravely forward. Hermitage stopped just behind Cwen.

'Wait a minute,' the Norman commanded. 'Is that a monk?' He pointed his sword at Hermitage.

'This monk?' Wat asked, turning and indicating Hermitage. 'Yes. This monk here is a monk.'

'Hm.' Perhaps the Norman had second thoughts about doing battle with a monk. Hermitage certainly hoped so.

'Right,' the man on the horse came to some sort of conclusion. 'Let's get on with it then. Where's the rest of you?'

'Rest of us?' Wat looked and sounded clueless. 'This is it.' He shrugged his apology.

'Three?' the armed man clearly thought this was either an insult or a joke.

'And one a monk,' Wat explained.

'We can't do battle with you lot.'

'Oh, that is a shame,' Wat sympathised.

'We were sent to do battle.' There was a definite complaining whine in the voice.

'You do look ready for it. Perhaps it's somewhere else? Can we give you directions?'

'This is the right place,' the man insisted, looking around from atop his beast.

'Not sure I can help,' Wat tried meek.

'This is really not good enough.' The man on the horse turned to his companions and through various noises and gestures indicated what the position was and how unsatisfactory the whole business was turning out to be. The grunts and sighs that were returned indicated that they shared his opinion.

'Do you know how far we've come?' the man asked in complaint.

'Er, no,' Wat confessed.

'A long way, I can tell you. And for this?' He took in Hermitage, Wat and Cwen with a sweeping and dismissive gesture. 'Isn't there anyone else you can go and get? Round up the village, something like that?'

'To come and do battle with you?' Wat made it sound as ridiculous as it was.

'That's right.' The Norman didn't think it was ridiculous at all.

'I think they're probably a bit busy at the moment. This time of day and all.' He turned and gave Hermitage and Cwen a look that said he thought these particular Normans were one shaft short of a quiver. 'Was it anyone in particular you were expecting?' he asked.

'A bit of decent opposition,' the horseman moaned. He dismounted his animal and wandered over towards the three of them in a desultory manner, his weapons clanking as he walked. 'What did you say you did?' he asked.

'Weaver,' Wat explained the name. 'Wat the Weaver.'

'Well, Wat the Weaver. Just think what it would be like if you travelled the length of the country to do some weaving and when you arrived, there wasn't any, what-do-you-call-it in your stupid language?'

'What do you call it?'

'You know.' The man made waving gestures with his arms and fiddly movements with his fingers that indicated nothing at all.

Wat shook his head with a blank expression.

'Sheep's covering.'

'Wool,' Wat suggested.

'That's the stuff. Think of that.'

'Sound awful,' Wat tried to look sombre.

'Too right. So we do battles. We're sent to do battle and there's no battle. What are we supposed to do?'

'Go home without killing anyone,' Cwen suggested, quite strongly.

'We could do that,' the man mused. 'But it doesn't look very good, you know.'

'Doesn't look very good?' Hermitage queried. Now that the man was on the ground he just seemed like an ordinary fellow. Still carrying more weapons than most villages possessed, but at least human.

'That's right. We can't go back and say there wasn't any battle. Not after we set off with such thunder. What will the others say? We'll have no tales of great fights, no wounds to display, none of us will be dead.'

Hermitage thought that sounded like a good thing, but then what did he know? He heard Cwen whisper in his ear. At least her hatred of the Normans was being tempered by plain common sense in the face of this many of them. 'We could kill one of them if it would help,' she hissed.

'You could say we ran away,' Hermitage offered, managing to ignore Cwen's outrageous offer.

'What?' the Norman seemed to think that was even worse.

'Yes. You could say that in the face of your overwhelming strength the enemy turned and ran.' He tried to make it sound as exciting as possible.

'Hm,' the man gave it some thought.

# The Case of the Curious Corpse

'Perhaps you shot several of them in the back while they were running,' Cwen suggested, brightly. 'Probably the women and children who couldn't run fast enough,' she added in a much quieter tone.

'There's nothing for you here anyway,' Wat pointed out, gesturing to his not very humble dwelling. 'It's only a weaver's workshop. Who sent you to have a battle here?'

'Le Pedvin.' The man said calmly.

Hermitage's insides stopped being calm straight away. The bits of him that were in charge of keeping his legs firm and solid were the first to leave. 'Le Pedvin,' he croaked, his breath having skipped off as well.

'That's right,' the man confirmed as if that were sufficient explanation.

Wat had a resigned and despondent look about him. 'Le Pedvin sent you,' he confirmed. 'William's right-hand man, who knows us well, too well, sent all of you to come and have a battle here. Right here.' He pointed out the space in front of his workshop, which was nothing like the size needed for any sort of battle.

'Yes.' The man was firm in his belief and his disappointment at what was on offer.

'You're sure he didn't just tell you to come and fetch the monk?'

Hermitage watched as a fleeting expression wandered onto the face of the Norman before being sent on its way. It was the sort of expression that said its owner may have just got something horribly wrong but has almost immediately worked out how he's going to get away with it.

'That's right,' the man said confidently. 'And he said not to let anyone get in our way.'

'I assume that means us,' Cwen said, who only really

came half-way up the side of one of the horses. 'Did Le Pedvin actually say there would be a battle?' she asked, through narrowed eyes.

'Well,' the man drawled, obviously thinking how he could say yes when the answer was no. 'It was King William's instruction.'

'And did King William say there would be a battle?'

'King William doesn't give details like that,' the Norman scoffed at Cwen for not understanding the ways of the king. 'He just asked who would fetch him this troublesome monk.'

'Troublesome?' Hermitage was offended. He'd never been troublesome in his life.

'So, Le Pedvin gathers us and dispatches us to fetch the monk.'

'So,' Cwen retorted, folding her arms as she presented her conclusion. 'No one told you there would be a battle. No one told you to come prepared for a battle. No one even told that the monk would be any trouble at all, let alone that there would be a force resisting you.'

'Might have been more,' the man mumbled his protest.

'More monks, perhaps,' Wat offered.

The man was shaking his head slowly from side to side with a look of despairing sympathy. 'It's not a very good show is it?'

Wat looked at him askance. 'This is our fault?'

'Of course. You might have put up a decent bit of resistance, instead of giving in like this. It's typical, that's what it is.'

'Well, I do beg your pardon,' Wat laid it on thick. 'Deepest apologies for not throwing ourselves in front of the horses and being dead before you could say good morning.'

The Norman gave a great, heavy and growling sigh and

turned back to his men. 'Bloody Saxons,' he said loud enough for everyone to hear.

'There could be a surprise attack on the way back,' one of his men sounded hopeful.

Ah, thought Hermitage. If that were the case he would be able to see what the difference was.

'Tell you what,' the Norman turned back to Hermitage, Wat and Cwen with a rather determined look on his face.

'What?' Cwen asked, very cautiously.

The Norman smiled a Norman smile: full of threat, built on a foundation of truly horrible thoughts. He gestured his men forward. 'You three can put up a bit of a fight before we carry you off.'

## Caput II

## Day Trip to the Body

Since becoming King's Investigator, Brother Hermitage had undertaken many journeys. Every one of them had been ghastly in one way or another. Many of them had been ghastly in several ways at the same time. He supposed that he should be grateful for this latest experience. Being thrown across the country on the back of a horse made his previous voyages feel like gentle ambles through a beneficent countryside.

Going anywhere near a horse was bad enough. Being on one was dreadful. A small pony could be avoided or frightened off, but the thing he was bouncing on was some sort of monster and clearly had no fear of anything – it even seemed to harbour a deep-seated hatred of monks in particular.

He had started the journey sitting on the hard wooden saddle behind one of the Norman soldiers but it became clear almost immediately that Hermitage was as capable of keeping this up as the Norman was of discussing the lexicography of the post-Exodus prophets.

He had been removed from the saddle and unceremoniously slung across the beast's neck. He was now sharing the hot breath and spittle of a war-horse at full gallop. To add injury to his insult, whenever the pace slowed to accommodate an incline or a particularly dense patch of woodland, the horse would turn its neck and try to bite the annoying irritation that was tickling it. Le Pedvin could have sent the horse on its own and Hermitage would have gone willingly.

At least this would provide the mark against which all of the ghastly travelling experiences of his life could be judged. Wherever he found himself in the future, he would be able to take comfort from the thought that at least he wasn't on that awful horse any more. Even upon his deathbed he would sigh, knowing that any chance of having to go near a horse again was now gone. Unless one turned up to give him last rites of course. He shook his head to get the subject of horses back in its place.

Wherever they were going and whatever it was William wanted done, however far it took them and no matter the length of time, Hermitage would walk back.

Wat was bouncing along behind his Norman and at least looked uncomfortable. All his worldliness had not prepared him for an experience like this and it was impossible to tell which bit he was finding most difficult, being thrown around on a horse, having to hang on to a Norman or getting his clothes creased.

Cwen was having a much better time of it. Perhaps it was because she was light and supple. It could be that she had more horse experience than the others. Most likely it was that she was on the front of the horse and the Norman was hanging on for dear life. When they stopped to rearrange Hermitage, she had somehow persuaded or cajoled her Norman to swap places. The man looked like he would be very pleased to swap places with anyone now.

The appalling journey seemed to last for hours, probably because it did last for hours. At several stages, Hermitage tried to ask where they were going but he couldn't make himself heard. Or the Norman couldn't make himself listen.

Either way, he had no information about their journey other than the fact the ground was thundering past only a foot or so from his face.

He couldn't even tell which direction they were travelling. King Harold's court had moved around the country but goodness knew where William would be. He might have some very strange ideas. They could even be going back to Hastings for all Hermitage could tell.

At one point he waved his arms about in a forlorn attempt to warn his rider that he was feeling very sick. At the point just after that, he was very sick. This didn't seem to bother the horse at all, but the man in the saddle got very cross and shouted that Hermitage would have to clean the beast when they stopped. Where you even began cleaning a horse, Hermitage had not the first clue.

As the intolerable became interminable, Hermitage noticed that sky around them was darkening to orange. Heaven forfend that they would have to stop anywhere overnight and then start this all over again in the morning. If it was possible, he'd even volunteer to carry the horse next time. It would have to be better than this. Or these Normans could just give him some very good directions and he would make his own way.

He never thought that he would be glad to see a camp of Normans looming ahead of him, but the sight and sound of two guards greeting the band of horsemen was music to his ears. And his stomach.

As the band drew to a halt, a strong hand grabbed Hermitage by the scruff of the neck and heaved him off the horse and to his feet. There was no way his feet were going to cooperate with this and he instantly collapsed into a heap of habit.

Cwen and Wat, released from their animals as well, rushed over and helped him up. Actually, they just held him up while his legs dangled uselessly beneath him.

'Poor Hermitage,' Cwen said with genuine sympathy.

'What a journey,' Wat groaned with less sympathy as he rubbed his own aching backside with his spare hand.

The three Saxons moaned and complained at their treatment and wondered what on earth could come next.

'The king awaits,' a Norman announced what would come next. This was a new man, and clearly one from the camp. He was so well dressed and presented that it was obvious he hadn't ridden anywhere. He was probably one of William's personal guards.

With a nod of his head, Wat pointed out the monk he was holding up. 'Hermitage can't walk,' he protested.

The Norman did at least look at the state of Hermitage and give the situation some thought. 'You'd better drag him then,' he instructed.

'Drag him?' Cwen expressed her outrage at the suggestion.

'Better people than you have been dragged before the king,' the Norman explained, with the authority of experience.

'He can't use his legs,' Wat tried again.

'Doesn't need to, if you drag him.' The Norman strode off and beckoned on the bald assumption that they would follow.

Hermitage indicated with a hopeless nod of the head that they had better do as instructed. The alternative was probably a Norman with a big sword slapping his legs until they came back to life. Or came off completely.

Making a very haphazard band, neither Wat nor Cwen being in the best condition, the three of them staggered after the Norman. The man led the way towards what was obviously King William's tent. It was big, it was clean and it had a contingent of smart but violent looking soldiers standing outside it, glaring at anyone who dared to let their eyes linger too long.

Hermitage took the place in and gave his sense of despairing resignation full flight. Events had happened so fast that he hadn't really had time to dwell on the fact that it was all happening again. The awful summons from the king, or Le Pedvin, or, in this case both. The inevitability that there would be a dead body at the bottom of it all somewhere. And that like flies round the body of a badger, the guilty and the just plain bad would be swarming.

There would doubtless only be one who had done whatever it was had been done, and it would be Hermitage's awful task to find that one. That wouldn't stop a whole host of the disgraceful, the disreputable and the downright disgusting meandering around confusing the picture no end. The nature of his summons made it likely that they would all be Norman as well, which made the whole thing even worse, somehow.

Once more he wondered how on earth he had ended up in this situation. What had he done? What plan did the Lord have for him that required such work? But he knew his duty. Most likely he would carry on doing it until he died. Then, with any luck, it would all be explained.

Hermitage was dragged through the entrance of the tent and into a short canvas corridor towards the middle of the place. The bouncing along the ground was bringing some of the feeling back to his legs and he was able to take wobbly steps, relieving Wat and Cwen of some of their burden.

That they were approaching a centre of activity was clear from the noise. There was obviously some sort of riotous

## The Case of the Curious Corpse

fight going on, which gave Hermitage fresh alarm. The clash of metal, shouts of aggression, insults and battle cries filled the air. Perhaps they had arrived at the moment of an attack. Could it be that the rebellion against William's rule had taken a decisive step? Had the various bands of Saxons around the country managed to join their forces in a coordinated move against the conqueror? Were they to be witness to the overthrow of William, such a short time after his victory?

And if that was the case, why wasn't their escort rushing to the aid of his king?

'Wait here,' the Norman instructed in what was a very calm voice for someone whose leader was under obvious attack. 'The king is at his meal. He will see you shortly.' And with that, the man straightened his helmet and stepped through a canvas flap that briefly revealed a scene of complete chaos.

The three Saxons looked shocked and at a complete loss. If that was how the Normans ate their meals it was amazing any of them survived breakfast. Hermitage knew that mealtimes could be raucous if the ale or the wine was flowing, but he was a monk. A raucous meal in a monastery usually involved someone rolling a loaf of bread between the tables and then not owning up.

The flap of canvas stood between them and the source of the noise and Hermitage had an uncomfortable urge to pull it to one side, just to study the detail of what on earth was going on.

Cwen pulled it to one side without hesitation and revealed the Normans at their table. Not all of them were at the table, several were on top of the tables and others had tipped the tables over and were using them as defensive shields. This raucous meal really looked like a full-fledged fight.

The people on the tables had knives in their hands, which may have started out cutting up the meat but were now being brandished at fellow diners. Several men had swords drawn and were holding them high. One of the tables was burning slowly in the centre of the room and the servants were cowering in a corner. There was shouting and shoving and blows were exchanged.

'Perhaps we'll leave them to it,' Hermitage suggested, not that they'd been invited in anyway.

The others nodded agreement, even Cwen showing some signs of concern at what a whole host of Normans looked like when their blood was raised.

They gently let the tent flap fall, hoping that no one had spotted them and was thinking about inviting them to join for the sweet-meats. There was nowhere to sit so they just had to stand and wait for whatever it was they were waiting for. Hermitage used the time to flex his legs and get some function back into them. He cautiously released himself from support and managed to stand unaided. He felt that he might be able to take a tentative step in a few more minutes, as long as it wasn't towards a horse.

Without any ceremony or announcement, the tent flap was thrown aside and two figures appeared, Le Pedvin and King William.

Both men had blood on their cheeks and bore signs of having just stepped from the melee. In William's case, the blood looked fresh and bold and simply enhanced his presence and stature and made anyone facing him accept that if he wanted some more blood he would get it from them.

In Le Pedvin's case it looked like the blood had only just managed to struggle to the surface of what was basically a standing corpse. Surely this cadaverous figure couldn't afford to spare any blood at all. The small trickle that slid reluctantly down a bony cheek must be vital to keeping the man functioning at even a basic level. It was made even more ghastly by the fact that it trickled down from just below the man's eye-patch, the black covering that probably hid the small space in which he kept his soul. Handy for taking out and putting to one side when he didn't need it. Yes, these two had just emerged from a meal but surely Le Pedvin hadn't actually eaten anything. Probably for several years now.

In all his encounters with the man since the Normans arrived, only now did Hermitage realise who Le Pedvin reminded him of; Death. And it was so appropriate. All those representations of death had clearly had Le Pedvin in mind. All the man needed was a pale horse and Hades at his back, and that would be that.

He reasoned that his fragile state was getting the better of him and his imagination was carrying him away. Of course, most people told him he didn't have any imagination so perhaps there was another explanation.

'Aha,' King William cried, clearly in good spirits from his meal/fight. 'It's the monk.'

Le Pedvin just raised an eyebrow, the one opposite the patch that covered the vacancy created by the departure of his other eye. Hermitage had always assumed that had happened in battle. Perhaps it had been over dinner.

'And the others,' Le Pedvin observed, without interest.

'Yes,' William said. 'The one who makes rude tapestry and his serving girl.'

Hermitage noted that Wat had a tight grip on Cwen's arm.

'Well, well.' William looked at them all in turn.

Hermitage waited for his instructions. He knew they'd be terrible but better to get it over with.

The king drew breath. 'What are you doing here then?'

It was all Hermitage could do to stop the squeak coming out of his gaping mouth. What were they doing here? They had been assaulted in their own home, dragged across the country in enormous discomfort at this man's behest and he didn't know why they were here?

'You, erm,' Wat spoke up, 'you sent for us?' It was half question, half prompt.

'Did I?' William asked, brightly. 'That'll be why you're here then.' He clearly understood that that was the explanation for their presence. But why he had sent for them was obviously a blank. He turned to Le Pedvin. 'Why did I send for them?'

'The body?' Le Pedvin reminded his king.

That was that then. Straight to the matter in hand.

'Which one?' the king plainly had a lot of them. Hermitage only hoped that would be allowed to deal with one at a time.

'The one in the tent,' Le Pedvin sighed.

'Ah, yes. The tent.' William had got it now. 'And I sent for the monk?'

'Your investigator,' Le Pedvin was sounding rather bored that his ruler wasn't keeping up.

'Exactly.' The king nodded but the recognition wasn't quite there.

'Your Majesty,' Hermitage bowed his head and took his courage in his hands. The experience on the horse was still rankling inside him. 'A whole band of your men came to us ready for battle. They reported that you had dispatched them on their mission and warned them to expect resistance.'

## The Case of the Curious Corpse

He took a breath. 'They demanded that we come out and fight them, even though there were only three of us. Then they took us by force, threw us on the back of their horses, galloped across the land without pause and deposited us here.' He shocked himself at this outrageous impudence in the face of the king.

The king gave a shrug. 'They can get a bit carried away,' he acknowledged, nodding as it came back to him. 'I do recall saying that you might be some use in a little problem we've got. They probably just wanted to impress me.'

Hermitage did squeak this time. Which only caused the king and Le Pedvin to give him a very odd look.

'Well.' The king clapped his hands. 'I suppose you're here now so we might as well get on.' He made it sound as if Hermitage was the one to cause him inconvenience by arriving in the middle of a meal. 'This way.' He beckoned them to follow back out of the tent while another guard led the way. Presumably, some guards had to be excluded from mealtime in case the death-toll got too high.

Hermitage looked to the others to check they shared his outrage that the hellish pace of their journey bore no relation to the nonchalant nature of the king's request.

Le Pedvin picked up the silent exchange. 'You're lucky it wasn't urgent,' he smiled his grim and horrible smile.

Once out of the tent, more guards joined the entourage, two of them bearing torches, and followed the king across the camp towards its outer edges. Passing tents and camp-fires on the way, men either stood to acknowledge William or waved their greeting - perhaps being the ones who knew William well.

The party halted at the entrance to a small and grubby construction, more lean-to than actual tent. It looked like a collection of left-over bits of canvas, hastily thrown together to shelter something from the rain. Hermitage had a deep, sinking feeling about what was being sheltered.

At the king's nodded command, one of the guards threw back a large section of the canvas and stepped inside, his torch illuminating what was bound to be a grizzly scene and immediately filling the place with acrid smoke.

There it was. A body. Of course it was a body. What else would it be? The king would not drag Hermitage to wherever it was they were without there being a body. Although, then again, maybe he would. It seemed quite possible he could send a bunch of violent horsemen to abduct Hermitage just to give them something to do.

At least the body wasn't exposed. There was a rough blanket covering it but it was plainly a dead person. It had the shape and the presence of a dead person, and sadly, Hermitage was starting to get used to them.

'There you are.' Impatiently, the king gestured Hermitage towards the blanket.

'Indeed Majesty.' Hermitage didn't move.

The king gave it a moment, only a short one. 'Get on with it then.'

Hermitage raised his eyes in question.

'Investigate,' the king instructed. 'That's what you're here for. No point standing there looking at it.' He waved a hand towards the body as if Hermitage would immediately step forward and do some investigation all over it. 'King's Investigator. I'm the king, you're the Investigator. So off you go.' The king with the investigator folded his arms and waited.

Le Pedvin also folded his arms, but it was harder to tell.

There was nothing for it then. Hermitage stepped

cautiously forward and bent to take one corner of the blanket. He thought about throwing it back in a grand sweeping gesture. He thought the king would like something like that. He also thought he might scream if the body was particularly nasty, so instead he just lifted the cover carefully and peeked underneath.

He caught sight of something rather odd, which intrigued him despite the fact that it was associated with a dead body and there was an audience urging him on.

He slowly removed the whole blanket until the body underneath was revealed. Now it was even more intriguing. He looked to Wat and Cwen as if they could give him some silent explanation. Cwen was looking as astonished as Hermitage felt. Wat looked equally surprised but with a hint of understanding beneath his expression.

Hermitage didn't know what to say, let alone do. 'What a curious corpse,' he said, with a lot more interest in his voice than he intended.

'Thoroughly fascinating.' The king looked confused about what monks found interesting. 'But never mind how entertaining he is, there is one thing that is absolutely vital.' He was now being very serious. People had died as a result of King William being very serious. He even went so far as to step forward, bend down and grab a handful of Hermitage's habit, the handful nearest his throat. He pulled his investigator up and close.

'Yes, your Majesty?' Hermitage nodded as best he could.

'As you sort this business out there is one fact that must be completely and utterly proved beyond the doubt of a whole host of saints, apostles and the other ones.'

Hermitage couldn't think who the other ones would be, but didn't like to interrupt.

The king looked him deep in the eye and spoke with fierce instruction. 'I didn't do it.'

## Caput III

## The Curious Corpse

'I didn't for a moment think you had, Majesty,' Hermitage replied, having thought that he had almost immediately.

'Good,' the king nodded and dropped Hermitage back to his feet.

'I expect you want me to find who did do it then.' He thought it best to offer his services before they were demanded.

The king shrugged, 'If you like.'

'If I like?' Being in the king's presence was confusing enough, not having an idea what the man was talking about was positively frightening.

'Do you think it will help?' The king asked. He seemed to be seeking Hermitage's professional advice, but about what exactly, was a mystery in its own right.

'Help, erm, how?' Hermitage asked. 'Majesty,' he added, thinking that the king might get a bit cross if he appeared not to understand.

At least he got that bit right. The king was cross.

'In proving that I didn't do it,' William screamed, helpfully.

'I told you he was an idiot,' Le Pedvin muttered.

'Yes, Majesty.' Hermitage tired to sound very sure about this. 'If we can show that someone else did it then of course, you couldn't have.'

'Hm.' The king gave it some careful thought and seemed

content that this complex argument might be the one he was looking for. 'And that's investigation, is it?'

'Er, yes Majesty.'

'Of course, I could have done it. If I wanted to.'

'Absolutely, your Majesty.' Hermitage couldn't make most people out but kings seemed designed to befuddle him. First of all the man was adamant that he hadn't killed this stranger, now he was saying he might have done.

'Kill who I want,' William grumbled that his prowess might be questioned.

Hermitage said nothing. He wasn't the one doing the questioning.

'Just didn't do this one.'

Hermitage nodded. He hoped that was right.

'Don't want you spreading word that the king has stopped killing people,' William growled.

'Of course not,' Hermitage now shook his head.

'Killed lots of people. I'm very good at it. Likely to do a lot more as well. Just not this one.'

'Not this one,' Hermitage nodded and shook his head at the same time. He desperately wanted to know why it was so important that William had not done this one. He already felt that it would be key to the disaster that was about to unfold in front of him. He also knew the king didn't take kindly to being asked "why" about anything. Such impertinence might well provoke him to demonstrate just how good he still was at killing people.

'That's right. So, you do whatever it is you do and prove that I didn't kill him.'

Hermitage stroked his chin. He thought that it might make the king think something was going on. In fact, Hermitage had a long list of questions he wanted to ask.

# The Case of the Curious Corpse

They were questions he needed to ask of the king if he was going to make any progress on this at all. They were also questions he knew would not be welcome and there was very little chance he would get an answer to any of them. He cast a glance at Le Pedvin and knew that source would be even more hopeless.

First of all, who was this man?

How did he get here? By the look of him, he was certainly not local.

Did they have any ideas who might have killed him?

When did he die?

How did he die? Although he thought the large wound on the head was probably a helpful indication.

And of course, the question that he suspected was never going to get an answer. Why did William want it proved that it wasn't him? What possible consequences could there be for King William if it was found out that he had killed someone? As he'd pointed out, he'd killed a lot of people, most of them very recently and the consequences of that had been that he was now King of England. Not bad, really.

The stroking of the chin had taken rather a long time by now and the gathering was starting to get impatient. Was there a question he dare ask? Just to get things going.

'So, Majesty.' He tried to sound insightful and penetrating. 'Erm, these clothes?' he gestured towards the corpse. It sounded pathetic, even to his own ears, but at least it was harmless.

'The clothes?' William roared.

Ah. Not harmless then.

'What the devil have the clothes got to do with anything?'

Hermitage had to think quickly because he really didn't know what the clothes had to do with anything either. 'They are, erm, unusual.'

William did not answer the question if there really was one. Instead, he gave Le Pedvin a look of hopelessness. Le Pedvin returned a shrug of I-never-expected-any-better.

'Is this really the best you can do?'

Hermitage stammered on. He'd just let his mind produce some words and hope for the best. 'The clothes being unusual indicate that this man is not from round here.'

'Of course he's not from round here, just look at him,' William said, most unfairly to Hermitage's mind.

'Which would, in turn, be an indication that he was not an enemy of your Majesty, your enemies being those nearby, I imagine. Mainly Saxon?'

Hermitage took the king's lack of response to this as an affirmative.

'And as most of them are Saxon they would be dressed as Saxons. This fellow is clearly no Saxon. And so you are unlikely to have killed him.' He heard the words he was speaking but could neither follow them nor believe any of it.

The king's frown said that he was a bit happier with this, but not much.

Hermitage took a deep swallow and ploughed in with the question he really wanted to ask. He tried to make it sound as light and nonchalant as possible, which only made it sound mostly squeaky and desperate. 'Was he, erm, in fact, that is, known to your Majesty? At all? In any way? A bit?'

At least the king didn't take this question quite so badly. 'Of course he was known to me,' he snapped. 'I don't accommodate just any dead body in my camp you know.'

'Of course not, Majesty,' Hermitage agreed immediately, having heard some very different stories about William and dead bodies. At least this gave an opportunity for another question he needed to ask. 'Did he actually die here your Majesty?'

'What?' the king seemed puzzled. 'Here?' He pointed at the spot on the ground.

'Well, not here, exactly.' Hermitage thought it hardly likely that the victim had conveniently died under a sheet in the corner of the camp. 'I mean, had he been alive around the camp and then came to his end, or was he brought in dead from somewhere else?'

The king looked like he was at least giving this enquiry some thought. 'What are you asking all these questions for?' he demanded.

Now Hermitage was truly at a loss. What was he asking questions for? How did the king think anything was going to be found out without asking questions?

'That's investigation, Majesty,' he said, wondering what the man thought was going to happen.

'Really?' William obviously had an entirely different idea of the process.

'Yes. From the Latin, *vestigare*, to track. I have to track the events that led to the death and can only do that by enquiring of those who have information.'

There was a pause while the king looked to Le Pedvin to seek confirmation that this ridiculous proposal was what was expected.

Le Pedvin gave half a nod, indicating that some questions might be an unfortunate necessity.

'Pah,' the king scoffed at the whole idea but at least looked prepared to give Hermitage something. 'If someone had told me an investigator was going to go round asking questions, I'd never have appointed one in the first place.'

That would have suited Hermitage down to the ground.

'Yes, he died here,' the king said with impatient resignation that he was going to have to provide some information. 'But he wasn't killed here,' he added, hastily.

Hermitage could only blink in the face of that contradictory statement.

'You mean he took a, er, fatal wound somewhere else, but died here,' Wat spoke up, nodding to the head of the corpse. The wound was clear although it looked old and not too deep. It certainly didn't look very healthy though. Not that it would, being on a corpse.

The king gave Wat a look that said he was ready to increase the number of corpses in the tent by one. Le Pedvin raised a calming hand.

'Brilliant,' William mocked this statement of the obvious. 'If we're done then?' He looked ready to move away and leave Hermitage to it.

'Majesty,' Hermitage pleaded. 'One more question.'

'Last one.' William raised a finger to emphasise the point.

'Who is he?' Hermitage asked this as if it was surely the most blindingly obvious question that everyone in the room wanted answered.

'Is it important?'

'Is it…?' Hermitage couldn't bring himself to repeat the question. It was clear that he and the king had very different ideas of what investigation actually was, but surely knowing who the dead body belonged to was pretty vital. 'Yes,' was all he could manage.

The king sighed deeply, clearly prepared to accommodate little more of this irrelevant rambling. 'You can see who he was.'

Hermitage couldn't see anything of the sort. There was no sign around the man's neck announcing his name. There was no sigil or armorial on any of his clothing to give a clue, albeit that clothing was truly bizarre.

The fellow was dressed in what seemed to be layers of flowing robes. Or at least robes that would flow if he was a bit less dead. A long scarf, made of some remarkable material, was wound around his neck It certainly wasn't coarse wool, the weave was far too fine, but neither was it a high-quality cloth, seeming to shimmer, even in the smoky light of the torch.

Hermitage was sure that the full light of day would give life to the remarkable colours that even in this gloomy place were vibrant. The main outer robe appeared to be yellow while the layers under that were cream with dark streaks, perhaps red or blue. The feet were clad with fine leather boots that made even Wat's extravagant footwear look like a pig farmer's clogs.

The face looked of middling age, worn by weather and the experiences of an active life, and a truly unusual beard appeared to have been painted across the chin. It was very finely shaped and clipped, nothing like the bushes favoured by Englishmen who simply couldn't be bothered to shave.

This was clearly a man of some wealth and, as a result, probably importance. That could go a long way to explaining why William was anxious not to be blamed for the death. If the common man was murdered there was usually a burial. When people of wealth and importance were killed there was frequently a war. William may be an immensely strong and powerful king but to some that made him even more of a target. Hermitage couldn't think who in the world would have the wherewithal to even think about taking on the Normans, but then it wasn't really his area of expertise.

'He is clothed very well,' was the only comment he could

think of.

'Saracens usually are.' Wat brought an intense silence to the scene.

Hermitage couldn't take it in straight away. Wat had obviously said the word, "Saracen" and there was an unusual dead body on the floor before them, but his first thought was that the weaver had come up with something else to talk about, just to take the heat out of the situation. He looked to Wat, then he looked to the body and then he looked back. He was gratified to see that Cwen was staring, open-mouthed at the dead man.

'That's a Saracen?' she asked as if the corpse would rise up from the dead and float around in the air at any moment.

'Was a Saracen,' Wat corrected. 'And the most Saracen looking Saracen I've ever seen.'

'And you've seen a lot have you, Master Weaver?' Le Pedvin asked this. It was one of those questions that was not going to have a right answer.

'One or two,' Wat acknowledged. 'Never a dead one though.' From the look on Le Pedvin's face that was definitely not the right answer. 'From what I've heard, they tend to make the most awful fuss when you try to kill them. God knows what happens if you succeed.'

'What's he doing here?' Hermitage blurted out before he could stop himself. It was a key question, but one almost certain to annoy the king even more. It also stopped Le Pedvin in mid-stride as he looked ready to thump Wat on the nose.

'Dying,' William grunted. 'That's what he's doing here. Going and bloody dying. In my camp of all places. Why the man couldn't have the decency to drop dead in a bush somewhere is beyond me. Instead, he staggers for miles until he gets here, then he dies. What good is that, I ask you?'

Hermitage glanced at the body again and tried to look disappointed that it had let the king down like this.

'Perhaps it was an illness, Majesty?' Hermitage suggested, with hopeless optimism as he tried to ignore the head wound. If this poor fellow had simply died of disease then all his problems would go away. William didn't spread disease that he knew of, and the death could simply be attributed to the will of God. Like all the other deaths from disease.

'Could be,' William acknowledged. 'Although I think having a sword stuck in his head didn't help.'

'Stuck in his head,' Hermitage repeated slowly. God didn't stick swords in people's heads. Only men did that.

'It would explain the hole,' Le Pedvin pointed out languorously.

Well, thought Hermitage, this had rapidly got exactly as bad as he had expected. He should learn never to get his hopes up. More death, more violence, and someone out there who stuck swords in other people. 'So, someone attacked him and then he came here before dying,' he said, shaking his head in sadness at the state of the world in general and this little bit of it in particular.

William simply looked at him with weighty disappointment. 'Is repeating everything part of investigation as well?' he asked.

Hermitage just gave an embarrassed smile. 'Getting things straight in my head, Majesty.'

'That'll be a miracle,' Le Pedvin suggested.

'Who is he?' Cwen asked the question that Hermitage still hadn't had an answer to. She had stepped closer to the body and was looking at it with naked interest.

'Like the weaver says,' William replied quickly. 'A Saracen.'

'But perhaps a particular one,' Wat suggested. 'Being in England and getting attacked and dying and all. Can't be many who've done that?'

'None at all,' William was clearly upset that even this one was here. 'He comes over here, starts skulking about making a nuisance of himself, and now this.'

'A nuisance of himself?' Hermitage asked. It sounded as if there was an awful lot more to this than the simple matter of a stranger being attacked and dying. And that awful lot more probably went a long way to explaining what had happened to the fellow. It certainly wasn't sounding like an accident or a routine mishap; wrong head in the wrong place at the wrong time. From the little that was being revealed, this Saracen was someone of significance and his death was a real source of trouble to William.

'You've had all your questions,' the king said, impatiently. 'Just get on with proving that I didn't do this.' He waved an annoyed hand at the corpse. 'I couldn't have anyway as the wretched man was done for somewhere else. You just have to show it's true.'

'Yes, your Majesty.' Hermitage saw that he wasn't going to get any more out of William.

'And you better get on with it,' the king urged. 'I've had to send word that this one is dead. That's bound to cause even more trouble. By the time any more visitors arrive, I want answers. Irrefutable answers.'

'Irrefutable,' Hermitage confirmed, with a very positive nod in which he had no confidence whatsoever.

The king and Le Pedvin gave Hermitage glares of instruction and swept from the place, leaving silence and confusion in their wake.

The three people left in the tent who were capable of

## The Case of the Curious Corpse

looking at one another did so. Then they looked at the one on the floor who wasn't doing anything.

'He did do it then,' Wat said, once William and Le Pedvin were well out of earshot. And he mumbled it in a quiet whisper, just to make sure.

'And why's it so important that he didn't?' Cwen asked. 'As he says, he doesn't usually mind killing people. What's so special about this one?'

'He does look very well dressed indeed.' Hermitage was now able to voice his earlier thought. 'Which doubtless means he's rich. Or was rich. Rich people getting killed always causes all sorts of problems. Perhaps even for kings like William.'

Wat stepped over to examine the body more closely and took the scarf between finger and thumb. 'My God,' he breathed. 'This thing's silk.'

'Silk?' Hermitage found that hard to believe. Perhaps it had a bit of silk in it. A tiny bit. After all, it was hugely expensive stuff, was in very short supply and it took years to make anything out of silk. For all those reasons it was usually reserved for church regalia.

'The whole thing is silk,' Wat was in quite a state now. 'And there are yards of it. Round his neck. Just draped about.'

Cwen went over and joined him. 'So this is silk,' she said, touching the scarf gently. 'I've only heard about it before. Never seen so much as a thread.'

'I'm not surprised.' Wat gave the corpse a fresh appraisal. 'This man was more than rich. Even the rich don't walk about strewn in yards of silk. They might have some but they don't wear it to go and get killed in.'

Hermitage let go of a little snort. 'I hardly think the fellow knew he was going to his death when he set off in the morning.'

Wat was serious, 'No one setting off in the morning puts on this amount of silk at all. You might wear it for a wedding and then it would be locked up again. This thing's worth more than my house.'

'So he's very rich,' Hermitage concluded.

Wat was down at the feet now, examining the boots and frowning.

'Don't say they're made of silk as well?'

'No,' Wat confirmed. 'Just the very finest leather I have ever seen. And what's even odder is that they're nearly worn out.'

'Worn out?' Hermitage couldn't see what the problem was. Everyone's shoes wore out.

'The most expensive pair of shoes in the country, and he's been using them to walk in.' Wat was astounded. 'If the Pope had a pair of shoes this good he probably wouldn't even stand up in them, let alone move about.'

'Maybe they were all he had?' Cwen suggested.

'If you've got a pair of boots like this, you've probably got a whole room somewhere just to keep the rest of your footwear in.' Wat shook his head in amazement. 'I'm not surprised William is worried. This man is beyond rich. He is going to be serious trouble.'

'I did wonder about that,' Hermitage mused. 'That's why William had to send word he was dead. And the man's friends might be quite upset about it and blame him. Hence he wants to show that he didn't do it.'

While this was all very reasonable, it didn't seem to be getting them anywhere. Hermitage was satisfied that a rich and important Saracen had died and that William didn't want to be held responsible. That all made perfect sense. Well, perfect as far as William and the Normans would be concerned, who seemed to have very strange ideas about most things. That just left him with the task William had laid out; prove that it wasn't him, probably by finding out who it was.

'It's a bit odd though, isn't it?' Cwen was frowning as she looked at the body.

A bit odd? Hermitage sincerely hoped this qualified as a lot more than just a bit odd.

Cwen went on, explaining the oddness with unfortunate clarity. 'What is a rich Saracen doing in the middle of England draped in finest silk and wearing the best boots in the land? What is he then doing getting himself struck on the head before staggering into William's camp where he inconveniently died?'

'And where are his men?' Wat added. 'No one this wealthy travels anywhere on their own. He must have been separated or singled out.'

'Oh, dear,' Hermitage said. 'Oh, my,' he added. 'Oh, dear. Oh, my,' he finished off.

'Spotted something?' Wat asked.

'It's what you said,' Hermitage explained with a quaking voice. 'And what William said.'

'What we said?' Cwen prompted him.

Hermitage explained his terrible conclusion, which he really didn't want to draw at all. 'What is the man doing here? One Saracen in the whole of the country, as far as we know. Is it really likely that William would not know him very well indeed?'

'I suppose not,' Wat replied. 'But he could have been off somewhere without the king knowing. Being this rich I think you can pretty much do whatever you want.'

'But William said he had staggered miles to get here.'

'So?'

'How did he know that? If the man just appeared at the camp gate, fell over and died he could have come from anywhere. He might have been just round the corner. How did William know it was miles away?'

They all looked at one another while Wat and Cwen contorted their faces to process this new piece of information. Those faces became expressionless as they drew their conclusions. Hermitage could see from their drawn and worried looks that they had arrived at the same conclusion. The conclusion that dare not speak its name.

Pale and quiet voices drifted from pale and quiet faces as they gave their awful answer in unison. 'William did do it.'

Wat blew long and slow. 'Now we really do have a problem.'

# Caput IV

## Tales from The East (Not Norwich)

'So,' Wat said, 'let us reconsider the king's request.'

They had escaped the presence of the dead Saracen leaving a Norman guard standing sentinel; probably not to stop the corpse leaving. With grumbling discontent, they were allocated a vacant tent. The camp Master said it was only because Le Pedvin had said so and that if it was up to him he'd kick them out into the darkness where they would be eaten by wolves.

Hermitage could not face explaining to this rough and angry man that people in England did not get eaten by wolves. He just shook his head at the ideas people got in their heads without a shred of evidence. Mind you, he had to accept that he didn't actually know that they were in England. For all he could tell they were in Scotland or Wales, where everyone knew people got eaten by wolves.

Needless to say, the tent had no comforts about it at all. There was one simple soldier's field bed, a wooden construction that could be easily dismantled and transported. There was the remnant of a fire but no fuel, and cooking utensils but no food. Hermitage did ask if the current occupant would be returning soon. The reply that he certainly wouldn't have any use for it any more was delivered in such a strange and hushed tone that he didn't like to enquire further.

Wat had scuttled off to locate something to eat and Cwen was allocated gathering wood for the fire. Hermitage was told to stay in the tent and not ask any questions about where the wood or the food came from. When Wat did return, he hastily drew the tent flap closed behind him and beckoned Hermitage to silence while a group of men, complaining loudly about thieves in the camp, went past without stopping.

Hermitage frowned at Wat and gave a little "tut" but he was very hungry.

Cwen's arrival was no better. She hastily dived into the tent carrying a wooden assembly that was clearly some sort of load-carrying apparatus. It was well made and solid, and obviously not intended for the fire.

'Where did you get that?' Hermitage demanded.

Cwen shrugged, 'Fell off the back of a Norman,' and she proceeded to stamp the thing into manageable sized pieces.

Wood quickly burned and food quickly heated and eaten, they could return to the matter in hand.

'I think what he is actually asking us to do is this.' Wat chewed a last piece of meat and drew a small bone from the corner of his mouth. 'Prove that he didn't kill the man that he did kill so that some Saracens won't come over and kill him in revenge. Or just to teach him a lesson.'

'But we don't actually know that he did do it,' Hermitage put in, although it did feel odd, defending King William against the accusation of murder. Particularly as they'd only just concluded that was guilty.

'Well, not exactly.' Cwen warmed her feet by the embers of the fire. 'But it's pretty, what's that word?'

'What word?'

'The one you use when you see a fox with chicken feathers round its mouth and the chicken is missing.'

'Suspicious?' Hermitage suggested.

## The Case of the Curious Corpse

'That's the one. It's pretty suspicious. I mean, really. King William, the man who has spent the last two years killing people claims not to have killed the one person who's lying dead in his camp?'

'True.' Hermitage had to acknowledge this. If you found any dead person with William close by there was only one conclusion. You'd need a mad man standing over the body with a dripping knife, doing a little dance and singing, "I did it, I did it" to perhaps raise a modicum of doubt. Even then you'd have to be very careful.

But of course, Hermitage wanted to be very careful and absolutely sure before coming to any firm conclusions in any circumstances whatsoever. If the experiences of his life were anything to go by that firm conclusion could be years away.

'But that's investigation,' he went on. 'There may well be suspicions about people. In all the horrible things we've had to deal with, there are suspicions. Only when you get the evidence can there be any certainty. At that point, all the suspicions you've held about other people fall away.'

Wat coughed. 'So, what happens when you've got the evidence that William did it?'

'Ah.' Hermitage hadn't thought that far ahead. 'That could be a problem.'

'I doubt it.' Wat was casual. 'Only two choices in that situation. One, keep it to ourselves and make something else up.'

'Wat, really,' Hermitage chided.

'Two, tell William and let him kill us straight away.'

Nobody had to say, "oh, he wouldn't", they knew he would.

'Of course, it's true that William's enemies are probably all around him,' Hermitage said. 'It's quite possible one of them did it.'

'Why?' Cwen asked.

'No idea,' Hermitage had to admit. 'But with a country swarming with people who want to kill one another, anything's possible.' After a pause for everyone to have a nice, introspective worry, he saw that there was nothing for it. 'Either way, we have to get on and find out what we can. William's not going to be very happy if we say we decided not to bother, or we can't find anything. He wants it proved that he didn't do this.'

The others gave him the looks the town drunk gets when he says he's off to fight a bear.

'We have to see what can be proved and take it from there. As I say, it could be that William is telling the truth. This time. Maybe he really didn't do it.'

'Pah,' Cwen dismissed the suggestion. 'Like he really didn't shoot Harold in the eye and instead let him escape from the battle near Hastings.'

They all had a laugh at that ridiculous tale.[1]

'Maybe he didn't do it personally,' Wat suggested, which seemed to give some hope. 'Maybe it was Le Pedvin?' That generated another silence. The thought of Le Pedvin dealing with them was somehow worse than William. At least the king was direct and decisive. Le Pedvin was just, well, nasty.

'Or any one of a thousand Normans just following their king's orders. We all saw how keen they were to come over to Derby and fetch us when it seems William had only mentioned it in passing. Imagine what they'd do if he said he would really, really like this Saracen dead?'

---

[1] A ridiculous tale that has been dragged out into a whole book; *The Domesday Book (No, Not That One)*

'At least that would mean it wasn't William who struck the fatal blow. I'm sure he'd quite happily throw one of his men to the Saracens to save his own skin.' Cwen's opinion of William was not improving.

'There's nothing for it,' Hermitage thought this discussion was getting them nowhere. 'We have to find out what happened. We have to investigate. When we come to an answer, we'll worry about it then.' He knew this was a bit rich coming from him, as he understood perfectly well that he would be worrying about it from now on. 'Who was this Saracen? Where has he been to get struck, and who did it? It should be easy enough to confirm whether he did stagger into the camp as William said. We just ask some of the guards.'

'William's guards,' Cwen pointed out.

'Who do what William tells them,' Wat added. 'And says what he tells them, probably.'

'We have to start somewhere,' Hermitage protested. 'In fact, we should really look at the body again.'

'Why?' Cwen asked, obviously not keen on the idea.

'Because we've only been told he was struck on the head.'

'Looked pretty obvious to me,' Wat said.

'But there might be something else. Other wounds?' He really didn't know anything about this and thought that being hit on the head with a sword would naturally lead to death.

'Do we have to?' Cwen turned up her nose.

'The alternative is to just believe what William has told us.'

'Ah,' Cwen saw the point.

'One thing does still puzzle me though.' Hermitage frowned.

'Only the one?' Wat gave a heartfelt laugh.

'Why is William going to all this trouble? I know this Saracen is incredibly rich and probably well connected, and his relatives might declare war,' as he said this he thought it did sound reason enough to go to some trouble. 'But William is having wars all the time. It's what he does. And he wins them all. He defeated Harold and the entire Saxon army. The greatest nation in the world fell before him. Surely he could deal with one Saracen and his family?'

'If it were only so simple,' Wat said.

'You know more?' Hermitage was intrigued. He knew Wat was a man of the world, after all, he was the one who had recognised a Saracen in the first place.

'Only what I've heard from merchants.' Wat looked around the tent to make sure they weren't being overheard, which was rather pointless as they were the only ones in it. 'A lot of very good trade comes from the east. It's a very unusual part of the world.'

'What, Norwich?' Hermitage asked, wondering why that place in particular, was so strange.

'No, not Norwich. For goodness sake, Hermitage.' Wat sighed heavily. 'The east where this body came from. Before it was a body of course. There's always a lot of talk with the merchants who've been out that way. Everyone wants tales of the mysterious east and the goings-on out there. Who's fighting who, who's rich and killing their relatives, what the very latest things coming to market are. And if what I've picked up is true, we might have a real problem.' He looked very sombre.

'A real one?' Hermitage thought that this problem was bad enough. He certainly didn't want to deal with any real ones.

'The Normans aren't just here you know,' Wat started his explanation in hushed tones as if it were some terrifying tale

## The Case of the Curious Corpse

around the camp-fire. Which Hermitage was pretty confident it would be. 'They're all over the place.' He made it sound like an infestation. 'North, south, east, west. Well, not west perhaps, but everywhere else. Swarming they are. They'll fight anyone, anywhere, any time. And when they've run out of opponents they fight one another. Apparently, there's one of them called William Iron Arm.'

'Are all Normans called William?' Hermitage asked, before recognising Wat's look, which told him to shut up.

'From what I hear, the two Williams do not get on at all well. If they so much as catch wind of one another there's a battle of some sort. Good job one is off killing southerners while ours does the same for the north. Anyway, this William Iron Arm was in the south, where the Saracens come from.' Wat looked them both in the eye to make sure they got the significance of this. 'And the Romans paid him to fight the Saracens on an island called Sicily.'

'Romans?' Hermitage was much more interested in that aspect. 'What Romans?'

'The ones in the east,' Wat said as if everyone knew that.

'There are Romans in the east?' Hermitage was amazed. The Romans had left Britain hundreds of years ago. It had never occurred to him that there might be some still out there.

'Except they don't call themselves Romans. They're,' Wat thought about it for a moment, 'Byzantines, or something like that. Apparently.'

'Oh, them.' Hermitage understood now. Poor Wat. He couldn't be expected to understand complex issues like this. The Byzantines were nothing to do with the old Romans. He'd explain it all later if they got the chance.

'Sicily?' Cwen was trying out the sound of the bizarre name.

'Where on earth is that?'

Wat shrugged that it didn't really matter. 'Somewhere off the coast of Kent, probably. Can I get on?'

Hermitage and Cwen nodded, silently.

'Thank you. The point is, these Saracens put up a fight and although the Byzantines and the Normans and some others won, they had to make peace.'

'I bet the Norman didn't like that,' Cwen observed from her understanding of Normans.

'Exactly. And there was probably all the usual negotiation around a peace. So, if these Saracens get to hear that William, our William, has killed one of their own, there's likely to be a whole world of trouble.'

'But this Sicily place sounds like it's miles away.' Cwen shrugged that it couldn't be their problem.

'It is. But then, being Normans, they couldn't leave a fight alone. Their friends the Byzantines had sort of won and so laid down their arms.'

'Quite right and proper,' Hermitage said, satisfied with an outcome for once.

Wat continued. 'Which the Normans saw as the perfect opportunity for an attack. After all, a friend with no weapons is much easier than a fully-armed enemy.'

Hermitage could only sigh.

'And they had some success, apparently. I suspect there isn't anyone left down there who doesn't count the Normans as their sworn enemy and would love any excuse to put them in their place. Never mind the Saxons nearby, there's a whole world of people who wish the Normans ill. If they don't all kill one another, one of these days someone will do it for them.'

Hermitage tried to take all of this in. He knew the world

extended beyond the monastery wall but most of the time he didn't like to think about it. It made him feel very small and insignificant. He knew that he was small and insignificant in the sight of God, but in the sight of everyone else as well was disconcerting.

'So, it's not just the family of this Saracen who might be out for William's blood,' Cwen noted, with some relish.

'No,' Wat was grim, 'It could be the whole Saracen nation, the Byzantines, the Pope and the King of Germany, for all I know.'

'Oh Lord,' Hermitage whimpered. He had an awful thought. Awful in its own right and awful for him. 'Why didn't William just bury the man and carry on as if nothing had happened? You know, say nothing, tell no one and hope it all turns out all right in the end.'

Cwen and Wat looked at him in amazement. 'Hermitage, I'm surprised at you,' Cwen said with the disappointment of a parent.

'I'm just trying to think like a Norman.'

'It is a good idea,' Wat said. 'Except that when it came out that our Saracen was dead and he hadn't told anyone, William could have no excuses at all. If he can get us to prove it wasn't him, he might survive.'

'Perhaps no one would find out at all?' Hermitage suggested.

'Unlikely,' Wat replied. 'Rich people don't die without someone noticing.'

Cwen was looking thoughtful. 'If we prove it was William, the whole world will come down on him, swords in hand.' She sounded quite pleased at the prospect.

'With us standing between them and him.' Wat sounded less keen.

'If it's possible to have less choice than no choice at all, that's what we've got. Investigation and the body of one dead Saracen await,' Hermitage sighed. 'Still, perhaps he'll keep until morning.' He lifted the tent flap and looked at the dark outside. The dark full of Normans, many of whom may have missed the instruction not to kill three Saxons wandering around the camp. If there had been any such instruction.

The fire was warm, their stomachs full and they had a tent to themselves. They all thought that this was probably as good as it was going to get over the next days and they had best make the most of it.

...

The following morning, despite some wishful thinking as he woke, Hermitage found that they were still in a tent in a camp full of Normans, ready to get on with proving the biggest murderer in the land had not committed murder. His wishful thinking was starting to get out of hand.

'Come on then,' Wat said. 'Not much chance of stealing food in broad daylight. Might as well get on with it.'

With all the enthusiasm of three little piggies going to market, they left the tent and headed back to the Saracen. Unsurprisingly the guard was still there, as was the body. The Norman started at the sight of three Saxons but apparently remembered something just before he drew his sword. He waved them past.

They paused before the body, perhaps as a mark of respect, perhaps as a final forlorn hope that all this was going to go away. Wat and Hermitage removed the covering sheet and revealed the man, who looked a lot like he had last night. Remarkably, the highly valuable silk scarf was still there.

'You'd think one of this lot would have robbed the dead.' Cwen snorted and nodded towards the camp full of corpse-robbing Normans.

'All too valuable to William as he is,' Wat said.

With great reluctance, Hermitage knelt at the head of the Saracen and looked at the wound. Yes, he could confirm it was a wound. Wat joined him and even went so far as to prod the red line that was drawn across the front of the man's head.

After a further pause, Cwen spoke up. 'That bit's true then,' she said.

It was indeed true that the man had been struck with something sharp. The large dark stain, which spread from his neck to his waist said that an awful lot of useful blood had come out.

Hermitage had to look to the wall as Wat pressed further onto the wound itself.

'Oh, nasty,' the weaver commented, reassuring Hermitage that he had been right not to look. 'It does look quite old. Very dry now but swollen and full of pox.'

Hermitage took a deep breath and swallowed.

'If pressed, I would say that he got this some time ago.'

'Then he could have staggered in from somewhere else and died here.' Cwen sounded reluctant to admit this.

'I'd have to say it was very likely.' Wat nodded his agreement. 'Doesn't look deep enough to be fatal at first blow. Unless he's been lying here for a week of course.'

Hermitage raised his eyebrows in interest. 'Which is always possible. We only have William's word that he came from outside. If William had struck him here, he might well have put him out of the way, hoping he got better.'

'Got better?' Cwen was disbelieving. 'Got better from getting a sword in the head?'

'If there was a good physick to hand.' Hermitage suggested,

although it did sound very weak. 'We need to ask someone else. We need some, erm, what would you call it?'

Cwen and Wat just looked at him. He was in charge of words.

Hermitage considered the best option. 'Corroboration,' he said.

'Who the what?' Cwen spluttered.

'Corroboration. From *corroborare*, to strengthen. It means we need to find someone else who can give us a version of events that strengthens William's explanation. If there is a separate telling, from someone who doesn't know what William has told us, it will corroborate.'

'If you say so.' Wat clearly didn't understand what he was talking about.

'The guard outside the tent will do.'

'Really?'

'Absolutely. A simple guard, just given his instruction and very seldom spoken to by the king, I expect. At least we can start with him and see how we get on.'

Leaving the Saracen with his wound, he led the way out of the tent and approached the Norman, who tried very hard to pretend that no one had appeared at all. Hermitage coughed. The guard's shoulders sagged and he turned to face the investigative party. He did not look happy to see them again.

'That man in there?' Hermitage asked with a nod.

'Which one?' the Norman asked aggressively.

Hermitage was taken aback rather. 'The dead one,' he specified, with unusual annoyance.

'What about him?'

'How long has he been here?'

'Well, he hasn't moved since he died.'

'All right.' Hermitage found himself sounding quite

# The Case of the Curious Corpse

demanding. 'Then how was he when he arrived?'

'Nearly dead.' This Norman was not being helpful. 'And later, he was dead.'

Hermitage had thought this corroboration business would be a lot less difficult than this. 'Well, when did he arrive?'

'Just before he died.'

Hermitage looked for help and Wat stepped in. He spoke casually and in an almost friendly manner to the guard. 'You do know that William and Le Pedvin have instructed us to look into the death of this man?'

The Norman did look a bit more worried than aggressive at this.

'And that if we get any more unhelpful comments there could be another dead body in the tent? One that looks quite a lot like a guard.'

The guard gave a quick look around to make sure no one saw him talking to Saxons. 'He came in a couple of days ago. Staggering along he was, calling out in some language or other. Le Pedvin had him put in the tent and sent for the physick, so that was that.'

'That was that?' Hermitage asked, thinking that sending for the physick would be a good thing.

'Our physick only tends to see people just before they die.'

'Then you should send for him earlier.'

'It's not that,' the guard explained, 'he's just not very good.'

Hermitage would have to think about that later. 'So, when the man arrived in the camp he was already wounded?'

'Either that or he'd fallen over in a pool of blood and banged his head on a sword.'

'Hm.' Hermitage turned to Wat and Cwen. 'This does seem to support William's story.'

'Unless William has instructed everyone to tell the same

story.' Cwen suggested that such large scale deceit would be common practice among Normans.

'The king doesn't talk to me at all any more,' the guard reported, with some mumbling shame and embarrassment.

'Why?' Hermitage wondered what on earth was going on in this place.

'I did a bad thing,' the guard muttered, looking at his feet and not going into any more detail, for which Hermitage was grateful. He shuddered to think what sort of behaviour would make William of Normandy stop talking to you.

'And you actually saw him arrive?' Hermitage checked.

'Yes. I always do guard duty because of the bad thing.' The way the man said "bad thing" really gave Hermitage the urge to move on.

'And does anyone know who he is?'

The guard frowned. 'What?' he asked, 'the dead man?'

'Yes, the dead man,' Hermitage's patience was generally deep and broad and accommodating but it seemed to have taken against this man for some reason.

'Of course,' the guard confirmed. 'We all know who he is. Or was.'

Hermitage was a bit stunned by that, he hadn't expected that answer and so hadn't prepared. 'So who is he then?'

'He's the hostage,' the guard replied, sounding rather proud that they had one.

'Oh, bloody hell,' Wat breathed and swore with real conviction.

'What?' Hermitage asked, not understanding why this was so interesting.

'They've only gone and killed the hostage,' Wat explained.

'Yes,' Hermitage said. 'I got that bit. Why the profanity?'

'Because you don't kill hostages. Not even Normans kill

hostages.'

'They killed all the nobles at Hastings,' Cwen pointed out, angrily.

'But only after they realised they weren't hostages because there was no one left alive to get ransom from. This hostage could be one from Sicily.'

Hermitage looked intrigued and ignorant at the same time.

'To keep the peace, armies exchange hostages. An important Norman goes to stay with the Saracens and an important Saracen comes the other way. Harold was a hostage in Normandy for a while, under the old king. Quite a nice life, being a hostage. You have to be looked after, you don't do any work and after a few years you get to go home.'

Hermitage shook his head at another whole new area of modern life he knew absolutely nothing about.

'Only if there's a big falling out and the war is about to start again do the hostages get killed. Even then it's more likely they get sent home so you can kill them on the battlefield instead.

'Killing a hostage without good reason is the very worst thing you can do. Bound to start a war. The hostage will be someone very important, probably a noble or the king's brother or something like that. His safety and protection would have been sworn to by the Normans. Probably by William in person.'

'Would a hostage dying by accident still be a problem?' Hermitage asked.

'Not necessarily. If you've got a really old one who's going to die anyway you can send the dead one back and get a replacement. Getting your hostage stabbed in the head doesn't count.'

'I see why William wants it shown that it wasn't him.'

Another thought occurred to Hermitage. 'And why would he do it anyway? If killing the hostage is such a bad thing?'

'He just does bad things?' Cwen offered.

'He's mad?' Wat suggested.

'The hostage got in his way one day?' Cwen said.

'All right.' Hermitage stopped the flow of perfectly sound reasons for King William killing the one man he shouldn't have killed. 'What was the hostage doing out of the camp anyway? If he's supposed to be safe and protected, shouldn't he be here?'

'Yes, he should.' Wat gave the guard a hard stare. 'Although hostages are pretty much free to do what they want, as long as they promise not to escape.'

'Do they do that?'

'Oh yes,' Wat nodded. 'Be very dishonourable to escape if you're a hostage. And this hostage is miles away from Sicily anyway, so he's hardly likely to walk back.'

'So, William's explanation could be entirely true,' Hermitage was quite surprised at that.

'It could,' Wat agreed. 'Although if your hostage has had his head connected to a sword and died in the camp of William the Bastard, what would you think?'

Hermitage saw that was a good point. None of them had believed a word of it.

'When the even more important Saracens come from Sicily for a bloody good explanation from William, they're going to want an awful lot of your collie borashon to believe any of it.'

'Corroboration,' Hermitage corrected. 'Yes,' he said thoughtfully. 'Would I be right in concluding that if they don't get it they'll be quite cross?'

'I think that would be fair.'

'And being cross could lead to a death or two.'

'Several, I should think. William and all those around him.'

'What's the problem, Hermitage?' Cwen asked. 'If they kill William we all win.'

'I suppose so.' Hermitage looked at the ground. 'I expect that when they find out the king has an Investigator who's been looking into it and hasn't come up with anything, they'll just let him go?'

Wat and Cwen had no reply to that, just rather pained looks on their faces.

## Caput V

## Le Pedvin Did What?

'We need to know where he'd been to get his head problem,' Hermitage said after they'd all had a quiet worry in their own way.

'Er, yes,' Cwen agreed. 'I think that will be a big step forward.' She rolled her eyes at Wat.

Hermitage turned to the guard. 'Did the Saracen often pass you on his way in and out of the camp?'

The guard looked horrified. 'I didn't do it,' he said.

'I didn't say you had.' Hermitage didn't know where the man had got that idea. 'I'm just asking you, as a guard, if you saw this man leave the camp on other occasions.'

'He was only attacked the once,' the guard explained, clearly thinking he was being blamed for something.

'Oh, for goodness sake,' Cwen huffed. 'Presumably, this Saracen has been with William for some time? Probably years.'

'Oh, yes,' the guard was confident of that.

'And what did he do all the time? Just sit around or did he go hunting and the like? Perhaps he was always going off on his own.'

'Oh, I see.' The guard was relieved that this was turning out to be someone else's problem.

'Well?'

'No idea.'

'What?'

'How should I know? I don't look after the hostages. I

stand guard. It's what I do. Might have seen him in and out a few times but I don't know how he spends his time. Not my place.'

'You must have seen him around,' Wat pressed. 'He must have been with William in Normandy.'

'Suppose.'

'Then what was he doing?'

'Being a hostage.'

'I think we need to talk to someone with a brain,' Wat concluded. 'What about his people?' he added, as an afterthought.

'People?'

'Yes. He must have had people to look after him. Hostages this rich don't come on their own. They have servants to do all the things they can't do themselves. Or don't want to do.'

'Oh, yes,' the guard was happy that he had some real information this time. 'There was only one though. King William won't have a whole troop of hostages where one will do. We provide for all he needs. He just had one of his men as a personal guard. Big, quiet fellow.'

'And where's he?' Hermitage asked.

The guard shrugged. 'Run off.'

'Run off?' Wat squeaked his surprise. 'A big Saracen fellow just ran off? Out of the well-guarded camp of the king?'

'When he saw his Master had come back dead, he probably thought he was next.' The guard seemed to consider this a perfectly reasonable conclusion.

'And the big fellow was the personal guard,' said Cwen. 'Didn't do a very good job, did he?'

'And he took his horse,' the guard complained.

'His horse?' Hermitage couldn't see that this was important.

'Magnificent beast,' the guard went rather teary-eyed. 'Sleek and fast. Could outrun anything in William's stable.'

'Very nice.' Cwen dismissed the horse. 'So, we have a rich Saracen with a nice horse and a big fellow to protect him, who goes wandering out of camp and comes back with a fatal blow to the head without anyone noticing.'

'I noticed,' the guard protested. 'I called Le Pedvin straight away.'

'I mean nobody noticed him leave.'

'Oh. Right. Yes.'

'Perhaps the big fellow did it?' Hermitage suggested. 'If the Saracen had a nice horse?' It sounded like reason enough for murder. After all, stealing a horse was reason enough for execution. He would have to ponder what it was about horses when he got a moment to himself.

Wat snorted. 'I hardly think his personal guard is going to wait years to kill him and then do it in the middle of a Norman camp.' He turned to the guard. 'Who was supposed to be looking after him? Who in William's court was responsible for the hostage?'

'Hostages,' the guard corrected.

'Sorry?'

'We've got quite a few you know,' the man went on with some pride. 'It's not just Saracens. We've got all sorts. Most of King William's neighbours have given him a hostage.'

'I bet they have,' Cwen said.

'It's hardly surprising that we wouldn't notice if the odd one went missing.'

'I don't think this Saracen counts as an odd one,' Wat said. 'Who looks after all the hostages then?'

'That'd be Mistress Le Pedvin.'

The silence was as stunned as the three Saxons who were

responsible for it. Eventually, just as the guard was starting to think something was wrong with them, Cwen found her voice. But it was a voice filled with such horror and disbelieving shock that it croaked out like the last breath of a dying frog. 'He's got a wife?'

Hermitage could not have brought himself to say those words. Le Pedvin, the man who brought as much fear to his sleeping hours as his waking, had a wife. He would not wish such a fate on anyone. Even that awful nun, Mildburgh, who had scared Hermitage pretty comprehensively, should not be forced to marry Le Pedvin as a punishment. No sin warranted such inhuman treatment.

'Good God,' was all Wat could say. For once, Hermitage was with him.

'I never dreamed.' Cwen's pale and drawn look said she had now heard of a fate that put all her gruesome plans for the Norman invaders in the shade. If one of them could marry Le Pedvin, what sort of beasts were they?

Hermitage knew there was only one thing he had to say next, but that didn't stop him dreading the words leaving his lips. He swallowed, closed his eyes and drew on his small reserves of courage. 'We have to talk to Mistress Le Pedvin.'

Wat and Cwen looked at him with a fine combination of fear and resignation, rather like people being led to the gallows by a large body of heavily armed men they knew there was no point in fighting. It was still hard to maintain even the semblance of dignity in the face of this horror.

'Where will we, erm, find her?' Hermitage asked, trying to sound nonchalant and hoping that the answer would be that the woman had gone away for a couple of years.

'She'll be in her tent. Can't miss it. Next to the king's, so she can be close at hand.'

...

'Next to the king,' Hermitage shivered. 'She would be. Along with Le Pedvin.'

'Perhaps he'll be out?' Cwen suggested.

They wandered the camp heading towards the centre, where King William's tented dwelling spread its canvas over its surroundings like a fog that hides something really horrible. Their journey was not direct, perhaps a result of them really not wanting to go anywhere near the place. They did not want to find Mistress Le Pedvin but knew they had to. The least they could do was avoid William and the Mistress's husband in the process.

'What sort of a woman would marry Le Pedvin?' Cwen gave a final shudder as they approached what must be the right tent.

It was actually quite a cheery-looking place. The canvas was clean and well-scrubbed, guy ropes were orderly and neatly arranged. There was even a stand outside where flaming wood could be deposited at night to lend heat and light.

'Probably to keep the hostages happy,' Wat observed.

Hermitage approached the threshold without going in. It was a large place with a gaping entrance shaded by a section of canvas that stretched out above their heads, supported by two equally spaced poles. 'Hello?' he called mildly, hoping that no one was in.

'Hello,' a bright and lively voice called back from the inside somewhere. A moment later a rotund and smiling woman greeted them with a broad smile and a twinkling eye. She had a mature, motherly look about her and was wiping flour off her hands with a cloth. She wore fine clothes, that much was

## The Case of the Curious Corpse

clear, but they were covered with a large, thick apron to protect them from what was obviously the morning bake.

'Aha, hello.' Hermitage was relieved that this woman was no threat and would at least give him a gentle introduction to the Le Pedvin family. The thought troubled his head of Le Pedvin having children. No, that was too foul to be accommodated and was sent on its way.

'We're, erm,' he even hesitated to make the request to another Norman. 'We're looking for Mistress Le Pedvin?'

The woman held her arms wide as if to hug them all, 'And you have found her, my dears,' she beamed.

Hermitage looked at Wat, who looked at Cwen, who looked at Hermitage.

'You're Mistress Le Pedvin?' He couldn't help the surprise making it sound like this was the most shocking thing he had ever heard.

'I am indeed. None other,' Mistress Le Pedvin's warm smile seemed to be a constant feature.

'Perhaps there's another Le Pedvin?' Cwen blurted out.

'Oh no, my dear. Just the one. There could only be one, couldn't there.' She even gave a little wink.

Hermitage still wasn't sure. 'Thin chap,' he described the one they were talking about. 'Very close to King William.'

'That's the one,' Mistress Le Pedvin confirmed. 'Do you know him?'

'Oh yes,' Wat confirmed. 'We know him.'

'He is a bit of a tinker, isn't he?'

'A tinker? Yes. Definitely a bit of a tinker.' Wat was shaking his head slowly in clear disbelief that this woman had anything to do with the Le Pedvin they knew.

'And you must be the people looking into poor Umair's death.' Mistress Le Pedvin let her head droop sadly.

'Who?' Hermitage asked before he answered his own question. 'Oh, the Saracen, yes, that's us.'

'My Marcel told me there'd be some people coming to find out who did that awful thing.'

Hermitage hoped she knew some of the awful things her Marcel did all on his own. Stabbing people in the head would be light entertainment to the Marcel Le Pedvin they were familiar with.

'One of the guards told us that you looked after the, erm..,' Hermitage had his doubts about how to express this. He couldn't believe this jolly, innocent-looking woman had the first clue about what went on around here. 'Guests?' he tried.

'The hostages you mean, my dear.' Mistress Le Pedvin smiled some more. 'Yes, that's right. Like my own little brood they are. Master Le Pedvin and I have never been blessed with children.'

Hermitage could have sworn he heard a muttered "thank God" from Wat's direction.

'I do look after them. Make sure they've got everything they need and everyone's as happy as the day is long.'

There appeared to be two options to Hermitage. The woman was either a well-meaning innocent or was completely mad. He didn't imagine that innocents lasted long in the Norman world. The thought of being as happy as the day was long was rather worrying as Hermitage's days were turning out to be very long and mostly miserable.

'So.' Hermitage went on. Whatever the woman was, she should be able to answer some questions. 'The Saracen.'

'Umair.'

'Umair, yes,' Hermitage tried to get his tongue round the very tricky name but it came out more Umaar than Umair. He was sure it was quite normal in the right parts of the

## The Case of the Curious Corpse

world but a simple Aethelred or Eorforwine would have been easier. 'We're told he came into the camp with his fatal wound. Do you think that's likely? Did he go off on his own a lot?'

'Oh, my, what a lot of questions you do ask.' Mistress Le Pedvin looked hugely amused by the whole process.

She beckoned them into the tent, which turned out to be a very comfortable spot. A thick carpet graced the floor and comfortable chairs with padded cushions were set about the place. Small tables held flagons of drink and open bowls of water for cleaning the hands. There were even plates of fruit - apples, pears and berries, as well as the smell of fresh bread baking somewhere.

'Take a seat, take a seat.' Mistress Le Pedvin bustled about and gestured that they should help themselves to whatever took their fancy. 'All that Umair's idea,' she smiled at the generous indulgences. 'Said if he was going to be held captive by the evil Norman warlords, the least he could do was put his feet up now and again.' She chuckled deeply at this, giving "evil Norman warlords" the tone of a cheeky tease from a close friend.

They settled themselves in the most luxurious surroundings they'd ever seen in a tent; actually, the most luxurious they'd seen in most houses. It became doubly hard to reconcile this Mistress Le Pedvin, who now went about straightening cushions and flicking dust from the tables, with the grizzled old Le Pedvin who did nothing but threaten them with death whenever he wanted something. She did seem to be in charge of the hostages though, whatever her state of mind.

Hermitage had a large apple thrust into one hand and a goblet of wine in the other before Mistress Le Pedvin sat in a chair opposite, perching on the edge as if it wasn't her place to be relaxing. 'Now then,' she indicated Hermitage could go on.

'Er, yes.' Hermitage put the apple and the wine down. He noticed Wat was on his second goblet and Cwen had a mouth full of pear and a handful of berries. 'We've heard that Umair was out of the camp when he was wounded.'

'That'd be right then,' Mistress Le Pedvin confirmed.

'Did he go out often?'

'He was a regular caution was Master Umair,' the Mistress said, which didn't seem to mean anything at all.

'Was he?'

She beckoned them to lean forward as she was about to reveal something private and probably embarrassing. 'Curious.'

'What is?'

'He was.'

'He was curious?'

'An enquiring mind, he called it.' Mistress Le Pedvin shook her head in sadness that anyone should be cursed in such a manner. 'Always wanting to find things out and understand things and know how they worked.'

Wat coughed into his wine. 'We know someone like that,' he muttered with an indulgent glance at Hermitage.

The monk ignored him, this Umair sounded a fascinating character.

'Oh, Master Umair, I'd say. Don't you go bothering your head about the whys and wherefores. It's not for the likes of us to know.'

'He asked a lot of questions then?'

'That he did. There wasn't a thing going on that he didn't want to know about. Why are you doing that? How does that happen? What's that you're building? Have you thought of doing it this way? He had a lot of new ideas about how to do things as well. Told the cook how to make the food better. Told the armourer how to improve the crossbows. Told the farrier how to make better horseshoes.'

'Sounds terribly useful,' Hermitage noted.

'Him and Master Ranulf never saw eye to eye.'

'Ranulf?' Hermitage asked. Where had he come from?

'Our own Master Ranulf is in charge of telling people what to do,' she informed them. 'So Umair was a terrible nuisance,' Mistress Le Pedvin smiled and laughed again. 'People liked it when Umair helped them out or told them things they didn't know.'

'Really?' Hermitage thought they were getting off the point.

Mistress Le Pedvin's face fell under a small shadow of its own devising. 'They don't like it when Ranulph tells them what to do.'

'Fascinating,' Hermitage felt he had to agree, not that he knew what he was agreeing with. 'Umair had lots of innovative thoughts then?'

'He did. But we wasn't going to have anything to do with changing things.' She said this as if it was the most outrageous suggestion. 'The old ways are the best.'

'And did he go off to find things out?' Hermitage asked with growing sympathy for the man. 'If no one here wanted anything to do with his ideas, perhaps he travelled? If he promised to return and the king would let him?'

'He was an honourable man, he was. He would no more dream of running off and betraying good King William than he would of not washing his hands before he ate.'

'He washed his hands before he ate?' Cwen spluttered a

mouthful of fruit.

'Every time,' Mistress le Pedvin reported, in tones of awe tinged with disgust.

'He did leave the camp then?' Hermitage confirmed, trying to put the bizarre hand washing business from his mind. 'Was he with you in Normandy? Before the, erm, trip to Hastings?'

'Oh, yes. He's been with us a good few years now.' Mistress Le Pedvin beamed. 'Real member of the family, he is. And always off finding things out and coming back with wild tales you wouldn't believe the half of.'

'Really?' This sounded more interesting. If the man was coming back with wild tales, perhaps he was getting into difficulties and making enemies out there. It could well be that he had a falling out with someone and that was that.

'He'd come back with arms full of plants, would you believe?'

'Plants?'

'That's right. And he'd take them to the physick and talk for hours about what do with them to make remedies for this and cures for that.' Mistress Le Pedvin laughed, heartily.

'How remarkable.'

'All a lot of nonsense of course, but we humoured him as best we could.'

Hermitage was starting to wonder if this Umair mightn't have stuck a sword in his own head, just to get away from Mistress Le Pedvin.

'No one would have passed comment on him leaving the camp then?'

'Bless my soul, no.' The Mistress beamed some more. 'He might even come back with some of his funny rocks. We always had a good laugh when he came back with his rocks.'

'Rocks?'

'Said how this one was this and that one was that. And if we put them in the furnace they'd make the metal stronger or lighter or some such witchcraft.'

Hermitage raised his eyebrows at that suggestion. The Saracen sounded very knowledgeable but it was an easy step from wisdom to witchcraft -   in which case a sword on the head might be the least he got away with.

'But you don't know what it was he was finding out about this time?'

'No one ever did, my dear. He'd come back with his little treasures and tell us all about them until we'd had enough. Then he'd go off on his own for hours on end.'

'What did he do when he was alone?'

'You won't believe this,' Mistress Le Pedvin said, with a hint of a confidence disclosed, 'he went away and wrote it all down.' She burst into a cacophony of laughter at such a ridiculous waste of time.

'He wrote it down?' Hermitage breathed.

'Books and books he made. Full of nonsense and squiggles but it kept him busy.'

He hesitated to ask the next question, in case the answer was not the one he wanted. 'And, erm, do you still have the books, at all, by chance?'

'Of course, my dear,' Mistress Le Pedvin smiled her smile. 'Poor Master Umair's only been dead a few days. We haven't had time to burn them yet.'

'No,' Hermitage burst out before he could control himself. 'Don't erm, burn them. They could be important.'

Mistress Le Pedvin looked very puzzled by this. 'If you say so, dearie.' She clearly thought she had a new idiot to look after.

'Are they here?' Hermitage could barely contain his enthusiasm, which never liked to be contained anyway.

'Only the new ones. Most of them are back in Normandy. The ones he made while we were there. He started some new ones when we came over here but they'll be about somewhere.' She made no sign of going to get them.

'Could we have a look then?' Hermitage asked. 'They could give us a clue as to how and why he died.'

'A book?'

'Yes, a book.'

'I've used one for killing rats before but never for finding things out.' Mistress Le Pedvin looked bemused by the whole idea. 'They'll be in his tent.'

Hermitage made a "now please" look with his face.

'Oh, very well.' Mistress Le Pedvin indulged her visitors and stood to lead the way through the back of the tent.

Across a short space of grass was another tent - if possible this one was even neater and better-presented than the last one.

Mistress Le Pedvin beckoned them to enter. 'No trouble to go in now, my dears. Not with him gone and his own man run off at the first hint of trouble. I don't suppose we even have to take our shoes off any more.'

Hermitage thought that your Master getting his head sliced was a bit more than a hint of trouble. He pushed his way through a gap in the canvas and stood in what was obviously Umair's personal tent. It was immaculate.

A simple cot was in one corner but it had lavish coverings and looked as if you would sink into it if you sat down. There was a large chair for relaxation and a smaller one drawn up at a desk, complete with quills and brushes and sheets of parchment neatly stacked. Hermitage had an overwhelming urge to sit down and start writing something.

Behind the desk, on a stand of their own, was a neat row of books. Each one a large volume, tall and thick and clearly made by a craftsman. Such was their order and uniformity that Hermitage was reluctant to disturb any of them.

'There you are then,' Mistress Le Pedvin waved towards these pointless wastes of space.

Hermitage took a breath and a step forward. 'I think this should be the most recent,' he said, reaching for the rightmost volume. He lifted it carefully, like pulling a baby from a well.

The others gathered round as he laid it gently on the desk and pulled open the front cover. The first page was revealed and drew a gasp from everyone.

'Well,' Hermitage said with complete confusion. 'What on earth do we make of that.'

## Caput VI

## If In Doubt, Read a Book

'What is it?' Cwen asked, peering at the page.

'It's writing,' Hermitage said.

'No.' Cwen thought that must be wrong.

'I've seen something like it in the books from the Monasterium Tenebrarii.' Hermitage smiled at the recollection of that great library that had fallen into his hands through the most bizarre set of circumstances.[2]

'Is it Saracen?' Cwen asked.

'It is. I can't read it myself but there's probably some scholar who can.'

'All them little lines?' Mistress Le Pedvin giggled at the very idea.

For some reason, an image sprang into Hermitage's mind. It was of Master and Mistress Le Pedvin gathered round the fire of an evening. He was telling her how many enemies he had dispatched that day, what method had proved most effective and what gurgling noises they made as they departed the world. She was spinning wool and saying how lovely it all sounded while she threw another priceless book on the fire. He turned a page, anxious to make his thoughts move on.

The second page contained some marvellous drawings. They could all understand these and gazed with interest. At

---

[2] Bizarre circumstances being the main feature of The Case of the Clerical Cadaver, yet another Chronicle of Brother Hermitage – there's a lot of them.

the top of the sheet, there was a very fine representation of the Betony plant. Its beautiful pink flowers were picked out exquisitely, indicating that this Umair was a fine artist, among his other talents.

'The cure for Chilly Need,' Hermitage announced, knowledgeably.

Below that was a very clear drawing of a rock. What it was, no one had a clue, but Umair had clearly thought it important. There was a lot of writing around it and there was even a small image of what the inside looked like when the rock was smashed in half.

At the bottom of the page was an image of something much more obvious. This was a fortification. The landscape around it was sketched out with simple lines but gave a very good impression of its position. The wooden fort itself was very accurately represented. A great wall rose up in the front with a gate firmly closed. Above that, dashes of ink, thrown on the surface with a brush, created very clear images of men peering over a strong wooden defence. There were smaller drawings of the sides and the back of the place and some writing below gave it a title of some sort.

'Now that is interesting.' Wat examined it closely. 'Do you know where this is?' he asked Mistress Le Pedvin.

The woman looked thoroughly confused.

'This looks like the drawing of a real fort somewhere. Do you know where?' Wat pressed.

'Probably somewhere Umair went on his travels. Perhaps he saw it once,' she said.

'I think he probably did.' Wat sighed. 'Unless he was in the habit of just drawing forts for entertainment.'

'Is it important?' Hermitage asked.

'I think it could be.' Wat was thoughtful. 'Tell me, mistress, did Umair ever have discussions with the king before he went off on one of his journeys?'

'Why, good King William had a kind word for him on many occasions.'

Wat looked thoroughly worn out that this woman could keep up the nonsense world she lived in. Le Pedvin the tinker and good King William had laid waste to more decent families than the plague. Perhaps Mistress Le Pedvin would realise what they were truly like when they chopped her head off for producing the wrong shaped loaf.

'Well, that's very useful, thank you very much indeed.' Wat was ushering her from the room. 'We'll just carry on looking at the books and see if we can find anything helpful. Don't let us hold you from your baking.'

'Baking?' Mistress Le Pedvin, asked with a happy smile, seemingly taking no offence that she was being invited to leave. 'Oh, I'm not baking. That'd be the girls in the cook tent.'

'But the flour?' Wat asked, indicating her apron and the white smears that covered it.

'Oh,' Mistress Le Pedvin saw his mistake and corrected him kindly. 'That's not flour my dearie, that's lime. I'm just slaking the bodies in the grave-pit out the back. And I'd better get on or the crows will be all over the place.' With a cheery wave, she left the three of them staring after her.

'You know,' Hermitage spoke after the longest of pauses. 'I actually think she's madder than her husband.'

'What a couple,' Wat breathed.

Cwen looked like she'd suddenly realised she may have eaten poisoned fruit.

They managed to remove the horrible images of the Le Pedvin's at play from their heads and got back to the matter in hand.

'If we're looking for someone who might have blunted their sword on Umair's head?' Wat suggested with a glance in the direction of the departed mistress. 'Could be he just left some rocks in the wrong place and she happened to have a blade in her hand.'

Hermitage could quite imagine that Mistress Le Pedvin was as capable of murder as her husband. She'd probably do it while smiling and telling the victim that she was going to make it all better. He didn't see her leaving the camp though. 'She seems firmly in her place here, somehow,' he said. 'It does seem that Umair was murdered outside the camp and came back. I can't see her wandering out with sword in hand.'

'Probably not,' Wat agreed. 'But it's just possible someone did.'

'Why were you trying to get rid of her?' Cwen asked. 'We didn't know she was a loon until then.'

'It's the drawing.' Wat directed them back to the book. They looked again at the page. 'The fort,' he pointed out.

'It's a very good one.' Hermitage admired the detailed representation.

'And the soldiers on the wall.'

'Yes, very lifelike.'

'And what sort of soldiers would you say they were?'

Hermitage looked but couldn't see anything other than soldiers. Granted, differentiation of fighting men was not something he'd turned his mind to. If they had a sword and shouted at him, it didn't really matter.

'Saxons,' Cwen concluded.

'Eh?' Hermitage couldn't see why that mattered.

'Exactly,' Wat said. 'This is a detailed drawing of a Saxon fort. One that has been done pretty recently.'

Hermitage still thought that it was a very nice drawing of a fort, no matter to whom it belonged.

Cwen snapped her fingers. 'Our Umair has been out drawing accurate pictures of the enemy.'

'And bringing them back to the Normans,' Wat nodded.

'That's very helpful of him,' Hermitage observed.

'Not if you're the ones in the fort, it isn't,' Cwen pointed out. 'They might not take kindly to people standing about doing drawings of their defences.'

'Oh.' Hermitage got it now.

'He could have been out sizing up the enemy, as it were,' Wat speculated, 'when one of them sized him up with something sharp and heavy.'

Hermitage gave this some consideration. It was all quite possible. It had been clearly established that this Umair went about all over the place without let or hindrance. He brought back plants and rocks and drawings of the places he had been. It was quite reasonable that someone might take exception to having their fort observed by a stranger and took the appropriate action. They stabbed the stranger. In which case…

'William didn't do it,' Hermitage concluded, very happily. 'The books show that Umair had been out and about. The guard said he saw him come back wounded. It all corroborates William's version of events.' He was very pleased about this. Even his wildest hopes had not been that this would all be resolved quite so quickly. Or that he'd be able to use "corroboration" quite so often.

'Except,' Wat said in a manner that gave Hermitage fresh cause for worry. 'Who sent him out to draw pictures of enemy fortifications?'

'Perhaps no one,' Hermitage suggested. 'Could be he just

enjoyed it.'

'I hardly think it's the sort of thing a Saracen hostage would do to pass the time.' Wat scoffed at the suggestion. 'And a bit of a coincidence isn't it? Here's a chap who likes going around drawing things, I can understand that. I've done a lot of sketches myself in my time.'

Hermitage scowled at this as he knew just what sort of sketches Wat did; the sort that needed to be thrown on the fire as soon as they were discovered.

'But he likes doing sketches of enemy positions while he's in the camp of the Normans during their campaign?'

'Could be he's simply on their side,' Hermitage suggested. 'Mistress Le Pedvin did say he was part of the family.'

Wat ignored him. 'And I think it's a bit odd to bring your hostages with you on a war anyway. Better to leave them at home safely locked up in a tower.'

'Good King William had many a kind word for him,' Cwen did a very good impression of mad Mistress Le Pedvin.

'And he does live very well, even for a hostage,' Wat said.

Hermitage looked from one to the other. He was clear that something was going on here, he just didn't know what it was yet.

Cwen sighed in the face of the innocent look. 'William has been deliberately sending Umair out to get information on enemy positions.'

'Ah.' Hermitage knew what it was now. 'I suppose that is quite clever. Finding out what the enemy is up to before you attack would certainly be very useful.'

'Indeed it would,' Wat agreed. 'And sending a Saracen would be a lot better than sending a Norman who would get shot as soon as he popped his head up. The Saxons wouldn't know who Umair was, so it would take them a while before they realised what he was up to.'

'I can see that a fellow who could do such good drawings would be an asset to William,' Hermitage said. He tried to think like a Norman for a moment. A specific Norman. Called William. What would the circumstances be when Umair went out to do his drawings? He found it all too easy to slip into Norman thinking. 'I suppose the question is, did he go really willingly, or was he pushed?'

'Was he threatened with death and burning to the ground you mean?' Cwen asked.

Wat scratched his head. And then his shoulder. Followed by the top of his leg and his left calf. 'What's that smell?' he asked.

This knocked Hermitage from his stream of thought and he looked around the room. 'There's a bowl here of dried plants and herbs.' He took the thing from the desk and held it to his nose. 'Ah, it smells wonderful.'

Wat peered at it from a distance. 'Is that lavender?'

Hermitage picked out the plant in question. 'Yes, it is. What a marvellous idea to put herbs in a bowl like this and fill the room with pleasing odours.'

'Always makes me itch, lavender,' Wat grumbled. 'Anyway, where was I? Oh yes. I don't think it matters if he went willingly or William threatened him. You're not supposed to use your hostages to fight for you.'

'Hardly fighting, just going to look at a fortification.'

'And taking a detailed drawing of it and then presenting it to the king of the army about to attack it? I don't think that would worry anyone who found him and attacked him for doing it. It might also explain why he wasn't killed on the spot. He was seen, got in a fight and took one good blow to the head while he was escaping.'

'And it won't make his relatives any happier to know that he was being put in danger,' Cwen added. 'Whatever the reason, even if William didn't stick the fatal knife in, it's all his fault.'

'Oh dear.' Hermitage saw the only obvious way to get to the bottom of this. 'Perhaps we'd better go and ask the king.'

Once Cwen and Wat had got over their shock at such a stupid suggestion, they both snorted.

'Excuse me, your Majesty,' Cwen practised the conversation. 'Did you send your hostage out to do drawings of your enemies or did he volunteer? Because it will make all the difference to the army of Saracens that is probably on its way. Oh, he wanted to but you didn't stop him. That's all right then. I'm sure they'll understand if we explain it nicely.'

'You may mock,' Hermitage chided her, 'but if we can show that he really did not kill Umair it must help.' The looks on their faces said no, it wouldn't. 'A bit?' he suggested. 'Maybe?'

'William swore to protect the hostage and he didn't. It's easy. War.' Cwen shrugged as if it really wasn't her problem.

Hermitage sagged. The whole experience had been as awful as it could be, and now the question they'd been told to answer turned out to be no help anyway. 'William's asked us to do the wrong thing then,' he sighed. 'He really should be wanting it shown that the death was absolutely nothing to do with the Normans at all.'

'Yes.' Cwen gave a hopeless laugh. 'That would probably do.'

Wat offered his opinion. 'I don't see there's any way he's going to get out of this one. Umair was his responsibility. He died in William's camp, which doesn't look good. He'd survived for years as a hostage until William brought him here, which doesn't look good. Between them they organised his going off to pry on the enemy position during which he got a sword in the head. All in all, I'd say it doesn't look good.'

'Well.' Hermitage tried to look on the bright side but couldn't see it from where he was standing. 'At least we can go and tell William that yes, we can show that he didn't kill the Saracen. Not personally, at least. That's all he's asked us to do.'

The others looked at him as if he was as mad as the hostage Mistress. 'Well, what else do you suggest?' he asked. 'Run away?' While it was very tempting, he knew it would be hopeless. They'd probably never make it out of the camp. 'And you know what William's like. We've already taken most of the morning, I expect he's getting ready to ask us why we haven't finished yet.'

Wat blew out long and slow and stared at the roof of the tent. 'I suppose it might help if we find him before he finds us.'

'Oh, yes.' Cwen's voice was heavy with mocking. 'If he has to come looking it might put him in a bad mood.'

Despite staying in Umair's tent and sitting, standing, walking about and holding their heads in their hands for at least half an hour, none of them could come up with a better idea than going to the king now.

'Let's get it over with,' Hermitage said.

'Whatever "it" might be,' Cwen complained as they left the tent.

. . .

Of course, getting to see the king, even though he would want to see them, was not a simple task. There were guards and officials who saw it as their life's duty to prevent anyone getting near the man who ran the country. Hermitage tried to explore how King William was supposed to make any decisions if people weren't allowed to talk to him, but the guards and officials only gave him funny looks and told him to stop babbling.

If there was anything the king needed to know, they would tell him. But what if there was something they didn't know? Hermitage asked. "Then the king certainly wouldn't need to know it", was the circular argument.

The fact that they had actually been brought here under the king's direct order and that they were close friends of the Le Pedvins - lovely couple - did get them to the officials closest to the king.

'We have news for King William,' Wat said in a most straightforward manner.

'What?' The young man in this particular part of the tented town seemed to have his hands full. Actually, he did have his hands full. Full of parchment, some of which spilled out of his grasp and onto the floor. Hermitage stooped to help gather the droppings.

'Thank you,' the man said, brusquely. 'Put them over there.' He beckoned to a table that was already straining under the weight of a small mountain of written material, while he tried to get his armful down without dropping the lot.

Hermitage tried to balance his handful on the top so that it wouldn't slide off back to the floor.

'I said, we have news for the king,' Wat repeated.

'Oh, marvellous,' the man said, sounding as if this was the very worst thing he could have heard. 'Just what we need,' he went on, 'more news.' He nodded his head to the table.

'We've got enough news, thank you very much. We're full now.' He turned his attention to the pile of parchments and started to read them quickly and get them in some sort of order. This seemed to mainly consist of moving individual pieces from one part of the massive pile to another.

Wat looked about the room. 'Our news isn't written down.'

'What?' The man stopped his bustling activity and looked at Wat with surprise. 'What do you mean, it's not written down?'

'Erm,' Wat gave the question some thought. 'In terms of parchment and ink, there isn't any.'

'Perhaps it would be more accurate to say we have word for the king,' Hermitage explained.

'What are you doing in here then?'

Hermitage, Wat and Cwen all looked at one another, sharing the thought that they had no idea what they were doing in here, mainly because they didn't know what "in here" was.

The man saw their confusion. 'This is submissions to the king,' he explained, as if to idiots. 'Submissions are in writing.' He turned back to his table.

Hermitage felt ashamed not to know that. Until he reasoned that he couldn't be expected to know it. What a rude man.

'So,' Wat said slowly and with a nicely insulting lilt to his voice, 'if we write it down, you'll deal with it?'

The man sighed the sigh of those being asked to do what they're supposed to do anyway. 'What's it about?'

'Murder,' Cwen said, with a horrible smile.

'Murder?' The man seemed to think this was some sort of joke.

# The Case of the Curious Corpse

'Murder by the king,' Wat added.

'Murder by the king. You have a submission to make about a murder committed by the king?' The tone of voice said the man thought this was completely ridiculous.

'Or not,' Hermitage added.

The man stopped his sorting and looked at them harshly. 'Get out,' he instructed. 'And stop wasting my time.'

'No, really,' Hermitage protested. 'We have news, I mean a submission about a murder that may have been committed by the king, but actually turns out not to have been.' He could see that said out loud, this didn't sound very sensible.

'Look,' the man said, at last giving them his undivided attention. 'You see this pile here?'

They nodded that yes, they did.

'This is just begging indulgences. Virtually every noble in the land, or their relatives, in the case of the dead ones, has written to the king begging his indulgence. Usually not to have them killed as well.' He waved a hand to the other side of the tent where more parchment was piled on the floor. 'That's cravings.' He moved his attention round. 'Over there is pleadings and I've managed to get most of the humble requests into a box.

'Demands are much less voluminous,' the man was clearly on his favourite topic. 'Which is wise really. Doesn't do to demand things from King William. But beseechings had to be put in the carpenter's shop, supplications are still on the cart and I suspect some of the entreaties have been used to start fires.' He was starting to get quite excited now.

'I can see that you have a lot to deal with,' Hermitage began, thinking he'd quite like to leave now.

'Piteous imploring is still being sorted and prayerful petitioning will be the death of me.' The man took a breath.

'So it won't surprise you to hear that submissions about murders the king might have done have their own tent! One about a murder he hasn't done will at least be unique. Which means I won't have to deal with it at all.' The man glared, inviting them to say a single word.

'Perhaps we'll just find the king on our own,' Wat said backing towards the entrance.

'Good luck with that.' The man returned to his work. 'If you find him, tell him he's got a year's worth of submissions to deal with.'

Back in the open of the camp, relieved to escape the company of the man of the submissions, they simply wandered around looking for someone they recognised. Ideally, someone who knew what they were here for. Of course, they got many glares of puzzlement, suspicion and downright hatred but Hermitage's habit seemed to act as a calming influence.

'Perhaps we should go and find Mistress Le Pedvin again?' he suggested, never having realised quite how many Normans there were. 'She could probably take us before the king.'

'Liming the corpses?' Cwen said. 'I'd rather not.'

'There,' Wat called out, spotting someone weaving between the tents. He set off, Hermitage and Cwen following. He dodged and skipped between ropes and canvas before emerging into what was the main thoroughfare of the camp, a wide avenue that ran through the middle of what seemed to be the random distribution of tents. He stopped and looked around in frustration. 'Where did he go?' he asked, as Hermitage and Cwen caught up.

'Where did who go?' Hermitage asked.

'Ah,' Le Pedvin said, seeming to appear out of thin air.

## The Case of the Curious Corpse

'There you are. Where have you been?'

Hermitage felt that was an unfair criticism, considering they had been looking for anyone for quite a while now.

'We have news for the king.' Hermitage was positive that it would be better received this time. 'We know that he did not kill Umair.'

'Who?' Le Pedvin seemed not to know who that was.

'The Saracen?'

'Oh, him. You better come and explain yourselves then, but I don't think it's going to help. There have been developments.'

That did not sound good.

'Developments?' Hermitage tried to make it sound like a light enquiry.

'Yes.' Le Pedvin spoke as he strode away. 'The Saracens have a very good navy and have developed a bit of a temper it seems. And now they're coming our way.'

## Caput VII

## The Mahuqiq Are Coming

'The Saracens are coming?' Hermitage asked, squeaked and fretted all at once. 'What does he mean, the Saracens are coming?' They were scurrying along after Le Pedvin, whose long legs strode across the camp as if he owned it.

'Probably that there are some Saracens,' Wat explained, 'and that they're coming.'

'What do they want?' Hermitage asked.

'Who knows?' Cwen sounded light and only mildly interested. 'Do some drawings of William and his camp? See what herbs grow in these parts? Wreak a horrible revenge for the death of Umair by killing everyone in their beds? Could be anything, really.'

'Oh my.' Hermitage was experiencing a whole new level of worry. The events close by were bad enough, now he knew that those on the other side of the world were after him as well. Just then they arrived at the king's tent, which didn't calm him in the slightest.

At least access to the king was a lot easier now. The arrival of a band of murderous Saracens had doubtless put the categorisation of William's correspondence in its place.

'Ah.' The king looked up from a parchment, which seemed to be a map of some sort. 'There you are.'

Hermitage bowed low. 'Your Majesty,' he tried to control the tremor in his voice.

'Well?' the king asked. 'What have you found out?'

Hermitage found the blunt question a bit of a surprise. He

didn't know why, after all, it was why they were here. He swallowed and dived in. 'From the information we have gathered we are satisfied that you did not personally kill the Saracen, Umair.' He folded his hands in front of him to indicate that that was that. No more to be said. They'd done what they were asked and perhaps they could go now.

'How nice.' The king's voice did not sound like he thought this was nice. 'But the Saracens are coming now, so that's going to be no bloody help at all. Is it?'

Hermitage didn't know whether answering or keeping quiet was the appropriate response. He had a feeling that whatever he did, it would be wrong. But he was never one to let silence have its own way for too long. 'As your investigator, I could say to the Saracens that I have looked into things and can confirm that you did not do it.'

'They'll still blame me,' William complained. 'They're always like that. Blaming people. They'll say that I was supposed to be looking after him. That it was my responsibility. That I should have made sure he was safe. Never mind who killed him, I should have stopped it happening.'

Hermitage thought that sounded like a very reasonable position to take. He knew better than to so much as cough.

'Completely outrageous,' the king concluded. 'And you're no use.' His anger at them looked strong enough to kill, but he obviously had bigger problems.

Hermitage wasn't about to contradict the king.

'And it won't be just one,' William went on. 'They'll be a whole force of them. Mahuqiq.'

Hermitage thought the king might be choking, but no one moved to help.

'Ma who?' he asked.

'Mahuqiq. They're sending their Mahuqiq.'

'And what are Mahuqiq, Majesty?' Hermitage asked, thinking it really wasn't his place to be questioning the king.

'No idea.' The king shrugged. 'Probably a whole troop of specially selected assassins.'

Hermitage frowned and looked around to see if anyone else thought the king had gone a bit mad. Well, a bit more mad. 'And what are assassins?'

'No idea either. But they kill people. Apparently very well.'

Hermitage had never seen King William this concerned by any threat before. He'd never seen him concerned by any threat at all. These Saracen Mahuqiq assassins must be truly terrifying if William the Bastard was worried about them. And if he was worried, Hermitage was not going to cope at all well.

William turned his attention back to his map and beckoned Le Pedvin to join him. Perhaps they were trying to work out where best to defend themselves against the imminent attack. Or which was the best direction to run way. Hermitage didn't think it would be running away.

A further thought occurred to him and he joined Wat and Cwen for a quiet discussion. It could be that there was one feature of their discovery that would be of help to the king.

There were two problems though. First of all, should they help the king at all? He really was a most unpleasant fellow and actually had killed an awful lot of people. Just because he may not have done this one did not make him any better in the eyes of the Lord. But then who was Hermitage to judge the eyes of the Lord?

Secondly, Hermitage didn't like to speak anyway. The king would probably shout at him. And thirdly, Hermitage, being quite capable of coming up with three problems when

## The Case of the Curious Corpse

he was only looking for two, the information was only going to make things worse.

Their conversation concluded that with King William, for all his faults and terrible sins, they were at least alive. If the Saracens took over, who could tell?

Mind made up, Hermitage turned back to William and Le Pedvin. 'Majesty?' he muttered rather quietly. 'Majesty!' he called out as Cwen thumped in the back and made him jump forward.

'Are you still here?' the king looked up. 'What do you want now? I'm busy.'

'Indeed, Majesty,' Hermitage wrung his hands. 'It's just that we found Master Umair's drawings.'

The king and Le Pedvin both gave him their attention now, which was very off-putting.

'Found his what?' the king asked, looking at Hermitage as if the monk was an even bigger idiot than he usually thought.

'His drawings, Majesty. We found his books with the drawings, including the ones of the fortifications.'

The king did frown now. 'And what has that to do with anything?'

'Well, Majesty,' Hermitage prepared his explanation.

'And keep it short,' Le Pedvin instructed.

Hermitage revised his explanation. 'It is clear that Umair had been out of the camp doing drawings of various things that he saw. Including fortifications.'

'What of it?'

'The fortifications of your enemies, Majesty.'

William's scowl deepened by several fathoms.

Hermitage hurried on before William could reach out and grab him by something. 'So, it seems highly probable that he was spotted while doing one of these drawings, and attacked.'

'By my enemies?' William drew the conclusion on his own.

'Exactly. If he was hiding somewhere, recording the details of the enemy position but was discovered, there could have been a fight. Umair was struck in the head but just made it back into camp before dying.'

William turned his gaze to Le Pedvin, who looked as impassive as normal. The king threw his hands in the air. 'I told him not to go poking around in the wrong places.' He paced up and down for a few short steps. 'Didn't I tell him?'

'You did,' Le Pedvin confirmed.

William now had an explanation for Hermitage. 'He was always wanting to go off finding things out. Wherever we stopped he'd be off with his brushes seeing what there was, and then coming back and telling us about it. Interminably. He even had pictures.' It sounded like an evening looking at pictures of Umair's latest travels was not the king's favourite pastime.

'Exploring?' Hermitage suggested.

'He was what?' the king sounded disgusted.

'Exploring,' Hermitage repeated. 'From *ex*, out and *plorare* to cry out. Usually associated with hunters searching out their prey. I did consider it for the function of discovering murderers and the like, but King's Explorer didn't feel quite right somehow.'

The king gave Hermitage an intense stare. 'Shut up,' he said. 'But we're in enemy territory now and so I forbade him leaving the camp. Seems he disobeyed my orders.'

'It seems so, Majesty.' Hermitage felt safe giving an expression of agreement.

'The fool.' The king spat, back to his normal, angry self. 'And now look what he's landed me in. It'll be no good me telling this band of Mahuqiq that he wandered off against my explicit order. They'll still blame me. I should have tied him down or something.'

'You had to treat the hostage fairly,' Le Pedvin pointed out. 'There would be hell to pay if you trussed him up and wouldn't let him do what he wanted.'

William just grumbled at this.

'And if what he wanted to do was go wandering into enemy territory, what could you do?'

'Did he not appreciate the danger, Majesty?' Hermitage asked.

'Never seemed to worry about it,' William was more even-tempered now. 'Seemed to think that all this was nothing to do with him so he wouldn't be injured. He wandered about doing drawings of the battle at Battle, would you believe.'

'Did he?'

'It was him gave me the idea for a tapestry of the whole thing.'

'Really.'

'He would insist on going right up to the enemy just to look at them. They probably thought he was mad and left him to it.'

'I see.' Hermitage was starting to feel a bit trapped in this conversation.

'But he did come back with some useful information now and again, which seemed to please him.'

'Had you seen the latest drawings Majesty?' Wat stepped forward with a humble question.

'Of course,' William replied. 'That took two whole evenings.' The king obviously took little pleasure from the experience, which was odd, considering he was being told about his enemies. 'But at least he never made it to another evening,' William sounded more cheerful. 'We were due to get details of all the local animals. All of them.'

'If he did this sort of thing regularly,' Hermitage pondered out loud, 'mayhap the enemy realised what he was doing and took some action.'

'Killed him, you mean?'

'If you saw someone from the enemy drawing your encampment, what would you do?'

'Kill them.' The king was clear on that. 'Eventually.'

The king's face was thoughtful and he was looking at Le Pedvin as if the answer was on that man's gaunt face. 'So,' he drew his conclusion slowly. 'What you're saying is that I did not kill the Saracen.'

'That's right, Majesty.'

'And not only that, but he was, in fact, killed by my enemies.'

'Just so.'

'Hm.'

Hermitage smiled that the king seemed content, at last, with the outcome of his investigation.

'So, when these Mahuqiq arrive we will be able to tell them that.'

Hermitage nodded.

'Excellent,' the king clapped his hands together and rubbed them, briskly. 'Off you go then.' He waved them away.

'Thank you, Majesty,' Hermitage said, the relief swimming through him like warm ale.

'The Saracens will probably arrive in a day or so. We'll need the killer back here by then.'

Hermitage's relief left him like ale as if he hadn't made it to the privy in time.

'Killer, your Majesty?' he managed to get out.

## The Case of the Curious Corpse

'Yes,' William said as if it was obvious. 'This killer in the enemy fortification? The one who did for Umair. Go and find him and bring him back here.' He gave his attention back to his map.

Hermitage turned to Wat and Cwen who were throwing him some very strange looks.

'Go into the enemy camp and find the killer,' Hermitage repeated, slowly.

'That's right,' the king said, brightly, not looking up. 'Good work, by the way,' he added as an afterthought.

'Right into the camp of the enemy and find the one who killed your hostage. Escape from said camp and return to your lines bringing the enemy with us?'

'Just the one of them. And I don't know how many more ways you want to say it.'

'Aha,' Hermitage gave a light laugh. 'And, erm, if we sort of get killed in the process?'

'I'll explain to the Saracens. You never know, it might help.'

Wat and Cwen were giving no assistance at all. In fact, Hermitage suspected they were going to be positively troublesome when they got out of here. 'Where, who, what?' Hermitage said, unable to string his words together. 'Enemy?' he got in at the end.

'You know where they are,' William explained, happily. 'You've seen the drawings so you'll recognise it when you get there. Who? Hereward the Wake. We're on the edge of his territory now. Going to wipe him out with any luck. That drawing will help.'

'Hereward,' Hermitage muttered, having heard the horrible tales of Hereward the Wake's resistance to the Normans.

'That's right. And if Hereward did kill the Saracen I might get their army to finish him and not have to bother myself. You should be able to join him easily enough. They're my enemies, not yours. You're all Saxons anyway. Hard to tell you apart sometimes.'

...

'Hereward the Wake,' Wat said as if this was Hermitage's fault. 'We have been dispatched to the camp of Hereward the Wake, no, I beg your pardon, the fortress of Hereward the Wake.'

They had returned to Umair's outer tent, which felt like a bit of a refuge in this place. Of course, they checked that Mistress Le Pedvin wasn't there first and reasoned that Norman soldiers weren't likely to go tramping through the place, looking for Saxons to kill.

Hermitage felt that a comment to Wat would be unhelpful. And he couldn't think of one anyway.

'Dispatched to find a killer, don't forget,' Cwen waded in now. 'One who is probably being congratulated for finishing off the Saracen who was prying on their camp in the first place. And then we have to take him back to King William.'

'Erm.' Hermitage wondered if there was any other way of interpreting their instructions. There wasn't.

'You never know,' Cwen went on, 'he might come along if we ask nicely.'

'Perhaps he'd like a go at trying to kill William as well,' Wat suggested.

Hermitage thought that William wouldn't be very happy about that at all. Then he saw that Wat was being sarcastic.

'Mind you.' Cwen was thoughtful. 'We are being sent off into Hereward's camp in the middle of a campaign to get rid

## The Case of the Curious Corpse

of him. Chances are we won't come back at all.'

Hermitage couldn't see any benefit in that outcome.

'So. Why don't we not come back at all?' she suggested.

No, Hermitage wasn't following this.

'You mean just disappear?' Wat had a sly look on his face.

'Who's to know?' Cwen said. 'William will just assume Hereward's done for us and that's what he'll tell the Saracens. With any luck, they won't believe a word of it and cut him into little bits.'

'Or Hereward cuts us into little bits first?' Wat put in.

'We don't go anywhere near Hereward. We head home and keep low until there's a new king.'

Now Hermitage got it. And it was positively dishonest.

'After all,' Cwen went on, seeming to anticipate Hermitage's objections, 'we've done what the king wanted, shown that he didn't kill Umair. It's a bit unfair to change the job once we've done it.'

Hermitage suspected that fairness seldom loitered long in the presence of the king.

'And what if he comes out of it all alive and finds we ran off?' Hermitage asked, heading straight for the worst possible outcome.

'The usual,' Wat said. 'Burn everything to the ground and kill us all.'

Hermitage considered the option. 'Just vanishing is a bit, erm, what's the word?'

'Risky?'

'I was going to say stupid.'

'Hermitage!' Cwen was clearly stunned by this most uncharacteristic outburst.

'Well, it is, isn't it? I mean, even if William doesn't get us personally and is killed by the Saracens, Le Pedvin will come after us just to express his disappointment. We still end up dead.'

'Of course, Le Pedvin might be killed as well?' Cwen sounded happy at the prospect.

'If he can be killed,' Wat said. 'And William might be having us watched already.'

Hermitage looked around. He couldn't see anyone watching them secretly, but then thought that secret watchers probably shouldn't be spotted anyway.

Cwen sighed her sigh of disappointment that the two men weren't prepared to take the brave, decisive and probably dangerous step. She tended to sigh it quite a lot. 'So, we go and find Hereward, do we? Just sort of wander out of camp, a bit like Umair, and when someone tries to knock us on the head with a sword, we'll know we've arrived?'

'I imagine the Normans know where he is,' Hermitage said. 'And if William wants us to go there it's only reasonable they should give us some directions.'

They both looked at him as if the idea of asking the Normans for directions was like asking King Harold for the name of a good archer.

'Let's take the book,' Hermitage blurted out, with a bit too much enthusiasm.

'Take the book?' Cwen sounded suspicious.

'You've got enough books, Hermitage.' Wat could clearly see his workshop filling up with the things.

'This one would be useful. If we take the one with the fortification in it, we can probably find our way from Umair's drawings.' He saw that this actually made very good sense. It also meant he could get another book. You could never have enough books.

'Go on then,' Wat said as if indulging the pestering child

who had seen some ducks on a pond and was insisting on stopping to throw stones at them.

Hermitage scurried off to Umair's inner sanctum and returned in no time, clutching the precious volume.

'Happy now?' Cwen asked.

'It's entirely practical,' Hermitage defended himself. He stood with book in arms and opened it to the page with the drawing of the Saxons behind their high wall. 'Here,' he said, turning the leaves. 'The land around the fort.' He held it out for the others to see. After the detailed drawing of the fortification, there was a series of images of the landscape, several of them with lines drawn, which seemed to show the route Umair had taken. 'What a remarkable innovation,' Hermitage observed.

The others obviously couldn't see anything.

'Rather than the map being a representation of the events that took place during his journey,' Hermitage explained what a proper map should be, which they knew anyway. 'Umair has drawn a picture of the ground over which he travelled.'

'What good is that going to be?' Cwen asked.

'It means we can follow,' Hermitage said simply. He gazed in awe at the image and wondered why no one had thought of doing this before.

'Excellent,' Wat sounded enthusiastic and despairing at the same time. 'Clear directions to the heart of the problem. Perhaps there's a picture of someone stabbing him in the head. Save us a lot of trouble.'

Hermitage considered this for a moment but concluded that capturing the image of someone who was hitting you on the head was probably quite tricky.

He turned the book around in his hands until he had the

small blob that looked a bit like the Norman camp, facing in the right direction. 'It's that way,' he announced, pointing out of the tent opening.

Wat and Cwen followed his pointing finger and squinted.

'I don't think we'll be able to see it from here,' Hermitage said. 'I imagine we have to walk quite a distance. I don't think even William would put his camp right at the enemy door.'

'Nothing would surprise me.' Wat put down the goblet of wine he had been using to fill the time.

They were very pleased to get the camp behind them. There was something quite oppressive about being in the midst of the Norman army. Probably because the Norman army kept oppressing everyone they came across.

It wasn't exactly a feeling of freedom, Hermitage wasn't sure he knew what that was like, but it was a sense that his life was under his control once more. It was only this one little bit of it and he was confident it would be taken away as soon as they found Hereward, but he could decide to put one foot in front of the other, instead of being told to do it.

'I don't suppose Umair's marvellous map tells us how far we have to go?' Cwen asked.

'It doesn't, I'm afraid.' Hermitage didn't need to open the book, having memorised the map. 'If we see a large fortification with Saxons on top, we're probably there.'

'That could be it then.' Wat nodded forward.

The landscape here was remarkably flat, which meant it was possible to see for miles. The land looked marshy and damp with clumps and larger patches of reeds filling their view in all directions.

The sight of nothing but Norman tents had not given Hermitage the chance to have even a wild guess at where they might be. Now it was clear. These must be the eastern marshes. Or the northern marshes. Or some other marshes he didn't know about. He knew what the eastern marshes looked like, he'd spent quite a while tramping through them. Now he looked with fresh eyes he realised all marshes looked the same. Wherever these were, there were miles of them.

That probably meant that there were secret paths winding through the deadly bogs. Paths known only to strange local people who didn't talk much and had a certain something about them; something that made decent folk shy away and bring their children indoors.

This would be excellent land for frustrating an enemy though. Land through which the men of the marshes could travel but lead their pursuers into danger. Of course, very few people pursued men of the marshes anywhere if they had any sense. There was nothing a man of the marsh had that those decent folk would want anything to do with. The personal habits of men of the marshes were not discussed in polite company. As the Rhyme of the Country Maid had it:

*As I was tripping to Willacombe fair*
*I saw a man of the marsh.*
*I said to the man of the marsh that day,*
*Why are you going there?*
*The man of the marsh he looked at me*
*With his eyes as grey as peat.*
*And he called me near and beckoned me close*
*....And that was my mistake.*
*So ye who hear this rhyme of mine,*
*Listen and take heed.*
*Stay away from the men of the marsh*
*They're disgusting.*

While Hermitage couldn't see any sign of men across these miles of marsh, he could see a large construction, sitting on what must be a very modest hill, so little did it lift above the blank horizon.

'I think that's too big,' he said, gazing into the distance. 'That looks so far away it must be pretty huge to be seen from here.'

Cwen peered as well, her younger eyes making better of the distance. 'It looks like a building, a proper one. Like an abbey or something.'

'An abbey?' Hermitage gave it some thought. 'Ely?'

'I can hardly tell from here,' Cwen protested.

'No, no. I mean it must be Ely. Hereward is fighting in the east if the rumours are true. And if William has brought us nearby, that must be Ely. It couldn't be anywhere else.'

'Lovely,' Wat said. 'We know we're near Ely.'

'Not lovely really,' Hermitage noted. 'Considering the Isle of Ely is regularly in the hands of the Vikings.'

'Out of the hands of Normans, looking for Saxons and jumped on by Vikings.' Wat's voice was heavy with resignation. 'What a perfect day. It'll be men of the marshes next.'

'I don't see any other fortification,' Hermitage observed, scanning the land in all directions. 'And you'd think it would stick out if there was one.'

The Norman camp was still clear at their back, and even though they'd only come a few miles, it was still the biggest thing close at hand.

'Maybe it's built out of reeds,' Cwen suggested flippantly.

'These things would hardly keep a Norman donkey at bay, never mind the whole army.' Wat kicked at the nearest reeds. 'Ah!' he reeled backwards as a large man with a spear rose up

## The Case of the Curious Corpse

from the ground.

Hermitage, Wat and Cwen formed a very small and ineffective defensive circle as more men appeared out of nowhere. They were clearly Saxon, or rather they were clearly not Viking or Norman, so what else could they be? They all had weapons in hand and were smeared with mud and bits of greenery, probably to hide them from sight. Which had worked very well.

'Aha,' one of the muddy men said, waving a long spear in their direction.

Hermitage looked at them all with fear but a touch of gratitude that they weren't already dead. These men didn't attack immediately so maybe they were just locals out to do something or other in the reeds. 'Eadig pec to metenne,' he tried, trying to sound as gruff and Saxon as he could.

'Nice to meet you too,' the nearest fearsome Saxon replied, looking a bit puzzled. 'What are you doing here?'

'Oh, you know.' Hermitage tried to think what on earth he was going to say.

'Escaping the Norman bastards,' Cwen announced, proudly.

'Yar,' all the men cheered and shook their weapons about.

'Come to join Hereward and rid the land of the evil invaders,' she went on.

'Yar,' the men repeated, with enthusiasm, their early aggression fading.

'You don't erm,' Hermitage hesitated to ask. 'You don't know where he is by any chance? Do you?'

## Caput VIII

## Hereward the Wake (Not)

'I am not Hereward the Wake,' Hereward the Wake said when they arrived at his camp.

The men leaping from the reeds to accost Hermitage, Wat and Cwen had known exactly where Hereward was because they were members of his band. Proud members of his band resisting the Norman plague and fighting to their death rather than give up an inch of land to that usurper and murderer of the rightful king.

There were quite a lot of descriptions of what they were, all involving fierceness of one type or another, and all of which took an interminable time to recite. They were still only halfway through a set of lurid descriptions of what they were going to do to William's livestock when they arrived.

'Not, erm,' Hermitage was confused. The man and his band seemed very happy that this was Hereward a few minutes ago. Now here he was, saying that he wasn't.

'The wretch William has already promised this land,' Hereward explained. 'Promised it to a family by the name of Wake. He calls me Hereward the Wake to make it sound like I'm related. He thinks this means there will be no objection to his plans.'

'Yar,' his band cried in unison; this "yar" being the defiant variety rather than the enthusiastic version. They seemed to have a "yar" for every occasion.

Hereward carried all the authority of any man who could

sit among a large group of devoted followers, all of whom cried "yar" at every opportunity. He was not a striking man though. His voice had a lilting, slightly distant tone as if talking to the people right in front of him was a bit of an effort.

Around King William, the aura of impending death hung like a heavy blade on a very thin string. Around Hereward, the aura was more, well, marshy. He looked fit and strong, probably about thirty years of age and appeared to be a man well used to dealing with trouble. He also looked like one who had been living among reeds for a bit too long. There was a tiny glint to his eye that seemed to be expecting something very peculiar to happen any moment now.

On their journey here, Wat had explained that all he knew of Hereward was that the man was trouble. Trouble to the Normans, certainly, but also trouble to his family, who had sent him into exile. The exile seemed to be effective because Hereward took up being trouble as a profession. There were legends that he had fought in every battle anyone could name and came out of them all alive. Which was very suspicious.

Hermitage well knew the rumour that Hereward's father was the old Earl of Mercia, a truly fearsome fellow who would certainly not tolerate a defiant son. If that was true it meant his mother was Lady Godiva, and if Hermitage's own mother had gone around town dressed like that, he'd probably have turned out trouble as well.

All this was hard to believe, looking at him now, lord of a wet and reedy demesne.

'So you've escaped this Norman blight then?' Hereward didn't sound doubtful about this. Hermitage would have done. Three Saxons turn up out of nowhere, right next to William's camp? It must count as odd, surely.

'That's right,' Cwen said loud and clear before Hermitage could say anything a bit more accurate. 'From the very heart of their camp.'

There were some impressed mutterings at this.

'Excellent,' Hereward commented. 'And now you join us to fight to the death.'

'Aha.' Hermitage hoped it sounded like "yes" without meaning it.

Hereward frowned at them all. 'I'm sure the woman will strike fear into their hearts.' He waved a hand at Cwen. 'Not sure about you two though.'

Cwen beamed like a burning brand.

'A monk and a whatever-you-are,' he looked at Wat in his fine clothes with clear confusion.

'Weaver,' Wat said. 'Wat the Weaver.'

This brought no reaction at all, which clearly disappointed Wat but made Hermitage happy that there was at least one band of men in the country who did not salivate at the thought of Wat's works.

'And are you a fighting monk?' Hereward asked Hermitage.

'Erm,' Hermitage wondered how to answer this. A blank "no" seemed a bit abrupt.

'No, then,' Hereward concluded. 'I shall have to introduce you to Leofric, he's a monk and very handy with a sword.'

Hermitage didn't like the sound of that. Perhaps he could offer his own skills and make a record of their exploits. A very neat record.

'We'll make Saxon terrors of you both, given time.' Hereward nodded at his own thought. 'Assuming you live long enough, of course.'

'Ha, ha,' Hermitage laughed lightly, with just the slightest hint of panic.

'But the day draws on. We'll retire for tonight. The Normans don't come out after dark.' Hereward's band gave vent to a triumphant "yar" this time, clearly taking credit for the fact that Normans didn't go out at night.

Not that it was actually dark yet. Their discussions with various Normans hadn't taken that long, and although they had walked for a good hour or two, it was still only late afternoon. A bit early to retire for the night, surely.

The camp they were in did seem to be a temporary place though, just a flattening of the reeds really, in which the men could rest without being seen. A very small fire sent wisps of smoke into the air but even if they were spotted, it would be easy to disappear into the greenery.

Hermitage knew very little about how fighting men organised themselves, but he imagined this was an expedition from Hereward's main stronghold. Doubtless, the men would sally forth to harry the enemy before retreating to safety each night.

He had absolutely no idea what sallying and harrying involved, but he could do retreating.

If this was the case, the man who killed Umair might be with them right now. Or then again, he might be back with the main body of men. Hermitage would have to accompany the force back to their home and take things from there. It did occur to him that if finding Hereward and joining him without being killed was tricky, "taking things from there" was going to a real problem. Only now did the strength of Cwen's argument rattle him. How on earth was he going to identify Umair's killer and then get him back to William?

Identifying him might not actually be a problem. He would probably be the one who went round shouting "yar" louder than the rest. As for getting him to come to William, Hermitage had not a clue. He doubted that the man would do so willingly. Why would he, knowing that William would only want to kill him?

Hermitage's general inclination was to work things out before he did them, or even to work them out and be so satisfied with the working out that the things didn't actually need doing at all. Many times he liked to work a lot of things out without the slightest intention of even starting most of them.

Now, he realised he was going to have to wait and see and then act. Once they were in Hereward's main camp he would have to see how the land lay. He would need to judge the state of things and appraise people's intentions and possible reactions. He would have to carefully observe comings and goings and listen for the little signals people gave off. All of the things that Wat and Cwen told him he was utterly incapable of. Cwen seemed to be fitting in quite well though. Perhaps she would be able to give him some ideas.

Hereward's men had quickly packed up their simple belongings and had stamped the fire to a smouldering heap. Swords in hand, spears on shoulders and packs on backs they strode off purposefully into the reeds.

They obviously weren't heading for Ely itself, which surprised Hermitage. Rather their path directed them in completely the other direction. They made for the west. Wherever this fortification of Hereward's was, it must be some distance. Perhaps it was going to take them the rest of the day's light to get there.

Hermitage nodded to himself thinking that this was a very clever move on Hereward's behalf. All the rumours were that he was fighting from the fens, if he wasn't actually there at all, it was no wonder no one had caught him. He prepared himself for a long and weary journey.

...

He was quite surprised then, that when they entered the first stretch of reasonable woodland and moved under the cover of the trees, Hereward's men dropped everything and started to make camp. Good heavens, was the centre of Hereward's power so far away that they would not get there in a day? How on earth did he attack the Normans in the fens if it took him two days to get there? He stood, feeling a bit confused and looking it.

'Come, Master Monk,' Hereward cried, with arms held wide to take in their surroundings. 'Avail yourself of the camp of Hereward Not The Wake. Tonight we shall camp beneath the trees of our land and hear tales to curdle the blood of every Norman.'

His men looked up, seemed to consider whether this required a "yar" or not, and gave a very muted one, just to be on the safe side.

Hermitage tried to look like this plan for the evening was just what he'd been hoping for. He glanced to Wat and Cwen for an indication of whether he should start asking all the questions that were starting to pile up. Wat's shrug and shake of his head indicated no, he should keep quiet. Cwen was already busying herself with the camp, helping to stack the bows and quivers of arrows for safekeeping.

Hereward came over and laid a strong hand on Hermitage's shoulder. 'Tomorrow, we shall return to plague the foul Normans, tonight we rest.' He pulled a small pouch from a belt at his waist and balanced it in the palm of his hand.

Hermitage looked at it, wondering what on earth this had to do with anything. He hoped it didn't contain some treasured trophy, a bit of a Norman perhaps. He really didn't want to see that.

Hereward carefully drew the string of the pouch open and moved it slightly in Hermitage's direction. He leaned in close and whispered so no one would hear. 'Fancy a mushroom?' he asked.

Hermitage looked from pouch to man to pouch. 'No thank you,' he said, in his firmest tone. 'I don't.'

'Oh,' Hereward said happily. 'They're very good. Hand-picked by the witch of Penda. Best quality.'

'I'm sure.' Hermitage tired to sound very aloof. 'But not the sort of thing a monk should indulge in.' He meant that it was not the sort of thing anyone should indulge in. He didn't feel that he was in a very good position to start lecturing the leader of a band of murderers.

'Please yourself.' Hereward took a small piece of something dry and brown from the pouch and popped it in his mouth. 'You don't know what you're missing.'

Hermitage knew very well what he was missing. Once, he had seen a young novice brought into the monastery who had been out foraging for mushrooms, both for the pot and for medicinal purposes. It seems the fellow had found a patch of a different kind altogether and had to be strapped into his bed, which he had claimed was going to eat him. Two days later the boy had regained his senses but could never go near moss again and kept insisting the pigs were keeping secrets.

Leaving Hereward to eat mushrooms while others organised his camp, Hermitage stood with Wat against a large oak. 'You know,' he commented, 'I'm beginning to have my doubts about Hereward. Do you think this is the sum total of his strength?'

'This lot?' Wat did not sound impressed. He nodded towards two men who had simply thrown a rough sheet of hide between two low hanging branches and were now sitting under it. 'I think it is. And I'm starting to think they couldn't find a Norman in Normandy. They seem more interested in moving around and making camp than striking at the heart of the enemy.'

'They've got a lot of weapons.'

'That they have. Enough to turn a young girl's head.' He nodded to Cwen who was bustling about, taking shields and laying them round the camp like some tourney.

'Do you really think they could have killed Umair? Hereward talks very proudly of his battles with the Normans.'

'But the weapons don't look very worn.' Wat indicated that the shields now forming a nice border to the camp were in excellent condition with barely a mark on them. And the swords, once the mud and grime had been washed off, looked in very good order.

'And if I was devoted to the defeat of the Normans I'd be at them night and day. Especially at night when they can't see you coming. Not exactly an aggressive tactic, leaving in the middle of the afternoon to go and have a lie down in the woods.'

'And where's the fortification that Umair drew?' Hermitage asked. 'Do you think we're on the way there?' He drew the book from under his habit where he was keeping it safe from the weather and anyone who saw it and might want to start a fire.

Wat sniffed. 'Could be it wasn't Hereward's at all. Perhaps there's some other band around. One a bit more, you know, effective.'

'William thinks he's fighting Hereward,' Hermitage whispered.

'Yes, he does, doesn't he?' Wat looked thoughtful and dropped his voice. 'And if I was a real fighting force of Saxons behind a fortification in say, Ely, and my enemy was busy chasing Hereward round the countryside, I might think that was for the best.'

'Perhaps it's a devious plan?' Hermitage didn't know anything about devious plans, but he was sure they would have a part to play. 'Hereward leads William's forces on a merry dance through the marshes while another band attacks in strength.'

'Not sure this bunch could manage devious or plan,' Wat said as some of the great warriors started to snore.

'We're no further forward,' Hermitage said with some despair. 'We've found the great enemies of William who are supposed to have killed Umair, but it could be they didn't do it after all. There's some other band of much more fearsome fighters we have to go and search out.' Searching out bands of fearsome fighters was not something Hermitage relished, and he certainly wasn't going to attempt more than one a day.

'So, Monk,' Hereward called, now that he was comfortably settled in front of a blazing fire. Comfortably settled in a grand camp chair that had come from somewhere. Perhaps it was left in this spot, which was their regular haunt. 'Come and tell us your tale of escape from the bowels of the enemy.'

Hermitage swallowed and threw a pleading look at Wat.

'I should just ask him if he's stabbed any Saracens recently,' Wat suggested. 'He doesn't look in a state to do anything about it.'

Hermitage was appalled at this suggestion.

'Did you meet a Saracen by any chance,' Wat prompted. 'And did you kill him at all? Easy enough.'

'You ask then,' Hermitage said.

'All right.' Wat strode over to the fire, Hermitage in his wake.

'So, Hereward, no relation to the Wakes,' Wat began.

'A book!' Hereward pointed at the volume under Hermitage's arm as if it was a magical object.

'Er,' Wat was put off his stride. 'Yes, it's a book.'

'Come, come,' Hereward waved Hermitage to come close, although the wave was rather haphazard and indecisive. 'I've not seen a book in many a long year. What's in it?'

'Oh, er,' Hermitage didn't quite know what to do. If he said what it really was it could cause all sorts of trouble. The Saxons might reason that Hermitage had been a guest of the Normans if he had been gifted such a great object as the book. He looked around the camp and, judging from the state of the men, concluded that most of the Saxons wouldn't be doing any reasoning at all for quite a while. That witch in Penda must have a mushroom workshop running night and day.

'It contains drawings and observations,' Hermitage explained.

Hereward held his hands out and Hermitage passed the book over. Not without a nervous glance at Wat.

Cwen joined them as Hereward sat back in his chair and opened the cover of the book. Hermitage was grateful to see that the man knew how to handle a treasure like this.

The Saxon leader turned the leaves slowly, frowning at the contents and tilting the book this way and that to see if he could make sense of it.   He paused at one page and

Hermitage felt his knees wobble as he saw a close examination of the image of the fort. After what seemed a very long and painful wait, Hereward closed the book with an awful finality, laid it on his lap and stared hard at Hermitage. 'You have some explaining to do, monk,' he said, fiercely.

'Indeed.' Hermitage tried to come up with a perfectly reasonable explanation of why he was carrying a book with a drawing of the Saxon defences in it. Unfortunately, all he could come up with was the truth, which wasn't going to help at all.

'Why do you have Umair's book?' Hereward demanded.

'I, er, pardon?' That wasn't what Hermitage was expecting at all.

'Umair's book,' Hereward repeated, firmly. 'This is Master Umair's book. How do you come to have it?'

Some of Hereward's men seemed to wake up to the fact that something was going on. They dragged themselves from their rest and wandered over to stand at the back of their Master, facing the three strangers. This did not help Hermitage's concentration at all.

'Did Umair give this to you?'

'Erm, in a way.' Hermitage found that fear for his life was a marvellous inspiration for taking a lot more care over his words than normal.

'It was in the Norman camp?' Hereward patted the volume on his knees, never dropping his gaze.

'Er, yes.' Hermitage didn't really have anything else he could say to that.

'Close to the hand of that devil's dropping William the Bastard?'

'Er, I suppose so.' Hermitage, never one to know what was

going on around him at the best of times, was now utterly lost.

How did Hereward know about Umair and the book? Of course, if you've stabbed someone in the head there's a good chance you'd know who they were, but the book wouldn't have been out of the camp, would it? Did Umair take the whole book with him on his wanderings? Hermitage imagined that he would have done the drawings from memory, or bound individual leaves into a book at his leisure. Wandering around the enemy position with a large book in your hands, doing drawings of their defences was almost certain to attract attention. Wasn't it? Hermitage was no longer sure he would know what was going on around him if someone wrote it down in his very own book.

'And you escaped that place?' Hereward asked.

Hermitage had to think for a moment what place they were talking about now. 'That's right.' he chanced a glance at Wat and Cwen, who were looking just as confused at Hereward's reaction to the book.

'You met Umair?'

'You could say so.'

'So why on earth did you remove the book? You have ruined everything. You fools!'

# Caput IX

## Friends in the Woods

Hermitage was well used to being told he had ruined everything. He seemed to have some innate talent for it. And most of the time he didn't even know what it was he had ruined, let alone how he'd done it. The accusation made so little connection to his own experience of events that he just let it wash over him. As a young boy, he would wander up to other children who were doing something or other, only to be told that he had just ruined everything.

As he grew into manhood he would be engaged in conversation, mainly with young women now he thought about it, and these would inevitably conclude with the woman in question telling Hermitage that he had ruined everything. Even he managed to discern that the last thing he should do was ask what "everything" was.

In his short years before taking the habit, various members of his close and more distant family would tell him that he was ruining everything. Right there and then he was actively ruining things. Even being told at the time he was doing it was no help.

And then in the monastery, his brothers would repeat the accusation. There might be a small gathering in one brother's cell; there might be a private conversation between an abbot and a novice; there could be an intense theological discussion behind closed doors between a priest and nun. Whatever it was, Hermitage would ruin it.

## The Case of the Curious Corpse

He had gone on so long not having a clue what it was he ruined, or how he managed to do it, that he had stopped worrying about it – or rather other worries had grown to take that one's place. At least in this situation, Hereward seemed to have something very specific in mind. Perhaps, at last, Hermitage would find out the details of something he had ruined and how he'd done it.

'Ruined what?' Wat asked.

Hermitage was glad that Wat couldn't see it either.

'Everything.'

No, still no help.

'You know about Umair and the book?' Wat asked.

'Of course, I know about Umair and the book,' Hereward snapped. 'What I don't know is what it's doing here. Why isn't it in the Norman camp? Why would Umair let you take this away?'

'You knew him well?' Wat asked, in the manner of someone exploring whether they should give away information and whether the person in front of them was trustworthy.

Hermitage thought that as Hereward was the man with all the weapons and several men at his back, he could be told anything.

Hereward's eyes narrowed. 'What do you mean, *knew* him?'

'Well,' Wat said bluntly. 'He's dead.'

'Dead?' Hereward choked the word out and looked genuinely distressed. 'Umair is dead?'

'He is,' Wat confirmed.

Hermitage saw that the men behind Hereward were as put out by this as their leader. They really looked like they had just received news that a dear friend had died. Which would be a bit odd, if they had killed him. He now felt comfortable that he didn't know what was going on around him because no one else did either.

Hereward's face took on the expression he probably used to frighten people. 'Who did it?' he asked. 'That bastard William,' he answered his own question.

'He says not.' Wat explained. 'Umair being his hostage and all.'

'He would say that, wouldn't he?' Hereward was clear. 'If you find a dead body near William, there's only one man who did it.'

'But he wasn't attacked in the camp. We discovered that he had been out in the country somewhere and came back with a wound to the head.'

Hereward shrugged. 'So William followed him out of camp, stabbed him and then claimed not to know anything about it.'

Hermitage noticed that none of the Saxons showed any signs of recognition at the mention of a wound. And Hereward's explanation of events was quite a good one. There was more that he had to know though. 'How did you know Umair?' he asked, as gently as he could.

Hereward was clearly conflicted between sadness and anger at this development. 'He was a good friend to us.'

Hermitage knew that the Normans weren't averse to stabbing their friends in the back, perhaps the Saxons did it as well, only in the front. At least it would be a bit more honest.

'Umair had a great knowledge of herbs and medicine. Treated many of us for wounds and the like. He'd been all over the known world and had tales that would fill many a dark and lonesome night.'

Hereward's men started to sit on the ground, some of them holding their heads and slowly shaking them in disbelief.

'And he knew about mushrooms,' Hereward added as if this was the most important feature of the man.

'He was a regular visitor?' Cwen asked, clearly as puzzled by all of this as the rest of them.

'Virtually lived here.' Hereward was sniffing and dabbing his eyes. 'Like a son he was. Well, a brother perhaps.'

'But he was William's hostage,' Cwen pointed out.

'If you were William's hostage, wouldn't you want to spend quite a lot of time somewhere else?'

'Well, yes, I suppose so. But here? To the Saxons? William's enemies?'

'Exactly.' Hereward nodded thoughtfully. 'This changes everything. Umair dead, the book here. We shall have to consider carefully.'

Cwen was screwing up her face in thought and slowly put a finger to her mouth. 'If Umair was a good friend of yours,' she said slowly, 'and was regularly coming from William's camp, perhaps he gave you information? About William's plans.'

What a thought. Hermitage was shocked.

'Of course he did,' Hereward confirmed, sadly. 'The very best. How do you think so few of us have managed to cause them so much trouble?'

'Umair was discovering William's movements and intentions and telling you about them,' Wat concluded.

'I just said that,' Hereward retorted.

'Interesting. William thinks he was doing the same to you.'

Hermitage was worried that Wat had revealed this. Making Hereward angry did not seem a very good idea.

'That's right.' Hereward smiled now.

A look of realisation swept across Wat and Cwen's faces and they grinned at one another. Hermitage sincerely hoped someone was going to explain something very soon.

'And a book with a drawing of a powerful Saxon fortress might be just the sort of thing to give William pause.'

Hereward clapped his hands to his knees and laughed heartily. 'If Umair brought me drawings of a Norman camp full of siege engines and mad dogs I wouldn't go anywhere near the place.'

Wat summarised with an amused smile on his face. 'William sends Umair to find out what the Saxons are up to so he can make his plans. Instead, Umair tells you all about William's plans and the two of you send back a load of nonsense about a massive Saxon army, giant fortresses and goodness knows what.'

'Witches,' Hereward said.

'Beg pardon?'

'We also sent word that the fens were full of Saxon witches who would curse any Norman who set foot in the place.'

'Very clever,' Wat even clapped his hands.

'We even caught one Norman, filled him with some of our best mushrooms and sent him back. After telling him that the owls would be watching.' The whole Saxon band had a good laugh at this memory. One of them even did an impersonation of a mushroom-addled Norman, staggering through the forest, swatting away owls.

It meant nothing to Hermitage, but the rest of the Saxons clearly thought it remarkably accurate. He just hoped that the witches and the owls weren't too close.

'Because Umair hated William?' Cwen suggested.

'Who doesn't?' Hereward replied simply. 'Umair was

supposed to be a valued hostage. Instead, William sends him out all over the place to find out what his enemies are up to. He's been doing it for years. Puts Umair in some rival family and demands reports. Takes him to negotiations and gets him to pretend he can't speak the language so he can listen in to private conversations. It's disgraceful.'

'And he did the same once the Normans got here.'

'He did,' Hereward confirmed. 'But this time Umair finds us and we find we have a very common enemy.'

'Do you think William could have found out what he was up to?' Cwen asked.

Hermitage had just got the idea of what Umair was up to. He looked, open-mouthed, around the camp. He knew people lied but he didn't know they could be quite so organised about it. And even the drawing in the book was a lie. That cut him more than anything. How could anyone bring an innocent book into such a murky pool of deception?

'Could be,' Hereward acknowledged. 'Although Umair always said his family was so powerful that William wouldn't dare actually do anything to him.'

Hermitage was about to open his mouth and say that this would explain William's desire to prove he was not guilty. He realised that the details of their connection to William would be more news to Hereward. And news that might not be welcome.

Hereward became lost in his thoughts and sat shaking his sad head slowly from side to side. Eventually, it came to a halt and a frown appeared. Hermitage didn't like the look of that frown.

'If Umair is dead,' the Saxon leader said, thoughtfully, 'and the book was in the Norman camp. What are you three doing with it back here?'

'That's a very interesting question,' Wat replied.

Yes, Hermitage thought it was very interesting as well. The answer would be even more interesting.

The pause while the answer to this was prepared was far too long for Hermitage's comfort.

'It all goes back to King Harold,' Wat said eventually.

Ah, thought Hermitage, that was a good move, bring the old Saxon King into it. After all, the men in the reeds had called him the rightful king.

'That bastard,' Hereward spat.

Perhaps not such a good move.

'The idiot who lost the country to the Normans? Should never have been king in the first place. It was only his foul family, the Godwinsons - God curse them - that forced him on us. We wouldn't be in this mess if we'd had a half-decent king. Hobnobbing with the Normans all his life, leading them on. It's no wonder they thought they could come over here and murder us all. Serve him right.'

'I thought Harold was a hostage of the Normans?' Hermitage asked, needing to get things clear his head.

'Hobnobbing,' Hereward insisted.

'Er, right.' Wat was clearly a bit worried that they weren't going to be able to say anything right. 'Anyway, Brother Hermitage here holds the high office of King's Investigator. It's his job to look into situations such as this and determine what's going on.'

Hereward looked at Hermitage as if expecting an extra head to pop out of the habit any moment. Hermitage smiled a humble acknowledgement of his position. Not that he'd ever thought of it as a high office before.

Hereward's frown wriggled about in concentration. 'You mean he finds out who killed Umair?'

'That's it exactly.' Wat smiled.

'So, if William did it,' Hereward speculated quite slowly, 'you could have him executed.'

'I wouldn't be sure about that,' Hermitage put in. He was actually very sure about that.

'Still doesn't explain why the book is back here,' Hereward grumbled.

Hermitage always found telling the truth was best. It was usually the only version of events he could remember. 'It's a clue,' he said.

'A clew?' Hereward asked. 'No, it isn't. It's a book.'

'I mean it's a clue, not a clew. I use the word to describe the pieces that lead to the explanation. Just as a clew is a ball of thread that leads from one end to another, a clue will lead us to the end of the tale of Umair's death.'

Hereward just looked at Hermitage but spoke to Cwen. 'Is he all right?'

She shrugged. 'It's investigation,' she explained. 'He knows what he's doing.'

'And how does this help?' Hereward asked. 'You said Umair had been struck on the head. If he'd been beaten to death with the book I could see the point.' He looked at the book to see if there were any signs that it had been used as a weapon.

'Well.' Hermitage was happy to have an opportunity to explain the process. 'Umair was attacked somewhere outside the Norman camp.'

'On the head.' Hereward looked pleased to help.

'Er, yes. On the head. But while he was outside the camp. We were told that he spent a lot of time wandering around and brought back drawings and descriptions of the things he had seen.'

'Like fortresses and witches,' Hereward grinned.

'Exactly. So, when we saw that he had a fine drawing of a Saxon fortress we imagined that he must have actually seen one. And that could be where he was hit.' Hermitage smiled at the neatness of his reasoning. He stopped smiling when he realised what he'd said.

Hereward had realised as well. 'Are you saying a Saxon did it?' He sounded very angry now. He pointed at Hermitage, 'Umair was fine and well when he last left us.'

'Of course, of course,' Hermitage put in, quickly. 'Now we know there wasn't actually a fortification at all, that's cleared up.' It obviously wasn't cleared up in the slightest but Hermitage wasn't about to say that. Not right now. He had another question he needed to ask. He didn't really like asking questions of important people, or those with weapons and bands of men at their back. Or anyone at all come to that. A bit of a hindrance to an investigator, he realised. 'Erm, when was that, exactly? Or roughly?'

'When was what?' Hereward snapped.

'When did Umair leave you?'

'What does that have to do with anything?' Hereward was really rather cross now, which helped Hermitage's state of mind not one bit.

'Erm,' he quivered. 'It's just that if we know when he was last alive and well we'll know how long William had to come out of the camp and do the deed.' He tried a smile.

Hereward lightened a little at this. 'Hm,' he didn't sound convinced. 'It would be about a week ago.' Some of his men nodded and mumbled their agreement at this.

'And now William wants to put the blame on the Saxons.' Hereward thumped a fist into his hand for emphasis. He thought some more and his face scowled. 'I'd bet a bag of mushrooms that he even sent you to prove that I did it so Umair's family will come after me instead of him.' He laughed heartily at this.

Hermitage, Wat and Cwen laughed as well, just not quite so heartily.

Hereward went on. 'If William wanted Umair dead, he couldn't do it himself. The Saracen's family would be after him in no time. If he can show that the Saxons did it he'd be safe. In fact, he might even get the Saracens to help him fight the Saxons thinking they were getting revenge. Bastard.'

'Yes, I know,' Hermitage said before he realised it was an accusation, not the use of William's name.

Hereward sat back in his chair and patted the book with one hand, obviously deep in thought. 'We only managed to battle the Normans with Umair's help,' he mused. 'And now we've lost him. Perhaps the time has come,' he nodded to himself, slowly and seriously.

Time for what? Hermitage wondered. Surrender? Surely not. They must know what William would do to them. Just stop fighting perhaps? Vanish into the reeds and the woods and never be heard of again. Or perhaps become a figure of legend. Hereward who fought the Normans and vanished mysteriously. Hermitage dragged his attention back to the moment. Or maybe they were going to mount a final, desperate frontal assault on the Normans. For reasons he couldn't quite put his finger on, Hermitage doubted this.

Hereward turned his head to address the men at his back. 'This could be the moment,' he said. 'The death of Umair is a grievous blow but there is one option. We could continue the fight against the invader another way.'

His men were all ears, although some of them were looking a bit suspicious.

'If we join with Eadric,' Hereward said quickly.

He had to say it quickly because the furore his men threw up at this suggestion was immediate, loud and quite rude.

Hermitage turned to Wat and Cwen and they all looked on as the band of Saxon fighting men started fighting. First of all, there were loud deprecations, then pushes and shoves and threats of worse. This seemed odd because as far as Hermitage could tell they were violently agreeing with one another. Hereward left his chair and stood to one side while his men went at it, but the clear mood of the group was that this Eadric fellow was the one they would fight alongside after the devil himself had turned them down three times.

One man said Eadric was a deceitful, cheating, two-faced liar who had betrayed his own family to the Welsh. Another took issue with this, pushing his fellow back quite violently while insisting that Eadric was a cowardly lackey of the Vikings and had surrendered his lands and those of his men at the first sign of trouble. A third joined in with a thump in the back of both of them, saying that he knew for certain that Eadric carried out unnatural practices when the moon was full and should not be left alone with cattle.

Whatever the truth of the matter, and Hermitage suspected it was none of this, the men were clearly against any suggestion of joining Eadric. He, Wat and Cwen just watched with amusement as the scramble to denigrate Eadric rolled around. The jostling moved away to another part of the clearing and Hereward was back sitting in his seat, but now had his head in his hands.

'Enough!' he barked eventually when some of the energy of his men was spent. 'How can we defeat the Norman scourge if you lot start on one another at the drop of a name?'

'But Eadric,' one of the men replied as if they could tolerate a lot but this really was going too far. 'Who wants to fight alongside someone called Eadric the Mild?'

Hereward looked at his man with incredulity. 'Wild, you idiot. Eadric the Wild, not Eadric the Mild.' His head went back in his hands form where a muttered "Ye God," emerged.

'Oh, right.' The man seemed to think this was at least an improvement.

'Eadric is fighting the Normans very effectively in the west,' Hereward reported. 'We don't have to actually join him, just work together.'

This suggestion did not generate another fracas but the volume of grumbling would be enough to attract any passing Normans.

'Let me just get this right; you'd all rather die alone in the marshes, slaughtered by William and his evil band, than work with Eadric to inflict a greater damage?'

The men were pretty clear that yes, that's exactly what they'd rather do.

'We'd prefer to join the Saracens,' one of the men piped up. 'At least that way we could avenge Umair. And there's a good chance they're a measure more trustworthy than Eadric.'

The other men grumbled their agreement at this proposition, even referencing some innovative sword-work Umair had taught them.

'And where are we going to find a band of Saracen warriors round here?'

Hermitage took the step of gritting his teeth to stop the words getting out. But they were stamping about angrily inside his head, demanding release.

Wat caught his eye and gave him a very hard stare. So hard that it would crush the words and Hermitage with them. He could see that telling Hereward that a band of Saracen warriors was expected very soon would not make things better. In fact, he was sure it would make things an awful lot worse. The Saxons would want to join the Saracens and attack the Normans. Alternatively, the Saracens would join the Normans and attack the Saxons. Either way, there would be death and bloodshed and it would all be his fault. He could see that. Really he could. But he had words.

Cwen joined the stare now. Her teeth were gritted as well but in a much more aggressive manner.

'What are you lot gurning at one another for?' Hereward demanded.

'Nothing,' Hermitage said, as lightly as he could.

'Are there Saracen warriors?' Hereward asked, very quickly connecting the conversation to the looks flying about.

'Um,' Hermitage said, which he felt wasn't really a word at all, so didn't count.

Hereward gave him a piercing stare now. These stares were starting to mount.

'William would have to send word that his hostage was dead,' Hereward reasoned. 'And I can imagine what the discussion was like when that news was received. "Shall we go and kill William personally, or shall we do his army at the same time?"'

Hermitage tried to look completely surprised by this suggestion. 'I suppose it's possible.' He also tried to sound like the sort of person who wouldn't know about things like that.

'In which case, Master monk investigator..,' Hereward had a very thoughtful look on his face, 'I might have a job for you.'

'Ah, yes?' Hermitage asked.

Wat and Cwen had stopped staring now and were just

standing there, looking very resigned.

'Indeed.' He held out the book so that Hermitage could take it. 'You put this back where you found it so William doesn't think anything's amiss. You carry on with your investigatoring to find out who killed Umair.'

'I see.'

'And what you'll find out is that William did it.'

Did Hereward have information about the death he hadn't passed on? 'Did he do it?'

'Probably.' Hereward shrugged. 'Him or one of his men. So when the Saracens arrive you'll be able to tell them William's the man, and they can kill him. Easy, See?'

'Erm.' Hermitage wondered if he'd just been told to lie. To Saracens. About King William.

'Did William have word who'd be coming?' Hereward asked.

'Er,' Hermitage was too confused by the whole situation to say anything but the truth. 'Mahuqiq, apparently.'

'Ooh.' Hereward grimaced. 'Nasty.'

'Are they? Do you know what it means?'

'No, but it sounds nasty. And you'd send something pretty nasty to avenge a death, wouldn't you?'

'I suppose so.' Hermitage really was the last person who would know.

'We're agreed then.' Hereward clapped his hands. 'We set off first thing in the morning. You return to the camp and prove William is the killer. We'll wait close by and keep watch for the Saracens. When the moment is right we join forces, swoop on the Normans and slaughter the lot of them.' His men cheered heartily at this new option.

Hermitage only saw swooping and slaughter.

Hereward stood and went to each of them, clasping them

in a tight hug, a tight hug that smelled quite strongly of mushrooms to Hermitage's nose. He slapped them heartily on the back. 'You will be doing England a great service and when William the bastard is dead, you will not be forgotten.'

Hermitage wished he had been forgotten quite some time ago.

## Caput X

### Deceive the Deceivers

'So,' Cwen said as the following dawn waited for them on the last portion of track back to the Norman camp. 'I hate to repeat things, but I want to make sure I understand.'

Hermitage thought that she had done nothing but understand last night, repeatedly making the same point about the situation they now found themselves in. The implication seemed pretty clear that it was Hermitage's fault. The detailed exposition had ruined what was already a pretty revolting meal. Hermitage suspected that some of the mushrooms had gone into the cook pot as he had some very strange dreams.

He could see now that their mission had been well and truly ruined. He even saw that just by talking about things, he had played some part in the ruin. If his simply talking ruined things it could explain a lot about life. Not that this mission had been a wild success since the Normans turned up at Wat's workshop in the first place.

William's men dragged them across the country, the king sent them to find murderous Saxons and now Hereward and the non-murderous Saxons were sending them back to the Normans. Was he never to have any say in the comings and goings of his own life?

As they reluctantly trod the last half mile, Hereward's mighty forces were lounging in the cover of yet another ditch, eating mushrooms and resting for the great battle that might be imminent. To Hermitage's eye, it had been a rather damp and nasty looking ditch, but the Saxon forces took to it as if they'd been given fresh linen. Somehow they even managed to light a fire in what was basically a hole with a puddle in the bottom. A lurid odour and very strangely coloured smoke started to emerge, which Hermitage thought might draw attention. The smell of mushrooms was strong and the giggles from the bottom of the ditch indicated that the Saxons were beyond worrying about the practicalities.

'We started off being instructed by King William to go and prove that he did not kill the Saracen.' Cwen was still going.

Hermitage didn't feel this required confirmation.

'And now we are instructed by the Saxons to prove that he did.'

'And the Saracen Mahuqiq army is about to arrive,' Wat added, helpfully. 'Who will doubtless want to know who to kill first.' He gave this some thought. 'Or maybe not.'

Hermitage took a crumb of comfort.

Wat sounded quite bright at his conclusion, 'Maybe they'll just kill everyone,' he said. 'That'll solve the problem of us being caught in the middle of it all.'

Hermitage's crumb crumbled.

'Don't suppose it'll really matter if the Saxons or the Normans get us first with the Saracens coming up behind.' He ran a hand through his hair and scratched hard. 'You know, Hermitage, before I met you only robbers tried to kill me. Along with the occasional customer and the other traders of course. Now I've got the whole country after me. Even the ones who want to kill one another will probably want to kill me as well.'

Hermitage did not know what to say. He had no useful contribution to make and the words that had been

## The Case of the Curious Corpse

clamouring to get out only yesterday, seemed to have packed up and left. This was simply an intolerable and insoluble situation and he had brought it upon them all, just by being King's Investigator, which he didn't want to be anyway.

He was familiar with the expression "the lesser of two evils", but now had the opportunity to consider it at first hand in a very practical situation. The Norman camp loomed in front and the Saxons pressed from behind. There were even Saracens coming in from the sides. He realised that having one evil slightly lesser than the other was no help to anyone. Better to have no evils at all.

And the evils in this situation were very real and all of them had swords. He knew that Hereward was the friendlier of the two, but frankly, the man would have to work very hard to be less friendly than William of Normandy. In the ranking of evils, Hermitage was quite happy with the nomination of William as leader. Which was also no help at all.

And then there were the Saracens. They might not be evil at all, but he thought that Hereward was probably right on this point; people sent to avenge deaths were hardly going to be charming company.

What could he do? There was no way out. No option presented itself that would make everyone go away. Umair was dead, that was certain, and someone had done it. It would be marvellous if it turned out to be an accident but Hermitage couldn't immediately imagine how anyone gave themselves a fatal wound in the head by accident. Perhaps Umair had been engaged in some sword practice and had misjudged a swing or something. Hermitage knew nothing about the handling of swords but imagined that if you were proficient enough to practice swings, you could probably manage not to hit yourself on the head.

If it was a case of accidental death, Hermitage would be able to confirm that William didn't do it, and neither did Hereward. The Saracens might be disappointed but they wouldn't have any excuse to start the slaughter. Everyone happy. Apart from Umair, of course. How would he be able to show it was an accident though? There would have to be pretty incontrovertible proof. Someone standing there watching it perhaps? He shook his head and tried to make himself go back to the beginning again. Lesser of two evils.

He hoisted the book back up under the cord of his habit from where it kept slipping. This great treasure and bright spot in an otherwise completely gloomy situation was turning out to be a bit of a burden. Reading books was marvellous. Holding them, smelling them, looking at them, counting them, cataloguing them; all wonderful tasks and treasured moments. Carrying quite a large one backwards and forwards through the forests of England was turning out not to be quite such a pleasure. If he could sit under a tree and just look at it for a few days he'd be much happier.

And a new worry tickled the place he kept his worries. When the Saracens arrived they'd be able to read the books. Then they'd know what Umair had been up to. This was such a complicated worry that he couldn't immediately work out whether the result would be good or bad. It would be complicated. Complicated was seldom good.

He now knew that if you were a hostage you weren't supposed to betray your captor. But if that captor was himself betraying the code of hostage-keeping? Not only was this a complicated worry but it encompassed so many aspects of human activity, about which Hermitage had not a clue, that he was tempted, once he'd put the book back, to that most shameful of all actions when the various forces finally came together; keep his head down and hope no one noticed him.

'Well?' Cwen asked, disturbing his thoughts. 'What's to do then? William or Hereward?'

'Or someone else completely,' Hermitage suggested. 'Or an accident.'

'An accident?' Wat's reaction to that suggestion was clear. 'If we try telling them the man accidentally cut his own head off at least they'll be laughing while they kill us.'

'He obviously didn't cut it off, just hit it a bit.' Hermitage protested.

'People who know how to handle swords do not hit their own heads.' Wat was clear. At least Hermitage had been right about that bit. Not an accident then.

'I don't think anyone else would be murdering passing Saracens,' Cwen said. 'Not when you've got two armies close at hand.' She thought. 'Well, one army and one loose assembly.'

'I'd go for Hereward, if I were you,' Wat suggested.

'What do you mean, "go for Hereward?"'

'Say he did it.' Wat nodded to himself. 'Huge great Norman army? We know they're mostly mad and wouldn't hesitate to finish us all off. Hereward though. Nice man and everything, but not much of a danger if it came to a fight without Umair's help.'

Hermitage looked at his friend with profound sadness and no little horror. He also reached a conclusion about what they had to do. It had been nagging at him for a while but he didn't dare speak it out loud. It was the only one that was possible in all the circumstances. It was always his favourite conclusion but never went down very well whenever he mentioned it. He would have to pick his moment. Something else he wasn't very good at. He could pick moments easily enough, there were plenty of them after all. He always managed to get the wrong one though.

'Are you suggesting that we say Hereward did it, just to save our skins?'

'Well,' Wat hummed, 'I wouldn't put it quite like that.'

'But that would be the outcome.' Cwen nodded her agreement to the plan.

'Regardless of whether he did it or not?' Hermitage checked.

'He's not likely to last long anyway,' Cwen argued. 'After all, no one's going to last long fighting Normans all the time. They'll get you in the end.'

'I thought you were the one who wanted to fight them, come what may?'

Cwen's look said that she might be going off that idea. Talk of killing Normans was easy when there weren't any Normans to hand.

Hermitage shook his head with slow sadness. 'There is only one thing for it.' He couldn't tell whether this was the moment or not. It was *a* moment, so it would have to do.

'And that is?'

He took breath and spoke the awful words. 'The truth.' He saw their mocking looks. 'We actually find out who really did it.'

'Yes,' Wat said, 'Hereward.'

'Not if he didn't. We find out who struck the blow. We find the truth.'

They both looked at him as if he had gone very slightly mad. 'Even if it's William?' Cwen asked.

'Even if it's William. He will have to face the truth. And if the army of Mahuqiqs is here he may not be able to do anything to us.

'Hm.' Wat was thoughtful. 'Not sure I'm quite happy about that "may not".'

'It's the only thing we can do,' Hermitage said firmly. 'It's no good trying to make up some story that wouldn't fit the facts, that would be exposed in no time. No. We find out who really killed Umair and we present our conclusion.'

'Who to?' Cwen asked.

'Beg pardon?'

'Who to? Who do we present this wonderful, truthful, actual, real conclusion to? William? We're in his camp, he seems to be in charge so it should probably be him. He's the king and asked you to investigate. I expect he'd be quite disappointed if you told someone else at the end of it all. You investigate away, find he did it and then tell him so? I think you'll last about a minute. I think he'll be so angry he won't even be able to draw his sword and will probably just punch you to death.'

'Erm.' The truth had seemed such a wonderful idea a moment ago. How to get it out though, without the person who didn't like the truth taking something vital out of them with a sharp thing? 'I have it,' he said, snapping his fingers. 'We find out what happened, then we gather everyone together and explain it all in one go. If the Saxons and the Saracens and the Normans are in the same place they can deal with one another and not with us.'

He could even picture the scene. All the different parties would be gathered in a circle around a camp-fire while he walked about explaining things. They would be in thrall to his exposition as first one, then another theory was postulated and then dismissed. Eventually, after quite a lot of walking and a very satisfying amount of exposition he would reveal the truth. The guilty party would have nowhere to run and the rest of them would marvel at his dissection of the facts.

There was another picture, in which all the different parties were fighting over the camp-fire and there were a lot more dead bodies than he had started out with. He could also make out an empty habit, smouldering on the fire.

'Can't see the Saxons and the Normans sitting down peacefully while you walk up and down in front of them explaining a murder,' Cwen scoffed.

'We'll deal with that problem when we get there,' Hermitage said rather hopelessly, confessing to himself that his second picture was the more likely. 'We haven't even worked out who did it yet.'

'Talking of problems when we get there,' Wat said. 'What, exactly, are we going to tell Good King William when we get back? Yes, we did find Hereward, had a nice meal with him but he says none of his men did it so we didn't bring the murderer you asked for? I don't think William cares whether any of them actually did it or not.'

Hermitage had given this some thought but considered a simple "the investigation continues" would suffice. Now they were a lot closer to the camp he could see that it wouldn't suffice at all.

'William's orders were to come back with the killer,' Cwen reminded him, unnecessarily. 'So unless one of us did it?'

'Oh, I don't think we need to bother William at the moment,' Hermitage said rather weakly.

'Not bother him?' Cwen asked.

'No. I mean, we don't have any information for him right now. What we need to do is gather some more facts, investigate Umair's movements a bit more thoroughly. Establish who knew about his comings and goings and who could have followed him.' As he randomly rambled on, he began to see that actually, this might be quite helpful. 'Where were people during the time Umair was away? What did they know of him and who hated him most. Was anyone actually given any orders concerning him?'

'And William's going to be fascinated by all of this, is he?' Wat asked. 'When we bump into him or Le Pedvin in their own camp, they're going to be happy with all of that instead of a trembling killer in front of them?'

Hermitage thought they had enough problems without Wat bringing up more, no matter how realistic they were. 'We could say that we've looked in one part of the country, couldn't find the Saxon fortress and so will be going out again tomorrow?' Hermitage offered.

They both looked at him with some awe. 'Hermitage!' Cwen shook her head. 'You mean, we lie?'

'Not at all,' Hermitage wanted to make sure this was clear. 'It's absolutely true. We didn't find the fortress.'

'We didn't find it because there isn't one.' Wat pointed out.

'And there isn't one because Umair and Hereward made the whole thing up,' Cwen reminded him.

'William doesn't know that,' Hermitage offered, feeling very bad at even having the thought.

'If that's not a lie, there must be another word for it.' Wat grinned.

'Dissembling?' Hermitage suggested, with a very weak smile, thinking that giving it a different word didn't make it any better.

...

Their return to the Norman camp was cautious and careful. Their last half mile from Hereward's men in the safety of their ditch felt as long as an English winter. Hermitage's nervousness reached new heights as the camp entrance came into view. What if William or Le Pedvin were standing there looking for them? Or just standing there? Or there was another guard who knew them? Or Mistress Le Pedvin? He thought that the three of them should have a quick discussion about what they should say when they were stopped. Obviously, there was the truth, but just now he felt that a slow approach to the truth might be best. So slow that they might never reach it at all. Well, not quite all of it, perhaps.

He noticed that the pace of the others was slowing as well but before he could organise a short meeting they came upon a Norman soldier. This one was further out from the camp than they had expected and the fear rippled through Hermitage like a fearsome wind. And the soldier was on a Norman horse.

'Who are you?' the Norman barked, while the horse gave them a very hard stare.

'Oh, no one, really.' Wat smiled.

The guard squinted and stared at the same time, somehow. 'Are you Saracens?' he asked.

'No,' Wat said as if so much should be obvious to anyone.

The Norman looked very thoughtful for a moment as he examined them to see if they matched some description he'd been given.

'We've just been out of the camp, at Le Pedvin's order.' Cwen kept a very straight face.

'Stop cluttering the place up then,' the Norman ordered.

# The Case of the Curious Corpse

'Get in camp and keep out of the way.'

Happy to follow direct orders, for once, they moved on down the track where their arrival was marked by no one whatsoever. The men posting some sort of guard seemed more interested in talking to one another than checking comings and goings. Hermitage thought that they could be a band of murderous Saxons and no one would have paid the slightest bit of attention. Then again, you probably needed more than three to make a murderous band.

'What's going on?' Cwen asked as a Norman with a bucket of steaming water scurried by.

It wasn't that the camp was in chaos, it was much more organised than that, but there was definitely something diverting attention from the day to day business of being a threatening invader.

'Could be the Saxons are attacking,' Hermitage suggested, with some worry.

'They must have run to get here before us,' Wat said. 'And to be honest, I can't see Hereward and his band mounting a frontal assault on the front of a thing with two fronts.'

'There could really be a second band who attack when Hereward retreats?'

Cwen looked around, 'They aren't being attacked,' she concluded. 'But they're certainly preparing for something.'

'Perhaps this is just the normal procedure for this time of day?' Hermitage naturally assumed that everyone organised their waking time. His own was ruled by the Orders of the day, or rather it had been before he moved to live with Wat and Cwen. He knew exactly what he would have to do at Vespers or Prime or Matins; he'd have to be in chapel.

He could see that the Normans spent very little time in chapel. They'd burned a few of them to the ground but in that situation, it was probably quite important not to be in the building at the time. The current flurry of activity was unlikely to have anything to do with worship or confession. It'd take a lot more organisation to make confession for all the things the Normans had done.

This was probably something to do with armies. He had no idea what they did when they weren't fighting - apart from shout at people nearby - and actually didn't have much idea what they were doing when they were fighting. He had heard that they practised though. Maybe this was practise.

Wat grabbed the arm of a passing soldier. 'What's happening?' he asked.

The soldier stopped and looked at him very blankly. It was the sort of look a smith, in the middle of making a horseshoe, gives to the man who wanders up and says "making a horseshoe then?"

'We're dead,' the man said as if this should be obvious. He ran off to get on with being dead.

'They're dead?' Hermitage asked, not understanding this at all, as the man plainly wasn't dead in the slightest.

'Sounds like William's in a bit of a mood,' Wat said.

The look on Hermitage's face clearly needed a better explanation.

'They've obviously done something wrong,' Wat went on. 'Like the guard who had done a bad thing and William stopped talking to him. This time someone's done something truly awful and their leader wants to simply kill the lot of them.'

'Probably put their tent pegs in the wrong way round,' Cwen mocked.

'And for that, they get killed?' Hermitage knew the soldier's life was one of discipline, but this did sound a bit

# The Case of the Curious Corpse

strict.

'You have met King William?' Cwen checked. 'Chap with a funny haircut and a lot of weapons. Threatens to kill people and burn everything to the ground quite a lot?'

'Of course I have,' Hermitage frowned. Cwen knew that perfectly well.

'So, why wouldn't he threaten to kill his own men now and again?'

'It doesn't sound very efficient,' was all Hermitage could come up with. How could you kill more people and burn extra things to the ground if you didn't have the men for the job?

'At least they aren't bothering us,' Wat observed. 'Perhaps we can get on with whatever it is we've come for and get out before anyone notices?' He directed this question straight at Hermitage, who smiled as he saw this was a very attractive prospect.

'So?' Wat pressed.

'Beg pardon?' Hermitage asked.

'What is it we've come for?' Wat sounded quite impatient.

'Oh. Yes, right,' Hermitage caught up. 'We need to put the book back and then find out some more about Umair's movements. Exactly when did he arrive back in camp with his fatal wound? We know he left Hereward's camp a week ago, but when did he actually leave and how long was it between that and the mystery of the sword in the head? When we have that time we can start narrowing down the possibilities.'

'Very clever,' Cwen said. 'Except we only have Hereward's word that it was a week ago.'

'And that Umair didn't have any holes in him when he left the Saxons,' Wat added.

'And that a Hereward full of mushrooms knows what day it is anyway,' Cwen complete the picture.

'But, but,' Hermitage said helpfully. He did wish people would stop confusing him once he'd made his mind up. 'I grant the week may only be an estimate,' he accepted, 'but I don't think Hereward's men killed Umair.'

'Very generous,' Cwen said. 'Why not?'

'Because they were genuinely upset when they heard about the death.'

'Perhaps they didn't know about it. Perhaps Hereward did it himself and is a very good liar.'

'Why would he?' Hermitage was pleading the case for the Saxon now.

'Falling out while the mushrooms were at their height?'

'Look.' Hermitage tried to bring some order to things, at least to the things in his head. 'Can we just believe the last person we spoke to until we find out any different?'

Wat and Cwen looked rather confused by this.

'Someone must be telling the truth in all of this. It could be William, it could be Hereward, it could be someone else completely. We're only going to confuse ourselves if we go around not believing anyone.'

'Hermitage,' Wat said quite seriously. 'In all of the investigations you've done, when did you ever find that anyone was telling the truth?'

'Well,' Hermitage began, almost immediately realizing that where murder was concerned most people lied most of the time, even the ones who turned out to have nothing to do with it. It really was rather disgraceful. 'That's only at the end,' he said. 'Once we've worked everything out. In the meantime, we have to have something to go on. I can't organize my thoughts if I think everyone is lying. Where would I begin?'

'So, if we talk to William again, we believe him, do we?' Cwen asked.

'Depends what he says,' Hermitage replied, wishing that his friends would stop making this any more difficult than it already was.

'Seems a funny way of investigating,' Cwen mumbled, but she didn't pursue the point.

'We need that guard,' Hermitage said. 'The one who said he saw Umair come back to camp. If we press him to tell us exactly when that was, we'll have something to go on.'

'Unless William has killed him already.' Wat wandered on, looking at all the activity around them.

As they meandered through the canvas alleys of the Norman encampment they continued to be comprehensively ignored, which was odd for the three Saxons who hadn't dared stick their heads out of the tent last time they were here.

Normans were scuttling about the place and appeared to be doing nothing more complicated than tidying up. Saddles and horse blankets were being stuffed into tents, cooking utensils were being rubbed clean with a good handful of earth and laid out around their fires, even boots were being brushed with a fresh layer of fat.

At one point they came across the camp barber who had a queue at his chair, waiting to have the strange circular mops that topped off most Normans, put back into shape. As that shape simply involved putting a dish on their head and cutting round it, it didn't take long.

'Could be an inspection of some sort,' Hermitage speculated.

'They've never bothered before,' Cwen said. 'Scruffy lot,

usually.'

'Whatever it is they've done, William's making them clean themselves up as a punishment. I shouldn't be surprised if he's promised to kill the worst dressed soldier, just to get their attention.' Wat straightened his immaculate jerkin to show that he would never be counted in such company.

'We're not going to get anywhere like this,' Hermitage complained. 'Even if we find the guard he's probably going to be too busy fettling his horse or something.'

Wat and Cwen both gave Hermitage the look that said he should not try to talk of things about which he knew nothing.

'Oh, my dears, my dears.' A shrill voice slapped their ears and Mistress Le Pedvin waddled across the camp towards them. All they could do was stand and wait for the arrival. At least her husband wasn't with her, demanding to have a killer presented to him.

'This will never do. Never do at all. Look at the state of you.' She held her arms out to illustrate that the state of them was not acceptable.

Hermitage looked and thought they were perfectly presentable. Wat was as well-dressed as usual, his fine-fitting clothes neat and clean. Certainly better than any Norman he'd ever come across. Cwen's dress was plain and functional – if your main function was to be ready for a fight at any moment. Plain brown leggings and a simple jerkin made her an anonymous figure. He could easily understand why people could mistake her for a boy. He less easily understood the things she did to anyone who made that mistake.

His own dress was the habit of his calling. What else would he be wearing? Granted, it was rather grubby and frayed around the edges, but that was expected of a monk. A neat and well-attired man of God would be quite wrong; although a lot of men of God did not seem to share his opinion.

'You'll just have to keep out of sight,' Mistress Le Pedvin dismissed them all. 'Wouldn't do to have Saxons around anyway,' she tutted. 'Good job I finished the liming,' she said to herself.

'What is going on?' Wat asked quite plainly, and quite loudly, right in Mistress Le Pedvin's face.

'What's going on?' she looked at Wat as at all idiots. 'We are preparing ourselves. Got to be in the very best of order. My Marcel says as how there could be the most awful consequences if we don't make the right impression.'

Hermitage thought that the impression made by Normans was pretty well established. He didn't think that cleaning up a bit would make murderous conquest any more appealing.

'The right impression?' Cwen asked. 'Who do you lot want to impress?' It came out sounding quite rude but it passed Mistress Le Pedvin by.

'Why, the Mahuqiq of course. We've only just had word that they landed yesterday. Good King William is not at all happy with his messengers.'

'They'll be the dead ones then,' Wat muttered.

'They could be here any moment,' Mistress Le Pedvin fretted. 'So shoo. Shoo away with you.'

'Suits us,' Cwen said as the Mistress worried her way across the camp, tutting quite regularly.

'Well, well.' Wat smiled. 'There's a turn-up. The great Saracen force here already. I'd love to have seen William's face when he got the news.'

'But not be the person delivering it,' Cwen said.

'Oh God, no.'

Hermitage was still trying to take this in. The arrival of the Saracen army so soon had surely destroyed any chance they had of resolving the death of Umair. William would doubtless report that Hereward was the killer and that would be that. A band of Saxons, albeit a rather small and ineffective one, would be wiped out by the descending hordes.

He knew he hadn't actually made any progress at all. He knew that he didn't want to be here in the first place and that he was no closer to knowing who had actually killed Umair. None of that stopped him having the overwhelming feeling that he had ruined everything.

## Caput XI

## Where's the Rest of Them?

'This should be exciting,' Cwen said with some relish.

They had gladly followed Mistress Le Pedvin's instructions and were hiding in the soldier's vacant tent once more. Whoever had used the place before was definitely not coming back, or if he did would be disappointed to find that his companions in arms had stolen everything. There was no bed, no cooking implements, even the unburned scraps of wood had been taken. Doubtless, the tent itself would be next.

'Exciting?' Hermitage asked as he peeped through the tent flap. It was not the word he would use to describe cowering behind a thin piece of canvas while two armies argued over which of them could kill all the Saxons.

'Seeing the mighty Normans cowed before a great army of Saracen warriors? What could be better?'

Hermitage just tutted.

'Maybe William will be shot in the eye,' Cwen suggested with disgraceful hope in her voice. 'That'd teach him.'

'We don't want anyone shot anywhere.' Hermitage was as stern as he could manage.

'Oh we do,' Cwen said. 'Really, we do.'

'I expect there will be a lot of talking first.' Wat was lying on the ground with his head against his pack and his eyes closed. 'That'll be followed by some shouting and pushing. The shooting might not start for hours.'

Hermitage's tut was getting heavy use.

'Better they start shooting at each other than at us,' Wat observed. 'If they all kill one another we can go home.'

'I'm sure it won't come to that.' Hermitage risked popping his head out of the tent to get a view of the entrance to the camp. Surely his tonsured hair would indicate that the head belonged to a monk and so didn't need chopping off.

He didn't have a clear view, but there was certainly quite a gathering of Normans. He ducked his head quickly away as he saw William and Le Pedvin striding towards the crowd. In the brief glimpse he caught, he thought they looked very smart, for once. William even had some sort of crown on his head and his accoutrements had been freshly buffed. Le Pedvin had obviously received the ministrations of his wife as his stick-thin figure was now well ordered with weapons and a shining helm topped him off. This thing was so bright and prominent that it made him look rather like a torch, waiting to be stuck in its sconce.

Once he'd given them enough time to pass, Hermitage peered out of the tent once more. 'William and Le Pedvin have just gone by, but I can't see any Saracen army,' he reported.

'The whole army won't turn up,' Wat explained. 'That really would be asking for a fight. No, they'll be camped somewhere. We'll just get a small band of the important people, come to find out what's going on.'

'They're not going to have much luck there then,' Cwen said.

'And if William's explanation isn't to their liking,' Wat added, 'then we get to see the army.'

'Oh dear.' Hermitage didn't want to be near any army, let alone between two of them,

'If it gets to that point,' Wat went on, 'we vacate the tent very quickly indeed, and run for the hills.'

'There aren't any hills,' Hermitage observed, dryly.

'We'll able to run faster and farther then,' Wat said without opening his eyes.

Hermitage was startled by a loud and well organized "hurrah" that rang out from the Normans.

'Welcoming their visitors,' Wat observed. 'Letting them know how very happy they are and how the arrival of a Saracen army was just what they'd been hoping for.'

Even Hermitage could tell that that simply wasn't true.

While he got on with some cowering, Wat's breathing steadied to indicate he was falling asleep and Cwen just sat with a look of eager anticipation on her face. Naturally, Hermitage had no idea what went on when two armies made first contact, nor how long it took. He had resigned himself to the fact that they might be here all night when the noise outside grew louder, but a bit less formal, somehow. He risked poking his head out once more. 'They're coming back,' he hissed.

'Probably off to sit in comfort and drink fine wine while they discuss who gets first go at the Saxons,' Cwen said.

'Eek.' Hermitage ducked very quickly back into the tent. 'They're coming right by,' he whispered.

'I don't think they'll be stopping for a tent inspection.' Cwen didn't sound concerned.

As the last word died on her lips the tent flap was thrown wide and an arm poked in. There was only one person that arm could belong to, looking as it did like the skeletal beckoning of the reaper himself. 'Come on then,' Le Pedvin said, sounding not the least surprised that the three of them were hiding in a tent in camp and not investigating Hereward at all. 'The Mahuqiq wants to see you lot.'

'Right oh.' Wat woke as if he had been alert all the time. Cwen and Hermitage exchanged looks, each expressing different reactions to their invitation; Hermitage was doing panic.

'Now it really is going to get exciting.' Cwen rubbed her hands.

...

'How can you be so calm?' Hermitage demanded of Wat as they walked along towards the back of the train of people heading into the centre of the camp.

'What's to worry about?' Wat asked.

'What's to worry about? Where shall I start? Normans, Saxons, Saracens, armies, death. Enough to be going on with, I'd have thought.'

'Not much we can do about it though, is there? Having a good worry isn't going to make them all go away.'

If having a good worry about things made them go away, Hermitage would be the only person in existence. 'But, but,' he tried to get his thoughts straight. 'You can't just decide not to worry. That's not how it works. Events occur and they set off the worry. You don't have any say. It's like deciding not to fall off a horse when you're halfway to the ground.'

Wat shrugged, 'Try to think of something else.'

Hermitage looked around at the phalanx of heavily armed men. The ones behind him with sharp swords drawn and eager looks on their faces got the bulk of his attention. Think of something else? Wat did say some ridiculous things.

As they approached the area of William's tent, the armed men began to disperse, which gave Hermitage some relief. It took a few moments before they drew towards the entrance of the tent, at which point Le Pedvin reappeared and ushered them away.

'Not needed now?' Wat said brightly.

'Not here.' Le Pedvin's tone was rather odd. 'This way.' He waved his air-thin arm in the direction of his wife's domain.

As they arrived, they were greeted by a very formal but obviously very happy Mistress Le Pedvin. 'King William is this way,' she said, the king being in her tents was clearly the greatest moment of her life. 'I should raise a pennant,' she went on. 'A royal pennant so that all may see where the king resides.'

'Good idea,' Cwen said equally serious. 'Then the Saxons will know where to shoot.' This got a very puzzled look from Mistress Le Pedvin, who clearly couldn't understand why anyone would want to shoot good King William.

'Get on with it,' her husband urged them forward.

They re-entered the tent of Umair where King William sat in one cushioned chair and a stranger sat in another. Le Pedvin strode across the space to take a third and sat looking at the standing Saxons as if waiting for the mummers to start.

The stranger rose as they entered and Hermitage could not contain a gasp. It looked like Umair had risen from the dead. This was clearly a different man, but the dress was the same and the neat, clean appearance was striking. And strikingly out of place in this particular camp.

This new man was older than Umair by a good few years. He had a look of wisdom and experience in his eyes and carried a comfort about him that showed he was not in the least put out by being in the presence of kings. In fact, the mood in the place made it feel that it was William who was the humble visitor.

Like Umair, the man was dressed in a bright white robe that dropped from neck to floor. How it managed to stay white in this place was a marvel. The head was wrapped in the same expensive silk and the beard was once more trimmed and neat. A broad smile greeted the three arrivals, and Hermitage couldn't remember the last time anyone connected to the Norman army had smiled at him. He was pretty sure it was never.

'Honoured friends,' the man said, as he gave a complicated bow that involved touching his stomach, his chest and his head.

Hermitage thought they must be in the wrong tent. Either that or this visitor had been seriously misinformed about who they were. The scowls of William and Le Pedvin were no help.

Hermitage led the reply by giving a deep bow of his own. Wat followed suit and even Cwen bowed, looking in some awe at the grand figure before them.

'What a sorry time we find ourselves in,' the man went on, face now sombre. He spoke the words very clearly with just a hint of an accent that told of distant mountains and sands and places where it didn't rain all the time. 'But,' he clapped his hands together and rubbed them with some enthusiasm. 'We shall get to the bottom of it, shall we not?' He said 'bottom of it' as if it was a fascinating phrase he'd been just taught and was happy for such an early opportunity to use it. He took a step forward and placed a friendly hand on Hermitage's shoulder.

'Er,' Hermitage said decisively.

William and Le Pedvin just growled, quietly.

'Introductions,' the man announced. 'The sooner we get on, the sooner we shall be done. My name is Abdul-Mateen al

# The Case of the Curious Corpse

Deir ez-Zor,' and he bowed his bow again as if giving them his name was a gift.

For reasons he couldn't put his finger on, Hermitage felt honoured to receive it. Even if he didn't understand it.

'You had better call me Abdul,' he smiled at their confusion. 'I am the Mahuqiq assigned to the death of Umair.'

'I am Brother Hermitage and this is Cwen,' Hermitage indicated with a bow of his head. Cwen was staring quite openly now, her eyes wide. Abdul responded with a warm smile full of white teeth. 'And this is Wat the Weaver.' Wat held up the flagon of wine he had found.

'*The* Wat the Weaver?' Abdul asked in some alarm.

'The only one,' Wat said with a grin. 'I see my reputation precedes me.'

'It does indeed.' Abdul sounded very much like he wanted to take several steps back from Wat and his reputation.

The pause after this was long and starting to get embarrassing. Abdul had been so friendly and welcoming and here they were with nothing to say. This was the Mahuqiq? The confusion was so profound it was stopping conversation.

'Where's the rest of you?' Cwen asked the question they were all thinking.

'Rest of me?'

'The army? The great force of Mahuqiq poised to lay waste to all that stand in their way.'

'There is only me,' Abdul held his hands out in apology for being so few in number.

'Beg pardon?' Hermitage managed.

'There is only me. There is no army of Mahuqiq. Who told you such a thing?' He gave a warm laugh. 'There are barely enough of us to make a small gathering, let alone an army. And what use would we be in a fight?' He laughed again at the very idea. Whatever in the world the very idea actually was.

'But then, what, how, who?' Hermitage ground to a halt.

'I am probably the only Mahuqiq in this country, just at the moment,' the man went on with his smile. 'We are spread thinly and go where the work calls and our Masters send us.'

That was no help at all. Hermitage couldn't see how one man was going to be able to defeat even a very small army.

'Ah,' Abdul said in apologetic realization. 'You are not familiar with our language. How remiss of me. I beg your forgiveness.'

This man did not belong anywhere near Normans.

'The word Mahuqiq has clearly not travelled to these shores. Let me think, how would you name me? The word is common for a variety of uses in my land. How would we translate? The Greek root perhaps, or the Latin?' he raised an eyebrow at Hermitage.

'Er, Latin?' he suggested, his Greek not being all it should be.

'Latin. Just so. How would it be then? Erm,' the man thought for a moment and then gave the translation. 'As I trace events in order to draw my conclusions, perhaps *vestigare,* to track? Yes. I believe I might be an investigator. How does that sound?'

Cwen looked wide-eyed. 'Hermitage,' she hissed, nodding her head towards Abdul, 'there's another one.' Hermitage gave her an empty look. 'And look at all that silk,' she added in a whisper and with what sounded like a sigh. Hermitage had never heard Cwen sigh before. He wasn't sure anyone had.

# The Case of the Curious Corpse

'Just so,' Abdul said, with a beaming smile that put his usual friendly visage to shame. 'As to my ruler, I am his investigator,' he spoke the word slowly and carefully, 'so, to King William, you are his. At least he tells me you look into events such as this.' He gave a respectful nod to William, who just bared his teeth, which were a lot less white, a lot less even and lot fewer in number than Abdul's.

'Yes, he tells me the same,' Hermitage said with little enthusiasm but sufficient obsequiousness to acknowledge that William was still in the room.

Abdul looked a little confused at this. 'It is good to meet a brother in the art of investigation. I am confident that, together, we will unravel the mystery of Umair's death and bring the perpetrator, if there is one, to justice.'

Hermitage was so taken with being this man's brother in an art that he had nothing to say.

'What do you mean, if there is one?' Wat asked.

Abdul held his hands out again, this time seeming to indicate that they were empty. 'I have no information yet. I know nothing other than the fact that Umair is dead, so I can draw no conclusions about the circumstances.'

'Didn't stop William,' Cwen muttered very quietly and carefully, making sure it was only for Hermitage's ear.

'We will need to examine the body, reconstruct his movements and encounters, determine the time of death, if possible, and the actual cause. We will interview those with any knowledge pertinent to the case and compare their versions of events.'

'He's very thorough, isn't he?' Cwen observed, sounding very impressed.

'I thought this one had done that,' William looked more unhappy than usual and waved an arm at Hermitage. 'At least, those were his instructions.' It was perfectly clear that Hermitage not following instructions was going to have consequences.

'And I am sure this is only what he has been doing already,' Abdul bowed to Hermitage's expertise.

'Oh, absolutely,' Hermitage replied. 'Only just got started really.' He shrugged apologetically, knowing that apologies were no use at all to the king.

'But as I mentioned,' Abdul said to William, sounding very apologetic, 'my Master has instructed me to draw my own conclusions. Although I am sure the brother's findings will be of great value.'

'If he had any findings,' Cwen muttered.

William simply growled as he stood and gave them all a regal glare. 'We have important business to get on with while you do whatever is you do. 'This one,' he waved at Hermitage once more, 'has already concluded that Umair was killed by the Saxons. He's singularly failed to bring me the culprit though. Perhaps you can do that.'

'Of course, Majesty,' Abdul said with another of his flamboyant bows. 'To find the culprit is the purpose of my attendance upon you. We will bring you news as soon as we have reached some preliminary conclusions.'

William grumbled something incoherent but rude-sounding at this and beckoned Le Pedvin to accompany him. That assembly of sticks in some clothes lifted himself from his chair and gave Hermitage a very close and personal glare of his own.

'As soon as I have ordered my thoughts I will bring my questions for you at your convenience.' Abdul nodded his head politely at the king.

'Questions for me?' William asked, in that tone that

usually had Hermitage trying to hide in his own habit.

'Of course,' Abdul said as if it was the most natural thing. He went on, very equitably, 'It is quite possible that you killed Umair, or had him killed, and this suggestion that he staggered into camp mortally wounded by the Saxons is all a ruse.'

Hermitage gave a little gasp as he saw William containing the most enormous rage within his body, which was starting to shake.

'And if that is the case,' Abdul continued, with a friendly smile, 'we shall prove it and the consequences will be what they are.'

They could all hear William's teeth grinding now.

'But it could be entirely true and you bear no responsibility at all,' Abdul beamed at them all. 'Either way, we shall find the truth.' A touch of steel edged his words now. 'And everyone will assist in our search.' He turned his eyes to Le Pedvin. 'Everyone,' he repeated.

William and Le Pedvin left the tent. They were in it one moment and then they weren't, but their leaving was a very heated affair with much huffing and throwing aside of canvas as they burst from the place like two very angry Normans who hadn't been allowed to kill anyone.

'Good heavens,' Hermitage said when he had managed to take in what had just happened.

'Thank goodness they have gone.' Abdul gave another of his broad smiles that revealed even more unnaturally white and even teeth. His mouth even seemed to have a complete set, which was remarkable considering he must be at least forty. 'Have you been in their tent?' He lowered himself back into his seat and indicated that the others should make themselves comfortable.

Hermitage took the moment to remove the book from his side and slip it back onto Umair's desk. He hadn't thought it would be so easy, but then Abdul wouldn't know anything about it. It was bound to come up later, no need to confuse everyone and start leaping to conclusions yet.

He didn't feel remotely comfortable sitting in William's chair so he just propped himself against its arm. Cwen sat where Le Pedvin had been and leant forward to take in what Abdul had to say. Wat immediately dropped into the king's vacant chair and reached for the wine.

'Yes,' Hermitage said. 'We arrived when they were at their evening meal, which seemed a very rough affair.'

'Disgusting place. Do these people never wash?'

'Er no.' Hermitage was happy to have a straightforward question. 'I don't think so.'

Wat was looking from the tent entrance to Abdul and back again. 'Did you just accuse King William of murder?' he checked, waving the wine in the direction of the departed Normans.

'Not at all,' Abdul confirmed, happily. 'I just made it clear that he is a suspect. Along with everyone else.'

None of the three Saxons in the tent could quite take in that anyone was allowed to call King William a suspect.

'So you think he did it?' Cwen said with quite a lot of pleasure.

'I think anyone could have done it,' Abdul replied. 'As I explained to William, I don't have any information yet. So far there is only one person in the world who could not possibly have done it.'

'Really.' Hermitage was fascinated by this approach to investigation. His method of wandering around mostly in a daze until something occurred to him seemed terribly primitive all of a sudden. 'And who is that?'

'Me,' Abdul answered. 'I know that I didn't do it, but that's all I know. It could have been one of you.' He gave them all an appraisal but it didn't look very threatening.

'Umair was dead when we arrived,' Hermitage pointed out.

'So you say,' Abdul replied with good humour.

Hermitage raised a finger, acknowledging the point. 'But of course, you need corroboration,' he said, with a confident nod.

'Corroboration?' Abdul tried out the word. 'From *corroborare*, to strengthen, yes I see. What an excellent concept.'

Hermitage beamed with pleasure while Wat and Cwen exchanged looks of resignation and were rolling their eyes for some reason.

'We will eliminate people one by one from our investigation until we have our killer.' Abdul sounded very confident that this would be no problem at all, just a question of time.

Cwen put her hand up. 'Can I eliminate William? Or Le Pedvin, I don't mind which.'

'Perhaps I should have said "exclude",' Abdul gave a light laugh.

'How can you accuse William though?' Wat pressed. 'If we did that it would be the end of the investigation.' He waved his arms about to demonstrate the end of things, careful not to spill any wine.

Abdul frowned at this.

'Because it would be the end of us walking around and breathing,' Cwen explained.

'Ah.' Abdul took the information in but didn't seem happy about it. 'You mean the king interferes with your work?'

Hermitage gave this some thought. The suggestion of interference seemed to be a bad thing, but he couldn't immediately think of another description. 'Um,' he said.

'If you mean does he tell us where to go and what to find out,' Wat said, 'yes. Yes, he does.' He took another swig to wash down this unpalatable fact.

Abdul tutted and shook his head slowly. 'Then how is the truth uncovered?'

Now it was Wat's turn to contemplate. Hermitage was about to say that steady persistence and a careful consideration of conflicting evidence ultimately revealed the facts. Wat got in first.

'Luck. Usually,' he said. 'Luck and Brother Hermitage,' he added with an extravagant nod to the monk on the arm of his chair. 'We end up surrounded by a bunch of liars and evaders giving us versions of events that wouldn't convince a fox with his head down the rabbit hole. I help to wheedle things out of people, Cwen drags it out of them and at some point, and for reasons only he understands, Hermitage says "aha" and explains everything.'

'Remarkable.' Abdul looked seriously impressed. 'I wish I had such a gift. For me it is a hard task of laboriously sifting through every detail, comparing every scintilla of information and coming to the conclusion I have most confidence in. Even then I frequently doubt I am right. After all, finding a man guilty does not mean he did it.' He bowed his head at Hermitage, 'I envy you, brother.'

Hermitage could only manage a weak smile. He wasn't altogether sure the "aha" theory of investigation was entirely correct.

'But if your "aha" moment indicates that William may be the perpetrator in this instance?' Abdul enquired.

'We won't let Hermitage say it,' Cwen said. 'We prefer to stay alive.'

Abdul shook his head, sadly. 'Then it is a good job I am here. I am not influenced by any. Even if I found that my own Master was to be accused, I would not hesitate. That is my duty before God. William was charged with the care of Umair and he appears to have failed in that. If he committed the murder as well, I shall name him.'

'And you won't be dead?' Cwen asked, in awe.

'Of course not. William would not dare anger my Master by such an act. And even the greatest in the land cannot hide the truth from God.'

'The greatest in this land can,' Cwen complained.

Wat was looking thoughtful. Either that or his third flagon of wine was having its effect. 'So what if you determine that William was the perpy what-not?' he asked.

'Then that shall be the conclusion,' Abdul confirmed.

'And then?' Cwen asked.

'And then I simply report the finding back to my Master.'

'And then?' she pressed.

'Ah,' Abdul paused significantly. 'That is when the army of assassins arrives to lay waste to all that stands in their path.'

Cwen broke the ensuing silence, rubbing her hands with glee as she did so. 'Excellent,' she said.

## Caput XII

## The Investigator Investigates

𝔄bdul stood in silent contemplation of Umair's body as it lay in its tent. He bowed his head and muttered some words in his own incomprehensible language. The others kept a respectable distance, although Wat was swaying about a bit, William's flagon of wine still in his hand.

The guard to this place had been sleeping across the entrance and had to be woken to grant them access. He had opened his bleary eyes, seen a fine Saracen figure standing before him and run howling off into the camp screaming that Umair had risen from the dead to punish them all.

Abdul had called that interesting but said no more.

'Let us examine the body then,' he said, having paid his respects. 'Of course, the Normans should have had the decency to bury him within the day, but they are heathens so perhaps we must make allowance.'

Hermitage nodded his agreement that the Normans were heathens. Then he thought that no, they weren't. They were as Christian as the next man. Well, perhaps not the next man, but the next appallingly bad Christian who never went to church and sinned pretty much constantly. Perhaps to Abdul even Hermitage, Wat and Cwen were heathens. Well, that was one thing he was wrong about. Hermitage would have to explain about heathens when he had a moment. Meanwhile, he moved to Umair's head and peered closely at the wound.

'A telling mark, my friend,' Abdul raised a cautionary hand. 'but there is much we can tell before we examine what we are told was the fatal wound.'

Hermitage didn't know what more information they needed to confirm that Umair was dead, other than his dead body.

Abdul knelt at his compatriot's side and lifted Umair's hand before letting it drop again. 'Hm,' he said.

'Hand,' Cwen said, apparently thinking he might not know the word.

'It is,' Abdul confirmed. 'And you note how it drops once lifted.'

'They usually do.'

'Depending on the time,' Abdul said, in a friendly, informative manner. 'You doubtless know that after death the body stiffens.'

'Surprise,' Cwen said, knowledgeably.

'I beg your pardon?' Abdul asked.

'Surprise,' Cwen repeated, explaining how this worked. 'That's why bodies go stiff. It's surprise at being dead.'

'Fascinating.' Abdul looked like was controlling a shaking that was going on somewhere in his body. 'But not the standard theory.' He even wiped a tear from his eye, doubtless at the sadness of the occasion. 'The Romans would call the process rigor mortis, and poor Umair here has passed through that stage. Meaning that he has probably been dead for at least four days. Given the low temperature in your country.'

Hermitage moved his attention to the arm. This Abdul seemed very knowledgeable. He wondered how many deaths the man had investigated.

'First comes pallor mortis, the loss of colour. Then algor mortis, the change of heat.' Abdul seemed to give this some careful thought. 'You know, I will risk a speculation that in your chilly surroundings the body may actually lose heat to become the same as its surroundings. In my country, the body heats up after death.'

Hermitage really wanted to know whether that gave rise to a risk of fire, but he was starting to feel that he had little he could tell Abdul that would be of any help.

'Which may be a useful factor in itself, preserving much information for us to consider.' Abdul mused. 'At home, we must bury our dead quickly before putrefaction begins, but here, I suspect the cold will keep all things fresh.'

'If you drop a joint of meat in a bucket of water in the winter and let it freeze, you can still eat it the next year,' Cwen contributed, keenly.

'How lovely,' Abdul said, although it didn't sound like he would be joining the meal.

'It's not very nice though,' Cwen confirmed.

Abdul stood again from his examination of Umair and looked the body over. 'While we also see evidence of blood, it is only on his clothes, not on the ground. And there is not so much as to indicate death from blood loss.' He nodded thoughtfully and held a hand up to stop Cwen's explanation of this before it had even started. 'Which tells me that the bleeding must have stopped before the return to the camp. If the wound had been fresh then livor mortis, the fourth stage of death would have seen the blood fall from it and spread to make quite a mark.' He indicated that the ground around the body was free of blood.

Hermitage was nodding because it seemed polite.

'Unless, of course, he was killed elsewhere and then brought back here after death?' Cwen suggested. 'And the guard who says he saw him stagger in, was lying.'

'An excellent suggestion, and quite possible,' Abdul

nodded. Cwen smiled broadly at everyone, which made Hermitage wonder if she was feeling ill. 'In which case, there will be witnesses to a body being brought back into camp.' Abdul concluded.

'Norman witnesses,' Wat slurred as he closed closing his eyes and hugged the wine close to his chest. 'Who might, you know, also lie?'

'Lies seldom stand for long,' Abdul was confident. 'The problem with a lie is that it has no foundation. When put to the test it will crumble.'

'You haven't been around Normans much, have you,' Wat observed. 'If they spot you crumbling their lies, they chop your head off.' He even giggled at this.

'Presumably,' Hermitage went on, ignoring Wat, 'if we find the place where Umair was killed we will also find the blood.'

'That is quite possible,' Abdul acknowledged. 'Although it is also possible that your rain has washed away all trace. I assume it has rained recently?'

'It always rains.' Hermitage didn't quite understand the question.

'Indeed it does.' Abdul gave a little shiver. He smiled his smile and turned to Hermitage. 'But of course, it depends on the volume of blood in this case. I must lend you my copy of Abū ʿAlī al-Ḥusayn ibn ʿAbd Allāh ibn Al-Hasan ibn Ali ibn Sīnā. He writes on *the pulse* and it is a fascinating volume of great value in our work.' He considered the blank faces staring at him, Umair's looked the most engaged of the lot. 'I think you call him Avicenna?'

'Ah, yes,' cried Hermitage, who had heard things.

'You have read his work?'

'Not exactly,' Hermitage confessed. 'But I know someone

who once saw a copy of his book locked up.'

'Locked up? A precious book then.'

'No, a forbidden one.'

Abdul just raised his eyebrows at this. 'I also see no sign of poison,' he went on. There are no unusual colourings and while rigor mortis has been and gone, there are no contortions or disfigurements.'

Wat snorted at this and Cwen gave him a hard look.

'And so we turn to the wound.' Abdul nodded to Hermitage to indicate that this was the time to consider the livid and unpleasant gash that ran across the right side of Umair's head. Cwen looked on while Wat decided to go and have a bit of a sit down in the corner of the tent. He got comfortable very quickly if the snoring was anything to go by.

Abdul moved Umair's robes around until he revealed the full extent of the wound. 'Ah,' he breathed as if some great revelation had occurred.

'Definitely a blade wound,' Hermitage commented, starting to feel that he was getting a bit left out of his own investigation. He reasoned that he didn't want to be an investigator anyway, and so should be quite happy, but it didn't seem to work that way.

'Most definitely,' Abdul agreed. 'But not a fatal one I fear.'

'Not fatal?' Hermitage asked. Surely anyone being stabbed in the head died. What was the point of doing it otherwise? And Umair was most definitely dead. And he had been stabbed in the head. There didn't seem much more to say.

'The wound is not deep,' Abdul demonstrated, in a quite revolting manner, that the wound was indeed a shallow one. 'It has not penetrated the skull at all.'

'Perhaps there are other wounds that have damaged the vital organs,' Abdul speculated, looking the body up and

## The Case of the Curious Corpse

down.

'I see.' Hermitage imagined rather too much than was good for his stomach. 'Organs, eh?' He hadn't a clue what the man was talking about but just hoped he would stop fiddling about with that wound very soon.

'Of course. The lungs, kidneys, gall bladder, liver and spleen.'

'Of course,' Hermitage agreed, trying to sound as if this was all perfectly normal.

'I once read of a dissection carried out by Abū Bakr Muhammad ibn Zakariyyā al-Rāz.'

Hermitage smiled politely.

'Rasis?' Abdul suggested. 'Perhaps that version of his name is more familiar?'

Hermitage just smiled some more.

'Anyway,' Abdul shook his head and carried on. 'It was most illuminating. Even the work of Galen would be valuable in this instance though.'

'Naturally.' Hermitage was very familiar with the work of that ancient medical authority. He had read as many of the relevant works as he could get hold of and familiarized himself with both the theory and the practical applications. As a well-read monk with an interest in such things, he had frequently been called upon to exercise very limited treatments in the case of ailment or injury.

The four humors were the backbone of much of his own medical practice, but that's where he drew the line. There was no way he wanted to see an actual backbone. Reading about the internal workings of the human body was fascinating. Actually looking for them sounded positively revolting.

Abdul was still poking around on Umair's head, which

brought a lump to Hermitage's throat; one that he tried to swallow before he embarrassed himself.

'I believe the disease of the wound may have been the deadly measure,' Abdul concluded. He stood again and held his hands out and up, careful not to touch anything. 'We know from the De Materia Medica that there are invisible living forces that can get into a wound such as this and lead to illness and death.'

'What?' Wat woke from his rest to hear this. 'Invisible animals climbing into wounds? Now I know you're making things up.'

'I assure you it is well-founded,' Abdul said. 'The great work of Pedanius Dioscordes refers to such matters. Not animals, exactly, but certainly things with a measure of life. That is how the damage is caused.'

Wat snorted.

'Call them miasma or evil humors, if you will,' Abdul explained.

'Ah,' Wat nodded, knowledgeably. 'Miasma. Evil humors, there you are then.' He went back to sleep.

Hermitage tutted at his friend's condition. 'Bald's Leechbook contains a fine recipe for a salve,' Hermitage said knowledgeably. 'It is well known as a cure for seeping eye.' Abdul looked suitably impressed. 'Of course,' Hermitage went on, 'it only works for eyes and it takes nine days to make, so perhaps not so much use if you've just been hit on the head.'

No one had anything useful to say to this.

'Or he could have used some Waybroad and old lard,' Hermitage suggested half-heartedly, realising it wasn't very likely that Umair would carry a bag of old lard with him on his trips.

Cwen still seemed to be paying the most rapt attention and had even knelt to study the wound more closely as Abdul examined it.

'I must wash my hands,' Abdul noted. 'If there is anywhere clean to wash in this place.'

'I doubt it,' Cwen sounded surprised at the very idea.

'Even some wine or vinegar would suffice if there's nothing more wholesome.'

'Wash in vinegar?' Hermitage asked.

'It is a good cleanser. As this wound is so superficial Umair would certainly have been able to treat it himself, if he had had the facilities.'

'Or could get someone to do it for him,' Hermitage suggested.

'Just so. This tells us that he was either prevented from treating it or was unable to do so.'

'The report was that he came into the camp of his own volition but died soon afterwards,' Hermitage reported.

'That could well be the case then. If he was wounded some way away, where there was no cleansing agent, the disease could have reached him before he could reach the camp. But then he would have been able to at least find appropriate herbs, even in this place.' Abdul sounded like he wasn't too impressed by their country. 'Which indicates that he was probably alone.'

'Which still gets us no closer to knowing who did it,' Cwen said.

'There is one more check we must do that will help us in that direction,' Abdul said. 'But for this you must leave us, mistress.' He inclined his head apologetically at Cwen. She glared in return.

'I have a stronger stomach than most,' she said, the

inclination of her head pointing straight at Hermitage.

'I do not doubt it,' Abdul agreed. 'But we must now remove Umair's clothing. It would not be seemly for you to stay.'

'Oh, er, right, yes.' Cwen turned bright red and hurried from the tent.

Hermitage rather wished he could go with her. Why on earth were they taking the man's clothes? Were they so precious that he could not be buried in them? In which case it was really none of his business to see what was underneath.

'Just the top half should do.' Abdul he lifted Umair to a sitting position and started to undo the robes.

Hermitage managed to find several interesting features of the inside of the tent to consider as this was carried out.

'As I thought.' Abdul brought Hermitage's attention to Umair's torso.

He chanced a short glance and saw two arms a chest and a stomach. All present and correct then. And all of the bits that should be on the inside were still where they belonged. Very good.

'You see there is no bruising or damage.' Abdul forced Hermitage to look again.

'Er, yes,' he said, thinking that surely one stab in the head was enough for anyone to put up with.

'Which, as we both know very well, indicates that this was no violent conflict. Umair did not defend himself or get the chance to do so. Otherwise, we would see the wounds of battle.'

'Ah.' Hermitage hadn't known it very well at all but did now. This Abdul really was quite clever and had obviously investigated many times before. It crossed Hermitage's mind to wonder if the man would like to stay on in William's service, leaving him free to get as far away as possible.

Abdul quickly re-covered the body and called Cwen to return. He stood and addressed them all. 'We now know that the single wound killed Umair and that he had no chance to defend himself against it. We can conclude that this was a loathsome and cowardly act, carried out by someone without honour.'

'Loathsome, cowardly and without honour eh?' Cwen mused, with an odd tone in her voice. 'Now, where on earth will we find someone like that in a camp full of Normans?'

Abdul raised a cautionary finger, 'We have no evidence that the wound was inflicted here though. The tale of him returning to camp could well be true.'

'We could talk to the guard again,' Hermitage suggested. 'He seems sure about things and is not in William's favour, so perhaps less likely to lie?'

'Or more likely?' Abdul suggested. 'Seeking to regain his Master's trust.'

'Oh, yes.' Hermitage felt rather deflated.

'It is not the time or nature of the return to camp that interests though, is it.'

'Isn't it?'

'Doubtless, you have already been analysing his time away from camp,' Abdul nodded, knowingly. Hermitage was grateful this wasn't a question. 'That will give us an indication of when this event could have taken place. Which will in turn point to the distance from camp Umair could have travelled. And that will raise some options concerning the perpetrator.'

'Unless he was stabbed here and then thrown out of camp?' Cwen offered.

'A good point, mistress.' Abdul brought a rather smug

smile to Cwen's face. 'My experience of these matters tells me that an injury such as Umair's if it went completed untreated, would not kill him for several days.'

'Or he never left camp at all,' Cwen was taking to the subject with some relish. 'They stabbed him here, tied him up so the wound would go rotten and then released him when he was ready to die.'

'There are no signs of ties on the body.' Abdul held up Umair's limp arm to prove the point.

'Hm,' Cwen didn't sound happy that the Normans might be getting away with this.

Abdul folded his arms in front of him and addressed his audience. 'I think we must accept that it is inherently unlikely that William would actually kill his own hostage.' He sounded like this was a reluctant admission. 'Of course, that doesn't rule him out,' he went on quickly, seeing the look on Cwen's face. 'We know the Normans are a violent and troublesome people everywhere they go but they are manipulative and scheming when the need arises. It would be a very stupid thing to kill a hostage and while he may be many things, William is not very stupid.

'Common sense would say that one of William's enemies did this or someone who did not know Umair's significance. And we know that the camp is surrounded by enemies.' He said this making it sound like a question and a statement at the same time.

'Perhaps not surrounded, exactly.' Hermitage felt that it was somehow betraying a trust to say anything about Hereward at the moment. 'I'm not sure there are enough enemies left to surround anything.'

'Hm.' Abdul stroked his beard as he thought. 'We must not leap to any conclusions. We must follow a straight and

# The Case of the Curious Corpse

steady course and take the only step that presents itself to us at this point.'

'And that is?' Hermitage asked.

'I interrogate the king.'

'Do what to him?' Cwen asked with some disturbing glee.

'Interrogate,' Abdul repeated. *Interrogare*, to question? We question him.'

'Interrogate the king,' Hermitage managed to get out before his voice gave way to fear, which always came out as an incoherent squeak.

'And Master Le Pedvin,' Abdul added for good measure. 'And anyone else with information that might be of assistance.'

'Mistress Le Pedvin,' Cwen said. 'Fat woman,' she went on, seeing Abdul's confusion.

Abdul looked surprised at this. 'That was Mistress Le Pedvin?'

'We know.' Cwen shared his horror at the thought. 'She was Umair's sort of housekeeper-jailer, it seems.'

'Then Mistress Le Pedvin must be interrogated as well,' Abdul confirmed.

Hermitage slowly raised his hand, hoping it would give him time to recover the power of speech.

'Yes, Brother?' Abdul asked.

Hermitage croaked out his whispered question, 'Do we have to come?'

## Caput XIII

## What a Rude Book

'While I'm all for intergutting the king,' Cwen said as they walked away from Umair's resting place, Wat weaving his way behind them and tripping over tent lines that weren't even in his way. 'I think there's more we'd better tell you. And you'd better see the books first.'

'Books?'

Hermitage was relieved that someone else had raised this, and it had not been left to his own judgement to choose the moment; a judgement that would almost certainly have been wrong in someone's eyes. Cwen seemed to be a new person in the presence of Abdul. Perhaps all of his knowledge was firing the learning in her. Hermitage had tried often enough but she never showed the slightest interest when he tried to discuss the post-Exodus prophets, a topic on which he could have given her a great deal of information.

'Yes,' Cwen went on. 'Umair made all these books.' She made it sound like a very personal and rather embarrassing pastime. 'Pictures and squiggles and all sorts.'

'A journal?' Abdul asked.

'Was he?' Cwen nodded. 'There you are then. Hermitage knows all about them.' She nodded that Hermitage could take over.

Hermitage opened his mouth to speak and then recalled that they were walking through the middle of a camp full of Norman soldiers, all of them in the service of their Master, which service mostly involved killing people who showed the least sign of causing trouble. 'Perhaps we should return to Umair's tent,' he suggested.

'As you wish.' Abdul beckoned that Hermitage could lead the way.

Cwen fell into step with Abdul and seemed fascinated by his robes. 'Does everyone wear silk where you come from?'

'Not everyone,' Abdul replied. 'It is more common where I come from because we are on the trade routes with China. But it is a light material, good for keeping cool in the heat.'

Cwen looked wistful. 'I live in England,' she said. 'I've never had to keep cool in the heat.'

'But it is less effective at keeping warm in the cool,' Abdul went on with a rather pained nod.

'You want some thick wool,' Cwen said. 'Sheep are everywhere, you don't need a trade route.'

'Thick wool?' Abdul said with some distaste, sounding as if it was the last thing he was going to put next to his skin. 'Can you answer a question of mine mistress?'

'If I can.'

'I am the one Mahuqiq. You asked where the rest of me was, and sometimes we do work with others, where the issue is complex. But you are three. I understood that Brother Hermitage was the investigator?'

'He is,' Cwen said. 'It's all rather complicated and I wasn't around at the very beginning. Wat and Hermitage got involved in some problem at a monastery, De'Ath's Dingle.'[3]

'De'Ath's Dingle?' Abdul repeated, in some wonder.

'It is as bad as it sounds, I'm told. Anyway, when that was all sorted out King Harold, he was King back then, made

---

[3] The problem is randomly explained in The Heretics of De'Ath.

Hermitage his investigator.'

'I see. A reward for his work.'

'Not the way Hermitage tells it. Apparently, there was some other monk who was claiming to be the investigator but Hermitage was given the job.'

Abdul just looked bemused.

'And Wat sort of took Hermitage under his wing. He is a bit, how can I put it?" Cwen paused and gave this complex question some thought. 'He'd be all right in a monastery,' she explained. 'But the real world isn't really ready for him.'

Abdul smiled.

'Don't get me wrong. He's very clever and he can read and write and everything, and he does piece together what's going on when the rest of us are completely lost, but he can be rather trusting.'

'A good quality surely.'

'Not round here.' Cwen gave a nod to their surroundings. 'After the monastery business Wat and Hermitage came to investigate something else and that's where I met them.[4]'

'And you have stayed together ever since.' Abdul smiled.

'Yes, I suppose we have.' Cwen said this as if she'd only just realised. 'I make tapestry as well, you see,' she went on hurriedly, 'so it makes sense for me to stay with Wat.'

'Not tapestries of Wat the Weaver's subject matter,' Abdul said, with certainty and a cursory nod back to Wat who was now humming to himself.

'Absolutely not,' Cwen said with some disgust in her voice, but a lot less certainty.

'I can see that it is useful to have a rich patron,' Abdul nodded again at Wat. 'But one must take care that the

---

[4] The something else is The Tapestry of Death.

patronage does not become influence.'

'Of course.'

'Or even corruption.'

'That would be terrible,' Cwen nodded and shook her head at the same time. 'Oh look, we're here.' She sounded relieved.

Back in Umair's tent, Hermitage went straight to the volume he had only just put back. He turned and handed it with all due reverence to Abdul who took it in his hands, spun it over and opened it at the back.

Wat deposited himself in one of the chairs and reached for more wine, which he simply hugged to his chest as he closed his eyes.

Cwen stood close at hand, looking with interest as Abdul examined the book.

'You'll find the most interesting material is at the front.' Hermitage left it to the Saracen to discover things for himself so that he wouldn't have to tell.

'This is the front,' Abdul said simply.

'Er.' Hermitage was unable to make his head accommodate this madness.

Abdul looked a bit puzzled and perhaps disappointed that Hermitage didn't understand this. 'Our script reads from right to left.' Abdul laid the book down on Umair's desk with the page open and ran his finger along the top line of script from the outer edge of the right-hand page towards the spine. 'This is the first line.'

Hermitage just gawped. How could that be the first line? The first line on a book was at the top on the left, everyone knew that. He somehow felt that his whole world had just been lifted up and put down in the wrong place. He didn't know where anything was any more, and also seemed to have lost the power of speech.

Books were more than just important, they were everything. They provided some solid ground while the rest of the world fell down whatever particular hole it was heading for at the time. You could always go back to a book to find it hadn't changed a bit. Words didn't move around or alter themselves when you weren't looking. To find that not all books were alike was very unsettling. He knew the script was a mystery to him, but he had at least thought it would behave properly.

Abdul shook his head lightly with a wry smile on his face. He moved his finger along the line once more and made some noises as he did so. To Hermitage's ear, it sounded like speech but nothing he'd ever heard before. He knew his Latin, of course, Norman French, Saxon and even had a smattering of the strange hooting noises that Vikings made, but which seemed to make sense to them. As he listened he thought he caught something that sounded a bit like "Umair", but only a bit.

Abdul went back to the start of the line. 'This is the thirty-third journal of Umair Ibn Abdullah Ibn Abd-Al-Aziz during his time as hostage to the Norseman William.'

'Was he a hostage as well?' Cwen asked, looking very confused.

'That was Umair's name,' Abdul sighed, heavily.

'Does it really say that?' Hermitage overcame his confusion and leaned over to peer at the book.

'Of course it does,' Abdul indicated with his finger.

'Where's "Umair?"'

'Here.' Abdul pointed out one section of script in the middle of everything else. Hermitage had no idea what it said, but the idea that these strange markings could be translated into recognizable words fired his curiosity. Here was something completely new. Something he had never come across before, and about which he knew nothing. It was quite fascinating.

'And thirty-three?' he asked. Abdul indicated the appropriate marks.

'You have three where you come from then?'

'I beg your pardon?' Abdul sounded very confused.

'Three,' Hermitage repeated. 'You have the number three?'

'Er, yes.' Abdul sounded rather lost himself. 'We use it to count the things that come between two and four.'

'How wonderful,' Hermitage said.

'We have all the numbers.' Abdul now sounded as if he were talking to a child. 'Right the way to the top.'

'Very good.' Hermitage was pleasantly surprised.

Abdul took a breath. 'We invented numbers,' he said, making it perfectly clear that anyone of education should know this.

'Invented numbers?' Hermitage knew that he was weak on numbers. Words were not a problem at all and it seemed unreasonable to expect anyone to do both. 'You don't invent numbers.'

'Not any more.' Abdul wiped a hand over his face. 'They've all been done.'

'Eh?'

'The Babylonians invented numbering systems thousands of years ago.'

'Ah, well, Babylon.' Hermitage made it quite clear that no one should be counting things using numbers from that wicked place.

'You still use our numbers to tell the time,' Abdul sounded like he was getting a bit impatient. 'On your clocks and sundials? Sixty minutes in an hour and sixty seconds in a minute?'

Now Hermitage was thoroughly confused.

'I admit that last one is only a recent development,' Abdul explained. He gazed at Hermitage, seemed satisfied that understanding was not going to emerge any time soon, and went back to the book with a shake of his head.

As he read on, a broad smile broke out that became a grin as he moved on to the second page. Halfway down this, he released a burst of laughter.

The others looked at him for some explanation.

'It's erm, about some people he met.' Abdul looked at the Saxons with a slightly apologetic look on his face. 'It's just a rather amusing description, that's all. You have to know the language.' He quickly returned to the book. As he turned the page, the laughter broke out again, this time much more sustained and forcing him to retreat to the chair, where he sat with the book on his lap.

With each page read and turned the laughter continued until tears started to run down Abdul's face. Three stony-faced Saxons, not having the first clue what was so funny, stood like all those do who don't get the joke. They didn't see the humour and found someone else who did get it intensely annoying. Not only did they not get the joke, it didn't look like Abdul was about to tell them.

Hermitage started to wonder what on earth Umair could have written about being a hostage that was so amusing. He reasoned that it must be some sort of commentary on his years with the Normans, but commentaries weren't supposed to be funny. He had read a commentary on Saint Botwulf once, that hadn't been funny at all. Quite miserable, really.

'Oh, ha, ha, ha,' Abdul burst out, throwing his head back

and giving the laughter full rein.

'What,' Cwen asked, clearly not wanting to be left out.

The others found themselves smiling in spite of themselves now. Abdul's laughter was so genuine and persistent that the sight of the laughing man became funny in itself. Whatever this joke was, it was so funny you didn't actually need to hear it in order to laugh, just be near someone who had.

Abdul gasped for breath and wiped the tears from his eyes. He tried to speak but couldn't get the words out between the convulsions that he was trying to control. He took deep breaths, clamped his mouth shut and forced a moment's control upon himself. He looked at them and took the plunge. 'Pudding woman,' he managed to squeak before the laughter got the better of him and he collapsed once more, all mysterious dignity abandoned.

The others looked at one another thinking that that didn't sound very funny.

Abdul slammed the book closed as if to contain the agonies it was putting him through, and he thumped the cover with his fist to make the laughter stop. 'He-calls-,' he started to stutter words out through his shattered breath. 'He-calls-mistress-Le-Pedvin-Pudding-woman.' This only brought deeper and more uncontrolled howls to the surface.

Hermitage shrugged. He could see that it was an amusing name for the woman, but not that funny, surely.

Abdul had regained some control now and took slower breaths. 'I do apologise,' he nodded to them all. 'But it seems Umair has been entertaining himself at the expense of his captors.' He patted the book on his lap. 'You have to read the whole thing, really. It is a fascinating insight into the Normans and their foibles. And they seem to have a lot of foibles.'

Hermitage smiled, politely.

'You should see what he calls William and Le Pedvin.' Abdul concluded. 'I don't think I dare read the rest, I'm not sure I could contain myself.'

'Towards the start, er, end,' Hermitage pointed at the book. 'There are some drawings.'

'Drawings eh? I hope they're not as funny as the text.' Abdul opened the book once more and turned the pages, left to right until he came to the cover at the other end. Here were the drawings that had directed enquiries towards Hereward. He raised an eyebrow at the picture of the fortress and quickly scanned the text. Another guffaw burst forth, which was quickly contained. 'Does King William know about this?' he asked with as much seriousness as he could muster.

'He knows about the drawing,' Hermitage replied, cautiously.

'And believes this fortification exists?'

'He does.' Hermitage longed to tell the whole story and everything that they knew. He usually longed to tell anyone everything that he knew, but they seldom listened. In the case of Abdul, he was cautious. There was no telling what the man would do. Perhaps he would drag them before the king and report that they had been cavorting with Hereward. It hadn't really been much of a cavort but Hermitage imagined that William wouldn't worry about the details.

'Do you know what this signifies?' Abdul asked, with as serious a tone as he could manage.

'Possibly.' Hermitage didn't have the confidence that he really knew anything at all.

'There is information here,' Abdul tapped the book to make sure they all knew what they were talking about. 'And

# The Case of the Curious Corpse

it is of great significance.'

'Indeed.' Hermitage thought that sounded suitably non-committal.

'It is very funny,' Abdul with a shake of his head. 'But very bad as well. It casts a whole new light on the situation here, and possibly on Umair's death. It also puts me in a very difficult position.'

'Ahum,' Hermitage said.

'It could be that you already know what it is, in which case you are also in the difficult position. Perhaps you do not know?'

'Maybe,' Hermitage replied if it was a reply.

'Can I ask you a question?'

'Of course.'

Abdul steepled his fingers and looked very thoughtful. 'Brother Hermitage,' he said, 'have you been out of this camp following your arrival? In fact, did you leave the camp following your discovery of this book. More particularly, this drawing?'

The look was piercing and intense and Hermitage felt obliged to answer honestly. 'Yes. Yes, we have. We saw the drawing and saw that it could well be connected to Umair's death.'

'Just so,' Abdul went on. 'And did you discover anything in the course of your inquiry? Did you discover anything about this?' He tapped the drawing of the fort very specifically.

'Possibly,' Hermitage said thinking ahead - for once.

'You discovered that the drawing was, what can we say? Imaginative?'

Hermitage dove in with a plain-speaking and positively blunt statement of the facts. 'One could be justified in determining that, in reality, there were perhaps slightly fewer

Saxon forts that might be concluded from a cursory examination of the illustration.' There, he had said it.

'Slightly fewer than one?' Abdul checked.

'Just so.'

'And fewer actual Saxons?'

'Markedly fewer,' Hermitage said, the urge for confession washing over him. 'At first, we thought that Umair might have been attacked by the Saxons for making drawings of their fortifications. William seemed very happy about that possibility and sent us to find them. When we saw that the fortifications were not as erm, *there*, as expected, we concluded that wasn't the case.'

'The problem being that if we told the king what we discovered he would probably be very cross,' Cwen said.

'Then we are in the same difficult position,' Abdul concluded, with a sigh.

'When King William gets very cross he tends to get a bit, you know, murderous?' Cwen added.

'I can imagine. If he found out that he had been fed false information about the Saxons he would be very, very cross, I expect.'

Hermitage took a breath. Abdul needed to know the rest, and he hadn't leapt to his feet denouncing them as traitors, yet. 'It seems Umair got on quite well with the Saxons. They say he left them fit and well, having come up with a few, erm, ideas for William. It takes very little to make him very cross, and this seems like quite a lot, so we didn't like to mention it. Not that we've had the chance.' Hermitage gave a hopeless shrug.

'And the whole Saxon force is actually feeble,' Abdul concluded.

'Well.' Hermitage wanted to defend his countrymen. 'I

wouldn't go so far as to call them feeble, but they're certainly not as well organised as the pictures indicate.'

'They're not as well anything,' Cwen added.

'The pictures are the least of it,' Abdul said. 'I can read the text. It says here that they're feeble.'

'Ah,' Hermitage said.

'In fact, it says a lot worse than feeble, but that will do for now.'

'What else does it say then?' Cwen asked.

'Erm,' Abdul hesitated for a moment. He scanned the page and selected a passage. He cleared his throat. 'I have today returned from another visit to the, erm, Saxons.' It sounded like Abdul was missing some words out on purpose. 'William,' Abdul stumbled over the word, 'sent me out once more to discover his enemy's strength.'

Hermitage looked at the script to see if he could spot what the name William looked like.

'It doesn't actually say "William",' Abdul explained. 'The word Umair uses for the king is revolting in most of the languages I know, so I think it best left silent.'

Cwen looked rather disappointed at this.

Abdul read on. '"And I have told the, erm, William, that the Saxons are a mighty force with a great fortress hidden the fens. Of course the idiots believed it, not knowing that these particular Saxons couldn't put one log on top of another, let alone build a fortress."' Abdul coughed, 'Sorry about that,' he said.

'Don't apologise,' Cwen said. 'Hereward and his men are pretty hopeless. On the mushrooms most of the time.'

'Yes,' Abdul said, 'there's quite a lot here about mushrooms.' He flipped over several pages. 'This does double our problems though. William should not have been using his hostage in this manner. That alone would be enough to bring my Master's wrath upon him. But then Umair should not have been lying to his captor, or writing of him in quite such disparaging terms.'

'If William found out,' Cwen suggested, 'he might have killed Umair for it. No, sorry, he *would* have killed Umair for it.'

Abdul gave this some thought. 'I don't doubt it at all mistress.'

Cwen smiled and rubbed her hands at what might come next.

'But I also doubt he did.'

'Oh,' Cwen's disappointment was that of the child told it was turnip for tea again.

Abdul explained. 'If William had discovered Umair he would have reported the same to my Master. He would have sent word that he had caught his hostage betraying him to his enemies and had justly dispatched him.'

'And please send a fresh hostage,' Wat spoke from somewhere in his stupor.

'Exactly,' Abdul agreed. 'That William has summoned you here to prove he did not do this is further evidence that he probably didn't. If he had good reason to deal with Umair, why deny it?'

'Unless he didn't have good reason and just killed him anyway?' Cwen put in.

'Hm,' Abdul hummed. 'That is still possible, I suppose. But I think there is further cause to conclude that William did not know what Umair was up to.'

'And that is?' Hermitage asked.

Abdul tapped the book. 'I don't think any of the Normans know how to open a book, let alone understand what's going on inside. They can obviously manage the pictures, but that's probably about it. If Umair didn't tell them in plain language, they would never find out. And I don't think he would have told them.'

They nodded their sombre agreement to this.

Abdul looked thoughtful and concerned, 'If we are going to discover Umair's killer, the Normans must not know the true content of his journals.'

'Mistress Le Pedvin was going to burn them,' Hermitage said, with a quiver in his voice.

'Ha,' Abdul gave a hollow laugh. 'From what I have read of that woman the only use she would have for a quill would be to stab the goose to death.'

'If William knew what's written in the journals,' Cwen did not conclude the thought.

'He may be Norman but he is one of the cleverer ones.' Abdul acknowledged. 'And if he does get a sniff of this he will send us all on our way, perfectly happy that Umair is dead, doubtless loudly claiming that he did it.'

'They think Umair mostly wrote nonsense about rocks and flowers and things.'

'Then we must keep it that way.'

'Unless someone asks you to read them out?' Hermitage suggested, with a shiver of worry.

'The Normans ask to be read to?' Abdul sounded surprised.

They all had a little laugh at this suggestion.

'Anyway, I can always say it's a strange dialect and I can't read it.' Abdul shrugged that this would not be a problem.

There was a silence, during which a lot of thinking went on, judging by the contortions on people's faces. Apart from Wat's, of course.

Abdul drew himself out of his chair and returned to the desk, carefully placing the journal back in its place. He turned to face Hermitage and Cwen. 'Our interrogation of William will have to be a very careful one,' he nodded from somewhere in his own thoughts. 'We still need to find out what he knew about Umair's movements before the fateful day. Doubtless, he will not want to reveal that he was sending his hostage to scry out the Saxons, but there may be some detail that gives us cause to think he knows more than he is saying.'

'Perhaps we should let the Pudding Woman burn the journals now,' Cwen suggested. 'Get them out of the way.'

'No!' Hermitage cried out.

'It would remove one problem,' Abdul said.

'You can't.' Hermitage was horrified at the very idea. 'You just can't. It would be like murdering Umair all over again.'

Abdul gave this some thought. 'Very well,' he said. 'I doubt the Normans will call for the books but we must keep it in mind if the need becomes urgent.'

'I'm sure it won't.' Hermitage tried to sound confident, but he was worried about the path things were taking. 'And surely we don't want the investigation to become as dishonest as those being investigated. Keeping information back, removing evidence? Surely these are things we'd expect from the Normans.'

Abdul shrugged and held his hands out as if there was nothing he could do. 'Sometimes it is necessary to, what shall we say? Encourage those with something to hide to reveal themselves.'

'He's always doing this,' Cwen scoffed at Hermitage. 'Wants to tell the truth all the time, to everyone. Even when it's the worst possible thing to do. We keep trying to tell

## The Case of the Curious Corpse

him.'

Now it was Hermitage's turn to shrug.

Deciding it was probably best to leave Wat where he was, they readied themselves for the interrogation of the king. It looked like it would be hard to wake the weaver and get him safely across the camp anyway, and Cwen also suggested that he would probably say something offensive to the king, which wouldn't help.

Taking a last look around, Abdul ducked out of the tent.

'There was one thing you said which I think we need to clarify,' Hermitage said as he followed his brother investigator.

'Ah, yes. And what is that?'

'When you mentioned it you said "I" will interrogate the king. Now you say it's *our* interrogation. What do you have in mind, exactly?'

# Caput XIV

## Haven't You Finished Yet?

The very sight of Abdul opened their passage to King William's tent as if the men guarding him had been given special orders. Hermitage was in two minds about this. It obviously removed a lot of problems but presented them in person to the man who seemed to be the main problem of his life much more quickly than he would have liked.

Of course, they were still kept waiting throughout the middle of the day, but that was just so William could show who was who, according to Abdul. According to Hermitage, it was rather rude and a complete waste of everyone's time.

When they were eventually admitted to the Royal presence, Hermitage was pleased to note that William was sitting behind a great oak table with a variety of parchments and half-eaten bits of animal around him. Hermitage's mind conjured an image of the nest of a very well-read rat. At least this meant that the man would have to jump over the table before attacking them, which might present an opportunity to run away.

Le Pedvin was to one side, at the end of the table, in a much better position to leap out and do something horrible. 'No weaver?' the man observed, slipping one eyebrow up his forehead.

'He's erm, resting,' Hermitage said with a quiver.

'Very tiring,' Le Pedvin observed, 'drinking all the king's wine like that.'

Hermitage felt a lump in his chest. Had they been watched?

# The Case of the Curious Corpse

Did the king and Le Pedvin know the secrets of the journal? Was their doom already written? He then reasoned that Wat had been staggering around the camp for a while now and so his state shouldn't really be a surprise to anyone. Quite why the weaver had taken to the wine with such vigour was a mystery in its own right. Just not the most important one at the moment.

King William said nothing. He just sat behind his table and looked at them all. He didn't invite them to sit, but then he and Le Pedvin occupied the only chairs and didn't look ready to give them up. This silence was somehow worse than the explosion Hermitage had been fearing. It felt like the king was saving something up for them. Or saving them up for something. Hermitage was like Daniel in the lion's den, except, in this case, every time he pulled a thorn out, the lion stuck it back in again.

'Your Majesty.' Abdul gave a deep and obsequious bow, which somehow managed to be impudent at the same time.

'Yes.' William confirmed the fact.

'Who killed him then?' Le Pedvin asked, nonchalantly.

'That, we do not yet know,' Abdul acknowledged with a lesser bow to Le Pedvin.

'Well that's not very good, is it?' William said. 'What have you been doing?'

'In the hours since I arrived, Majesty?' Abdul asked with his quiet and polite impertinence.

'You're no better than what's-his-name.' The king waved a hand at his investigator.

Hermitage felt a sudden and enormous comfort that the king couldn't even remember his name.

'We believe Umair was struck some time ago and that it could well have happened out of the camp,' Abdul reported.

'I told you that,' William pointed out. 'In fact, that's what I said in my report to your Master. Hardly worth the bother coming all this way just to find out what you know already.'

'And that on occasion he brought back information about the disposition of your enemies,' Abdul went on as if William hadn't spoken.

William shrugged this away. 'He liked being helpful.'

'Helpful?'

William spoke down to them through one of his regal stares, 'I treat my hostages properly. I don't lock them in towers or chain them to posts or remove their, erm, privileges. They can do what they like. As long as they stay hostage, I don't care. Your Umair liked wandering off and exploding all over the place.'

'Exploding?' Abdul asked. He looked to Hermitage.

'Exploring,' Hermitage mouthed.

Abdul frowned as he considered the word, then nodded that he understood. 'So, he explored outside the camp, even when you were surrounded by enemy forces?'

'I told him not to go.' William sounded very reasonable. 'I told these two that I told him not to go.' He waved again at Hermitage and Cwen.

'But he went anyway.'

'What am I supposed to do, tie him up?'

'Leave him in Normandy, away from the field of battle?'

'I may treat hostages very well, but I want them where I can see them.' William was starting to get a bit less reasonable.

Abdul calmly contemplated this. 'And when did you see him last?' he asked.

'Days ago.' William waved the question away. 'Long before he had any fatal wounds.'

'He was in good health when you saw him?'

'That's what the king just said,' Le Pedvin stepped in quickly before William's reasonableness left completely.

'Indeed.' Abdul nodded, grateful for the confirmation. 'And was he leaving the camp on that occasion?'

'How should I know?' William ground out. It was clearly taking a lot of effort to contain his desire to strike out.

'Because you were telling him not to go?' Abdul reminded the king of what he had just said.

'I don't stand guard of my own camp,' William barked out. He then took a deep breath, tried something like a smile at Abdul and continued. 'I have guards for that. I told Umair when we got here that he should not leave the camp. My instructions are usually followed. First time.'

'Quite right too,' Abdul commented. 'So, when Umair returned from his journeys with information about the Saxons, I imagine you reminded him that he shouldn't be going out.'

William's glare headed straight for Hermitage, who quaked under the onslaught. 'Of course,' the king grunted.

'Nevertheless, Umair retrieved information about your enemies and delivered it to you against your express orders,' Abdul shook his head in disappointment. 'That was most improper of him.'

'It certainly was,' the king was happy to agree with this.

Abdul spoke as if talking to himself, just to get the ideas straight in his head. 'Just as you would never send him out on such a mission, as that would be an improper way to use a hostage.'

'Absolutely,' William confirmed.

Hermitage paid special attention to the way the king said this, knowing that it was a lie, having heard the truth from

Umair's own record. He thought that there might be some physical indication of the falsehood in the king's demeanour and that being able to spot when people were lying could be quite handy, particularly for an investigator.

People lied to him with alarming regularity, but he only ever found that out later. This was the opportunity to see the lie in action. And it was no help at all. The king might as well have been calling for wine. Hermitage could see no hint of discomfort, no aversion of the eyes, no fidget, no slip of speech. The king could obviously lie very well indeed, or just spoke and it didn't matter in the least to him whether it was true or not.

Unless Umair was lying in his book? He brushed that thought away. Why would the man lie in his own language, knowing no one else could read it? And anyway, books didn't lie.

Abdul was looking very thoughtful, stroking his beard. 'You may not have seen Umair before he left on his final journey then.' It sounded like he was supporting the king's version of events.

'Probably not,' William gave a relaxed shrug, 'you?' he asked Le Pedvin who was now lounging with his feet on the table.

'I always did my best to avoid him,' Le Pedvin drawled.

'Why so, my Lord?' Abdul asked.

'My wife may have found his reports on everything from flowers to frogs fascinating, I did not.'

'Then he could have left without anyone seeing him go.'

'Quite possible,' William said. 'And it matters why, exactly?'

'A very good question Majesty,' Abdul nodded thoughtfully. 'We are told that he came back into the camp

## The Case of the Curious Corpse

wounded. What we do not know is whether he left in that condition.'

'Eh?' Le Pedvin scowled. 'Why would anyone who'd been struck a grievous blow on the head go for a walk?'

'If his attacker was here, he may have been escaping.'

William had found his glare again. He gave it added strength by standing up and struggling against the urge to bang his fists on the table. It was quite clear he was going to bang them on something before the day was out. Hermitage jumped back a good foot but Abdul seemed not to notice the king's anger at all. 'Are you suggesting that a Norman did it?'

'Not necessarily, Majesty,' Abdul remained calm. 'It is possible that someone got into the camp from outside, seeking a significant victim, perhaps even yourself. An assassination attempt.'

'A what?' William demanded.

'A killing, Majesty, of a specific person. Usually by a lone assailant.'

'Mahuqiq assassins,' Hermitage reminded the king, unnecessarily.

'Hardly,' Abdul said with a puzzled frown. He shook his head gently, almost as if in amusement. Hermitage found nothing amusing about this situation at all.

'A killer may have entered the camp, looking for you, or another noble,' Abdul explained to William. 'If they could remove the leader, the rest of the force may crumble.'

William frowned as he thought about this. 'Pretty cowardly way to go about things but nothing surprises me where Saxons are involved,' he said with dripping contempt, completely ignoring the Saxons in the room. 'Bit of a mistake to make though, stabbing a Saracen instead of a Norman. Not much of an assassin to get that wrong.'

'Perhaps they failed in their attempt on you and selected Umair as an easy target?' Hermitage offered. He was feeling left out of all of this, for which he knew he should be grateful, but his urge to speak was in control, as usual.

'You know what?' William asked, and it was clear he was going to answer almost immediately. 'It's perfectly possible a Saxon assassin crawled into my camp on his backside and stabbed the wrong person, or they got hold of him out there,' he waved in the general direction of outside the camp to give the right idea. 'And they did it on purpose. No Norman had anything to do with his death and the sooner you satisfy yourself of that, the sooner we can get on with dealing with the Saxons.' He sat back in his chair, which at least let Hermitage breathe again.

'Someone will have seen Umair leave,' Le Pedvin said as if he hadn't really been listening to anything that had been going on. 'The guards are mostly useless but they do spot comings and goings. Or at least they do after I've reminded them that's their job.' He said this last with a very unpleasant smile.

'Excellent,' Abdul thanked Le Pedvin for the information. 'If we speak to the right person and find that Umair was either wounded or not when he left, we can pursue the inquiry.'

William coughed. 'If one of my guards let him go wandering off with a knife in his head you can watch the execution.'

Abdul simply nodded at this.

'Come on then.' Le Pedvin gave a weary sigh that this was asking a lot of him and he really couldn't be bothered. He pulled himself to his feet and beckoned that the investigative party should follow him out of the tent.

## The Case of the Curious Corpse

Grateful to leave the image and the person of King William behind, Hermitage drew up the rear, behind Cwen, as they exited.

'Of course,' Le Pedvin said as they walked, 'we don't know how long ago he left so it might mean asking everyone.' He waved his arms around to take in the whole camp.

'We do know that he has been dead about four or five days,' Abdul explained. 'And before that, the wound might take a few days to kill him. So sometime around a week ago?'

'Hm.' It wasn't clear whether Le Pedvin was working out what this meant for the questioning, or was annoyed at a stranger telling him what to do. 'We can ignore the bulk of the men then. They only got back three days ago from scouring the countryside.'

Hermitage had an urge to ask what they'd been scouring for, but he was pretty sure he already knew the answer and wouldn't like it if it was said out loud. 'There was one guard,' he said, meekly, hating to interrupt Le Pedvin's walking. 'He said he saw Umair come into camp. Perhaps he was on guard when he left as well.'

Le Pedvin scowled a bit, then realisation dawned. 'Oh him,' he said with disparagement, which was a bad sign coming from a Norman warlord.

'He, erm, said he'd done a bad thing?' Hermitage offered.

'He certainly had.' Le Pedvin gave a very disappointed sigh. 'Lucky to be alive if you ask me. Getting a crown's made William soft.'

Hermitage just swallowed at that thought.

'At least he'll be easy to find,' Le Pedvin grumbled, striding off in a new direction.

'Ah, good,' Hermitage tried.

'He'll still be on guard if he knows what's good for him.'

'He is a regular guard then?' Abdul asked, clearly thinking that such a man might be useful.

'He's a permanent guard,' Le Pedvin said. 'All day, all night, every day, every night. It's easy to remember. Part of the punishment.' He snorted at this gentle and generous treatment.

'When does he eat and sleep then?' Hermitage asked, thinking that the gaps in the man's duties might cover Umair's departure.

'Don't know. Don't care,' Le Pedvin explained, carefully. 'He'll be over there,' he waved towards the outer edge of the camp, which was about fifty yards away. 'I've just spotted someone else who needs correction,' he nodded away to their left. 'I'll be there in a moment.'

Slightly puzzled, they moved off to the edge of the camp, where the familiar guard stood, slumped against a long pikestaff that he was holding up. When they got closer it was clear that the pikestaff was holding the guard up. The snores, whimpers and mutterings of a man on the edge of sleep, and possibly the edge of madness from trying to sleep standing up, spluttered from his lips.

From the slight, wavering movement of the pikestaff Hermitage could tell that the guard would slip at any moment and be shocked back to wakefulness. He thought it wise to wait until that happened before making any enquiries.

He had once been sent to visit a very devout monk, Brother Ur, who went without food, drink or sleep for prolonged periods. While this behaviour was, of course, laudable and praiseworthy, his behaviour when approached by strangers explained why people only ever visited him once. He could understand that in Ur's addled state he needed to

## The Case of the Curious Corpse

touch people to make sure they were real. Why he had to touch them just *there*, and for quite so long was never fully explained.

'The easily startled fellow,' Abdul observed. 'You say he saw Umair enter camp.'

'So he says,' Cwen said, not willing to believe a Norman about anything.

'He seems to appear quite regularly in our considerations.' Abdul's expression was thoughtful. 'Guarding the body. Saw Umair arrive with his wound. Now the one we talk to about the departure.'

'Do you think it's significant?' Hermitage asked.

'In my experience,' Abdul replied, 'and doubtless in yours as well, the people who keep turning up in investigations frequently have some important part to play.'

'Like King William,' Cwen suggested.

Abdul gave a hearty cough as they approached the slumping guard who leapt to an upright position as if Hereward the Wake had fallen from the top of his pike.

'Whassat? Who? Halt.'

Abdul held his hands out and up to indicate that there was no cause for alarm, and the three of them approached the still bleary looking guard.

The guard blinked his eyes a few times and eventually recognised the visitors. He still looked quite alarmed at the sight of Abdul, but seemed to conclude that this was not the dead Saracen; there must be two of them.

His expression at this recognition was not a happy one. He put on his best snarling Norman guard look and spoke with vicious intent. 'What do you want?' he snapped. 'Clear off. Bad enough I'm on guard all my life without you lot keep turning up.' He lowered his pike, the pointy end towards them. 'Go on, I've got nothing to tell you, get away before I spike the lot of you.'

'I sent them,' Le Pedvin's quiet voice interrupted the tirade.

Hermitage had never heard a Norman guard scream before. He didn't know they could. He imagined that in the heat of battle, or upon receipt of some terrible wound they would cry out, but not like this. Not like the piercing shriek of a cat that's just snagged something very delicate on the blade of a scythe. If the man could have climbed up his own pikestaff he would.

'Yes, it's me,' Le Pedvin said with horrible satisfaction.

'Aha, my lord,' the guard gave the sort of squeak that indicated he would rather run gibbering into the Saxon-infested woods than have a conversation with his leader.

'These people have some questions for you. Apparently.'

The guard just smiled the smile of a man looking forward to the moment when all the troubles of the world would fade away as he went completely mad.

'You'll answer them properly,' Le Pedvin added. 'And I shall watch.'

Hermitage noted that he had not said that the questions should be answered honestly.

Abdul had observed the exchange without comment but now stepped forward and put a hand on the guard's shoulder. Hermitage expected the man to recoil at the touch but instead, he just slumped, as if this was the final declaration of his doom.

'You have been on guard for many days,' Abdul said, with genuine sounding sympathy.

'All of them,' the guard replied with a muted whimper. 'Every day there is to do guarding, I do it.'

## The Case of the Curious Corpse

'And we know why, don't we?' Le Pedvin put in.

'Yes, my lord.' The guard seemed resigned that his fate was a just one.

Hermitage's curiosity was really irritating him as it demanded to know what the "bad thing" the guard had done actually was.

'And you saw Umair return to camp with his wound.'

'I did.'

'And you sent for your Master?'

'What else was there to do? He was mumbling away in that language of his and wouldn't let anyone get close. I sent for…,' he couldn't bring himself to say the name, but just gave a submissive nod towards Le Pedvin.

Abdul gave this some thought. 'It sounds like the wound had already progressed significantly. Which would mean it had been delivered several days before.' He turned back to the guard. 'And did you see him leave camp?'

'Oh, yes,' the guard confirmed, brightly.

'Just a minute,' Cwen said angrily. 'When we asked you said you didn't know.'

'Ah, well.' the guard had a genuinely confused look on his face. 'I forget things, you see.' He gazed at them without seeing anyone. 'The more duty I do, the more I forget things.'

'You did see Umair leave?' Abdul checked.

'Yes,' the guard said with resignation. 'I saw him leave lots of times.'

Abdul stroked his beard in that way Hermitage had come to recognise as impatient. 'Did you see him leave on the occasion before he came back wounded?' He spoke the words slowly and clearly.

'Well, I don't know, do I?' the guard had recovered his snappiness. 'I can't say I saw him every time he left.'

'But you were on guard all the time,' Abdul's voice had taken on a sort of strangulated squeak.

'Oh, yes,' the guard remembered. 'I probably did then.'

Abdul just made a noise this time. 'If you think back about a week before Umair's return,' he prompted the guard.

Le Pedvin snorted as if this was an outrageously optimistic request.

'Umair left the camp in his normal manner?'

The guard looked at Abdul as if the investigator hadn't spoken at all. The look was so blank that Hermitage was concerned the man had finally left his senses. There was no reply to the question and Hermitage felt an overwhelming urge to prompt one. 'You never saw Umair leave camp with a wound?'

The guard turned his face to Hermitage but his eye wandered to Le Pedvin.

'A wound?' the guard asked as if he'd never heard of such an idea.

'Yes, a wound,' Hermitage repeated, feeling a little impatience of his own that this guard appeared not to know what they were talking about, even though they'd been talking about nothing but. 'The wound that he came back to camp with?'

'Oh, right,' the guard nodded his recognition and now gazed into the sky as if thinking deeply about the question. Hermitage found this suspicious in its own right. He'd never seen any sign of profound thought in the man before.

'A wound?' the guard checked.

'Yes, a wound,' Cwen said fiercely. 'Like the one you might get if you don't answer the question.' Hermitage frowned at her but was a little grateful for some edge being given to the demand.

# The Case of the Curious Corpse

The guard glanced at Le Pedvin once more, who appeared to have no interest in the question. 'You'd better answer,' he drawled, slowly folding his arms with some insidious intent.

The guard's eyes seemed to fill with worry at his leader's words. He looked around as if wondering if a magical gate might open, through which he could step to whatever paradise Normans looked forward to. Hermitage didn't like to ponder that topic.

'Absolutely not,' the guard said, with some professional pride, or at least what professional pride he had left. 'I wouldn't let him go wandering away from camp with a knife sticking out of his head.'

Abdul sighed. 'The knife may not have been actually sticking out of his head. But he may have had the wound. He could have been in some distress, or staggering about a bit.' As he said this, he subtly moved position so that he was blocking the guard's view of Le Pedvin.

'He didn't drink at all,' the guard reported, clearly thinking such strange behaviour was a problem in its own right. He too moved position so that he could see his leader again.

'Not staggering from drink, you idiot,' Cwen burst out, 'staggering because he'd just been stabbed.'

'No,' the guard confirmed, firmly. 'No staggering, no stabbing. Just leaving camp like normal.'

'Did he say where he was going, or when he would be back?' Hermitage enquired. He thought it unlikely that Umair would have reported that he was just popping off to meet the Saxons, but he might have said something.

'No,' the guard was firm. 'Just went wandering off like normal.'

'How long was he usually gone?' Abdul asked, 'you being the guard on guard all the time,' he added before the guard could say he had no idea.

'Could be anything. Few hours, couple of days.'

'And how long was it this time?' Abdul pressed. 'How long was it between you last seeing Umair leaving with no wounds at all and him coming back with his final one?'

The guard scratched his head and screwed up his face as if this would make his head generate the answer. 'Days,' he came up with.

'How many?'

'How many?' The guard seemed to consider this question ridiculous. 'I've been on guard so long I don't know what day it is now, never mind how many have passed since I started.'

A grumble from Le Pedvin's throat brought the man back to his senses. 'Several days, but I can't tell you exactly.'

'Several days,' Abdul pondered. 'This was a longer absence than normal then.'

'I suppose it was,' the guard acknowledged.

'And he said nothing when he came back?'

'Nothing I understood. Just rambling really. Well, you would if you'd been stabbed in the head, wouldn't you?'

Abdul let out a deep breath and looked to Hermitage and Cwen with a look of disappointment that this was getting them nowhere.

'What did the rambling sound like?' Hermitage asked. Having only just heard the language of Umair and Abdul spoken aloud himself, he could well understand why a Norman guard about to fall over the edge of his senses would make no sense of it.

'Eh?' the guard looked slightly more lost than normal.

'Was it just urgh, and argh and some gurgles, or was he making other sounds?'

The guard looked at him as if Hermitage was the mad one.

'You must remember,' Hermitage encouraged. 'Not every day you get a wounded Saracen staggering into camp.'

The guard wasn't at all interested but answered anyway. 'Sounded like "my head has a knee."'

'My head has a knee?' Hermitage repeated, very disappointed with the result.

'Like that. Mind you, I bet his head hurt by the look of it so not surprising he was confused,' the guard explained. 'Except he said it all together. Like "myheadhasaknee".'

Hermitage tried it, putting different emphasis on the syllables and speeding it up and slowing it down. It didn't help.

'Ma 'adhashini,' Abdul said fluently.

'That's it.' The guard was pleased that someone had got it. 'That's what he said.'

'What does it mean?' Cwen asked.

Abdul pursed his lips and glanced at Le Pedvin. 'It means, they struck me.'

## Caput XV

## The Green Man

Hereward not the Wake was not a happy man. And when Hereward not the Wake was not happy, his men were not happy. They had been lying in their ditch for a lot longer than they'd expected and the mushrooms had run out hours ago.

When one of his men had the temerity to suggest that he was cold and wet it set off a whole debate about the benefits of ditches and why they spent so much of their time in them. The fact that the ditches were an essential part of this flat landscape and stopped the whole place vanishing under the water had no impact. It was even proposed that if the land flooded perhaps William would drown and they wouldn't have to fight him at all.

Hereward reminded them of their pledge to resist the Norman invader by all means possible but the mood had changed.

Several voices suggested that there must be a lot of "means possible" that didn't involve ditches and perhaps they could try some of them for a bit. There might even be some that required high ground. There was very general and vocal support for the prospect of high ground, all of which sounded rather wistful.

This even started a series of reminiscences about high ground and which bits were particular favourites. One of the older members of the band told some ridiculous tales of cliffs and how someone had once fallen from a piece of high

## The Case of the Curious Corpse

ground that was so high he nearly died.

Such defeatist and frankly ungrateful attitudes drove Hereward to distraction. He knew that wandering up and down the ditch slapping the men never went down very well and might cause such a disturbance that they would be spotted. Instead, he settled for a grumbling sulk full of muttered complaint. It sounded like he was talking to himself but his men knew very well what it meant; things would be bad for days to come.

There would be no talking to the man. You wouldn't even be able to offer him food or drink without getting a bad-tempered and insincere "thank you" in response. Most of the time this behaviour brought them to some sort of order. Putting up with Hereward in one of these moods was usually not worth the satisfaction of having a good moan about their lot.

Perhaps it was his suggestion of teaming up with the awful Eadric that had set their minds to more committed complaint this time. Whatever the cause, the atmosphere in this specific ditch was positively frosty and perhaps explained how a stranger managed to wander in without anyone noticing.

It didn't help that it was Hereward himself who first noticed, once he looked up from sulking at the mud on the far side of the ditch. There was a new figure sitting right in front of him. There really would be no living with him now.

'What the devil?' he cried out when he eventually focussed his attention on the figure who was dressed entirely in green. 'Which one of you idiots is supposed to be guarding the ditch?' He called to his men and got no reply.

The figure gave a simple nod and the eyes crinkled in what might be a friendly gesture. Any other gestures would have to be a complete guess. Apart from the eyes, the green swathing covered everything. A slip of cloth was wrapped across the nose and mouth as if the man was about to rob them, or was avoiding being infected by plague. A hooded green cloak covered the head and hung from the shoulders, wrapping a slim body, dressed in a plain green jerkin and leggings. The boots may be brown leather, but they too were hung with strips of green cloth.

Hereward just naturally assumed this new arrival was a man. He'd never found a woman willing to spend much time in one of his ditches.

'Who are you?' he demanded.

'A friend,' the green man replied in a voice muffled by the cloth across his mouth.

'What sort of friend goes wandering around ditches dressed in green?' Hereward asked.

The figure shrugged. 'A green one.'

The other men of Hereward's band had gathered close now and were peering with undisguised menace towards the new arrival.

The arrival gave them a friendly nod and casually drew a long, shining dagger from a scabbard at his belt. He made no threatening move with it, rather he simply twiddled it in his hands. The simple twiddling involved spinning it around rapidly on one finger, throwing it a few inches into the air before catching it, point first, on his index finger and then flipping it over to the other hand from where it appeared to vanish completely. Without anyone seeing how it happened the knife reappeared in the other hand from where it was thrown neatly back into its scabbard.

The men in the ditch settled back and started to try and look a lot less menacing.

'What do you want, green friend?' Hereward asked, not sounding very friendly at all, but obviously not willing to try and take the knife away.

'Want?' the green man shrugged. 'I don't want anything. I bring you news.' The voice was light and seemed unconcerned about being in a hole with a band of Saxon fighters. The accent was plainly Saxon, which helped the assembly relax.

A lone voice piped from the back of the crowd. 'If it involves more ditches, you can clear off.'

Hereward grunted his dismay at this. 'What news?' he asked with a frown. 'Who from? The monk and the weaver?' He brightened considerably at this thought. 'Have the Saracens arrived? Is this the signal to attack?'

'*A* Saracen has arrived,' the man in green explained.

'One?' a voice squeaked in disappointment. 'What good is one Saracen going to be?' This was the same voice that expressed discontent with the role of the ditch in the rebellion against the Norman invasion.

'He's supposed to find out who killed Umair,' the green man explained

'I thought the monk was going to do that,' Hereward replied, suspiciously.

The green man just gave his verdant shrug.

'And that's your news, is it? One Saracen has arrived.' Hereward was clearly disappointed. 'No army?'

'No army, but there is more.'

'Well?' Hereward asked when the rest of the news was not forthcoming.

'There's more than Saracens,' the man explained. 'You are not alone,' he added mysteriously.

Hereward turned and raised a finger to his band. 'If

anyone is considering a smart remark about ditches at this point, I'd advise against it.' He turned to the man in green. 'What do you mean, not alone?'

'William has enemies,' the green man said significantly.

'You don't say.'

'I mean apart from you. His enemies gather.'

'That's usually how he gets rid of them,' the voice from the back put in.

'What enemies gather?' Hereward asked, sounding both cautious and a bit worried.

'Many. Many enemies gather.'

There was a muffled "I bet they're not gathering in wet ditches" from the back.

Hereward stood up at this, his patience finally gone. He took three long strides down the ditch, there was a very un-muffled thump followed by a squeak. He returned to the green man.

'So this *is* the signal?' he asked.

'It could be *a* signal,' the man in green nodded.

'Not going to be much good with just one Saracen though, is it,' Hereward said. 'With a good Saracen army at our back we might have a chance. Need more than a few people who don't like William to drive this lot out of the country completely.'

The green man leant forward, conspiratorially. 'They are here, though,' he said.

Hereward glanced up and down his ditch.

'I have been talking with them,' the man went on, pulling his green hood even lower over his face. 'And they are ready to talk with you.'

Hereward frowned hard at this. 'Oh yes,' he said as if seeing through a ploy. 'If I just come with you we can have a moot. But I have to come on my own, without any weapons or guards.'

'Not at all,' the green man sounded that he thought this would be pretty stupid. 'Their representatives are ready to talk now. I have brought them here.'

Hereward hissed angrily 'You've brought them here? To my secret location?'

The green man looked up and down the ditch himself, clearly not thinking much of it as a secret location. 'Only one person has come from each force. They acknowledge your leadership of the fight against the Normans in these parts and seek audience.'

That seemed to placate Hereward. 'Still shouldn't have brought them here. Neutral ground is what we need.' He gave it some thought, 'Go on then,' he muttered.

The green man gave a low whistle and a few moments later there was a disturbance at the top of the ditch. Hereward's force stepped back and made way as four new arrivals slid down the ditch, clearly intent on not being spotted by anyone who might be observing the local ditches.

There was muttering from the forces in the ditch as, while three of the new men were plainly Saxon, the third was not. A good foot taller than the rest of them, built like an oak tree with extra oak, and as blond as a Viking, this man was plainly a Viking.

'What the hell?' Hereward burst out. 'What have you brought a bloody Viking for?'

'He is William's enemy.'

'He's probably everyone's enemy.'

Despite the lack of a warm welcome, the Viking made no move to do anything and simply stood there, his head sticking out the top of the ditch. 'You don't want to rid the country of the Normans then?' the Viking said, in a broad northern accent.

'Not to have it all turn to Danelaw,' Hereward retorted. 'Have us ruled from Denmark instead of Normandy? What's the difference?'

'I'm not a Viking,' said the man who looked the most like a Viking of them all. 'I was born in Kendal.'

'Look,' the green man interrupted, 'there's no point arguing with one another now. There's a camp full of Normans out there. A camp with the king himself in the middle of it. This could be the best opportunity there is. When are you next going to get this close to William?'

'Hm,' Hereward reluctantly accepted the situation. 'And who are this lot?' he gestured at the others.

'I am Aelfstan,' the first spoke, and he sounded rather proud of the fact. 'And I speak with the voice of the king,' he announced grandly. He was of middling age, well dressed in fine garments and stood erect and proper. There was something about him that said he had never been in a ditch before and that this would most likely be his last visit. This was a man more used to the corridors of castles and the halls of court. While he didn't exactly look down his nose at them all, he clearly didn't want to spend any more time with these people than he had to.

'Which king?' Hereward asked, bringing the man back down to the ditch.

'The only one,' Aelfstan said, with confidence. 'The king appointed by the Witan upon the death of Harold. King Aedgar Aethling.'

The men already in the ditch dropped to one knee at this. The Viking did not.

'How fares the king?' Hereward asked, with some

reverence.

'He fares well, and safely,' Aelfstan replied.

'He fares about three hundred miles away,' the Viking grumbled, with undisguised contempt. 'We'd all be safe if we were in Scotland.'

Everyone gave the Viking very hard stares but no one seemed ready to correct his manners in person.

'And I am Bleddyn,' the third of the number came forward, speaking with a pronounced Welsh accent. This was a small and young fellow. Doubtless, he could slip through the country unnoticed by Norman patrols but he didn't look like he'd be much good in a fight with one. He had tousled hair and bright brown eyes that said the realities of life had yet to bite.

'The Welsh?' Hereward sounded shocked. 'What are the Welsh doing here? What do you want?'

'The same as you,' Bleddyn complained. 'Normans are turning up all over the place. We want rid of them as well. You can be sure they'll be marching on Wales once they've finished here.'

Hereward was shaking his head as if this was all getting completely out of hand. 'And you?' he asked the last man.

The last man did look like an experienced fighter. In fact, it looked like he'd been in a lot of fights and there was no telling what the losers looked like; probably a bit more dead. About the same age as Aelfstan he had led a much more physical life. He was short and squat and looked like he'd be very hard to knock over. Scars on face and arms were worn with some pride and his mouth had long since forgotten how to smile. 'I am Cenric. Liege man to my Lord Eadric the Wild.'

This nearly brought the ditch down on itself. Hereward's

men, having welcomed the king's representative, noted the Welsh and put up with a Viking were being pushed too far.

'This is your doing Hereward,' one of them called, defiantly. 'You said we needed to fight with Eadric. Lo and behold, here he is.'

'I didn't send for him' Hereward protested. 'It's all this one's doing.' He waved an arm at the green man.

'We all want the same thing,' the man said through his green covering.

'That's as may be,' one of Hereward's men spoke. 'But we don't want it with Eadric.'

'My Lord Eadric has done more to damage the Norman forces than skulk about in ditches,' Cenric said, which was not helpful.

'You can skulk around in the bottom of a ditch with your head under the water,' the Saxon retorted.

'We are here to talk about the Normans,' the man in green protested.

'Typical,' the Viking put in from his great height. 'Stick two Saxons in a ditch and get three fights.'

'You are all subject to the rightful king anyway,' Aelfstan said with what dignity he could muster in a ditch.

'We're not,' Bleddyn responded, quite forcibly.

'You'd all be better off under Danelaw anyway,' the Viking said. 'Look at you.'

The argument in the ditch developed both pace and volume with participants expressing their views with gestures, insults and the stamping of feet. The first blow would not be far away.

Hereward sat himself back on the side of the ditch with the man in green and watched the melee developing with resigned disappointment.

'What would Umair say if he could see this?' Hereward called to his men as he shook his head. 'Never mind sending false stories to the Normans, you lot can't even face the same direction.'

The disturbance quieted.

'What did you say?' the Viking asked.

'Won't mean anything to you,' Hereward replied. 'Fellow called Umair. Great help to us in our fight against the Normans. He'd be ashamed.'

'Umair Ibn Abdullah?' the Viking asked.

Hereward looked nonplussed. 'Could be.'

'Umair Al-Aziz?' Aelfstan asked.

'Umair the travelled?' Cenric enquired.

'Must be Umair,' Bleddyn finished off.

'You all know this man?' the one in green asked, sounding very puzzled.

'Of course,' the Viking replied. 'He gives us all the information we need about the Normans. Through him, we are able to get our men to the right place and prepare for the coming onslaught.'

'He tells us when any Normans are venturing west,' Bleddyn explained. 'Then we make sure they don't get home again.'

'Umair's news is vital to the king,' said Aelfstan. 'The time and place of rebellion depend upon him.'

'And Eadric needs Umair's knowledge to attack at the weakest spots.' Cenric concluded.

'Well, well,' the man in green said with interest.

Hereward took a few moments to look at the gathering around him, which had at least stopped fighting itself now. 'We all have cause for sorrow and anger then,' he said.

Nobody said anything, but all of the faces were

questioning.

'Umair is dead,' Hereward said.

There were gasps in the ditch at this. Although Hereward's men took some pleasure from the fact that they knew this before everyone else.

'Dead?' Aelfstan broke the silence. 'How? When?' Then he frowned. 'How do you know?' he asked very suspiciously.

'I had word from the camp of William itself.'

'And you believed this?'

'It came from Saxons. A monk, a weaver and a young girl.'

'What were a Saxon monk, weaver and young girl doing in the camp of William?' Cenric asked, clearly thinking this tale had the whiff of mushrooms about it.

'The monk had been summoned to find out who killed Umair,' Hereward explained. 'He's the king's impertinator or something.'

'Ah,' Aelfstan said with some recognition. 'King's Investigator.'

'That was it.'

'You know him?' the Viking asked.

'I know of him. Appointed by Harold and then again by William it seems. Very little known about him, apart from that. Most of the Bishops I've asked have never heard of him.'

'Could all be a ruse?' Bleddyn suggested.

They pondered this for a moment.

'Has anyone seen this Umair recently?' the man in green asked.

There was a general shaking of heads.

'He left us fine and well about a week ago,' Hereward reported.

'And us a day or two before that,' the Viking added.

'We saw him the week before,' said Cenric.

# The Case of the Curious Corpse

'And us,' Aelfstan and Bleddyn concluded.

'Must have been doing the rounds,' the man in green noted.

'I'm not surprised the Normans killed him then, if he was a regular visitor to all of us, coming laden with William' secrets,' Aelfstan noted, with the nonchalance only a man of court could muster.

'And you all gathered his information regularly?' the green man enquired.

Various mutterings of "that's right" and "wouldn't stay here for any other reason" floated round the ditch.

'It certainly wouldn't make sense for any of you to kill him then,' the green man said.

This brought loud complaint that Umair had been like a brother/son/informant to all of them and they would never have dreamed of such a thing.

'It'll definitely be the Normans,' the Viking observed. 'Just the sort of thing they'd do. Especially if they found out he'd given away all their secrets.'

'They say not, apparently,' Hereward observed. 'The monk said he'd been called to show that William didn't have anything to do with it. Stop the Saracens descending on him and removing his head.'

'Well, he would say that, wouldn't he?' Bleddyn noted. 'If a Saracen asked me if I'd killed any of their own, I'd probably say no.'

The others all agreed that this would be the sensible course of action.

'Umair was William's hostage,' Hereward pointed out. 'Pretty stupid idea to kill any hostage, let alone a Saracen.'

The group seemed to think that being a stupid idea would not stop William doing the deed.

'If it wasn't the Normans, and it wasn't any of you?' the man in green pondered.

'Robbers?' someone suggested. 'Lot of them about at the moment.'

'Another Saracen?' Cenric suggested. 'Not that I've ever seen another one, but we don't know if they get on with one another.'

General mutterings and increasingly ludicrous speculations got nowhere. The overall conclusion was that without Umair's information there was no hope of mounting a realistic attack on the Normans.

The Viking suggested that even an unrealistic attack was better than nothing, but he was shouted down.

Everyone seemed ready to disperse, taking the news of Umair's death back to their various Masters. The green man was particularly despondent that all his efforts had come to nothing. 'Is there no one else who could have done it? Anyone who didn't actually think Umair was the greatest person in the woods?' he asked.

'You can wait until the ravaging Saracen army turns up,' Cenric replied. 'They might know.'

Hereward's men's comments about the reliability of Eadric resurfaced but were waved away by their leader.

'How many more do you want?' Hereward asked with a tone of complaint. 'You've got Vikings, three lots of Saxons and the Welsh. Unless we invite the bloody Romans back I think this is your lot.'

'Hm,' the green man didn't seem satisfied. 'I was asking around and heard of another group way out in the marshes.'

'We've all heard of people way out in the marshes,' Hereward scoffed. 'Did these ones have webbed feet and six fingers?'

## The Case of the Curious Corpse

'Nothing like that. A tinker told me he'd sold them some pots. Very strange men, apparently.'

'Well, you go off into the marshes and have a look then. You'll find quite a few strange people I expect. They're that way.' Hereward pointed away across the top of the ditch. 'Come to think of it,' he went on. 'Do any of us actually know who you are?' He turned his back and addressed the others preparing to leave the ditch and got blank looks. 'You could be a Norman leading us into a trap.' He turned back to the green man and saw an empty space where he had been. 'Where did he go?' he demanded.

# Caput XVI

## Discoveries All Round

'I think it's time we spoke to these Saxons,' Abdul said as they left the king's presence, having been told to find who out this "they" were, under the clear instruction that they certainly wouldn't be Normans.

'*They struck me*,' Hermitage repeated the translation. 'More than one then.'

'Indeed.' Abdul was thoughtful. 'And the only other group we are sure Umair met were the Saxons.'

'Who said he left them fit and well.'

'They did say that,' Abdul noted. 'But people say all sorts of things.'

'The news of Umair's death appeared to genuinely upset them.' Cwen sounded ready to defend the band of Saxons she had already branded as useless.

Abdul stroked the beard in his familiar way. 'It is the only information we have. It is possible there are other enemies but we have no idea who they may be. We have to follow the only information available.'

'A sort of lead, you might say,' Hermitage suggested. 'Leading us to the next stage of the investigation.

'If you like.' Abdul clearly didn't see the point. 'I think I must look further at Umair's journals first though. I only studied the one. It could be that there is more information in the others. Perhaps mention of more meetings.'

'Yes.' Hermitage was always happy to turn to a book and preferably stay there. 'There were several volumes and we

## The Case of the Curious Corpse

only looked at the most recent one.'

'Or the oldest one,' Abdul said, 'depending whether you started at the wrong end or not.'

'Aha.' Hermitage nodded but was still doubtful as he followed Abdul's lead back towards the tent. If the books went backwards as well as the pages, he wasn't sure he'd be able to cope.

When they arrived, Mistress Le Pedvin appeared to have cooled towards them considerably. She was almost abrupt when she allowed them back into the tent. Doubtless, she had heard from her husband that the investigators were not behaving themselves. She bustled about the place, removing the fruit and wine and even taking the cushions away.

'Where's Wat?' Cwen asked her, in her own, very effective brusque manner.

'Who?' Mistress Le Pedvin asked, without a single "my dear".

'The drunken weaver,' Cwen explained. 'We left him propped up over there.' She nodded to the corner of the tent.

'I'm sure I don't know. Not for me to go keeping watch on your friends.' And she left.

'I think we might be irritating the Normans,' Hermitage said with some concern.

'Excellent,' Abdul and Cwen chimed together.

'I find that if people are disturbed from their normal ways, any lies they may be concocting fall apart more quickly,' Abdul said.

'And I just like irritating Normans,' Cwen added as she sat in an un-cushioned chair and drew another one up to put her rather muddy feet on. 'But where has Wat gone?'

'Probably for a lie down in that tent we had.' Hermitage was disappointed at the weaver's behaviour.

'We left him lying down in this one,' Cwen said. 'Not like him to bother moving when he doesn't have to.'

'Most likely Mistress Le Pedvin did move him on, stop him cluttering up her nice, neat tent. But she does seem to be a lot less friendly towards us.'

'Doubtless her husband's doing.' Cwen seemed content with the explanation.

Abdul turned to the books at the desk and Hermitage joined him. He knew that all he could do was look at the pictures, but perhaps Abdul would explain more of the writing to him.

The Saracen investigator pulled one book out of its place and opened it on the desk. He quickly flicked through the pages - once more in the wrong direction, which gave Hermitage the shivers - but didn't read any of it out this time.

'This one is more routine in nature,' he explained. 'A lot about plants and minerals and some observations on the length of days this far north. You could well be right that the book we looked at was the most recent.

'In this volume, Umair makes no comment about the Normans or their habits. Perhaps he had not taken so much against them at this point.' He took another volume down and opened this one. Once more he rapidly passed through the pages, although this time he went back to one after he had passed it. 'Hm,' he said.

'Hm?' Hermitage enquired.

'Vikings,' Abdul said.

Even though Hermitage knew he was talking about the book he could not prevent a tremor running down his back as he thought there might be a Viking behind him. 'He mentions Vikings?'

## The Case of the Curious Corpse

'Just briefly. No mention of actually meeting any, more of an observation that the Normans are Viking in origin and some speculation about why all the different Vikings end up fighting one another on different sides.'

'Really?'

'Yes. He reports that when the Vikings invaded the east of England half the army fighting against them were Viking themselves.'

'Did they know?' Hermitage asked.

'I believe so,' Abdul said with a slightly confused look. 'Umair concludes that the Vikings like fighting everyone, even their own.'

'No surprises there then,' Cwen observed. 'It's probably where the Normans get it from.'

Abdul turned to another volume. This one he turned more slowly, clearly reading passages of the text before moving on. 'Ah,' he said, stabbing his finger on to one part of the page. 'I think we see the start of things here. Umair reports that William has a job for him. Something to help him make use of his hours of idleness. He already speculates that this is going to be trouble.'

'Does he say what it is?' Hermitage asked, peering at the page.

'No. At this point he doesn't know, he is just making a note that he has been sent for. He does say that he hopes it isn't going to be like the business with the French all over again. He had told William he wasn't going to do that any more.' Abdul shrugged. 'Must be in a different book. Perhaps left in Normandy.'

'What's that?' Hermitage asked, pointing to what appeared to be a very small drawing in the margin of the page.

Abdul peered closely. Then he looked rather shocked,

drew his head back and turned the page quickly. 'I, er, think it might be a rather crude representation of what he had to do with the French. No need to concern ourselves with that at the moment.' He moved quickly on. 'Here we are. He says that William has instructed him to go out into the country, just as he has been doing, but this time see if he can spot any Saxons gathering nearby.'

'Doesn't sound like a very direct instruction,' said Cwen.

'No, indeed. William would be careful not to make it too explicit. Just enough to be plain about what he expects.'

'And what does Umair have to say about it?' Hermitage asked.

'Ah.' Abdul went quiet.

'Something rude?'

'No. Something troubling though. He says that he will go and find some Saxons.'

'I see.'

'And as many other people who hate William as he can locate.'

'Oh, yes?'

'And he will make William regret the day he dragged him here from Normandy.'

Even Hermitage could see the significance of this comment. Umair had set himself against William, which was probably something else that hostages weren't supposed to do. In effect he had joined the enemy and William would be well with his rights to put a knife in his head, if not somewhere far worse.

'Umair chose a very dangerous path,' Abdul reflected.

'It is the sort of behaviour that frequently leads to a surprise knife, although usually in the back,' Cwen said with more knowledge than she ought to have. 'Often in the dark and when you least expect it.'

Hermitage frowned at her, part of him wondering what the situation would be if someone was expecting a knife in the back.

'From what I've heard,' she added quickly.

Abdul was pulling all the volumes of Umair's journal onto the desk now and quickly stepping through them. With each new piece of information he discovered, his face became more grim and his beard stroking more fretful. 'Ah, brother Umair, what have you done?'

'More trouble?' Hermitage asked.

Abdul sighed, moved away from the books and sat in a chair, brushing Cwen's feet away in the process. 'What might have been difficult before is now very troubling indeed.'

'Umair obviously made contact with the Saxons,' Hermitage concluded.

'Oh, it's much worse than that.' Abdul shook his head. 'We shouldn't be surprised I suppose, but the country surrounding William's camp seems littered with those opposing him. If they aren't here in force they have sent men to watch and wait and report back to their Masters. Umair seems to have found them all.'

'And given them all information?' Cwen asked.

'Exactly. As far as I can tell the only false details he has fed to William concern the Saxons, but then perhaps the king doesn't even know the others are close by.'

'What others?' Hermitage asked. He understood wars and battles and the like were between enemies, but only one of each, surely. How would anyone keep note of what was going on if the enemies were all vying with one another at the same time? How would anything get done? It would all be horribly inefficient if the enemies spent their strength disturbing one another, instead of focussing on the problem in hand.

'Other Saxons, it seems,' Abdul explained. 'Ones who don't even get on with one another. Someone called Eadric the Wild.'

'Yes,' Cwen said. 'Heard of him, but I thought he was in the west.'

'He is. But he has a man here, watching William. And there's another group from the Witan-appointed English king, Aedgar Aethling.'

'I thought he'd run away,' Cwen noted, in an unfriendly tone.

'He gathers his strength,' Abdul replied, referring to the notes.

'Tires you out, running away,' Cwen scoffed.

'And then there's a Viking.' Abdul got back to the topic in hand.

'There is a Viking then?' Hermitage trembled slightly.

'Representative of the North,' Abdul said. 'And Umair makes the point that this Viking is probably related to William in some way, but that won't stop them trying to kill one another.' He shrugged his despair at the whole situation. 'And there's the Welsh,' he added, 'for good measure.'

'The Welsh?' Hermitage couldn't understand any of this. 'What are the Welsh doing here?'

'Same as everyone else,' Abdul reported. 'Looks like you couldn't stick a spear in a bush out there without scratching someone who wants William removed. Umair even mentions some band of locals out in the marshes who have declared themselves against William but at least he didn't bother with them as well. He says there's enough madness about without going looking for the people even the mad ones think are mad.'

'I imagine none of these people are working together,' Cwen speculated.

'Oh, heavens, no.' Abdul gave a wry smile. 'Umair noted that if they took an hour off denigrating one another they might make some progress against their real foe.'

Hermitage just shook his head in complete confusion at the motivations of men. And their lack of basic organisation.

'They all want William defeated,' Abdul explained. 'They just don't want any of the others to do it.'

'Then how will it get done?' Hermitage couldn't even formulate the right question properly.

'Not at all, is the usual outcome. The one at the head of the trouble, in this case William, benefits from the confusions of his enemies. And in the case of a well-established ruler, he probably spends a lot of his time and effort making sure his enemies remain confused. And of course, the enemies help him enormously by trying to make sure that none of them come out on top.

'I doubt Hereward wants the northern forces and their Vikings in charge. The Vikings won't want Aedgar because they'd rather have the place for themselves. And no one wants the Welsh. So, most of their time goes into making sure their friends don't get an advantage, even if it's at the expense of letting William win.'

'Madness.' Hermitage shook his head.

Abdul shrugged. 'Umair's very word. But perfectly normal, I assure you. I even hear that your church is Master at the art.'

'Surely not.'

'Popes and Bishops and the like all get along terribly well and do what's best then?'

'Ah, I see what you mean.' Hermitage tried to think about

how conflict might work at a personal level, but he'd never met anyone who wanted what he had, and he had never wanted what others had. He could conceive that such a situation might give rise to discord, but he couldn't actually envisage it. His discord usually arose from people who wanted him to go away.

He would have to have a chat with Wat, he could usually explain the way the world worked in words that made sense. Of course, they'd have to find Wat first. And get out of this horrible confusing and dangerous situation.

'Why would any of these people want to stab Umair though?' he asked. 'If he was giving them information to aid their cause?'

'Any number of reasons,' Abdul said. 'They didn't like the fact he was giving information to everyone? Someone did it thinking they could put the blame on one of the others? One of them is actually in league with William?'

'Really?' Hermitage was horrified at this.

'Or is pretending to be in league with William in order to gain some advantage over one of the other groups, while in fact being in an arrangement with a third party to betray Umair and so gain William's trust in order to exploit that as a weakness.'

Hermitage's head was spinning.

'It's all quite usual,' Abdul didn't seem in the least concerned.

'How do people live like this?' Hermitage asked, with profound despair.

'Not for very long, usually,' Cwen put in.

'All right, why do they live like this? Surely it would be better just to get along with one another and live a peaceful, harmonious life.'

## The Case of the Curious Corpse

'Like they did in De'Ath's Dingle?' Cwen asked.

Hermitage shivered at the memory of that awful monastery, which was not an example of harmonious living between the stones of the place, never mind the people.'[5]

'And there are just plain bad people in the world,' Abdul remarked, without rancour. 'People who want everything for themselves and to trample everyone else beneath their feet. It's just the way they are.'

'Why would God create such monsters?' Hermitage speculated.

'Oh,' Abdul said, 'I don't think God had anything to do with them. They come from a different place altogether.'

There was a momentary pause while they each considered the implications of this, although Hermitage seemed to be the only one who had the slightest concern about it at all. He also had a mounting concern about what their next steps were going to be, now that there was a growing collection of people who might have done for Umair.

'Well.' Abdul rose from his chair and fulfilled all of Hermitage's fears with one simple sentence. 'Time to go and find some bad people.'

---

[5] The inharmonious stones of De'Ath's Dingle are considered in the treatise, *The Heretics of De'Ath*

## Caput XVII

## Suspect Number One Please.

'You know where to find the Saxons?' Abdul asked quietly as they walked across the camp.

'If they've stayed where we left them,' Hermitage replied.

'Not that they can be relied on for much,' Cwen added. 'But if they brought a good supply of mushrooms they won't be capable of going far.'

They were threading their way between the tents and accoutrements of the camp, getting the odd strange look from Normans who had probably heard about what was going on but hadn't seen it for themselves.

At one point a single Norman soldier scurried over to them in a rather surreptitious manner. They were stopped in their tracks as he looked around to make sure no one was watching as he addressed the strange band. Hermitage wondered if this man had some information for them that he didn't want his fellows to know about. Having been told how the deceptions of the world worked in practice, he wouldn't be surprised by anything.

'Here.' The Norman's voice was low and gruff. He didn't look at any of them, his head was turned back towards the camp, but for some reason, it seemed that the words were addressed to Abdul.

'Yes?' the Saracen asked, also quietly in case some secret information was about to be passed.

'Is it true?' the Norman asked in what Hermitage could

only take as a very disreputable manner.

'Is what true?' Abdul asked.

'You lot.' The Norman waved in Abdul's direction.

'What about us?' Abdul was starting to sound impatient.

'Is it true,' the Norman looked about once more. 'That you can cure warts?'

'What?' Abdul sounded as confused as Hermitage usually was.

'Only I've got this horrible one right on my…,'

'No, we cannot cure warts.' Abdul shook his head in disbelief. 'Nor do we fly, steal babies or turn into cranes when we die.'

The Norman looked very disappointed. 'Only asked,' he complained. 'No need to get difficult about it.' He shambled off, muttering to himself. 'Anyway,' he called back, 'I know the last one's true. My brother's seen it happen.'

Abdul, Hermitage and Cwen just gave one another looks of resigned disbelief.

'Talking of idiots,' Cwen said. 'I think we'd better drop by the other tent, see what state our weaver is in.'

'Will he be of some use in our enquiries?' Abdul asked.

'I very much doubt that, but I'd feel terrible if he'd drowned in wine and we didn't know.'

'Why would he take to the flagon with such vigour?' Hermitage asked. 'It's not like him.'

'Oh, it is,' Cwen said. 'Most particularly when the flagon has someone else's wine in it. Maybe drinking all William's wine is his way of resisting the Normans.' She peered around the camp, trying to get her bearings to lead back to the tent they had already hidden in twice. 'This way, I think,' she pointed and led not too far off their path.

Recognising the tent from its position rather than

distinguishing features it didn't possess, Hermitage was first to arrive and threw back the opening.

'Ah,' Wat said, 'there you are.'

He looked a little dishevelled, for him, and was pulling and tugging his clothes into order, as if he had just got up from sleeping in them.

'Not dead from wine then?' Cwen asked, sounding a bit disappointed.

'Of course not.' There was no hint of a slur in his voice. 'What on earth would make you think that?'

'From the amount of it you were putting down your throat.' Cwen folded her arms.

'Ah, but was I?' Wat sounded mysterious. 'I've been busy, not lying down all day.' He stepped out of the tent and pulled his pack after him. Sticking from the top, not quite packed properly, was a small square of green cloth.

'What have you been up to?' Cwen asked, more suspiciously than if she had been questioning a Norman with a guilty face.

'Finding out,' Wat said.

'I don't understand.' Hermitage didn't understand.

'I wasn't drunk at all,' Wat explained. 'Half the wine I poured out, I tipped away.'

'Why?' The explanation had not helped at all.

'So that I could wander at will. If everyone thinks you're lying drunk in a corner somewhere, no one bothers about you. You can listen to what people are talking about, ask a few questions of people who don't know who you are and generally gather information.'

'Very clever, Master weaver,' Abdul said. 'But surely those people recognise a stranger and are cautious.'

'They would be,' Wat said with a glint in his eye, 'if my

# The Case of the Curious Corpse

pack here didn't include my disguise.'

'Your what?' Hermitage asked.

'Aha,' Wat crowed. 'Not the only one with clever words, eh Hermitage? I picked it up in France a few years ago. They use the word to describe changing your appearance.'

'What were you doing in France?' Cwen asked, quite forcefully.

'Another story.' Wat was not going to explain that. 'Suffice to say, I change my clothes and people don't recognise me. It's remarkable. You'd think they would. After all, it's still me. Why should a change of clothing make people stupid?'

'Very clever indeed.' Abdul nodded appreciatively. 'I think if I cast off my robes and shaved my beard people wouldn't give me two glances.'

'I think you'd have to be a bit less clean as well,' Cwen suggested.

'And what do you dress as?' Hermitage asked, all sorts of bizarre images creeping into his mind.

'I've got two,' Wat said proudly. 'One is a dirty old beggar. You know, torn clothes, boots more hole than boot.'

'I can't imagine you dressed like that.' Hermitage had always been slightly in awe of Wat's immaculate dress.

'It is a bit nasty,' Wat acknowledged. 'But very useful if you want to be ignored. How many people do you know who see a beggar coming and look forward to spending time with them?'

'They're usually sent on their way,' Hermitage noted. He had every appreciation for the condition of the poor. Those who could not work through illness injury or age should be given alms by any caring Christian. If they didn't want to work they should be hounded from the streets. Even as he thought this, he concluded it didn't sound very Christian.

'Yes, but they never leave you alone. They can sit and mumble to themselves and listen to everything that's going on. And no one expects a beggar to understand the Normans.'

'And your other, what did you call it?'

'Disguise. I like that one. It's all green. Like some spirit of the woods. Puts the shakes up some people. I've even got a scarf for my face.'

'How long have you been doing this?' Cwen asked, sounding a bit disturbed now. 'Dressing up and wandering around talking to strangers.'

'Wouldn't be much of a disguise if everyone knew about it.' Wat smiled broadly.

'Anything else we don't know?' Cwen asked

'Very probably.' Wat gave a mischievous shrug.

Abdul was looking bemused by all of this. 'And what did you find out in your disguises?'

Wat looked confident and successful now. Much more like the normal Wat. 'William's enemies are numerous.'

'Ah.' Abdul, sounded impressed. 'You mean the Viking from the north and King Aedgar's man along with Eadric's and the Welsh.'

Wat looked completely crestfallen. 'How did you know that?' he asked plaintively.

'We read a book,' Hermitage said with smug satisfaction and the accompanying guilt at such a feeling. 'Or rather, Abdul did. Umair had written it all down. He's been giving information to everyone.'

'And they've all been relying on him.' Wat got some of his swagger back. 'While you were hanging around here...,'

'Interrogating the king,' Cwen corrected.

'All right,' Wat accepted, 'interrogating the king. I've been

## The Case of the Curious Corpse

out and about. Finding Hereward again was no problem, right where we left him. But it wasn't hard to spot that he was being watched as well. A few cautious introductions to the man in green and I got them all together. Turns out they all knew Umair. Even King Aedgar was relying on him for planning a rebellion. They all seemed saddened and a bit confused at the loss. It was only Eadric's man who got cross and tried to take my head off.'

'And did you find any men of the marshes?' Abdul asked.

'No,' Wat dismissed this. 'No one takes them seriously. Just some locals with sharp sticks. Spend all their time in the damp following their "great man of the marsh" apparently.'

'Great man of the marsh?' Abdul enquired with interest.

'Probably the one who's supposed to lead them out of the marshes. They've been there for years. Well known to the locals for stealing anything left out overnight. Wouldn't you, if you lived in a marsh?'

'Hm,' Abdul seemed to store this information away for later consideration. 'And all claim to have seen Umair alive and well and were dismayed to hear he was dead,' Abdul made a statement.

'Exactly,' Wat confirmed. 'Not a hint of anything but support and need for the man. He was alive and well when he left Hereward. It all fits. They were getting all their information from him, why kill him?'

'Unless you were a Norman who discovered he was giving everything away,' Cwen suggested.

'We just go round in a circle,' Hermitage complained. 'If William knew what he was doing he would have every right to kill him. So why claim you didn't?'

'Could be a different Norman,' Cwen suggested. 'There's lots of them.'

'I'm sure he'd have gone to the king to claim the credit. Finding out your hostage was giving away all your secrets?' Wat clearly wasn't convinced.

'Speculation is not accusation,' Abdul cautioned. 'We must speak to these people and trace Umair's movements. We know when he left the camp and when he came back. We must fill the gap.'

No one had anything more to say so the movement to leave resumed.

As they clambered from the tent, Hermitage had an overwhelming urge to talk through the long list of questions that he needed to give to the air. Usually, this was enough to let the stream flow freely but he did realise that discussing the details of Norman enemies while in the middle of the Norman camp was probably not wise. He also realised that realising this probably was quite wise as well.

The small group walked on in silence. Abdul's robe attracting stares from the men in the camp but at least keeping them at a distance. Perhaps word that the cure for warts was not in the camp had spread.

'And where do we start?' Hermitage burst out when he thought they were far enough out of camp. Abdul waved him quiet. They obviously weren't far enough yet. He contained himself for several more steps. 'With Hereward?' he couldn't go on. 'At least we know where he is.'

'I know where they all are,' Wat boasted.

'I think we do not start with Hereward,' Abdul responded carefully. 'As far as we know he was the last to see Umair alive. I think we get information from the others and then see how Hereward's tale fits.'

'Or we could get them all together,' Hermitage suggested, returning to his idea of striding up and down explaining things to people.

'That could be a very bad idea,' Abdul said although he managed not to sound critical at the same time. 'If they are all able to listen to one another's versions of events, they may be tempted to adjust their stories accordingly. We need to find out where their explanations differ and holes appear. In those holes, we may hope to find the truth.'

'Ah, yes,' Hermitage said. He really must start being less trustful of suspected murderers. He should know by now.

'Perhaps we start with the least significant and work our way up.'

'The Welsh,' Wat said. 'Their man really does seem to be here only to watch. They've got Normans on their borders already, been there for years without much trouble. Their worry is that with William running things the locals will start their own war.'

'The Welsh eh?' Abdul said. 'I shall be intrigued to meet someone from the lands of the west.'

'I could try and find an Irishman if you like?' Wat offered.

'Perhaps later.' Abdul gave him a frown. 'And after the Welshman? Who next?'

'Move east a bit, I'd suggest,' Wat said. 'Get closer to William and the impact he can have on people. Cross into England and you bump into Eadric. Just as the individual Normans along the Welsh border might get a bit lively, Eadric sees the arrival of William as his chance to, what shall we say, expand the borders of his own demesne?'

'Ah.' Abdul gave a knowing nod. 'It is just as I told you, Brother,' he said to Hermitage. 'The games within games. I imagine Eadric might quite like the fact that William and his Normans make all Normans fair game. Under the guise of defending England against the Normans, he can go and kill some of his neighbours.'

'Oh, Lord,' Hermitage groaned, new depths of human behaviour opening up before him. 'If Eadric wants William alive and well, he might not like Umair giving away the secrets and making Norman defeat more likely.'

'It is possible.'

'No wonder they call him "The Wild". What a way to behave.'

'Who next, the Viking?' Abdul asked.

'Probably,' Wat agreed. 'A lot of power behind him but perhaps less than Aedgar.'

'And do they want William alive?' Hermitage asked, in some despair.

Abdul pondered this one.

'I suspect yes,' Cwen said. 'But not for long.'

They all raised eyebrows at her.

'If William could finish off most of the resistance in the south, but be seriously weakened by it, they could swoop down and take over. Finish him off at the last.'

'This really is getting worse and worse,' Hermitage moaned.

'You do know that the Saxons invaded this land in the first place?' Abdul enquired. 'And before that, it was the Romans?'

'Well, yes,' Hermitage admitted. 'But that's history, it's not like real life. I read about the Saxon invasion in a book. I'd rather read about invasions in books than see them first hand, let alone be in the middle of the woods while one is going on around me.'

Abdul didn't seem to have anything to say to this. 'Waiting until your enemy is weakened is a sound idea,' he nodded at the thought. 'But the Vikings would also have Aedgar to

# The Case of the Curious Corpse

worry about.'

'Better just Aedgar than Aedgar and William,' Cwen observed.

'The Viking next then. Followed by Aedgar's man.'

'Aelfstan,' Wat said. 'Slippery character, as you'd expect from someone near the king. Uses a lot of words but then you find he hasn't actually said anything. At least nothing that you could hold him to afterwards.'

'I wouldn't describe Le Pedvin as slippery,' Hermitage noted from the depths of his despair at the state of the world.

'True,' Wat agreed. 'But then William is just a mad fighter who wound up King. Aedgar's been bred for it.'

Abdul was nodding as if this type of person was well known to him. 'And finally, Hereward.'

'Finally, Hereward,' Wat confirmed. 'Actually the least significant of the lot.'

'How so?' Hermitage asked, thinking that Hereward was the only one they'd seen putting up any real resistance to the Normans. Well, they hadn't really seen any resistance but he was sure it was going on somewhere. Probably in a ditch.

'Hereward's useless?' Cwen suggested. 'He happens to be here but he really doesn't have an effective fighting force, not like the northerners or Aedgar. And while the Welsh might be a distant issue now, they could be trouble in the future.'

'But for our purposes, he is the most important if he really did see Umair last.' Abdul raised a finger. 'We must remember that we are not here to resolve the problems of the Norman invasion of England. Our task is to find out who killed Umair.'

'And if it was William, that resolves the problem of the Norman invasion of England,' Cwen said with an unhealthy smile.

They were well beyond camp now and Wat took them off to the left of the path into an area of low bushes and sparse spiky grasses. He wound a way that seemed familiar to him but only led through more of the same landscape.

'How do so many people manage to hide from William and one another in this place?' Hermitage asked. 'I can't even see a ditch for Hereward.'

'You would be surprised,' Abdul said. 'In my land, a whole army can hide in a desert, if they know what they're doing.'

Hermitage didn't like to admit he had no idea what a desert looked like. Deserted, probably.

'This one's in a bush,' Wat said. 'No mention of the green man please,' he cautioned the others. He walked a few more paces and gave a nearby bush a healthy kick. It was quite a large bush and had spread its branches along the ground and doubtless left a small space in the middle in which someone could hide.

'Ow,' a voice came from the middle of the bush.

Cwen snorted. 'What sort of idiot hides in a holly bush?'

Amid much scrabbling and various cries of "ouch", "oh" and one plaintive "oh no, not there again," a young head appeared on the ground at the side of the bush. They all looked at it and it looked at them.

'Who are you?' a Welsh accent asked.

'We need to ask you some questions about Umair.' Abdul made no comment that everything but the head was still inside the bush.

'I'm a bit busy at the moment,' the head explained.

'Bit stuck, you mean,' Cwen said unkindly.

'I can get out if I want to,' the man complained. 'Just don't want to.'

There was a cracking sound from inside the bush

## The Case of the Curious Corpse

somewhere and the rest of the Welshman joined his head on the ground.

'There we are.' Abdul smiled.

The man stood up and brushed himself off as if this method of arrival had been exactly what he'd planned. 'Why does everyone want to know about Umair?' he asked, in a strange, strangled tone, as he appraised the crowd before him. He peered hard at Wat. 'Haven't I seen you before?'

'Definitely not,' Wat said in a slightly lower tone of voice than was normal.

Removing a holly leaf from his hair, the man turned his attention to Abdul, not that the sight of a monk and a contemptuous looking young woman didn't give him pause. 'Are you the other Saracen then?' He put a finger into his mouth, fiddled around a bit and pulled out another holly leaf.

'The other one?' Abdul queried.

'Apart from Umair.' The Welshman spat and cleared his throat.

'Aha, yes. There are more of us at home though.'

'There's more of me as well,' the Welshman said as if this comment had been some sort of threat.

'I am,' he paused over his name, 'Abdul,' he said, clearly thinking that this would be sufficient. 'I am here to discover how Umair met his death, and to take what steps are appropriate thereafter.'

'I'm Bleddyn.' The Welshman was content to swap names. 'The green man told us Umair was dead.' He said this with a sad shake of his head.

'Green man?' Abdul asked, managing to sound intrigued.

'Well, some strange fellow who goes around dressed in green, anyway. Don't ask me why.' He made the universal symbol of the madman, which got a snort from Cwen.

Hermitage appraised the fellow and could see Wat's point. The man was very young indeed, no more than a grown boy really. This could be an indication of any number of things. He could be a highly intelligent individual, the best of his nation, and this mission was one completely suited to his talents and insights.

That he had just found a holly leaf in his mouth and had looked at it as if he'd never seen one before, never mind hidden in a tree full of them, persuaded Hermitage that this was probably not the case.

Mayhap he was the only one who could be spared from important matters in Wales and so had been sent across the land to report back to his leaders. From the rather vacant look on his face Hermitage doubted that an accurate report was anything more than wishful thinking.

More likely he had put his hand up and volunteered for a mission about which he knew nothing. When he heard that it would mean going to England he probably jumped at the chance. Young people always found excitement in the things their elders had long since concluded were stupid and dangerous. By this reasoning, Hermitage had never been young at all.

'Why do you want to find out who killed him?' Bleddyn asked. 'Lots of people die and no one asks who did it.'

'Umair was an important figure,' Abdul explained. 'I have been sent to find his killer and bring them to justice.'

Bleddyn shrugged. If Abdul wanted to waste his time like that, it was up to him. 'Easy to say who killed him then, isn't it?'

'Is it?' Abdul sounded as if he was expecting a wrong answer to the problem any moment now.

'Of course it is. Place like this, situation like this. Umair bringing information out of the Norman camp.'

'The Normans,' Cwen concluded.

'Normans? No,' Bleddyn clearly thought this a ridiculous suggestion. 'Why would they want to kill him? There's hundreds of Normans you know. They tend to kill in large numbers. Wouldn't bother with one man.'

'Who then?' Hermitage asked.

'Obvious, isn't it. It was the English.'

# Caput XVIII

## Not Him Then

The silence at this accusation was quite a long one. People's faces were creased in thought, clearly trying to work out why the English would want to kill Umair.

Hermitage had one question of clarification that he needed to ask. A lot of his questions were of clarification but when answers came they seldom clarified anything. 'Which English in particular?' he enquired. 'The Saxons under Hereward, those under Eadric, the ones under King Aedgar or the Vikings?'

'Oh.' Bleddyn sounded rather crestfallen. 'You know about them then?'

'Yes,' Wat said, 'we do.' He gave a little scowl at Hermitage who realised that he probably shouldn't have said anything. 'And why would any of them want to kill Umair?'

Bleddyn looked defiant. 'Stands to reason,' he said.

'What reason?' Abdul asked.

'I don't know what reason, do I?' Bleddyn now sounded resentful that he was being asked all these questions. 'But there's loads of English skulking about and that's what the English do.'

'Kill people?' Cwen demanded.

'Of course. That's what they do to the Welsh. And to everyone else.'

'And the Vikings?' Wat clearly thought Bleddyn's suggestion was ridiculous.

# The Case of the Curious Corpse

'Saxons, Vikings, you're all English to me. You want to live in a little farm on the Welsh border, you do.' Bleddyn's defiance was back. 'Won't matter an owl's hoot whether the men coming over the hill have swords or axes. They're both bloody sharp.'

Abdul raised his hands and closed his eyes, effectively bringing the lively debate to a halt. 'You didn't actually see anyone kill Umair though? English, Viking or anyone else?'

'Well, not exactly,' Bleddyn admitted.

'Exactly?'

'No,' Bleddyn admitted.

'And you've heard no one talk of killing him? No one boasting of their deed.'

'Erm,' Bleddyn gave this long and careful thought. 'No.'

Abdul let out a long sigh. 'When did you last see him? Alive?'

'Be days back now.' Bleddyn seemed happy that the topic had moved on a bit. 'Last word I had from him was that William was interested in Wales but didn't have any plans at the moment. Well, that suited me down to the ground. He was due to finish off the English first. Hereward and the nobles in the north as well as Eadric.'

Hermitage drew on his learning from the most recent conversations. 'So you could join forces with them and defend against the Normans.'

Bleddyn was shocked. 'Not bloody likely,' he said. 'Let William have the lot of them, that's what I say.'

Hermitage was completely bewildered. The others didn't seem to be so, at all. 'But then he'll come to Wales unopposed.'

'Maybe not,' Bleddyn wasn't concerned. 'Perhaps he'll be so weakened that we can deal with him. Or he'll just go back to

Normandy.'

Cwen laughed out loud at this. In fact, she laughed so long and hard that Bleddyn started to look quite uncomfortable. Hermitage had no idea what was so funny and Abdul and Wat just stood looking on. 'He will not go back to Normandy, you idiot,' she eventually got out. 'He will come to Wales and he'll do to you what he's done to everyone else.'

'He might get killed,' Bleddyn protested.

'He's got sons,' Cwen pointed out. 'And he's not been killed in any of the other massive battles he's been in.'

'We've met him,' Wat added. 'He's not the getting killed type.'

Cwen controlled her mirth and gave Bleddyn a rather hard stare now. If the laughter had been disconcerting, the stare made the Welshman shift about on his feet.

'What?' he asked, resentful at being stared at.

'Maybe you killed Umair,' Cwen said quite matter of fact.

'Me?' Bleddyn burst out a squeak of denial.

'Of course. You want William to leave Wales alone. He'd have to do that if he was dead. That's less likely if Umair is feeding false information to the Normans. Getting them to chase their tales instead of attacking the right places.'

'Eh, what?' Bleddyn looked genuinely confused. 'Umair was giving us information about William. Why would I want him dead? That would stop us knowing what was going on. What false information are you going on about?'

Hermitage saw Cwen give a very subtle glance to Abdul who returned an almost imperceptible nod. He was feeling as confused as Bleddyn.

'Umair was taking false stories back to William. Stories that would stop him coming out to attack. That was no good for you. You wanted William to attack. That way either he'd be killed or the English would. Both would suit you. One happy Welshman.'

Bleddyn looked at the others for some support against this mad accusation. 'What false stories?' he cried, quite plaintively. 'I don't know anything about any false stories.'

'Oh, come on,' Wat chimed in. 'You're seriously telling us that you didn't know what was going on? You? A Welshman sent all this way specifically to discover what was happening over here and you didn't spot that? You claim not to know that Umair was telling William that the Saxons were here in great force? When you had regular meetings with Umair? It's very hard to believe.'

Both Bleddyn and Hermitage were rapidly looking backwards and forwards to try and get some understanding of what was being said.

'I didn't know any of that,' Bleddyn protested, sounding very worried. 'What forces? I hadn't even met the Saxons until the man in green turned up.'

'But you must have been here for days, if not weeks.' Now Abdul joined in. 'Surely it is your job to descry the goings-on of everyone? How can you report back to your leaders if you have not gathered very fulsome information on how all the parties are behaving and what their plans are?'

Bleddyn seemed on the edge of something. His hands were fidgeting about, his feet couldn't keep still and his eyes were darting all over the place, perhaps looking for a route of escape. His breath was coming in short bursts and Hermitage wondered if they really had pierced the problem with their first encounter.

This Welshman seemed very young for such a mission but then perhaps that was the point, he could deceive much more effectively if he had a naturally trustworthy appearance. And

Umair might also have trusted him and so not have expected the fatal blow at all.

At no prompting in particular, Bleddyn suddenly collapsed on to the ground, sat cross-legged and held his head in his hands.

'Well?' Cwen snapped out.

The Welshman dropped his hands from his now pale face, which had tears running down its cheeks.

The tears of the guilty man? Hermitage wondered. He'd never seen any guilty men cry before. At least not until the executioner turned up.

Bleddyn wailed out for all to hear. 'I don't know what I'm doing,' he said, bursting into sobs.

'Thought not,' Cwen said, which Hermitage considered rather heartless.

Bleddyn's confession, if such it was, continued at some volume. 'They just asked if anyone wanted to go to England on a secret mission.'

'And you put your hand up?' Wat sounded very disappointed at such stupidity.

'Myfanwy was looking at me.' Bleddyn howled.

'Myfanwy?' Abdul asked.

'Girl's name,' Cwen explained.

'Ah.' Abdul understood fully.

'Without knowing what you were doing, you came to the camp of the Normans.' Wat shook his head. 'Right to the edges of King William's force as he goes about the conquest of the country.'

'I didn't mean to,' Bleddyn protested through his increasingly wet face. 'I thought I'd wander around Gloucester for a bit, pick up some gossip about the Normans and then go home.'

'And Myfanwy would be very impressed.' Cwen's arms were folded and impassive.

Bleddyn just nodded. 'But people would keep sending me in the right direction. They were all going on about how the Normans were just down the road and if I went a bit further I'd find some. Before I know it, I end up here. And there they are.'

'Scary,' Cwen noted.

'I was hiding in a tree when Umair found me.' Bleddyn muttered.

Hermitage felt a profound sympathy for the unfortunate young man. He knew how easy it was to be led by events into some truly horrible situation. Or even just to end up in a horrible situation without having the first clue how you got there.

The look of youthful innocence around Bleddyn was just that then. It sprang from genuine youthful innocence. In this place, with these people. Hermitage shivered. He knew that his own curse, being King's Investigator, was bad enough. To be sent on a mission by your whole country must be even worse. If he had any advice for Bleddyn it would be to go home, find Myfanwy and hide in a cave.

'Could be you killed him by accident?' Cwen suggested. Much to the horror of both Bleddyn and Hermitage.

'Umair saved my life,' Bleddyn's tears bubbled once more. 'He looked after me. He said he knew what it was like to be away from kith and kin. He gave me real information about the Normans that I could take home. And he told me to stay away from Hereward.'

'Very wise,' Cwen said.

'He taught me how to find hiding places and avoid Norman patrols. He told me about plants and rocks and cures and all sorts. When I heard he was dead, it was horrible. I was going to head home tonight, after dark. I didn't kill him. I couldn't have.'

Abdul, Wat and Cwen were exchanging glances full of understanding and intent. Hermitage watched them go by, full of neither.

'Of course,' Abdul said, 'this could all be a ruse. A cleverly constructed tale, full of tears and confession, deliberately designed to throw us off the scent of the true killer.' He looked hard at Bleddyn, demanding an answer.

Bleddyn put his head back in his hands and the sobs burst forth once more. He shook head and hands from side to side as if refusing to let some awful truth out into the air.

'Come, boy.' Abdul's was the voice of a strict father. 'Out with it.'

Bleddyn mumbled something into his hands and his shoulders shook.

'We can't hear you,' Abdul pressed.

Bleddyn released his head and gave them all a tearful glare. 'All right,' he half-shouted. 'I'm sixteen, and I've never…' he sobbed some more as if about to confess that he had yet to kiss Myfanwy. 'I've never killed anyone. Satisfied now?'

Abdul, Cwen and Wat were all shaking their heads at the effort it had taken to get this simple truth.

'Well, that's good,' Hermitage responded quickly, with half a glance to the others. 'Surprising as it may seem, not everyone has killed people. In fact, most people haven't killed anyone. It's not something you have to do. You should be proud of the fact that you're a fine young man, with a girl at home and no deaths on your conscience.'

Bleddyn didn't look satisfied with this.

'I've never killed anyone,' Hermitage added.

## The Case of the Curious Corpse

'Of course you haven't,' Bleddyn replied. 'You're a monk. You're not supposed to.'

'Maybe, when you're older, the need will arise,' Wat encouraged.

'If you can manage it then,' Cwen muttered.

Hermitage scowled at them both. 'If you go through life never having killed anyone, it will be good.'

'Hm,' Bleddyn grunted.

'Look at it this way,' Cwen said. 'You go back to Wales with your news of the Normans. They won't be that far behind and when they turn up you can kill all the people you like.'

'Really, Cwen,' Hermitage began.

'I think.' Abdul raised his voice, 'that we can be satisfied young Bleddyn here is not our killer.'

This got half a smile from the accused.

'For one thing, it is clear he is not yet capable of taking a life. For another, I think Umair would have been able to deal with him in the blink of an eye.'

Bleddyn didn't look so happy about this. 'I was right about it being the English though,' he put in.

'How so?' Abdul asked, in all seriousness.

'He was worried about them.'

'He told you this?'

'He told me all sorts. He said it would be good for me to understand them. I should study them as they were all hardened warriors who knew what they were about.'

'Including Hereward?' Cwen asked, in disbelief.

'Except Hereward,' Bleddyn admitted. 'He said it would be good for my, what did he call it, education?'

'Learning,' Abdul explained to the vacant-looking Saxons.

'But he said there was one band worried him more than

the others, and that they might be trouble.'

'Which one?' Wat asked.

'He didn't say. Told me I shouldn't know as it might put me in danger.'

'Well,' Hermitage said in some exasperation. 'That's going to drag this investigation out a bit, isn't it. He didn't even give you a hint?'

'I'm afraid not. I don't think it was Hereward though.'

'That man would only be a danger to a one-legged mushroom gatherer,' Cwen snorted.

'I think you'd better go home now, young man.' Abdul's tones were more gentle. 'We are here to find out who killed Umair and bring them to justice. If you are caught up in that it may not go well. King William will doubtless attack sooner or later and you have all the information you need. The times that are upon us are not ones for the young. Go back to your Myfanwy.'

Bleddyn dragged himself back to his feet and looked at them all, wiping the mess from his face. 'If you're sure,' he said, clearly hoping that they were very sure indeed.

Abdul waved him away and with a not-very-reluctant shrug, young Bleddyn turned gratefully to the west.

'And don't talk to strangers,' Cwen called after him.

Alone again, the investigative band exchanged looks, acknowledging that one of their possible killers was now out of the picture.

'Eadric, Aedgar or the Viking then.' Wat clapped his hands together enthusiastically. 'Who shall we do next?'

...

'Say that again,' Cenric instructed, very clearly.

## The Case of the Curious Corpse

Wat couldn't say it again as his throat was currently being squeezed shut while his feet dangled a few inches from the floor. Cenric was holding his back hard up against a tree, so at least he didn't have to worry about falling over.

Cwen was beating Eadric's representative repeatedly on the back, which appeared to have no effect whatsoever. Hermitage was protesting most strongly at this unfortunate development.

The pressure was released when Abdul took hold of Cenric's arm. He did so in a very peculiar manner, only lightly touching the man's elbow, but the effect was immediate. Cenric let out a howl and fell to his knees, grimacing in pain. Abdul released his grip and stepped back to let Cenric regain his feet.

'What the devil?' Eadric's representative snarled at Abdul as he rubbed his elbow.

'Just a simple technique,' Abdul smiled. 'Our weaver needs his hands for his trade but his throat keeps him alive.'

'Accusing me of killing Umair,' Cenric was still very angry but cautious about dealing directly with Abdul. Instead, he pointed, very hard, at Wat.

The weaver was on his hands and knees coughing and gasping as he recovered his breath. 'Only a possibility,' he croaked out. Cwen turned her attention to him and rubbed his back as he recovered his breath. Hermitage stood back, looking very disappointed and shaking his head at Cenric, but not so much as to raise the man to fresh anger.

'Well, think again, weaver,' Cenric's finger was now stabbing at Wat. 'I've heard all about you.'

Wat managed a strangled croak in acknowledgement.

'Disgusting,' was Cenric's conclusion. 'All those disgusting tapestries and now disgusting suggestions. Why would I kill

Umair? He was bringing useful information about William's plans. As soon as I got a hint about him moving west I could alert Eadric and we'd be ready.'

'But no such hint was forthcoming?' Abdul asked, in a neutral manner.

'No,' Cenric replied, brusquely, but then he did most things brusquely. 'All we heard was that the Normans were after Hereward's forces. Didn't seem to know the rest of us were here.'

'And you know Hereward has no real forces anyway.' This was a statement from Abdul.

'I do now,' Cenric grunted. 'That loon in green got us all together so I can see Hereward wouldn't put up an effective fight against a couple of water rats. Skulking about in their ditches all the time. Ditches, I ask you? They ought to fight for a real land of rolling green hills, not some swamp with a few paths through it.'

'And you didn't think it odd that they had held William at bay for so long?' Abdul enquired.

'God knows what goes on in a Norman's head,' the Saxon shrugged his shoulders, he even managed this brusquely.

Abdul continued his discussion. 'Perhaps William thought Hereward's forces were greater than they were?'

Hermitage was fascinated by this. Abdul wasn't asking Cenric a direct question about Umair's activities. He was trying to see if the Saxon would let slip that he knew false information was going back to the Normans.

'He couldn't have thought they were any less,' Cenric gave a harsh laugh. 'He could have come out and trampled them in a morning if he'd known.'

'And then he'd have been heading west,' Abdul suggested.

'Umair reckoned the north was more likely, all of those

troublesome earls and the like. Most of 'em related to William, probably. Still, wherever they go we'd be ready for them. Take 'em head-on or harry as they head north.'

Abdul had nothing more to say to this and simply stood in contemplation, a slight frown indicating that all he had heard was being carefully considered. Cwen was helping Wat to lean back against the tree and recover his breathing while Hermitage tried to think whether anything they'd heard was any help at all. If it was, he couldn't quite spot it yet.

He was perfectly satisfied that Bleddyn had nothing to do with Umair's death, that poor young man seemed incapable of most things. Even hiding in a small tree had tested him beyond his abilities. Striking a real live Saracen with an actual sword called for competence too far.

And now this Cenric was ruling himself out as well. The man appeared to have every reason to wish Umair alive. He clearly had no idea of the two-way information flowing back and forth with the Normans and so what would he gain from the death of the Saracen? He did appear to be the sort of man quite capable of hitting people with swords and probably boasted of the fact afterwards.

There was nothing for it but to move on to King Aedgar's man and the Viking. Hermitage was very clear on his hopes for these encounters; they would find out that the king's man did it and wouldn't have to talk to a Viking.

'What about you lot?' Cenric interrupted Hermitage's thoughts.

Hermitage turned his attention back to Eadric's man, who was looking very thoughtful himself now.

'I don't know who you are.' It was very clear that this was a bad thing. 'Apart from the disgusting weaver, obviously.'

'Erm,' Hermitage said.

'You turn up out of nowhere asking a lot of questions about Umair. Just after that idiot in green arrived.' At this, he gave Wat a piercing gaze as if trying to solve a problem in his head.

'We're just trying to find out who killed him,' Hermitage said, genuinely puzzled why anyone would think otherwise.

'So you say.' Cenric's stare was now moving among them. 'Perhaps it was you,' he announced with an air of triumph.

'Us?' Hermitage's genuine reactions had now moved on to shock.

'He's a Saracen,' Cenric said waving a hand at Abdul. 'And who's more likely to kill a Saracen than another Saracen.' The lines of thought on his face deepened. 'Especially one who finds out one of his own has been betraying King William.' He spat as he said the word "king" without even pausing, which Hermitage thought was quite a trick.

'That's not what's happened,' Hermitage protested.

'And this weaver tries to accuse me,' Cenric drove his argument on. 'Trying to divert attention, eh? We were all perfectly happy until you lot turned up. Well Umair was, now he's dead. Answer me that then.'

Hermitage didn't have a clue what the question was, never mind what the answer was supposed to be.

'I can assure you,' Abdul spoke calmly, 'that we have all been summoned here after the death of Umair. Brother Hermitage and his companions called by William and me at the behest of my Master to find out who killed Umair.'

'Hm,' Cenric didn't sound convinced.

'It has been suggested that it could have been William himself. If that is the case he must face the consequences.'

'Ha,' Cenric dismissed this. 'William face consequences? It'll be the first time.'

'But these consequences will be delivered in person by the Saracen armies. Probably with the support of your pope if it is found that William killed such an important hostage.'

Cenric gave this serious consideration, looking hard at Abdul to see if he believed the words. He came to a conclusion. 'Definitely William then. In which case, why are you bothering me? You've got a killer in a camp over there.' He waved in the wrong direction. 'And Umair was his hostage.'

'He says he didn't do it,' Hermitage blurted out.

'Aha.' Cenric was triumphant. 'Been talking to William, have you? Good friends of his then? No wonder you're trying to find someone else to blame.' He threw his hands up and grinned. 'Normans, I might have known.'

'Now,' Abdul began, holding his hands out to calm the situation. He dropped his hands as there was a high risk that Cenric would do them some damage with the large sword he had just drawn.

'All is clear,' Cenric was happy with his conclusion, whatever it was. 'William the Bastard has killed his hostage and has sent his lackeys to find someone to blame. Even inveigled a Saracen to join his plan.' He jabbed his sword in a very professional manner towards Abdul, keeping him at a safe distance. 'I don't doubt that the Saracen army is on its way to avenge the death, but William will have found his killer, won't he?'

Hermitage desperately wanted to explain the situation but Cenric was in such a state that all he could was put his hand up. He quickly put it down again when the sword moved in his direction.

'Except, of course, you chose the wrong man with me.' Cenric beat his chest.

Hermitage hoped that Abdul had one of his clever moves that would work on a fearsome and well-prepared Saxon holding a sword. It didn't look like it.

'So.' Cenric smiled broadly at them all. 'This is what's going to happen now.'

# Caput XIX

## Tied Up at the Moment

'Explain this to me again,' Wat said.

'Well.' Hermitage wondered why it was necessary to repeat this when he thought he had already covered it quite comprehensively. If Wat and Cwen paid more attention the first time, he wouldn't have to keep repeating things.

'We are all tied up against the tree because Cenric thinks we killed Umair and are William's spies. He has gone to get the others, the Viking, Hereward and so forth, to come back here and deal with us. Abdul, who seems to know a lot about ropes and knots and tying things up, says that Cenric has done a very good job indeed and is obviously well practised.'

'We now stand accused of the murder we came to investigate,' Wat checked.

'Sitting accused, really. But yes, I suppose you could say that.'

'Seems to happen quite a lot, Hermitage,' Wat sounded weary. 'There comes a point in each of the investigations you do when someone accuses you of being the killer.'

Hermitage thought that this couldn't be right, but then he didn't have the full catalogue of his works readily to hand.

'In this case, it seems to be different. This time there are several people accusing all of us.' Wat seemed to get a bit excited at this point. 'And Abdul has been dragged into it. A man we only just met!'

Hermitage could tell that if Wat's hands were free he would be waving them about.

'We weren't even here at the time.' Wat appeared to be jumping up and down inside his ties now and was thumping his feet on the ground, albeit they were firmly lashed together at the ankles. 'We didn't even know the wretched man was dead until half the Norman army turned up and dragged us from our beds.'

'We weren't in bed,' Hermitage explained, wondering where Wat got that idea. 'And I don't think it was actually half the army. From what we can tell, that seems to be quite large in number.'

'That's not the point, Hermitage,' Wat's excitement seemed to die as quickly as it had arrived. His head hung now. 'Oh, God,' he sighed. 'Why does this always happen?'

'Always?' Abdul asked, sounding puzzled and worried at the same time.

Hermitage couldn't see his fellow investigator as they were tied to opposite sides of the large tree. The four of them were like great roots, spreading out from the trunk in each direction. He thought it might be quite nice if the ground swallowed them just now.

'Pretty much,' Cwen answered the question. 'Before we get to the "aha" moment, someone involved usually suggests that Hermitage is to blame for the whole thing.'

'When I first met him his own prior, piece of work called Athan, was already blaming him for a death,' Wat grunted.

'Yes,' Hermitage acknowledged. 'But then Prior Athan blamed me for everything anyway.'

'This is very interesting,' Abdul said, slowly.[6]

'Is it?' Wat didn't sound interested.

---

[6] It is very interesting, isn't it? The Heretics of De'Ath is the book you need....

'Of course. It is to be expected that those responsible would seek to avoid the blame. Particularly if they feel that discovery is close.'

'You mean Cenric did it?' Cwen sounded surprised and disappointed.

'It is another element to be considered,' Abdul explained. 'Of course, it is always possible that he genuinely believes we had something to do with Umair's death and is seeking retribution. But it is also possible he knows something and seeks to divert attention.'

The other three roots of the tree thought about this for a moment.

'One question,' Cwen said.

'Yes?'

'What's an element?'

'What's a what?' Abdul sounded confused for a moment. 'Erm, it's the smallest bit of a thing.'

'Is it?'

'Yes.'

'There you are then.' Cwen didn't sound very enlightened.

Abdul muttered something in his own language, something that carried an air of desperation about it, even though they couldn't understand a word.

'It means that it is just part of the whole picture. When the time comes to gather everything together, it is a feature that must be explained.'

'We're all tied to the tree,' Wat pointed out. 'How likely is it that we get a chance to explain anything? When Cenric comes back with his friends they're likely to decide who killed Umair just by the look of us.' He craned his head in the direction of Abdul.

'Hardly the path of reason,' the Saracen observed.

'You've met two of them,' Wat said. 'Do you think reason troubles them much?'

Abdul's silence said he was considering their position quite carefully.

'At least everyone we've met so far is upset at the death of Umair.' Hermitage thought that sounded like an encouraging fact.

'And that helps how, exactly?' Cwen asked from her side of the tree. 'It means they'd all be quite happy to find the killer and chop them up.'

That sounded a lot less encouraging.

'And you know how keen William is to get this all finished off. If someone told him that his investigator did it, I'm sure he'd be quite happy. He could give your body to the Saracen army.'

'I would know that Brother Hermitage is not our murderer,' Abdul said.

Wat shrugged within his binding. 'They'd better do you as well then.'

'In fact.' Cwen picked up the theme. 'He can say that the Saxons did for the lot of us, Umair and Abdul included. I bet killing two Saracens more than doubles the trouble.'

Abdul was silent, but the two nearest him, Wat and Cwen, could see that he was shaking his head slowly from side to side.

'I don't expect you've come across an investigation like this before,' Wat said with a smile so wry it was audible. 'One where the investigator gets tied up and accused of the murder. One where the possible killers all get together in a happy band. One where the king doesn't really care who did it, as long as it wasn't him?'

'Erm.' Abdul had no ready reply.

# The Case of the Curious Corpse

'I wouldn't say it happens like this all the time,' Cwen added, nonchalantly. 'But most of ours go seriously wrong at one point or another. Quite often several points at once.'

Abdul sounded a bit of a loss. 'We haven't even gathered any real evidence yet. All we know is that Umair left the camp and that he's dead. We haven't found out anything else useful at all. Apart from the fact the woods are crawling with people who might have done it.'

'Welcome to England,' Cwen said. 'Most of the woods are crawling with people who've done something or other.'

'That's why they stay in the woods,' Wat explained.

'But, but.' Abdul was clearly trying to get something out of this. 'Brother Hermitage's "aha" moment?'

'It'll come,' Wat was confident. 'No telling when, and it doesn't seem to bear any connection to what's going on at the time anyway.'

'Just got to hope it arrives before the axeman,' Cwen said.

'This is no way to conduct an investigation at all.' It now sounded as if Abdul was talking to himself. Not a good sign. 'We must gather information. Times, dates, people, movements. We must compare explanations and eliminate the innocent. We must find the inconsistencies and confront the accused. We must present our findings to those in authority so they can take action.'

'We usually just wait until we're accused of the crime and then hope for the best.' Wat gave a hollow-sounding laugh.

'Oh,' Hermitage said, getting their attention immediately.

'Is this the "aha I know who did it?"' Abdul asked, with just a hint of desperation in his voice.

'No,' Hermitage said. 'This is "oh, here come all the possible killers."'

There was a crashing of undergrowth and a clamour of

voices as Cenric returned to their tree, accompanied by a full band, judging from all the noise.

Hermitage couldn't back away as the tree was in his way. And he was tied to it. He would have loved to climb up it as the gaggle of men emerged from the brush in front of him. This seemed to be a small army, with Cenric at the head. Hereward led his men who looked just as lost and vague as usual. They were followed by a very well dressed fellow who appeared to be tip-toeing through the woods so he wouldn't stand in anything. Bringing up the rear was a Viking. No mistaking it, a real, live Viking.

'Here they are,' the Saxon warrior called out as if he'd just found his grandchildren, lost in the forest. 'All tied up where I left them,'   - it being quite possible he was still referring to his grandchildren.

'There's a Saracen,' one of Hereward's men called out. 'Is it Umair?'

'Of course it isn't Umair, you idiot,' Hereward reprimanded. 'This one's much taller.'

'You said you'd caught the killers.' A very educated voice came from the well-dressed man. It carried a fair degree of contempt for Cenric.

'And here we are, Aelfstan.' Cenric covered the prisoners with a wave of an arm. 'Umair's murderers.'

'This lot?' Aelfstan sounded very doubtful. 'I know for sure that the one on the left is Wat the Weaver. He's committed many sins himself and made tapestries of most of the others, but I doubt he's a killer.'

'And that's the monk.' Hereward pointed at Hermitage. 'He's the king's whatnot. Come to find out who killed Umair.'

'So he says,' Cenric sounded confident in his conclusions.

'And a maiden,' the Viking said with a rather strange tone to his voice.

'Who are you calling a maiden?' Cwen demanded.

'I, er,' the Viking started and then stopped. The others all gave him impatient looks.

'Look,' Cenric said firmly. 'Umair's dead and then these three turn up pretending to ask who did it.'

'They did ask who did it,' Hereward's man explained.

'Yes, but only at William's behest.' Cenric explained, as if to idiots. 'The monk is William's man. He's come to prove that the Bastard didn't do it. And how does he do that? By finding someone to blame. One of us.'

'I assure you' Hermitage began.

'Shut up, you,' Cenric instructed. 'It's obvious, isn't it? Umair was alive and well until this band arrived.' He took to pacing up and down in front of the tree and its captives. 'It's just as you say,' he nodded to Hereward. 'The monk is the king's what-not.'

'William, please, if you must, or just the Bastard,' Aelfstan corrected. 'The true king is Aedgar.'

Cenric waved the error away. 'This monk comes along at William's behest and does what he's told; show that someone else killed Umair.'

'I thought you said we did it?' Abdul enquired.

Cenric did not look happy at being interrupted by one of the accused. 'Doesn't matter. Either you did it or he did. Makes no difference to Umair.'

'But Umair was not alive and well before we arrived. He was dead. Had been for several days. Even Saracens can't murder people when they're already dead.'

'Be silent.' Cenric paused for a moment. 'All right. Maybe William had already done it, or he sent for these three to do it for him and you were just late. The outcome's the same. Umair is dead. Realising that the Saracens will have his head if he's found out, he sends the monk to find someone to blame.'

'And he sends another Saracen?' Aelfstan did not sound convinced as he nodded towards Abdul.

Cenric looked a bit panicked for a moment. 'Ah,' he said, reaching an answer quickly. 'That's the clever bit. Who'd think a Saracen would kill another Saracen? Eh?'

'I would,' Aelfstan said. 'They probably do it all the time.'

'But how do we know he's even a Saracen?' Cenric now changed his argument with a leap.

'He looks like one?' Hereward's man suggested.

'Anyone can look like one,' Cenric dismissed the man.

Abdul said something fast and complicated in his own language. And insulting and disparaging if tone was anything to go by.

'And anyone can sound like one.' Cenric snapped at Abdul.

'So what you're saying is…,' the Viking spoke now, a deep frown bothering his brow. He explained events as he now understood them in a rather slow and ponderous manner. 'King, beg pardon, William the Bastard either killed Umair or had one of these do it for him. A monk, a weaver, a maid, er woman, and a Norman dressed up as a Saracen.'

'Exactly,' Cenric nodded.

'And they did it after Umair was already dead?'

Cenric just pointed a finger at him now. A slightly shaky and barely controlled finger. All he had for the rest of the group was a glare, his explanations seemed to have run out.

The sounds of contemplation rustled around the group. There was some humming and a bit of grumbling as well as an impatient huff or two from Aelfstan.

# The Case of the Curious Corpse

'Excuse me,' Wat spoke up.

'And you can be quiet as well,' Cenric growled. 'We're not listening to any of your explanations. Killer.'

'I was only going to ask how you know Umair is dead at all.'

The contemplative noises went very quiet.

'What?'

'How do you know he's dead? Umair? The dead one? The one we've come to find out about. I was just wondering how you knew he was dead. That's all.' Wat sounded as if he had just run out of polite conversation with a market trader he didn't want to talk to.

The band of accusers gathered around the tree looked at one another, seeing if anyone else had the answer to this.

'Erm,' one of Hereward's men sounded thoughtful. 'You told us?'

'That's right.' Wat congratulated the man on his memory. 'We told you. We came and told you that Umair was dead. Now. Let's have a think about this. If we had killed him, would we have come and told you?'

There was no immediate answer.

'I think not,' Wat sounded very thoughtful. 'If I had killed Umair, I think I'd be miles away by now.'

'All right,' Cenric snapped. 'Perhaps you didn't do it yourself. You're still trying to help William get away with it.'

Wat shook his head. 'No, not doing that either. What we are trying to do is find out who really did it. If it turns out to be William then Abdul here will deal with him. Well, he will if you untie him. If we find it was someone else Abdul will still deal with them. And William will probably want to as well.'

'Ha,' Cenric dismissed this and turned away.

'All we've heard is that Umair really was alive and well in William's camp. Living very well, it seems. It was only when he came to England and started visiting you lot that he got dead.'

That got the gathering around the tree looking at one another.

'You see,' Cenric crowed in triumph. 'Trying to blame us.'

'Not necessarily,' Wat went on, 'it could still be anyone. Though it could have been one of you for all we know.'

The members of the band passed glances around.

'I can see your problem.' Wat sounded sympathetic. 'You've never seen us before and we arrive from William's camp with news that Umair is dead. It's a problem. I'd be suspicious if I was in your shoes. And of course, you all know one another so well that you can trust that none of you did it. You've probably been together for years.'

The glances now included a narrowing of eyes.

'Oh.' Wat said in great surprise. 'You don't know one another either?'

'The green man got us together,' Hereward's man explained. He quietened under the scowl of Cenric.

'Green man?' Wat sounded thoroughly bemused. 'What, the fellow with trees coming out of his mouth?'

'No,' Cenric said. 'Just some loon dressed in green.'

'I see,' Wat said slowly. He paused as if giving this information careful thought. 'A loon dressed in green comes skipping out of the woods and introduces you to one another.'

'He wasn't skipping,' Hereward pointed out.

'Still. Make an interesting tale when the rest of the Saracens turn up looking for Abdul. I imagine there's only so many of their people they see vanish before they all arrive.

# The Case of the Curious Corpse

Can't keep sending investigators forever.'

'No, indeed,' Abdul confirmed in a deep and serious tone.

Hermitage really wished that they would have this conversation on his side of the tree. He couldn't see expressions on faces and usually relied on Wat's knowing winks to give him a clue what on earth was going on.

Preparations could be underway to release them all or chop their heads off. The discussions gave him no hint of the way the group was thinking. But then it was hard to get hints from what people were saying when he couldn't see them. Come to think of it he seldom got hints when people told him things directly.

Wriggling around in the ropes did no good at all, his chest and waist were firmly lashed to the tree. He craned his neck round to the right but the best he could do was catch a glimpse of someone's leg. The left was worse, all he could see there was a sword dangling from someone's belt. Resigned to waiting for his fate to be unveiled he rested his head against the tree and stared at the bushes opposite.

'Aha,' he said.

'Aha?' Abdul, Cwen and Wat called out, hopefully.

'Sorry,' he called out. 'I meant "aha, here are some more people."' As he said it he wondered just how many were hiding in these woods. There seemed to be more in there than in the Norman camp.

Three figures emerged to add to this growing crowd and they bore a strong similarity to the marsh they emerged from. Hermitage had thought that Hereward's band was a rough collection of men of the ditch but the latest additions brought the tone of the whole gathering down by a very long way. Hermitage had seen men of their ilk before, but his father had dragged him away and told him not to go near in case he caught something.

Every area of the country had tales and legends of men who lived in the wild. Those who shunned the gatherings of civilized folk and survived on their wits and the provisions of the land. Snaring rabbits, picking berries and fruits, building homes of wood and wattle. In all of those stories there was something grand about that life. That men and women could live by their own hands and without the support of others was a mark of the nobility of the human spirit.

The marks on these men of the marshes did not bear close examination. There was absolutely nothing grand about them at all, although several bits appeared knobbly.

One of their number stood slightly in front of the others, doubtless their leader. There was nothing to distinguish him from his fellows apart from where he stood. The manner of his standing, and that of his fellows, said that there was something very wrong with their legs. If this was the great man of the marshes, he dreaded to think what a humble one looked like.

Their clothes, assuming that once upon a time they had been clothes, were ragged and hung patched and mended with twine pulled fresh from the ivy by the look of it. Their feet were wrapped with rough animal hide, the animal in question having been very rough indeed - and probably in such poor health that it was incapable of running away.

Their faces told their own tales of months under the open skies as the rain fell, the sun shone and then the rain fell some more. Followed by more rain. Strangely, this quantity of water falling upon them had absolutely no effect on the grime that caked their skin.

Hermitage's mind naturally turned to Matthew chapter 5 verse 13. These men were indeed the salt of the earth as the

## The Case of the Curious Corpse

Gospel says. Unfortunately, that verse concluded with the good for nothing being trodden under the feet of men. This triumvirate encapsulated the verse from start to finish. And as they drew close to Hermitage, who was nearest, the odours of the marsh came with them. Mainly the odours of things that had died in the marsh, things that made even the magpies turned their beaks up.

The leader spoke. Well, he made a noise. 'Grargh,' or something like that.

'What do you want?' Cenric demanded. Even Hermitage, still out of sight behind the tree, could tell that the Saxon warrior was pretty disgusted by the sight before him.

'You,' the leader of the marshland folk said, his accent a thick Saxon, which said he spent little time speaking anything else. He raised a gnarled and knobbly finger and pointed at Cenric and the others. It was also a dirty and scabrous finger that looked like it had been places no finger should go.

'What about us?' Aelfric asked, sounding as positively revolted as only a man who lives in court can be by the sight of the ordinary folk - although this particular group gave ordinary folk a very bad name.

The pointing finger still pointed and there was an accusatory angle to it. 'You killed Umair.'

# Caput XX

## Accusation

'Told you,' Wat said, which Hermitage felt was less than helpful.

'What do you mean, we killed him?' Cenric shouted, taking an aggressive step towards the men of the marsh. He got within range of their perfume and took a quick couple of steps back again.

'The friend,' the man explained who Umair was. 'Dead.' He was clearly a fellow of few words. Probably because he didn't know many.

'We didn't do it,' Cenric barked. 'It was this lot.' He waved towards the tree and its captives.

'It wasn't them, it was William the Bastard,' Hereward put in.

'Could be that one from Wales,' the Viking put in. 'Don't know where he's gone.'

'He, erm, had to report back,' Cwen explained.

'We're satisfied he didn't do it,' Abdul said.

'Thought as much,' Cenric snorted. 'Boy couldn't stamp on a hedgehog, let alone strike a blow on a living man. And it certainly wasn't us,' he was adamant.

'Must have been William,' Hereward grumbled.

After this exchange of views, things descended into a bit of a shouting competition. Even the men of the marshes had their say. They tended to use the same words over and over again but at least they were contributing. No one was coming to any sort of conclusion, or even an agreed position. If anything, William was coming out as favourite, probably the first time in this company.

Everyone protested that they were Umair's greatest friends and would never have harmed a hair on his head, let alone put a sword in it. They all relied on him as one of their own and he supported them in their aims against the invader.

Hermitage began to wonder how much time Umair spent out of the camp. The number of people he had to supply with information was increasing with every passing hour. Getting round them all must take days, particularly as none of them knew about the others.

He also thought that with so many people to keep in order it would be easy to make a mistake. Perhaps he said the wrong thing to the wrong person at some point and raised their ire. Or perhaps they fell out over him, like jealous lovers they didn't like to see him cavorting with someone else.

He also thought that he was getting carried away again. Things would turn out to be much more simple than this. Someone simply hit Umair with a sword. All he had to do was find out who. Which is all he'd been trying to do since they arrived - with no measurable success.

The hubbub was increasing in volume when it came to a complete halt.

'Silence,' Abdul shouted in a loud and commanding voice.

The effect was immediate. Some turned to see what the noise was. Others looked shocked that the man tied to the tree was ordering them about.

'Thank you.' Abdul's voice was back to its calm authority. 'Friends,' he nodded his head to them all. 'We all want to know who killed Umair. That includes those of us currently tied to the tree. If you all claim that you did not do it then we are left with William. Unless there are any more of you out in the woods and marshes?' He glanced around the group, who all shook their heads.

'I didn't even know there were this many,' the Viking shrugged.

'If it is William, I shall report this to my Master who will deal with him accordingly.'

Everyone seemed more content with this conclusion now.

'But we need proof. It will be insufficient to simply say it was William, we need evidence.'

The puzzled looks said that this was an entirely new concept.

'We need something that shows it was William,' Hermitage explained. The group shuffled round until they could see him. Although he had heard all the conversations it was still a surprise to see there were quite so many people. He just hoped one of William's patrols didn't turn up at this moment. He didn't want to be caught in the middle of a battle while he was tied to a tree.

'Like a sword,' Hereward's man suggested.

'Only if it was William's personal sword,' Hermitage said.

That didn't help.

Hermitage pondered how much more simple he could make this. 'If it was William's personal sword and we could show that it was the one that killed Umair,' he left the idea hanging in the air. Surely someone would make the connection.

'William did it?' the Viking suggested, tentatively.

'Indeed,' Hermitage confirmed.

'Ah,' the rest of the group appreciated the revelation.

'So, what we need to do is work through all the possibilities and determine exactly what happened.'

Blank looks again.

'If you untie us we can discuss what happened when you all saw Umair last, and who might possibly have done the deed.' Abdul explained.

The group didn't respond immediately but looked to Cenric and Hereward for a decision.

'We can always kill them if they try anything,' the Viking suggested. 'There's enough of us.'

'And they don't have any weapons,' one of Hereward's men added.

Cenric grumbled and complained but bent to the ropes and started to untie the bindings. 'If you try and make a run for it I can throw a dagger in your back from twenty paces.'

'I don't doubt it for a moment,' Abdul said as he squirmed out of the bindings and rubbed the parts of him that had taken the brunt of the ropes.

The best Hermitage could manage was to roll over onto his hands and knees and stretch like a dog. Using the tree as a prop, he dragged himself up to his feet.

Cwen was as quick to her feet as only the young can manage, and as quick to glare at her captors as only Cwen could manage.

Wat spent a lot of time cleaning the dust off the floor from his clothes.

Hermitage was rather alarmed to notice just how many of the crowd now stood with their arms folded looking at the released investigators very expectantly. He had thought that gathering everyone together, striding up and down in front of them explaining everything would be a lot less worrying than this. Principally because he imagined that he would have something to explain. As it was, he had not the first idea. His only relief was that this was Abdul's idea. Presumably, the Saracen had everything sorted out. Hermitage looked forward to hearing what it was.

'So, gentlemen,' Abdul held his arms out to draw them all in. 'Shall we explore what we know?'

Everyone frowned at him and the marsh-men added some grunts.

'Let's find out who killed Umair,' Abdul clarified.

Ah, they understood now.

Abdul straightened his robes, stretched his neck and his arms and then descended to sit, cross-legged on the floor. Hermitage did likewise, his legs still not really up to the task of holding him up. One by one the others followed suit until only Wat remained standing. The look on his face said that there were no circumstances in which he was going to get down in the dirt again.

'Excellent.' Abdul smiled at them all. 'We are now comfortable and no one will be able to reach out and do anyone to death if they hear anything they don't like.' He said this with a smile but it sounded like a very good reason to have everyone sitting down.

'Get on with it,' Cenric said. 'Whatever it is.'

'Just so.' Abdul bowed his head to the Saxon and cleared his throat. 'William did it.'

There was much roaring and approbation for this statement, several "I told you so's" and the start of one conversation about what the Saracen army would do to him when they got here and if anyone else would be allowed to join in.

Hermitage was very puzzled at this. He had certainly seen nothing that proved William to be the killer. What had Abdul spotted that he had not?

Abdul went on, 'The only questions remaining are how and when and why.'

## The Case of the Curious Corpse

Hermitage thought that if those were the questions remaining, which ones had actually been answered? The rest of the audience seemed a lot less concerned about these minor details.

'How? Well, we know that don't we,' Abdul explained. 'A blow to the head. We have seen the body and can confirm that this is the case.'

Some of Hereward's men wanted quite a lot more detail about the body and what it had looked like but Abdul waved them away.

'The wound on the head was consistent with a sword or heavy blade of some sort. It was not such that would deliver instant death but certainly began Umair's journey to meet God.'

That brought a certain sombre mood to the group.

'When? Again, we now know that Umair was killed outside of the Norman camp and that the blow was struck some days before he made it back there.'

'William followed him,' Cenric asserted.

'Quite possibly. The Norman guard we spoke to reported Umair's words as he returned with his deadly wound. Words he could not possibly have known as they were in my language. Umair said "they struck me."'

'So there was more than one,' Hereward sneered. 'Typical Norman trick.'

'He didn't say "the Normans have struck me", or name anyone in particular. He simply said, "they struck me". And we know it was someone outside the camp.' He paused after he said this and looked very thoughtful, even moving his head slowly from side to side as if this would stir his ideas.

'So,' the Viking said slowly and carefully, 'it could have been anyone.'

'I suppose it could,' Abdul accepted. 'Although,' he frowned hard as if the thought was only just occurring to him. 'Of the people gathered here, only Master Hereward has a band. The rest of you are alone.'

'Don't you look at me,' Hereward growled. 'I've told you Umair was our friend. Last thing I would do is kill him.'

'Probably the last thing you were capable of,' Cwen's mutter reached only Hermitage's ear.

'But you said it was William,' Cenric protested.

'Indeed,' Abdul confirmed. 'This brings us to why? Why would anyone kill Umair?'

Hermitage was very impressed with this. Abdul had brought this gathering of dangerous men to consider all the possibilities without one of them threatening to kill him at all. He saw that he had a lot to learn from this man about investigation and dealing with the accused. In dealing with anyone at all, really. If it turned out at the end of all this talk that they still didn't know who did it, things could get ugly. The sort of ugly that involved knives and wounds.

'If William had good reason to kill Umair he wouldn't be trying to show he didn't do it,' he put in, hoping it was the sort of thing that would help.

Abdul quickly raised a finger. 'A very good point,' he said. Hermitage smiled at everyone, hoping they'd recall that he'd said it. 'Which leads us to conclude that William did not know that Umair was speaking to all of you.'

'Unless, of course, he did know, and was using it to his own ends,' Wat threw in.

The audience looked thoroughly confused at this.

'Could William have sent Umair to scout out his enemies?' Cwen asked, sounding as innocent as she ever had.

'What an awful thought, mistress,' Abdul sounded

shocked at the suggestion.

'He was telling us about William, not the other way round,' Cenric objected.

'Master Hereward?' Abdul asked. 'I think you can tell us some more about this?'

All eyes turned to Hereward, who just looked confused, 'What?' he asked.

'Umair's book?' Hermitage prompted.

'Oh, right. The book, yes,' Hereward got it now. He grinned at the others. 'We fed false stories back to William about the enormous strength of the Saxon forces out here. Fortresses, witches, the whole place was crawling with dangerously armed men ready for war.'

'Instead of you lot.' Cenric nodded to the paltry Saxon forces, one of whom was asleep.

'Exactly.'

'Ha, ha!' Cenric laughed heartily at this. 'No wonder he kept to his camp. I could never understand why he didn't just march out here and trample the lot of you.'

'By the Gods,' the Viking said. 'If William found out he'd have done for Umair then and there.'

'By the Gods?' Cenric grunted. 'Not a Viking? Ha.'

'You didn't know of these tales going back to William?' Abdul asked.

'No, of course not,' Cenric replied.

'And you sent no similar information back through Umair?'

'No we did not.' Cenric looked cross. Again. 'We agreed that William was not to know we were here at all. We'd be better able to deal with the bastard if he didn't know we were out here. And ready for him.'

'The information Umair brought you about William was

genuine?' Abdul asked the wider group.

They all nodded at this. 'Sizes of patrols, directions, all good and helpful,' Cenric confirmed. 'He never led us astray.'

'The details of William's long-term plans seemed to be in accord with that gathered from alternative sources, which presented a coherent picture of his wider strategy,' Aelfstan confirmed.

'What?' the Viking asked, looking thoroughly confused.

'The information was true,' Aelfstan explained with a magnanimous sigh.

'Ah, right.' Viking still didn't sound too convinced. 'Yes,' he added, 'true for us as well.'

'And you?' Abdul asked the leader of the marsh-men, who looked surprised to be included.

'Was the information Umair gave you true?'

The man's eyes moved about as if waiting for one of the others to answer.

'You said Umair was your friend?' Abdul prompted.

This got a gruff nod of confirmation.

'And he told you things? He told you about William and what he was up to?'

'William?' the man asked. 'Who is William?'

'Erm.' Abdul was nonplussed by this response. 'King William of the Normans? The one who has recently invaded the country? The one all the fuss is about?'

'I know no William.' The marsh man folded his arms, signifying that he wasn't going to talk about people he'd never heard of.

'Who in God's name do you think we've been talking about?' Cenric bawled at him.

The men of the marsh looked at one another, clearly very puzzled why the strange man was shouting at them.

## The Case of the Curious Corpse

'We just spent a good long time arguing over whether William killed Umair or not. Did it never occur to you to say you didn't know who William was?'

The leader's look was clear, no it had not occurred to him and he still didn't seem to understand why it was important, or interesting. 'We thought one of you was William.'

No one had anything to say to that at all.

'They've been in the marshes too long,' Hereward eventually commented. 'They're no use to us.'

'But they still knew Umair,' Hermitage raised a timid hand. 'Why would he go and see them? Particularly if they had no knowledge of or interest in William?'

'Get away from all talk of the man, probably,' the Viking observed.

Hermitage directed his question at the marsh men. 'What did Umair do then? When he came to see you?'

'Healing,' the marsh leader grunted.

'Healing? He brought healing?'

Nods of assent. 'Great man of the marshes.'

'Sorry,' Hermitage corrected himself. It seemed even men of the marshes could quibble over titles. 'He brought healing, great man of the marshes.' He even bowed his head as he addressed the leader. Why the three men burst out laughing at this confused Hermitage no end.

'We are not great man,' the marsh leader scoffed at their ignorance. 'Great man is in the marshes.'

'Ah.' Hermitage nodded his understanding without understanding anything at all.

'Friend brought healing for the great man.'

'I see.' Hermitage actually did see this time. 'The great man of the marshes was sick?'

'Many who come to the marshes are sick.'

'There's a reason for that.' Cenric gave a contemptuous snort.

Hermitage ignored him. 'If Umair healed their great man, they are hardly likely to kill him, are they?'

'Wouldn't put anything past them. They could have sacrificed Umair to the marsh.'

'If we can get back to the matter in hand?' Abdul, asked, politely. Everyone ignored the marsh men once more and turned their attention back to the Saracen.

'We still see no one with anything to gain from the death of Umair. Hereward you relied on his information to keep up your action against the Normans. And of course, he was sending his tales back to William, who appeared to be accepting them. Cenric, you and the others gained from what Umair told you.' He paused for a moment and Hermitage could see that he was thinking about whether he should say what he had in mind.

'Unless of course, one of you wanted Umair dead to bring pressure on William from the Saracens. Or even all of you together? Unable to defeat William by yourselves you thought about provoking a greater strength.'

He definitely shouldn't have said it. The uproar was instantaneous and the language was positively disgraceful. Everyone got so angry so quickly that Hermitage thought Abdul must be well wide of hitting the truth. He'd hit something though, and they all looked like they wanted to hit him back.

He held his hands out, as if in surrender to their arguments. 'We have to consider every option. King Aedgar would no doubt gain from having the Saracens attack William. As would you all.'

Aelfric waved the accusation away. 'The king doesn't keep

track of William's hostages.'

'But you do,' Abdul still sounded very polite. 'You knew Umair was here because you met him. Perhaps you thought that if William could be implicated in his murder, the Saracen army would spring to your aid.'

Hermitage thought that was the most appalling suggestion. Surely no one would behave in such a despicable manner.

'It's just the sort of behaviour kings and their courts get up to,' Wat said as if stating a truth of nature.

'Not in this case.' Aelfric's tone was a very serious tone. 'We could have sought allies with the Saracens if we wanted but quite frankly who needs an army of Saracens in your country? They would probably never go home again.'

'And Eadric,' Abdul went on. 'Any force attacking William would dent his strength.'

'We don't need his strength dented,' Cenric became very war-like. 'We'll defeat him alone. We're hardly likely to join league with the Saracens when we won't even have anything to do with a hopeless group of ditch dwellers.'

The hopeless group of ditch dwellers in question took umbrage at this and raised the pitch of the noise once more as people got to their feet to make the arguments. To Hermitage's eyes there seemed to be an immediate danger of even more deaths. Surely it wouldn't be long before one of these people drew a sword. Perhaps the sword that killed Umair? There was some pushing and shoving but nobody actually pulled out a weapon.

That was a thought. If, even in a loud and aggressive argument like this no one pulled out a sword to threaten their opponents, why would anyone do it to Umair? It had to be a planned and deliberate act, not one taking place in the heat of a fight. But of all the groups currently readying their fists to join the argument, which would deliberately and cold-bloodedly strike Umair on the head? Unless there were yet more people out here that they hadn't met yet.

Now that was another thought.

All of the information Hermitage had picked up over the time he had been involved in this sorry business washed around inside his head. Places, people, swords, Umair.

The sword and Umair. He could picture poor Umair receiving the fateful blow. He could even see the sword. Well, he could see *a* sword, not being able to discern one long, sharp piece of metal from another. Whose hand was that on the sword? He peered deeply inside his own head and was completely surprised by what he saw. Or rather what he didn't see. He also had a fascinating thought about the "they" that Umair had reported.

He also heard words. Words that Wat and Cwen had said that dropped into the scene in his head like blackbirds into a pie.

'Aha,' he said.

'Aha?' Cwen asked, with no enthusiasm for what was going to be yet another false "Aha".

'Yes,' Hermitage confirmed. 'Exactly. Aha!'

Abdul, Wat and Cwen all turned to see a wide and not very modest smile on his face.

'Aha,' Le Pedvin said as he strode into the assembly with a not very modest force of men at his back.

# Caput XXI

## Doom

𝕭efore Hermitage could even register the arrival of the awful Norman, he registered the departure of Hereward. Or at least the end of his left foot as it disappeared from sight into the bushes. Maybe that was how the man kept one step ahead of the invaders; he ran away whenever he saw one.

'What have we here then?' Le Pedvin appraised them with his eye. 'Looks like a conspiracy against the king to me.' He was in a very good position to make whatever accusations he liked. Six heavily armed and armoured men took up station to his left and right. They even started growling at the assembly, which Hermitage thought was rather unnecessary.

He could see that Cenric was biting his tongue. Quite hard by the expression of pain on his face. Hereward's men looked largely vacant while the men of the marshes were gazing at Le Pedvin with very strange expressions. They were pointing at him and having some discussion in their own version of Saxon, or whatever noises they called language. They'd probably never seen anything like him before. The Viking simply stood, defiantly. If just standing could have any effect, he would be driving Le Pedvin back into the woods.

'Nothing of the sort, I assure you, sir.' Aelfric stepped up. 'Just a gathering of friends and travellers discussing issues of import with these people here,' he included Hermitage, Abdul, Wat and Cwen in his gesture.

'And what issues would those be?' Le Pedvin asked, clearly expecting a wrong answer.

'We hear there has been an awful murder. Of a Saracen no less.' Aelfric sounded as if he had never heard of such a thing in his life. 'These folk were asking us if we knew anything of it.'

'And do you?' Le Pedvin stared at Aelfric as if had found his killer.

The look bounced off King Aedgar's man, who was clearly used to this sort of thing.

'Nothing at all,' Aelfric apologised. 'Such sorry times we live in.'

'About to get a lot sorrier,' Le Pedvin said with a slight smile. 'I think you are all here festering revolt against the king.' He turned his head to take them all in. He dismissed Aelfric easily. 'You look like you've just stepped out of court and don't belong anywhere in the open.' He turned to the marsh men. 'That lot could have been dragged from the bottom of the marshes.'

'We walked,' the marsh man corrected.

'The one over there,' Le Pedvin nodded at Cenric. 'The one who is giving me all sorts of looks and is barely holding himself back from attacking must be some sort of Saxon soldier. We don't like Saxon soldiers in these parts.' He looked to the last of the number. 'And a Viking?'

'I am not a Viking,' the Viking complained.

'And I'm not a Norman with a lot of men and a penchant for killing people.' Le Pedvin made the noise that he passed off as a laugh. 'And you,' Le Pedvin turned his attention to the investigators. 'Conspiring with the enemy eh? There must be a good punishment for that.' He gave it a moment's thought. 'It's probably death, come to think of it.'

'I don't think killing another Saracen is going help,' Wat suggested.

# The Case of the Curious Corpse

Le Pedvin's face, normally a featureless sheet of indifference, dropped into an icy bath of anger. 'We didn't kill the first one,' he pointed a gloved finger at Wat, giving the clear impression that the glove was going to be let loose on the weaver any moment now.

'I know you didn't,' Hermitage spoke up.

At least that had the benefit of stopping Le Pedvin in whatever murderous tracks he was getting on to. 'What?' he said, confused and sounding as if he'd just been accused.

'I know you didn't do it,' Hermitage said. 'You didn't kill Umair.'

Le Pedvin looked confused and disappointed that someone was agreeing with him. It must be difficult, killing people who agreed with you. 'Well, that's good then.' he said.

'Who did, Hermitage?' Cwen asked.

'I don't know,' Hermitage replied simply.

'What!?' Wat shrieked his frustration. 'You just gave us an authentic "aha" and now you say you don't know?'

'Well, I do and I don't.'

'You're not helping yourself you know,' Le Pedvin drawled, back to normal now.

'I mean I know who did it, but I don't know who they are.'

Everyone gave this a moment's thought.

'No,' Le Pedvin said, 'that's no better.'

'It's a simple process of, what could you call it?' Hermitage considered the appropriate expression. 'Ex liminare?'

'Eggs who?' the Viking queried.

'Removal of those who could not have done it, to leave the one who could,' Abdul said with some interest.

'Exactly,' Hermitage nodded appreciatively.

'I have had to use such a method on occasion,' Abdul went on. 'Sometimes there is simply not enough evidence to convince you that one individual is the guilty party, and so you have to find which one of them has the least evidence in their favour.'

'Could one call it,' Hermitage considered the options, '*elimination?*'

'An excellent proposal,' Abdul smiled and nodded. 'We eliminate all those who could not have done the deed until we are left with the one who must have.'

'Or at least the one who is most likely.'

'Naturally,' Abdul acknowledged. 'And then we can test a range of…'

'Shut UP,' Le Pedvin barked. His men adding their growl as supporting background. 'You.' The glove pointed at Hermitage. 'And you.' Now it found Abdul. 'Shut up.'

They shut up.

'Right,' Le Pedvin took a breath. 'You know that we did not kill the Saracen?'

'I do,' Hermitage confirmed.

'But you don't know who did, even though you said you do.'

'Not exactly.'

Le Pedvin closed his eye and clenched both his gloves so tight they looked ready to squeak.

'Shall I explain?' Hermitage offered, brightly.

'That would be good,' Le Pedvin ground out. 'And it would probably be very wise to do it quickly.'

'Well.' Hermitage wondered if he should stand to stride up and down a bit. He looked at Le Pedvin and decided that any additional delay would not be well received. This exposition was proving to be a lot less enjoyable than he had imagined. But then that was true of most things.

'We know that Umair returned to the camp with his

wound, crying out "they struck me". We have this from the guard at the camp who would seem to have no reason make something up and who would not know the exact words anyway. Thus we can conclude that Umair was indeed struck outside the Norman camp by a mysterious "they."'

'Still could have been Normans,' Cenric muttered.

'I'm watching you,' Le Pedvin called over, his glove doing its business once more.

'So,' Hermitage went on. 'Someone outside the camp did it and as erm, the gentlemen over there says, it could still have been some Normans.' He held one hand up to acknowledge the threatening hiss that was now coming from Le Pedvin. 'But there are a lot of people outside the camp.'

'More than there ought to be,' Le Pedvin noted.

'It is actually more likely that one of these outsiders did it. After all, Umair was William's hostage and was well known to his men. Hardly likely that one of them would kill him, even by mistake. They would not want to raise William's ire.'

'King William,' Le Pedvin specified.

'But who, out here, would want to kill Umair. That's what's been puzzling me. Master Abdul has told us all about the awful situations in which groups scheme and plot against one another, but I don't think that is enough here. These people were all strangers to one another until today.' He waved a hand to encompass the various individuals. Le Pedvin snorted at this. 'I assure you it is the case,' Hermitage said, imagining that the simple truth would be enough.

'I think we can rule out accident. Even when everyone was arguing a moment ago I noticed that no one drew their weapons.'

'We had a lively discussion about what sort of shocking person would do such a thing,' Aelfric smiled at Le Pedvin.

Le Pedvin did not smile back.

'It was a deliberate act then,' Hermitage concluded. 'Someone took their sword and struck Umair on the head. Not so badly as to kill him on the spot, but enough to be a fatal wound. And he said "they struck me" suggesting there was more than one.'

'It usually does,' Wat observed.

'Usually, yes.' Hermitage said mysteriously. He had to think carefully about how he was going to approach the next bit of his argument, particularly with Le Pedvin present. He couldn't give away the knowledge that Umair had been telling everyone about William's plans. He could see that Le Pedvin's reaction to that piece of news would have that glove reaching for his sword in an instant. But he couldn't lie. Surely? 'None of the people here had any reason to strike Umair. They, erm, hardly knew him.'

'Hardly?' Le Pedvin questioned.

'Only heard about him, really,' Aelfric put in.

'Just so.' Hermitage nodded and moved on quickly. 'Why would any of them kill a complete stranger. Especially a Saracen?'

Le Pedvin started looking a lot less convinced that anyone in this gathering was innocent. And he hadn't looked convinced in the first place.

Hermitage raised a hand towards Le Pedvin, fending off the response that was going to come with his next statement. 'Of course, we know Umair was out and about taking drawings and notes and then returning to William with them.'

'Rocks and flowers,' Le Pedvin dismissed the matter with a wave.

'And perhaps some information about the Saxon forces,

none of whom are actually here,' Wat added, rather nonchalantly. 'Obviously different Saxons,' he added. 'Must be somewhere else. No fortifications or armies in these parts.'

Le Pedvin pinched his face into an instrument of terror and pointed it at Hermitage.

'Just so,' Hermitage confirmed. 'It seems that Umair may have been reporting back what he had heard, rather than what he had actually seen?'

Le Pedvin's glare fell on Abdul, who reflected it straight back. 'It's a good job William didn't send Umair out to gather information. That would be a shocking misuse of a hostage that would demand immediate action.'

Hermitage had never felt sympathy for Le Pedvin before, but the man looked like he wanted to burst. All over everyone standing in front of him. It was a good job Umair was dead, or Le Pedvin would have killed him.

'But it's all part of the picture. One of the elements, as Abdul would have it.' Hermitage tried a smile but he knew it didn't come out right. He pressed on. 'Of course, if the Saxons knew that Umair was taking any information to William they might have wanted to do him harm, but we have discovered that they, erm, didn't know at all.' He felt the lie throughout his body, from the knot in his stomach to taste of it in his mouth. As he spoke he felt that he was shouting out "I'm lying" at the same time. Surely someone would spot that.

'They didn't?' Le Pedvin hadn't spotted the blatant untruth. How remarkable. Perhaps Hermitage could do lying after all.

'We did manage to find Hereward, briefly, and are sure that he had no reason to attack Umair.' He left it at that. Surely not saying something wasn't the same as a lie. An omission, perhaps. A selection of the truth. He wasn't convincing himself.

He moved on quickly before Le Pedvin had a chance to draw any conclusions of his own. 'All of which means, using our new *process of elimination*,' he liked the sound of that, 'there must be another. If none of William's men did it and none of the people outside the camp did it, there must be someone else.'

'Could be anyone,' Cwen said. 'There could be dozens of people out here capable of the deed.'

'I don't think that's the case,' Hermitage nodded to himself. 'We know that Umair got on well with everyone. He made friendships quickly and with the widest variety of people. From the Norman nobles,' he nodded at Le Pedvin, 'to the humble men of the marshes.' An acknowledgement in their direction. 'Umair could meet anyone and not be attacked with a sword. So it was someone who actually wanted to attack him in person. And, of course, the blow was a very particular one. Bad enough to kill but not quickly.'

'Someone who knew exactly what they were doing,' Abdul concluded.

'Precisely. And more than that, someone who knew that the outcome would be serious trouble for William. It would bring the Saracen forces down on him and possibly see the Normans completely defeated.'

'Pah,' Le Pedvin snorted at this but it was a bit of a half-hearted snort.

'We now have someone who attacked Umair with a skilful blow and who wants to damage William. And we know it wasn't Hereward and the local Saxons. King, sorry, erm, Aedgar, we hear, is away in Scotland so hardly likely to be his forces.' Hermitage wasn't even convincing himself about this

## The Case of the Curious Corpse

but the rest of them seemed happy enough.

'Who does that leave then?' Wat sounded frustrated that all this careful argument still hadn't got them anywhere.

'It left me thinking who else hated the Normans enough to go to such trouble. If, like Hereward say, you just want them defeated, you try to attack, or beat them in battle.'

'Ha,' Le Pedvin mocked. 'That didn't go so well for the last king who tried.'

Hermitage ignored him. 'Why go to all the trouble of attacking an important hostage in the hope that someone else will be infuriated? It's too complicated. It had to be some group or individual who wanted the William dealt with, but didn't want to be seen doing so.'

'I'm confused,' Cwen complained.

'I know,' Hermitage sounded as lost as everyone else. 'But then I had another thought. It wasn't necessarily the Normans in general. What we were looking for was someone who hated William in particular. Enough to attack Umair.'

'We could be back to a long list.' Wat complained, with a smile at Le Pedvin, as it was only a joke.

'Who else hates William enough to go to all this trouble?' Hermitage asked. He looked around the gathering. Surely someone had got it. He cast a glance at Abdul who was frowning hard and stroking the beard at the same time.

'Who else have we mentioned?' Hermitage was surprised no one else was following him., The gathering in the woods looked like a group of novices who have just been asked to step to the lectern for scripture practice, who then confess that they can't actually read.

'One we haven't mentioned yet?' Hermitage prompted again. The silence continued as people looked up into the trees as if the answer was up there somewhere. Hermitage shook his head and directed his comment to Wat and Cwen. 'Those you told me about.'

'Eh, what? Me?' Wat got very defensive all of a sudden.

'I never mentioned anyone,' Cwen protested.

'But you did,' Hermitage said, assuming that they saw it all now.

He paused to let them get to the conclusion on their own. It was always much more satisfying that way. No one was saying anything and the silence dragged on as some puzzled faces squirmed.

'*They* struck me?' Hermitage prompted. 'Who could *they* be?'

'A band of killers,' Cwen said.

'Could be. But "they" can also mean a much wider group.'

Still no luck.

'Oh for goodness sake,' Hermitage huffed. 'The Normans.'

Le Pedvin looked horrified. 'I told you it wasn't us,' he snapped.

'And it wasn't,' Hermitage confirmed, which didn't seem to help. 'Cwen, you said there are lots of Normans, and that it might not have been William who actually did it. Wat, you told us all about a whole army of Normans who don't like William at all.'

'Normans who hate William?' Wat asked.

'Yes, the ones from the south. The other William, the one who got in all the fights.'

'Iron Arm,' Le Pedvin sounded gleeful and appalled at the same time.

'But they're in, what do you call it, Silicia,' said Cwen.

'Sicily,' Abdul said thoughtfully.

'They were,' Hermitage agreed. 'But if Abdul could travel all the way here, anyone could. And who else would wish

# The Case of the Curious Corpse

William harm and want to kill his hostage to bring the fury of the Saracens down on his head? Who would even know about the hostage in the first place? And be able to strike someone so they didn't die immediately. It must be a hardened killer.'

'It's a bit of a long shot isn't it?' Wat sounded very doubtful. 'There just happens to be another Norman out here, one who wants William in trouble. We haven't actually got any, what's it? Evidence.'

'But we do have some corroboration,' he said the word with a disgraceful amount of pride and smiled at Abdul. 'If my thinking is right, you can see why I would say that I know who did it but I don't know who they are. Well, apart from it being the great man of the marsh of course.'

This brought more silence. It was broken by the men of the marsh when they eventually realised what Hermitage had said. They made noises but no one could really tell what they meant.

'Umair had to heal the great man because he was sick,' Hermitage explained. 'And the men from the marsh told us that people get sick when they come to the marsh. So the great man had come to the marsh. He's not one of their number. He's a great man, who happens to be in the marsh. He's not a great man *of* the marsh. See?'

'Still mostly guesses.' Wat sounded very sceptical.

'But then the men of the marsh recognised Le Pedvin.'

'Did they?' Cwen asked.

'They did. They pointed at him and had a little discussion. At first, I thought it could be because they'd never seen anyone like him before, but then I thought that perhaps it was exactly the opposite. They'd seen someone very like him before. In fact, they've got one of their own, back in the marshes.' He called over to the men who were still babbling to themselves. 'Does this look like your great man?' He held an arm out towards Le Pedvin.

The leader shuffled forward and stood, just out of sword reach, while he examined the Norman. He paid particular attention to counting the number of eyes, looking at them several times to make sure he got his sums right.

'Not great man,' he eventually concluded.

'But he looks like the great man?' Hermitage asked.

The marsh man shrugged. 'Brother, maybe.'

'There we are,' Hermitage said, feeling an enormous relief that the man had said the right thing. 'There's a Norman in the marshes.'

'And who else is likely to kill strangers,' Cenric muttered.

'Iron Arm,' Le Pedvin repeated, this time with pleasurable malice, happily ignoring Cenric completely.

'Unlikely to be him in person,' Abdul said.

'But one of his men,' Le Pedvin's voice was dark with intent; the unpleasant sort. 'And I think the Saracen nation will want to rise up against him for this outrage. And quite right too. It's disgraceful.'

Hermitage thought that was a bit much, considering how much fuss they'd made over the possibility it might have been them.

Le Pedvin signalled for his men to join him and they gathered around. 'Go with these,' he indicated the men of the marsh with a distasteful gesture. 'Find their great man, who is probably one of Iron Arm's men, and bring him back alive. Well, alive-ish.'

The Norman soldiers, apparently happy with a task to their liking, strode over and herded the marsh men into order before disappearing into the undergrowth.

# The Case of the Curious Corpse

'Well, well,' Aelfric said, breaking into Le Pedvin's gloating silence. 'This is a fine to do, eh? What is an innocent man to do when the woods and the marshes of the country are not safe.'

'If you're an innocent man, I'm the pope,' Le Pedvin said. He drew his sword and insouciantly directed the point at them all in turn. 'This will make a fascinating tale when we take it all before the king.'

'I'm sure it would,' Cenric said, not sounding very concerned at all.

Hermitage wondered what was going on. He was now feeling very bad that although he had found the killer, he had led various Saxons and one Viking straight into the hands of the Normans.

He now noticed that, following Cenric's lead, the various Saxons and the Viking all had swords in their hands as well.

'You appear to have sent your men off into the marshes, leaving you alone,' Cenric observed. 'Out here in the woods, long way from camp, and threatening people with a sword?'

Hermitage noticed that Le Pedvin was now looking a bit less insouciant.

'Of course, William's hostage being killed had the potential to cause him all sorts of trouble. I wonder what would happen if his right-hand man didn't make it back at all.'

'All strangers eh?' Le Pedvin said with a nasty look at Hermitage.

'We were until we found a common enemy,' Cenric replied.

Hermitage looked backwards and forwards between the factions, and to Wat, Cwen and Abdul who all wore worried expressions. He stepped forward.

'Gentlemen, gentlemen,' he raised his hands to try and calm things.

'No gentlemen here,' Cenric said. 'Gentlemen at arms, perhaps.'

'This is not the way.'

'Tell that to William.'

Hermitage didn't know what to do. A group of armed men was about to attack one man alone. Granted, that particular man was the curse of his life. He thought that things would improve considerably if Le Pedvin were dead, but still. He couldn't stand by while murder was done. He could also imagine William instructing him to investigate the death of Le Pedvin when he had been there at the time. It was intolerable.

And Le Pedvin was a hardened fighter, he would probably take several of the Saxons with him, if not actually win. If the man came out of this alive, Hermitage dreaded to contemplate the conversation they would have.

Le Pedvin crouched slightly into a fighting stance and smiled horribly at his opponents.

Cenric and the Viking looked ready for the attack, the rest of them less so. Aelfric had taken several steps back and looked ready to report on events later, a long way away. Hereward's remaining men did have their weapons to hand but looked like they were quite ready to lend them to someone else who might want to take their place.

The chances of a Le Pedvin victory seemed quite high all of a sudden.

'Is this him?' a voice called through the bushes as the first of Le Pedvin's men reappeared. 'He was only hiding back there...' The man stopped short as he took in the scene before him. 'What's going on here?'

## The Case of the Curious Corpse

He was soon joined by two more Normans who were dragging a third between them. Although the accoutrements and clothing said this one was clearly Norman, he had a definite look of the south about him, not being as pale as everyone else. He didn't look at all well though. Umair's cures had clearly not had a great effect yet.

Cenric and the Viking responded quickly to the new arrivals. 'We were just leaving,' he said as he stepped smartly back into the bushes, followed almost immediately by the Viking, Aelfric and Hereward's band.

'If I find you again, I will kill you,' Le Pedvin called after them.

'You can try,' Cenric's voice shouted back.

'Shall we go after them?' the Norman guard asked.

'No,' Le Pedvin instructed. 'This one's more important.' He gestured at the sick Norman being held up. 'Better get him back to William. Don't want him dying before we can kill him.'

He turned to the others. 'I suppose that was well done, monk,' he said with reluctant gratitude. 'Consorting with the enemy is not wise but finding one of Iron Arm's men is some compensation.'

Hermitage thought that some acknowledgement of trying to save the man's life might have been appropriate.

'William is going be delighted at this. And Master Abdul-Mateen al Deir ez-Zor,' he pronounced the name perfectly, 'perhaps we can discuss the content of the message going back to your Master.' He clapped Abdul on the shoulder and led him back towards the camp.

Hermitage, Wat and Cwen exchanged looks with clear intent. Should they follow back to the camp, or vanish into the woods with the rest of William's enemies?

'There are still some Saxons out there with swords who are probably quite cross,' Hermitage noted.

'And a Viking,' Wat added.

'Could be they're not too happy that I tried to stop them killing Le Pedvin.'

'And I didn't like the way that Viking kept looking at me,' Cwen said.

'They might think that finishing off William's own investigator would annoy him a bit. Considering they didn't get to do Le Pedvin,' Wat speculated.

Hermitage gave it a moment's thought. 'Perhaps we'll just go back to camp. Make sure everything is cleared up.'

The other two reluctantly agreed, without much reluctance.

'There is one more thing I've got to find out anyway,' Hermitage added, as they followed Abdul, Le Pedvin and the Normans like forgotten lambs.

'What's that?' Cwen asked.

'It's another mystery, but thankfully one that doesn't matter in the slightest,' Hermitage said. 'I'm just curious, that's all.' He didn't want to explain any further as he felt slightly ashamed.

They walked on, Hermitage's relief that this was all over finally getting up its courage to wash through him.

'Aha, eh?' Cwen noted with a smile.

'I knew you'd get it eventually,' Wat said. 'And we only got accused of the murder once. Perhaps things are on the up.'

# Epilogue

'There's one thing that I still have to know,' Hermitage said as they were getting ready to leave the camp.

'Hermitage,' Cwen complained. 'William and Le Pedvin have told us we can go.'

'Well, they've told us to get out of their sight, actually,' Wat pointed out.

Cwen gave him one of the softest of her hard looks. 'We need to go. If we hang around someone else will get murdered and then where will we be?'

'It won't take a moment,' Hermitage protested. 'And it's on our way.' He stepped away from the now waving Mistress Le Pedvin, who had obviously taken them back into her favour.

Cwen and Wat followed, exchanging looks of reluctant indulgence. 'What is it you want to know?' Cwen asked. 'Surely finding the killer is enough.'

Hermitage had felt some shame when he saw the Norman from the marshes dragged into camp. It was soon overwhelmed by the enormous relief that his investigation had been right and he wasn't going to be threatened with death once more.

Abdul, on the other hand, was now being treated as an honoured guest of King William. He had been given Umair's tent and Mistress Le Pedvin was fussing over him such that the expressions he wore said he wanted to get back to the empty desert as soon as possible.

He bade them all fond farewells, saving the most effusive for Hermitage. He said that he learned so much from the young monk that his future investigations would be much more effective. He even hoped that one day he would develop his own "aha" approach, but he still wasn't clear how Hermitage had done it.

Hermitage in his turn expressed his gratitude to the Saracen and expressed the wish that his future work might present more opportunity for thought and organisation. He also confessed that he hoped there wouldn't actually be any future work. This business may be Abdul's natural calling but it was the Normans who kept calling on Hermitage, and he wished they would stop.

'We have an expression in my language for situations such as this,' Abdul had said, and though it sounded awful, Hermitage got the intent of the words perfectly.

'*Hal yumkinuna la yltqyan 'abadaan marratan 'ukhraa,*' Abdul said as he took Hermitage's shoulders. 'May we never meet again.'

...

'Here we are,' Hermitage said as he stepped over to a guard.

After all the time that had passed the man was now on his knees. He was still holding his pikestaff but it was clear he was going to be no use at all if any actual enemies turned up. The glazed look said that he had either fallen asleep with his eyes open or was in the middle of some waking dream. It wasn't a very nice dream, judging by the noises he was making.

Hermitage knelt at the man's side and got no acknowledgement. 'I must ask you something,' he said quite gently.

The guard did look up at this, although it wasn't clear what he was seeing if anything at all.

'There is a question to which I have to know the answer. It

# The Case of the Curious Corpse

has been bothering me throughout this whole business and I know will only get worse and rob me of sleep for weeks to come.'

The guard blinked a few times and seemed to come as near to consciousness as he was likely to get.

Hermitage sat on the ground now and tried to look into his eyes. When he felt he had got all the attention there was, he asked his question. 'What was the bad thing you did?'

This did bring the guard to his senses.

'What was the bad thing that made Le Pedvin put you on permanent guard duty? The thing he thought you should have been executed for?'

The guard frowned. He moved parched lips and drew struggling breath. When he had enough air in his chest he released one hand from the staff and beckoned Hermitage to draw near. Just as a man on his death bed might call the priest to hear his final confession. He muttered something inaudible and Hermitage leant forward to hear.

'What was that? I couldn't hear,' he pleaded with the man to repeat himself. This time he put his ear right up against the man's mouth so that he could catch the words. With a supreme effort, the guard croaked into Hermitage's ear exactly what the bad thing had been.

Hermitage leapt up from the ground and stood looking with horror at the sad figure before him. 'That's disgraceful,' he said. 'And disgusting.'

Was that a shrug from the guard, just before he finally collapsed onto the floor and fell into a sleep from which even an executioner couldn't wake him?

'What did he say?' Cwen asked, urgently. 'What was the bad thing?'

Hermitage looked at her and Wat with a serious, sombre

and slightly bilious face. 'I wish I'd never asked,' he said. 'And I'm certainly not going to repeat it.'

**Finis.**

> Brother Hermitage's travails continue in
> **The Case of the Cantankerous Carcass.**
> The first chapter beckons below…

# The Case of the Cantankerous Carcass

## Caput I

### Visitation

'Run away and hide, you mean.' Cwen scowled as they sat around the table in Wat the Weaver's kitchen.

'Not at all,' Brother Hermitage replied. It was no surprise that they didn't understand detailed theological issues like this. Cwen, while being an excellent young tapestrier, was not imbued with a cautious, careful and thoughtful approach to the world. If she could approach it, there was a good chance she would try to hit it, despite her diminutive stature and only seventeen years of age behind her. She'd even try to hit a well-armed Norman soldier. They seemed to be her favourite.

Wat himself was a worldly-wise weaver, far too worldly-wise in Hermitage's opinion. There was something in his eyes and in the nonchalant tousle of black hair sitting comfortably on his head that said he knew things. All sorts of things. Mainly the wrong sorts of things. He was only a few years older than Hermitage's twenty-something, so by rights should not know much more at all. Hermitage's knowledge was wide, but it was of an entirely different nature. A much better one.

Wat put far too much of his worldly knowledge into the

images he made. They included fine detail of things no decent person ought to have heard of, let alone seen. Lots of knowledge but very little wisdom.

It was a good job Wat was a naturally persuasive fellow. His skill at persuading people to part with large sums of money in exchange for disgraceful tapestries came in useful when he persuaded well-armed Norman soldiers not to chop Cwen to bits for her impudence, or Hermitage just for being a monk.

'Becoming a hermit is not hiding at all,' Hermitage explained. 'It is simply removing oneself from the world and living in solitude as a religious discipline. After all, my given name indicates that this should be my calling.'

'It would also mean removing oneself from the Normans and any of your duties as the King's Investigator,' Wat observed. 'And I'm not sure King William will be very supportive of that.'

'Or actually take any notice at all,' Cwen added.

'Oh, he's a hermit now is he?' Wat did a rather good impression of King William's gruff accent. 'Good, he won't put up a fight when you go and get him.'

Hermitage had to admit that the life of the hermit was attractive for that very reason. It was pure chance that he happened to have worked out one or two murders and for that he was expected to do it all the time. He had never asked to be King's Investigator. In fact, on a few occasions he'd specifically asked not to be. It didn't seem to make any difference to the king.

He countered his own argument by considering that if the life of the hermit was attractive then he shouldn't be doing it. Surely no hermit should actually enjoy being a hermit, what was the point in that?

# The Case of the Cantankerous Carcass

He looked at the pair of young faces opposite and appreciated their argument. He also appreciated that all three of them were still in their early years and had long, productive lives ahead of them. The thought of spending them all as King's Investigator really did make him want to hide at the back of a cave.

He stared at the kitchen table as if it would supply his inspiration. He sat back from its surface as he thought it would more likely give him something rather nasty.

Mrs Grod, Wat's cook, had disappeared for the evening, making the kitchen a safe place to be. She prepared meals on this surface and had just fed the apprentices, several of whom were now forcing themselves through the labour of digestion. Hermitage knew that dirt and grime were good for you, but he wasn't so sure it should be used quite so copiously in cooking. While the structure in front of them was called a table, it most strongly resembled a rotten tree stump. The rot being one of Mrs Grod's most frequent ingredients.

In a reflective frame of mind, Hermitage speculated that if you could scrape the layers of the surface away one by one you could probably work out what the apprentices had eaten going back several years. He suspected the results would be quite horrific.

Needless to say, none of them had eaten from Mrs Grod's hand, although eating from her hands would probably be more healthy than eating from her plates. They had their meals delivered from the local inn, a place Hermitage was pleased to avoid with its reputation for drunkenness, violence and debauchery. The innkeeper was happy to take Wat's money and to bring their food up. He said that having Wat anywhere near his inn would lower the tone.

'And what good would being a hermit do anyway?' Wat

pressed. 'You're better off with us two around. I dread to think what would happen if you ended up dragged away by William to investigate on your own.'

Cwen nodded sagely at this comment.

'How so?' Hermitage asked. He knew Wat and Cwen were always a great help, but they relied on him to resolve the mysteries at the end of the day. It usually was at the end. Just when everyone's patience was running out and before something horrible happened.

Wat sighed and smiled some encouragement. 'You usually end up accused of the murder you're investigating, you know.'

'And if we weren't there, you'd probably end up found guilty and executed.' Cwen gave a helpful shrug.

'Oh,' Hermitage said, 'I'm not sure it would come to that.'

Their looks said that they were quite confident that was exactly what it would come to. He had noted that when it came to murder and the like, the people involved could be really rather difficult. On occasion, they did turn their ire on Hermitage but he'd never murdered anyone, or even come close, so it was surely nothing to worry about. Hermitage had long practise at worrying about things that were nothing to worry about.

He pondered some more and tried to think what he could do that would legitimately get him out of any more investigations. He knew that it might be his duty, a sign from God that investigation was to be his task in life. But if that were the case, God would make it unavoidable. If he could come up with a way of avoiding it, it couldn't be God's will.

Even he thought that this reasoning was rather doubtful. He cast his mind around to try and come up with something that could explain the absence of a monk when you wanted

# The Case of the Cantankerous Carcass

one. An image of his old abbot leapt into his head.

'Pilgrimage!' he cried out.

'What?' Cwen frowned.

'Next time William sends for me to investigate, you could say I've gone on pilgrimage. He couldn't possibly object to that. Stopping a man doing pilgrimage is the most awful sin.'

'Tell him you're on a pilgrimage?' Wat checked.

'That's right.'

'Even if you're hiding under your cot?' Cwen asked.

'No, no.' Hermitage was shocked at the very idea of such dishonesty. 'I really will go on a pilgrimage.'

The frowns said that Wat and Cwen were as concerned about letting Hermitage go on a pilgrimage on his own, as they were about him dealing with murderers.

'Where to?' Wat asked.

Hermitage hadn't thought that far.

'Jerusalem?' Cwen suggested.

'Compostela?' Wat threw in.

They were all quite a long way away and probably quite dangerous. And he had met some pilgrims who claimed to have visited those places and they were most disreputable fellows. In fact, their claim to be pilgrims just because they walked about a lot, was extremely questionable.[7]

'I've heard very interesting things about Walsingham,' Hermitage said.

'The one near Norwich?' Wat asked, sounding unimpressed.

'That's the place,' Hermitage nodded. 'A vision of the Virgin Mary, apparently. They've built a replica of the very

---

[7] Perhaps unsurprisingly, this meeting is recounted in a Chronicle of Brother Hermitage: *Hermitage, Wat and Some Druids* is the volume you need.

place Our Saviour was born and have a vial of the virgin's milk.'

'Yeuch.' Wat turned his nose up at that.

'Yeuch?' Hermitage was appalled at this reaction to a sacred relic. He knew that the common folk took their devotions very seriously - when they were doing them - but could be lax and positively sacrilegious when out of sight of the church. But Wat was an intelligent man. He should know better.

'It's not very, erm, what's the word?' Cwen moved the conversation on. 'Not very far away. That's it. For a pilgrimage, it's not very far away. Not very pilgrimmy, if you see what I mean.'

Hermitage shook his head. 'The people who live near Jerusalem or Compostela are not thought less of because they don't have far to go.'

'I bet they are,' Wat muttered. 'And in any case, if William's men turn up and we say you've gone to Walsingham they'll be after you like an arrow to a Saxon's eyeball.'

'And you're going to walk to Walsingham?' Cwen asked.

'That is normal for a pilgrimage,' Hermitage said without a hint of sarcasm, which he couldn't do anyway.

'Through the open countryside full of Norman soldiers and robbers and worse.'

'They wouldn't attack a pilgrim.' Hermitage was confident.

'And you wonder why we think you'll come to harm.' Wat shook his head gently.

'When are you thinking of leaving?' Cwen asked.

'Oh,' Hermitage said. He hadn't really got as far as thinking about the details. Or about the implications of leaving at all, really. Pilgrimage sounded like a marvellous idea. He liked marvellous ideas and frequently had several in one week. Fundamental to the nature of their being marvellous was that you didn't have to actually do anything about them. As soon as one idea was fully rounded you could put it aside and wait for another one.

The marvellous element of this one was that he wouldn't be in when the king sent for him again. He could see straight away that just having the idea of not being in would be little use in dealing with a group of armed and angry Normans. He would actually have to leave. Such men were never willing to engage in intellectual speculation, no matter how fascinating. And they always seemed to be armed and angry. He sometimes wondered why they invaded the country at all, they didn't seem to be enjoying it much.

Perhaps he could just get ready for his pilgrimage and then be off as soon as he saw someone coming. That didn't sound terribly devout, somehow.

'Won't take long for you to pack,' Wat interrupted his thoughts. 'Only got that little book of yours and your sandals. You could be off first thing.'

'If not tonight,' Cwen put in. 'Must be very holy, setting off on pilgrimage in the dark.'

The idea wasn't sounding quite so marvellous any more.

'And if you keep up a good pace and don't get robbed or murdered or anything, you could be there in a week.'

'I expect there's lots of monasteries on the way that you can stop in.' Wat said.

Of course, a monk on pilgrimage would be expected to take lodgings at monasteries along the way. Which was another drawback. Hermitage had never got on terribly well with other monks.

He always considered that staying at Wat's workshop with

Cwen, the apprentices and Hartle, the old weaving teacher, was fulfilling his Godly duty as he persuaded the place away from creation of the extremely rude images Wat tended to produce if he was left alone. While it meant that he didn't have to go anywhere near a monastery, he reasoned that this was a sacrifice he was prepared to make.

The truth was that he didn't like monasteries very much, which was not a very positive trait for a monk. More accurately it was that the monasteries didn't like him. Or rather the people inhabiting the monasteries didn't like him. The other monks. If he could find a monastery without any other monks he would be fine. He had never managed to put his finger on it exactly, but there was something about everything he said and everything he did that just rankled with his brothers.

And if the brothers were rankled, the more senior members of the community, priors and abbots and the like, could be downright difficult.

At one extreme sat the old abbot who had given Hermitage his name. He had been a very kindly fellow and recognised the impact Hermitage could have on his brothers. And the impacts they subsequently had on him. He suggested that if the young monk went and lived on his own in a cave it might be best for everyone.

At the other end of the scale sat Prior Athan.[8] "Relatively kindly" could still cover the most appalling behaviour when weighed against Athan. If Hermitage could take a crumb of comfort from the fact that Athan was horrible to everyone, close examination would reveal that the crumb was mouldy.

---

[8] Prior Athan appears in a number of the Chronicles and would probably get a series of his own if he wasn't quite so revolting.

# The Case of the Cantankerous Carcass

A pilgrimage could be a real trial if it involved several nights in the company of other monks. Or even other pilgrims.

Once more he seemed faced with a choice between the lesser of two evils; a dilemma he was never able to satisfactorily resolve. It was only reasonable that a pilgrimage should not be thought of as an evil at all. Just because he didn't like the idea, didn't make it evil, as such. The Normans on the other hand, definitely evil. Pilgrimage it was then.

'There's no chance of sitting here and the king forgetting about me altogether,' he reasoned.

'I don't know,' Wat mused. 'He couldn't even remember your name last time we met.'[9]

'That's true. But he always seems to recall that he has an investigator when he wants one. I don't think that remembering names bothers him much.'

'And as soon as some horrible murder turns up, he'll send for you anyway,' Cwen said.

'Yes, thank you. I think that summarises the problem neatly.' Hermitage returned to his fretful cogitation.

A silence joined them at the table as they considered the problem.

'Couldn't you invent something religious?' Wat asked.

Hermitage gave him the blankest look he possessed. 'Invent something religious?' Wat was spouting gibberish again.

'Yes, you know.'

'No, I most certainly do not know. What on earth are you

---

[9] A meeting *The Case of The Curious Corpse* covers in considerable detail; some of it relevant.

talking about?'

'Well.' Wat pursed his lips as he worked through his argument. 'The Normans don't seem terribly church-minded.'

'Church-minded?'

'I know they have priests and bishops and what-not, and they go on about sanctity and supporting the church all the time. But William himself, and his man Le Pedvin. They're not very holy men.'

'Absolutely not.' Hermitage couldn't immediately bring to mind anyone less holy. Yes, William had got blessing from the Pope for the invasion of England, but that was not the same as being a good Christian.

'So they won't know if you're having to do something religious. Something that would prevent you investigating.'

'Such as?'

'Well, pilgrimage would be one, but that seems a bit drastic. What about a festival?'

'Festival?'

'The church has lots of festivals. This could be the middle of the festival of something or other. The festival that quite categorically prohibits investigation.'

Cwen was nodding that this seemed to be a very good idea.

Hermitage checked what was being suggested. 'So I make something up and tell the Norman soldiers that I can't possibly investigate because it's the middle of the Festival of, I don't know, the recumbent postulant?'

'Is it? There you are then. Perfect.'

Hermitage just looked at them both. 'No, it isn't. There's no such thing. Recumbent postulant? It's nonsense.'

'Ah, but they don't know that,' Wat argued.

'But I do. You know my views on dishonesty.'

# The Case of the Cantankerous Carcass

Wat and Cwen now took to rolling their eyes at one another. Something they did quite frequently.

'Pick a real one then,' Cwen suggested. 'It's always some saint's day or other. Just tell them that you're not allowed out because it's saint Oswald's day or something.'

'Saint Oswald's day or something,' Hermitage repeated slowly. 'You're suggesting I should use the holy saints to trick the Normans into not taking me away for investigation?' He hoped that the horror at such an idea was clear from his voice.

'It wouldn't be a trick, would it? Not if you used a real saint. What did Oswald do anyway?'

'The Blessed Oswald,' Hermitage emphasised the name. 'Was bishop of Worcester and died during Lent when he was washing the feet of the poor.'

'Perfect,' Cwen beamed. 'You can say that you can't go out because you're washing your feet.'

Hermitage shook his head in sorrow. 'I'm not sure which is worse. The Normans with all their death and destruction, or you two.'

'Us?' Wat sounded offended. 'What did we do?'

'Probably blasphemy.' Hermitage glared hard, which only got a shrug from the two weavers.

'I don't know how you two can kneel in church and then come up with ideas like this.'

'If you don't want our help, you'd better go and pack,' Cwen smiled. 'Pilgrimage or Normans. They'll both get you out of the house.'

Hermitage returned to staring at the table. He would just have to take his normal approach to the problem. Do nothing and just hope for the best.

It had been several weeks since his last encounter with the

Normans. Perhaps they had forgotten about him. Or not had any murders. He thought that unlikely. They'd doubtless had lots of murders, just didn't want them investigating. Which suited him.

Such was the depth of his reflections that he failed to respond to a knock on the outer door. It was not the hammering of Norman, nor was the door simply thrown aside by someone who thought they were entitled to just walk in.

Cwen rose from her seat and went to answer. Hermitage did now look up and felt a shiver of anticipation. It was only reasonable that this would be nothing to do with him, but that didn't help. Many people knocked at the weaver's door for a whole variety of reasons. Suppliers, other tradesmen, customers, there was a regular coming and going.

He did think that someone knocking after dark would most likely be a disreputable fellow at least. Probably after some of Wat's old works, and few people wanted to be seen making those sorts of enquiries in daylight.

He leant back on his seat to look down the corridor to the front door to see if he could spot who the visitor was. All he could see was Cwen's back.

'It's all right,' she called back. 'It's only a monk.'

Hermitage felt the relief flood through him. It was probably a Brother seeking alms or a place to rest for the night. A Brother who clearly had no idea who Wat the Weaver was or the sorts of work the man produced. A fellow monk would be an interesting visitor. It was fine when monks were visitors, it was when he had to live with them that things started to go wrong.

'Monk?' A strong, mature voice queried the title with no little offence in its tone. Offence and overt criticism of the person who had used the word.

Hermitage frowned as that single word set off a distant reminiscence.

'I am no monk, girl.' The voice clearly thought little of Cwen if she couldn't spot this.

Not a monk? Hermitage thought. The visitor must be dressed as a monk or Cwen wouldn't have reached the conclusion. And that voice really was skittering around inside his head, trying to tell him something. The recollection sprang into instant clarity with the next words.

'I am looking for Brother Hermitage.'

'Hermitage?' Cwen sounded very puzzled. 'Funny name for a monk.'

'It's all right, it's all right,' Hermitage called out as he jumped from his chair and sprang towards the door. 'It's Abbot Abbo.'

'Abbot Abbo?' Wat smirked.

Hermitage was deaf to everything as he almost bowled Cwen aside to greet the arrival. He smiled and nearly skipped with joy as he appraised the figure of the abbot.

It was a slight and old figure, the face creased by the years and the tonsure whitened by time. The habit dropping from neck to floor was neat and well presented, although it was little troubled by the narrow frame of the abbot, which was doubtless as thin and drawn as the face.

'Ah, Hermitage my boy,' the abbot held his arms wide and beamed as brightly as a summer's day, his scornful treatment of Cwen forgotten.

Hermitage happily entered the embrace and the two men exchanged enthusiastic slaps on the back. After a couple of these, he realised that this was entirely inappropriate behaviour for a monk and his abbot and so he withdrew.

Nevertheless, he felt a level of security and comfort that he had forgotten existed. If the Normans turned up now he would simply turn to his old abbot who would send them on their way with a massive flea in their ears.

He turned to see Wat and Cwen looking at them with wry amusement. 'It's Abbot Abbo.'

'So we gather,' Wat nodded.

The demeanour of the abbot dropped to mid-winter. 'This must be Wat the Weaver,' he noted with disapproval. Not the simple disapproval of a parent who doesn't like their child's choice of friend. No, this was the disapproval of a man who has years of experience disapproving of things and knows how to do it very well.

Wat tried a smile, but it was like sending a mouse in to stop a cat fight.

'It will be interesting to hear about your connection with this man.' "Interesting" was clearly not a good thing.

'Come in, come in,' Hermitage stepped back and beckoned the abbot to enter. 'It is so good to see you.'

Abbot Abbo did step over the threshold, but not without crossing himself first. He looked around the place, which was comfortable, clean and expensive. Disapproval obviously extended to comfort, cleanliness and expense as he managed to turn his nose up while simultaneously smiling at Hermitage.

'We can go to the upper chamber,' Wat offered. 'I'll bring some wine.' He seemed quite keen to leave the abbot's company and beckoned Cwen to help him.

Still overcome by the sight of his abbot, Hermitage didn't notice that the atmosphere had enough frost to open a fair. He led the way up the rickety stairs to the large chamber Wat used for greeting customers and preparing his larger

# The Case of the Cantankerous Carcass

works. He gestured that the abbot should take the most comfortable chair by the window. The window with real glass.

The man did so with the sigh of someone who has had a long and tiresome journey. He closed his eyes for a moment but then opened them to gaze upon Hermitage once more. 'Brother Hermitage,' he nodded gently.

'Abbot Abbo,' Hermitage replied as part of this very informative conversation.

'You look well,' the abbot commented.

'Ah,' Hermitage said, feeling guilty about this. 'The weavers are kind to me.'

'Yes,' the abbot made it clear that this was not the sort of thing a decent monk would confess to.

Hermitage needed to get his explanation in early. 'And I believe that I have spent my time constructively, moving Wat away from his previous works. He and Cwen now produce tapestries of a much more wholesome nature.'

'Really?' At least this seemed to be news to the abbot.

'Oh, absolutely. They are currently working on a representation of Saint George slaughtering the dragon in a most pious manner.' He didn't mention that he had had to insist on a lot more clothing for the maiden chained to the rock.

'Hm.' The abbot looked like he might be willing to accept this. 'At least it's better for you than that ghastly De'Ath's Dingle place.'[10]

Wat and Cwen arrived bearing wine in the best cups and distributed it.

---

[10] It was ghastly, but the book's not so bad: *The Heretics of De'Ath* - where it all began.

'We'll, erm, leave you to it then,' Wat was keen to get away.

'This may concern you, weaver,' the abbot raised a hand. 'If what I've heard is true.'

What you've heard? Hermitage thought. People tended to hear only bad things about Wat.

'You have news then?' Hermitage asked, without concern. Abbot Abbo was the only man in Hermitage's life who had ever given him any support, encouragement or even civility. It was he who had suggested the life of the hermit in the first place. He always seemed to have Hermitage's best interests at heart and if there was news, it was almost certain to be good. Perhaps he was going to invite Hermitage to join him in some theological adventure.

'Much as it is a pleasure to see you again, young Hermitage, my visit is not purely social.'

'I see.' Perhaps a ticklish point had come up concerning the post-Exodus prophets and only Hermitage could resolve it.

'I have always followed your progress with great interest and am pleased to note that you continue to prosper.'

Hermitage wouldn't have called the few years of his life before meeting Wat as prospering. He had survived, but then he supposed that was as much as some can hope for.

'And I hear that you have come to the notice of the king?'

'Ah, yes.' Hermitage was modest. 'I did meet King Harold just before the events of Hastings, and then William.'

'They gave you an official appointment?'

'King's Investigator, yes. It is an appointment but is more burden than benefit.'

'You investigate deaths I understand.'

'I do. And most disturbing it is. The things I have had to look into do not bear repetition. Why do you ask?'

# The Case of the Cantankerous Carcass

The abbot looked thoughtful and took a breath. 'I ask because I need you to investigate a death.'

Once he had managed to take the words in, Hermitage felt thoroughly conflicted. Of course, he wanted to help his abbot in any way he could. And of course, he hated investigating deaths. Perhaps without King William breathing down his neck it wouldn't be so bad. And being for the abbot it was bound to be a straightforward matter. Perhaps something about a bequest that was in dispute.

'I see,' Hermitage was cautious. 'Erm, whose death would you like me to investigate?'

'Mine,' the abbot said.


You can read the rest of the book in the rest of the book...

<u>The Case of the Cantankerous Carcass</u>

Printed in Great Britain
by Amazon